Nocturne for a Nondescript

Ill-starred love, duplicity and danger entwine in Paris and the Yorkshire Moors

By

SHEILA HEYWOOD

THE CHOIR PRESS

First published in the United Kingdom in 2022 by
The Choir Press

ISBN 978-1-78963-319-1

Dedication and acknowledgements

———

I dedicate this novel to my friends in Yorkshire and France, in particular Barbara Husband and Monica Munoz, for years of friendship, kindness and generosity, fun and support in not-such-fun times. You have always been there.

And to my wonderful partner, Chris Robinson, simply for being you. Thank you for all your patience and assistance with the computing aspects of my work and for putting up with my *impatience* and occasional explosions! Thank you also for assisting with the cover design.

I would like to express my gratitude to former Governor Jones of HM Prison, Armley, Leeds, who answered all my questions, provided information that I wouldn't have thought of, and allowed me to visit the prison. My thanks also to Prison Officer Jack Conway who guided me around the prison and introduced me to many inmates.

I would like to thank saxophonist Peter Corser and his Trio who gave advice on music, musicians and invited me to attend their rehearsals.

My thanks to Shoreh Gonzalez, a beautician and friend whose help and encouragement were indispensable, including allowing me to participate in her various appointments.

A special thank you to Sophia Samuels, Debbie Russell and Kathy Ross for reading my novel and all your positive comments and encouragement, which were a tremendous help. Thank you also to Alison Walters for all your ideas on marketing.

Prologue

I didn't do it. How many times has that short and necessary sentence gone round and round in my head, along with the other one that means exactly the same? I'm not guilty.

Not this time.

'Yes, sir, I'm coming.'

Politely – from four years' practice and a knowledge of what's good for me – I reply to the screw's imperious summons as he sits down at a table next to the wall, a rather charming lady companion sitting opposite him looking a tad nervous, a tad on the uncomfortable side. Don't worry, darling, you might be surrounded by poor bastards who've been locked up for years and who haven't touched a woman for as long, but you couldn't be in safer hands. Prison walls are safer than any chastity belt, believe me.

'Yes, sir, what can I do for you?'

The screw, I have to give him his due, is decent as screws go. We've got to know each other pretty damn well over the past four years, Harry Tyler and me. Under different circumstances, I reckon he and I could've been cronies. It was Harry Tyler who got me this job in the visitors' room. We all have work to do, if you can call it work: tedious, mindless jobs that we wouldn't give the time of day for in the sits. vac. column, but they get you out of the cell for a couple of hours a day. I used to do a bit of cleaning and then I had a 'promotion', if you like, making cups of tea and coffee in the visitors' room and cleaning the tables when their time was up. Well, it's not the kind of job that sets the old grey matter alight, but as I say, it gets me out of my cell a few hours a day. And, in a fashion, I get to meet people ...

'Two cups of coffee, pal, one black and you know 'ow I like mine. And then come and sit down for a few minutes – this young lady would like to 'ave a chat with you.'

Harry doesn't tell me who the 'young lady' is or what she wants to chat about and she and I look at each other warily, eye each other up and down. I pour two spoonsful of coffee into two mugs and watch the other inmates (I hate that word!) snatching a few last words with their wives, girlfriends, lovers ... who've probably by now got other lovers in the outside world. I don't blame them; you can't expect a woman to wait for ever. I suppose I'd be singing a different tune, though, if my wife/girlfriend/lover were sitting facing me and about to leave. But I wouldn't know about that. Visitors of any description have been a bit thin on the ground at my table and zero as far as women are concerned. Women. Woman. She-wolf. I feel two mugs shaking in my two hands and put them down again, trying to steady myself. I have to give a reasonably good impression now; this woman just might be my civil saviour.

'There you are – sir.'

I smile and at the same time I want to throw up. I still choke on the word even after four years' practice.

'Thanks, pal. Now – sit yourself down.'

I do as I'm told and Harry turns to the woman who's smiling (a bit nervously, I reckon) across the table at him and picking up her drink. Pretty smile, gorgeous eyes. Beautiful, silky, touchable hair. Probably a she-wolf in women's clothing.

'This young lady's going to ask you a lot of questions,' Harry Tyler's saying, 'and I want you to answer – truthfully. Okay? Right, love, you can ask 'im whatever you want – feel free – don't be inhibited.' He slurps his coffee noisily. 'Off you go, then, love.'

Harry still doesn't tell me who she is or why she's going to ask me a lot of questions. And it's not my place to ask. He settles back in his wooden chair; the keys, hanging at his side, jangle as he moves. He puts his chipped and stained mug down and his small grey eyes underneath thick grey brows move slowly, slyly, between the good-looking she-wolf and me. She turns her pretty, nervous (I reckon it's nervous) smile on me and I'm all too aware that I haven't touched a female for four years. Correction – more than four years.

'First of all,' she says, clearing her throat and looking a bit embarrassed, a bit wary. She has beautiful hair, beautiful … God, how I'd love to touch that hair, feel it in my penal-chaste but erstwhile experienced fingers, touch that smile. 'What are you in prison for?'

I look straight into her wary, questioning eyes.

'Rape.'

She doesn't even flinch. She doesn't shriek or faint or even move her chair further away from mine.

'I see. And – were you guilty of rape?'

'No.'

'Huh-huh. And how long have you been in prison?'

'Four years.'

She frowns slightly, stops scribbling and clears her pretty little throat.

'For something you didn't do?'

'Exactly. For something I didn't do.'

I hear the tone of my voice and feel Harry Tyler's small grey eyes on my face. So, I smile. The she-wolf starts scribbling again. There's a short silence while she and Harry sip their coffee. I don't have any coffee to sip. I lick my lips.

'Okay.' It seems like after the coffee she's crisp, efficient and business-like. 'Can you tell me what happened?'

I look at Harry Tyler. He looks at me and nods, enjoying himself, I reckon. I turn and watch the wives and girlfriends and lovers leaving and I hear the boom of a cell door, although the men aren't back in their cells yet. I slowly, pointedly, tell the she-wolf what happened and she writes all the time, occasionally looking up at me but never flinching. Harry starts to drum his fat fingers on the table and his keys join in a clinking chorus at his side. I cough. I've been talking for a long time; for God's sake, I need a drink.

'And when are you going to be ... released?'

I look at Harry whose fat fingers are now fanning out on the table. A small smile creases his face and he looks down at his hands. I look at the she-wolf in women's clothing and this time my smile is almost natural.

'Tomorrow.'

'Tomorrow?' For some reason, she looks stunned.

Tomorrow. She asks how I feel, how I've been feeling for the past four years. How would anybody feel who's been locked up for four bloody years for something he didn't do? I suddenly feel a queer churning in the pit of my stomach, a bit like cramp or a screw (excuse the pun – unintentional) turning. At the same time, I experience a sort of giddiness, rather like a kid on Christmas Eve, I suppose, or a tiger in the zoo who's just discovered a hole in the railings.

'I'm ecstatic,' I say, knowing that both my face and my voice are deadpan. She stops scribbling, looks at me and smiles.

'I'm sure you are,' she says. 'I'm so happy for you.'

And, do you know, she actually sounds genuine.

Harry Tyler scrapes his chair across the floor as he heaves himself up and asks her if she's finished, only more politely than that. She says she has and thanks him and then turns to me and starts to speak again, and after a while I start to pay attention. Then I hear the keys at Harry's side start jangling, although they're as silent as the tomb, and I hear the boom of a cell door. The lady smiles at me again – a really gorgeous smile – and thanks me again and I tell her it's a pleasure; a word that's been absent from my vocabulary for a long time. Anyway, I suppose it's what she expects me to say. Harry walks to the door with her and they shake hands. Her heels play a kind of military tune as she disappears down the corridor. Harry looks at me, nods, and I follow him out of the room.

Boom.

II

The sun rose in a cloudless blue sky and the warmth and growing light woke the ex-nun from her light summer slumber before the alarm clock trilled at her single bedside. She stretched her short, thin body beneath the cotton sheet and flickered her pale grey, myopic eyes into life. She yawned loudly and rubbed her heavy, crêpey eyelids before getting out of the old iron bed that had belonged to her mother when she was a girl. Many moons ago. The window was already open but she unlocked the wooden shutter and pushed it to welcome more sunlight and the view that never ceased to delight her eighty-year-old eyes. The geraniums glowed blood-red in their ceramic pots, tumbling along the terrace and forming a frame for the distant, snow-capped peaks of the Mont Blanc range; while in the foreground lower and inferior but no less beautiful mountains displayed clusters of pine trees, wooden chalets and a multitude of chaotic flowers. Bénédicte went into the bathroom and after her simple ablutions put on a long, blue flannel dressing gown and a pair of plain, steel-framed and thick-lensed glasses and hurried downstairs to prepare her equally plain breakfast, freshly-percolated coffee and toast made from yesterday's bread. Before sitting down at the kitchen table, Bénédicte glanced at the ugly but practical plastic and hugely-numbered clock on the yellow wall. Not yet six-thirty. She had time to eat her breakfast and put crumbs out for the birds (Well! They'd have something to say if she didn't!) before getting the Citroën Deux Chevaux out of the garage. Helen's train didn't leave till seven-thirty; they had plenty of time. She had only to drive down to the chalet a little further down the mountain, toot her horn and help Helen put her luggage in the boot. After that, they'd be at the station in fifteen minutes – plenty of time for Helen to buy a newspaper or whatever for the journey. And after Bénédicte had seen Helen comfortably settled into her carriage and waved her off, she'd have time for another cup of coffee and a change of clothes before Mass, which was exactly how she'd planned her morning.

The ex-nun dressed in her usual casual Sunday clothes: a pair of pink cotton trousers that finished just below the knee, a white, loose-fitting cotton blouse with long sleeves that she rolled up to the elbow and a pair of clean but well-worn trainers with a pair of pink and white striped socks. She picked her car keys off the kitchen table and skipped down the geranium-bedecked stairs at the side of the chalet and, acknowledging another early riser and hiker with a wave of her thin, arthritic hand, she pulled open the garage door and less than five minutes later was sitting in the red Deux Chevaux and taking the narrow, winding road that snaked down the mountain. Arriving at her neighbours' chalet she quickly braked and tooted the horn loudly, as planned. She sat and waited, feeling the heat of the Alpine sun penetrating the windows of her vehicle, penetrating her thin, parchment-like skin. She rolled the window down and turned her bespectacled eyes to the chalet on her right.

A beautiful dwelling, one of the most beautiful on the mountain. Almost totally surrounded by fir trees, the windows and balconies were an extravaganza of geraniums and other flowers exploding out of ceramic and terra cotta pots and trailing from hanging wicker baskets and hand-painted urns. The wooden shutters boasted engravings of fir trees and flowers and behind them, delicate lace curtains would be moving slightly in the soft mountain breeze. The shutters should have been open by now but they weren't. Bénédicte pressed the horn again, louder this time, and leaned out of the window, her eyes straining to see signs of life, but there were none. She muttered under her breath as she got out of the car and strode up the short gravel drive to the door. If Helen missed this train there wasn't another one till after midday, and with the change she'd have to make in Lyon she wouldn't get home till very late in the evening. Bénédicte didn't like the idea of Helen alone at night in a Paris railway station. She tutted and muttered to herself about the closed shutters and the silence and pressed the doorbell with a thin, fragile finger. Oh, if only she hadn't invited Helen for dinner yesterday evening ... if only they hadn't stayed up talking and putting the world to rights ... oh, where on earth was she? She was definitely going to miss that train and ... Bénédicte pressed the bell once more and, at the same time, pushed the door. Surprisingly, it opened.

'Helen! Bonjour ... Helen! Are you ready? You're going to miss your train!'

The chalet was dark in spite of the increasing sunlight. Bénédicte stood for a while in the doorway, listening to her own words as they echoed around the kitchen. Her eyes, getting accustomed to the strange light and the unexpected stillness, saw the remnants of yesterday's dinner on the cooker, on the table, in the sink. Pans, a plate, cutlery, one dirty napkin, a half-empty bottle of Bordeaux and a dish of dried, crusty cheeses.

But Helen hadn't eaten there yesterday evening; she'd had dinner with her, with Bénédicte. Their farewell dinner and Helen had given her a beautiful ... oh but, maybe ... of course, that was it, how silly of her, there was really no mystery at all, it was only her over-active imagination. Bénédicte called 'Helen!' again and then two more names echoed around the empty kitchen; she was greeted with yet more silence. She felt her eighty-year-old heart beginning to beat more quickly and the perspiration running down her forehead. She took off her glasses and rubbed her eyes with the back of her now trembling hand, giving herself time to think. She looked around her, as though searching for help or some kind of clue, but all she saw was the debris of a spectral dinner. She moved out of the kitchen and into the living room and her eyes fell on the old cottage piano standing upright against the wall to her right. She noticed that it was open and sheets of music lay scattered on the floor. Bénédicte could almost hear the thumping of the piano keys together with the thumping of her heart.

'Helen.'

The name stuck in her throat and Bénédicte tried to cough but that, too, refused to come. She swallowed several times and then walked to the back of the chalet where a winding wooden staircase led to the bedrooms. At the foot of the stairs she once again heard herself call Helen's name and then she heard the wood creak slightly as her foot touched the bottom step. She made her slow and very wary way upstairs and stood for a while on the landing, not knowing whether to turn back downstairs to fresh air, her car and cowardly escape, or to investigate what she knew to be the guest bedroom, the one that Helen had been sleeping in for the past ... she didn't know how many weeks.

The door stood ajar and it moaned as she pushed it wide open. The room was in semi-darkness as the shutters were still firmly closed and Helen's open and half-empty suitcase lay to her right on the polished parquet floor. The ex-nun blinked several times before her old, myopic eyes fell on the naked, battered, bleeding and unconscious body outstretched on the unmade bed.

Chapter One

Her suitcase was particularly heavy as it contained not only clothes, underwear and essential toiletries, but necessary documents, books and her precious unpublished poetry occupied a large part. She shuffled forward with the queue, dragging the blue case on wheels behind her, juggling with her handbag, passport and train ticket and hoping it was all going to be worth it. The passenger in front of her reclaimed his minimal luggage off the scanner and walked away, obviously knowing exactly what he was doing, where he was going and why. Unlike her; unlike Helen Hartnell.

'Put your handbag and suitcase on the scanner please, madam.'

She had no difficulty putting her handbag on the scanner but the suitcase was a very different kettle of fish. She should have brought another bag, she told herself. She should have put all her books and papers in a different bag. How stupid of her ... why hadn't she thought ...? Sometimes she thought her mother must have been right, after all ... 'You've no gumption, lass ...' She tried to pick the case up but it really was impossible. She heaved and pushed and turned red and looked apologetically at the bemused official standing opposite her. She pulled the case in its upright position again, took a deep breath, prayed, and then felt the cumbersome piece of luggage being lifted – not without some difficulty – on to the scanner. She turned around and smiled her thanks at the man who pulled a face as if to say, 'What the hell have you got in there, Big Ben?' She moved forward, ready to recuperate her case and the man followed with his own luggage – a light holdall and a briefcase.

'Don't even attempt to take it off there,' he grinned at her. 'Instead of going to Paris you'll be heading straight for A and E. There you go – it's all yours.'

'Thanks very much,' Helen smiled and blushed, and he nodded at her, preoccupied then with his own meagre belongings.

Helen moved forward, looked around her and suddenly wished she were back in Yorkshire, from where she had set off that morning. Back with Jill and Tom and the kids. Jill, her best friend, who had offered to come to London and see her off at Waterloo ... She was so pleased that she hadn't allowed her to do that. It had been bad enough waving goodbye to her in Bradford; God knows what it would have been like if she'd come to London. Helen choked back the tears that were threatening yet again and tried to concentrate on the present instead of the past, not to mention the future; whatever that would turn out to be. She looked around her and wondered if she'd done the right thing in travelling first class on the Eurostar. It had been a spontaneous decision when she'd booked her ticket. She'd never travelled first class anywhere; hadn't a clue what first class meant, really ... but now was her chance to find out. It was probably a once-in-a-lifetime experience, anyway, and now there was no one to question and carp and criticise and ... Well, it was her one extravagance and she'd probably never have the money or the opportunity to do so again.

So, Helen Hartnell was a first-class passenger aboard the Eurostar from London to Paris; at least she was about to be, but what was she supposed to do before she got on the train? She couldn't stand here looking like a waif and stray for the next hour or so. Her eyes then noticed a sign for the first-class coffee lounge and she dragged her luggage in that direction. She shuffled through the door rather nervously, squeamishly feeling that she certainly didn't belong in such a place, and headed towards a nearby table. Feeling more than self-conscious she slipped into a chair and opened her new, black patent handbag just for something to do. She didn't notice the man sitting at the next table because her eyes were focused on her bag's belongings and she jumped when a voice said, 'Hello again. So, you're travelling first class, too. Do you mind if I join you?'

Helen smiled into the kindly brown eyes of the man who'd helped with her luggage and murmured that no, she didn't mind at all. If the truth were known, she was grateful not to have to sit alone and, as she thought, conspicuous in the first-class lounge ... or any other lounge, for that matter.

'What would you like to drink?' the man asked, settling himself into the chair opposite hers. 'A glass of champagne?'

Helen gazed at him with astonished, wide blue eyes.

'Oh no,' she murmured, 'Not at this time. It's too early for ... well.' She looked at the black, leather-strapped watch on her left wrist. 'It's not even lunchtime yet. Are you drinking champagne?'

'Certainly not,' the man smiled, 'not at this time. It's far too early. I'm having a glass of rather delicious orange juice. Would you like the same or would you prefer a nice cup of English tea?'

'Certainly not!' Helen imitated him. 'I'd prefer coffee.'

'With milk and sugar, I suppose?'

'You suppose wrong. Black, please. And very strong.'

The waitress approached the table with a polite smile and the man ordered another fruit juice for himself and a cup of black coffee.

'Thanks very much,' Helen said when it arrived, with a chocolate. She couldn't think of anything else to say to her companion and immediately picked up her cup. The man was studying her and she looked around the room in order to avoid his probing eyes. He didn't offer to speak and Helen felt obliged to break the rather embarrassing silence and told him that the coffee was very good. He nodded.

'And now are you going to tell me what's in your suitcase? I'm afraid I'm going to break my arm when I heave it on to the train.'

'You don't have to ...'

'I know I don't have to. I want to. And I insist. Let me guess what you're taking to Paris with you. I imagine there's no hashish in there otherwise you wouldn't have got through customs; ditto the Crown Jewels. Clothes don't weigh that much. If yours *do* I'm afraid you'll be walking round Paris like the hunchback of Notre Dame. So ... own up, Miss... or maybe Missus ... Or probably Ms. What is your name, by the way?'

'Helen Hartnell,' she almost whispered. 'Miss,' the thirty-nine-year-old Helen Hartnell confessed, telling herself she wasn't ashamed of her single state; not at all. Never had been, never would be. Not in this day and age, and it wasn't as if she hadn't been ...

'Miss Helen Hartnell. Nice name. It has a ring to it. Now, Miss Helen Hartnell, are you going to tell me why your suitcase weighs a ton or ...'

'Why are you so interested?' Helen asked, beginning to feel slightly irritated with this curious bloke. He had an attractive voice. Not only was it gentle and deep but he also had a strange accent that she couldn't quite place. Not that she was an expert on accents. His brown eyes were soft and gentle when he smiled. His smile was warm, his teeth good, and his grey hair thick and shiny and just touching his collar. They were staring at each other, she suddenly realised, and when she looked away, she saw the thick gold band on the third finger of his left hand.

'I'm not really,' he suddenly laughed. 'It's none of my goddam business what you're taking to Paris with you. I'm making conversation ... small talk ... maybe trying to get to know you a little. After all, maybe we'll be travelling in the tunnel together, having lunch and a glass of champagne together. You wouldn't refuse me that, would you? A champagne aperitif before a delicious Eurostar lunch?'

Helen laughed, beginning to enjoy this man's company.

'You haven't told me *your* name,' she said. 'How can I have lunch with a man whose name I don't know?'

He looked away from her, finished his fruit juice and signalled the waitress. He paid for their drinks and indicated to Helen that it was time to start moving if they didn't want to miss their train.

'What carriage will you be travelling in?' he asked her.

Helen checked her ticket.

'Erm ... carriage number twenty-eight.'

'Ah. And I'm in number twenty-seven. Well, we'll remedy that when we arrive on the platform.'

Helen frowned at him and shook her head.

'Remedy what? What do you mean?'

'I'll ask to change my carriage to number twenty-eight. What's your seat number? Thirty-two? Okay, I'll make sure I'll be sitting in thirty-one. Let's go. No, let me drag your suitcase; you may carry my holdall. It contains my underwear and shaving equipment. Oh, and half a dozen pairs of unmatched and dirty socks.'

Helen laughed, followed him out of the lounge and towards the escalators that took them to the platform and the grey-uniformed hostesses who were ready to welcome them aboard the train. Helen did as she was told and waited while her intriguing companion arranged with a hostess to change his accommodation and then she watched as he hauled her case on to the train and found a suitable niche in the luggage compartment. He placed his own luggage on top. She followed him down the aisle and, after taking off her grey woollen coat, sank into the window seat and he settled himself beside her, stretched out his legs and rested his head on the back of his seat. He closed his eyes and a smile played on his rather thin lips.

'Are you quite comfortable, Miss Hartnell?' he asked, opening his eyes and looking at her.

'I'm very comfortable,' she smiled back at him. 'Mr ... Mr ... oh ... erm ... you still haven't told me your name.'

Helen wasn't sure if she imagined the brief silence that followed. He cleared his throat and muttered,

'You can call me Ben.'

Helen smiled rather wistfully. 'I always wanted a dog when I was a kid but wasn't allowed.' She paused. 'I would have called him Ben.'

'Fortunately, Helen Hartnell, I have a sense of humour. So, you never had a dog?'

'No. No pets ...'

'No pets when you were a kid. Not even a hamster? No? Well, Helen, I think that's very sad.'

You think right, Ben. It was very sad. That and a lot of other things.

'So, your name's Ben,' she said. 'But Ben what? Ben Down? Ben Evolent?'

The man whose first name was Ben briefly frowned and then chuckled.

'I love a lady with a sense of humour – especially a British sense of humour.' He paused for what seemed like a long time. 'My name's Beaulac. Benjamin Beaulac.'

At first it didn't sink in. After a few seconds, possibly minutes, however, Helen slowly turned towards her travelling companion and, blushing deeply, she said,

'Benjamin Beaulac. You're not Benjamin Beaulac the musician, are you? The composer?'

'That's me,' he confirmed, closing his eyes again. 'Like I said, you can call me Ben. Now, how about a glass of that delicious Eurostar champagne?'

***

'There's a name for women like 'er. You know what it is, don't you? Trollop. That's what they call women who lead men on, and don't you forget it. Trollop. Amongst other things.'

Her mother had said that about a young neighbour who hadn't said no when a passing hiker had invited her to accompany him across the moor and the poor girl had got more than she'd bargained for. Most of the street, the village, had been sympathetic; she'd been very young, naïve, inexperienced, it hadn't been her fault. But not Helen's mother. Oh no, not Dorothy Hartnell. So, what would her mother make of this, then? Sitting in a first-class carriage with a glass of champagne in her hand and giggling with an internationally famous composer and pianist? And on her way to Paris and a completely, more or less, unknown future, thanks to the money she'd received on the sale of the house. But her mother didn't know anything about that either, of course.

The house – an old, small and cramped terraced house – stood at the end of a long street in Firley, a village on the edge of the moor in the Yorkshire Pennines. Helen, an only child, had lived there since her birth, thirty-nine years before. Her beloved but rather distant and totally undemonstrative father had died of a heart attack when Helen was just twelve, and Helen thus lost her emotional and intellectual ally whenever the domestic war erupted between her mother and herself. Dorothy's constantly carping and critical tongue had accompanied Helen down the years with inevitable harmful and calamitous consequences. But Dorothy Hartnell would never have claimed responsibility.

After Frank Hartnell passed away, his widow didn't look to her daughter for solace and companionship. Instead, she complained that the house was too small for the two of them and they were always 'under each other's feet'. Dorothy needed her own space and encouraged her young daughter to 'play outside on the moor'; 'see your friends'; 'stay in your room'. Whenever they did spend time together Helen's initial eager, childish chatter fell on deaf ears and her mother sought escape in television soap operas, women's weekly magazines and gossiping neighbours. Helen always had the impression that her mam preferred chatting to the neighbours than spending time with her. And her impression was right. When Helen showed her mother good results at school, brought new friends and, later, boyfriends home the acknowledgement was always the same. A terse nod of the prematurely greying head, the semblance of a smile on her thin lips but not in her eyes, a caustic comment and an excuse to disappear.

Because of domestic financial need and maternal pressure, and much against academic advice, Helen left school when she was fifteen and subsequently drifted in and out of unsuitable and unsatisfactory jobs, either leaving of her own free will or getting the sack. Her mother's reaction to both was the same: total indifference. Helen later drifted in and out of relationships with the opposite sex with the same regularity and much the same pattern, either leaving them of her own free will or 'getting the push', as her mother called it. She used the same expression in both cases; 'Our 'Elen's got the push again.'

Jill Mooney asked Helen to be her chief bridesmaid when she and Tom Hopkins got married in June, 1981. Both young women were twenty-two years old and had been friends for nearly as many years. Tom had almost grown up with Jill, too. In Dorothy's words the wedding was 'a big splash'. After the church ceremony in Firley ('Four bridesmaids, page boy, "queer" photographer – all the typical trimmings. Must 'ave cost Jack Mooney a bloody fortune. And Jill'll never look as nice as that again. That's it now.'), a big reception at one of the best hotels in Bradford. Sit-down meal, fancy, three-tier cake, speeches, dancing. Honeymoon in Venice. ('What do they want to go to Venice for? Waste o' money, if you ask me. They'd be better off puttin' that money down on a ...' 'But nobody's asking you, Mam,' Helen had wanted to say.) She'd sat next to Tom's best man at the reception and danced with him quite a lot, and it was obvious that everyone had been hoping ... keeping their fingers crossed. Helen had met Michael many times in the past, him being Tom's cousin, but it was as plain as the nose on your face that he wasn't interested in her. Of course, he was nice to her at the wedding, he didn't have much choice, did he? But as her mam said later when they were unlocking the door and Helen nearly tripped up over her long, lilac dress, "E only danced wi' you cos you were the chief bridesmaid. His eyes were clapped on that friend o' Tom's sister all day, but she were flashin' an engagement ring. I wouldn't 'old out any 'ope, if I were you.'

6

Jill and Tom had three children, two girls and a boy, and eventually moved from their temporary rented flat in Keighley into a semi-detached, heavily mortgaged house in Firley, not a stone's throw away from Theresa and Jack Mooney.

'It's a good job I get on with the in-laws,' Tom often quipped.

Michael married a girl he met on a climbing holiday in Scotland and moved to Inverness. Helen continued living in the cramped terraced house with her mother, drifting in and out of unsuitable jobs and relationships, writing the poetry that she never showed to a soul except Jill (and no longer to her mam after she'd nearly split her sides that time), and wondering if her life would ever change.

Her life and, to a certain extent, her negative self-image, started to change when she decided to become a beautician and left home to follow a rigorous training course at a renowned school in London. Her life completely changed when Dorothy Hartnell was found dead at the bottom of the bedroom stairs, the tell-tale and fatal text still scrunched up in her stiffening fingers. Helen had completed the training course by this time and she was selling perfume on a temporary basis in a Bradford department store. She was just thirty-nine years old, a sibling-less orphan with no other family to speak of, friends with families of their own, and no real ties – not even a dog. As a child she would have given her right arm to have a dog and her dad had been on her side, as usual, but her mam said no. What did they want with a dog? They were only 'ard work, you 'ad to tek 'em out every day and when you went away you 'ad to find somebody to look after 'em ... But we never go away, Mam ... No, not even a pet. She was free. And it was time to re-think her life before it was too late. In spite of the profound guilt that had travelled with her to Dorothy Hartnell's grave, and the subsequent and seemingly permanent intellectual handicap that travelled with her everywhere.

***

Helen suddenly felt confused, embarrassed, ridiculous. Had she been flirting, however mildly, with a celebrated, much appreciated musician? Was she, Helen Hartnell the Nondescript, sitting next to, travelling with and regretting the wedding ring of the illustrious Franco/American composer? She had a lot of his CDs tucked away in her crammed case, along with her own non-illustrious compositions. The lively but gentle and harmonious melodies could often be heard in the terraced house in Firley. Benjamin Beaulac had written the scores for a couple of films, too, which were also in her music collection. She had seen his photograph many times, of course, had watched him being interviewed on television but would never have associated that distinguished personage with the easy-going, amusing man sitting next to her on the train. The man who'd helped her with her suitcase and bought her a coffee ... and changed his carriage in order to travel with her, for God's sake. A voice suddenly announced that the train was about to leave Waterloo.

They sat in silence for a while as the train moved slowly down the track and Helen turned her head to the right, concentrating on the grim grey scenery and the similar November weather. The smart and smiling 'chef de cabine' was suddenly standing in front of them, introduced herself as Maxine and asked to take their order for aperitif and lunch. Without consulting Helen, Benjamin Beaulac ordered two more glasses of champagne and passed the very tempting menu to his companion. Helen smiled her thanks and they both ordered a salmon lunch. They lapsed into a silence brought on by Helen's sudden and profound embarrassment and shyness. If Ben didn't speak to her any more, she knew that now she'd be absolutely incapable of prompting a conversation. Whatever nonsense came into her head would have to stay there, and that could only be a good thing. However, as he clinked his champagne flute with hers, Ben said, or rather whispered,

'Helen, what did the guy say who found his wife in bed with a Frenchman?'

Helen gazed at him and blinked. She thought she must have misheard him.

'Sorry?' She cleared her throat. 'What did you say?'

Ben grinned and repeated his very odd question.

'I don't know,' Helen murmured, blushing. 'What did he say?'

'Eiffel towered out; you'd better carry on.'

Helen continued to gaze at her companion, who was chuckling into his champagne flute.

'Have you just made that up?' she managed to giggle, but shyly.

'Yeah, I hope you're as impressed as I am. Okay,' he said, leaning his head a little closer to hers and lowering his attractive voice again. 'Here's another one. What did the man say who found his wife in bed with an Italian?'

'I don't know,' Helen grinned. 'Please tell me.'

'I'll give him a Pisa my mind.'

'Pisa or pizza his mind?'

'All the same to the poor old cuckold. Okay ... now it's your turn.'

Helen's turn was interrupted by Maxine, the chef de cabine, asking if they required anything else. After she'd moved on, Ben turned to Helen and raised an eyebrow, expectantly. Helen took a deep breath and played with her still-full flute, ignoring the blood that had rushed to her cheeks.

'What did ...' She coughed and started again. 'What did the man say who found his wife in bed with an ... an American?'

'Erm ... let me think ... "Good choice, my good lady-wife?" No, maybe not. Okay, I've no idea. Tell me.'

'Texas time, doesn't he?'

'Hey ... you know, that's not bad. For a Yorkshire-woman.'

Helen stared at him again and sipped the cool drink.

'How do you know I'm from ... from Yorkshire?'

Suddenly, it was Ben's turn to fiddle with the champagne glass and look uneasy. Helen waited quite a while before he replied, 'Your accent is quite strong.'

'Not as strong as it used to be,' Helen smiled, 'before I ... lived in London. But how on earth can you recognise a Yorkshire accent? Have you ever been there?'

Ben looked distinctly uncomfortable now and made a play of fiddling with and gazing at his glass.

'Yes,' he eventually replied, 'I've been there. Now ... tell me what's taking you to the City of Light. We've been travelling for ... what? Twenty minutes together, not to mention our little tryst in the coffee lounge, and I don't even know why or how long or because of whom you're going to Paris. Is a tall, dark and handsome Frenchman going to knock me out in a fit of jealousy when we say goodbye at the Gare du Nord?'

Helen had no idea why, but she blushed scarlet again and slightly turned away from the man who was slowly but surely beginning to get under her skin.

'No,' she smiled. 'No one's meeting me at the Gare du Nord. In fact, I don't know a soul in ... the City of Light. I'm going to work for a French beautician who I've never met and I'll be staying in hotel recommended and paid for by her until I find my own accommodation.'

'That sounds pretty brave of you. I guess you know Paris well if you're ready to live there, not knowing a soul and never having met your future boss? You must know your way around?'

Helen reddened, shook her head and at that moment the lunch arrived and their conversation was forgotten for a few busy moments. When they settled back in their seats again, a crab and crudité starter in front of them, together with a glass of Sauterne, Ben continued his verbal investigation.

'So ... how many times have you been to Paris?'

'I've never been to Paris.'

'You have to be kidding me?'

'Unfortunately, I'm not.'

Not for the first time, Helen suddenly wished she could leap off the train and run back to where she'd come from.

'Well, I'll be darned.'

***

The train had just entered the Channel Tunnel when Ben, after what seemed like an achingly long silence, looked at Helen again.

'I guess you're not married, Helen?'

'You guess right.' Her voice was a whisper.

'Divorced?'

'Not even.'

'You've never been married?'

'Is that a terrible admission?'

'No more terrible than never having a dog.'

And my mother is to blame for both deprivations. No, that's not fair; not really ...

'You *are* married, aren't you?'

'Yes, Helen, I am.'

'Have you got any children?'

'Yes, I have two wonderful children. Jeremy is eighteen and Amy is sixteen.'

'That's nice.'

Helen's voice was barely audible and she felt ridiculous. She would have felt ridiculous feeling like this before she knew the man's name, but now ...

'And your wife. What's her name?'

And is she wonderful, too?

'I'm sorry?'

'What's your ... your wife's name?' She coughed and it was followed by a brief silence. Ben didn't look at her.

'Do you realise we're surrounded by water out there? The English Channel. Deep, wide, cold ... Can you swim, Helen?'

Don't change the subject, Ben.

'Don't say things like that, Ben. I'm trying not to think too much about being under water.'

They enjoyed and finished their starter in silence and then the smiling chef de cabine came to take their dishes away. Ben suddenly shuffled in his seat, pressed a button and the arm that separated him from his companion disappeared. He turned a little towards her and gently touched her cheek with one long index finger.

'My wife's name is Kimberley. I'm going to stay at our apartment in Paris for a few days and then I'll be taking a train to the Alps where my wife and I are spending the winter. Amy and Jeremy will be joining us at Christmas. They're in the States at the moment; they haven't finished school yet.'

Helen realised that she was nodding her head at the same time she realised that he was stroking her cheek with the same index finger.

'Oh, right. And where will you be staying in … in the Alps? In a fabulous five-star hotel?'

'Not at all,' Ben laughed, removing his finger and settling back into his seat. 'My family has a chalet there … near Chamonix. And Mont Blanc. I'm going to be working over the winter, writing the score for a musical comedy that's going to take the world by storm next year.'

'And your wife? Will she be staying with you while you … while you work?'

His wife. Kimberley Beaulac. No doubt beautiful, accomplished, gifted. A Cordon Bleu cook. An expert skier. A whore in his bed.

'Oh yes. Of course.'

Helen turned her face to the window and the clear November countryside that was suddenly speeding by. Speeding them towards the French capital; a precarious future for her and another train journey for him, with a waiting wife at the other end.

'By the way, do you speak the language?' Ben suddenly asked her and Helen had the strange feeling that he'd been racking his brains for something to say to her. Then she reprimanded herself for being downright daft and tried not to show her confusion. 'Do you speak French?'

'I've been taking lessons. I think I know enough to get by.'

'Well,' Ben smiled at her, 'you'll be plunged in at the deep end if you're starting work next week. You'll have no choice but to get by.'

'I'm trying hard not to think about that at the moment. Being plunged in at the deep end, I mean. I'm trying to think of some good things, some positive things.'

'Oh, there'll be plenty of those, you know, Helen.'

His voice was a low, soft drawl with a smile to match.

'You think so? I'm not feeling very convinced at the moment. Tell me about them.'

Ben told her about the magnificent museums, theatres, restaurants, parks, not to mention the shops … and as he talked and smiled, his left hand, the one with the simple gold band, suddenly reached out and touched hers. And it stayed there, the big square hand with the long sensitive fingers rested on her small, ringless one, as he talked about her future in his favourite city. When he eventually stopped speaking Helen almost whispered, 'I must admit, I'm a bit scared,' and she inwardly chided herself for sounding like a little girl on her first day at school. Ben smiled and the long sensitive fingers coiled around hers and he leaned slightly to the right and kissed her burning cheek.

***

The train pulled into the Gare du Nord, Paris, at exactly two o'clock p.m. on that cold clear Saturday in early November, 1998. As the high-speed French train started to slow down, passengers stood up, reached for discarded coats and luggage, prepared to disembark. Some began to amble down the aisle towards the main luggage compartment and the doors. Only two figures sat motionless in their seats. Ben Beaulac's head was once more resting on the back of his seat and his travelling companion's head rested on his shoulder.

'Come on,' Ben finally said, his eyes following the disappearing passengers, his senses aware of the activity of another busy station, another city, another country, another life. 'Unfortunately, Helen Hartnell, it's time to move.'

Helen just needed time. Time to adjust to this new life she was about to embark upon, time to think about what lay ahead; what successes, what failures, what meetings, what partings. Time to find her hotel, time to find somewhere to live. Time to cling a little longer to this man she hadn't known five hours before. Time to kiss him just one more time, time to hear that strange but attractive accent taking its leave of her. Time to watch him walking down the platform to another station, another town, another woman. Time to think about the three hours she'd just spent with an incredible man she would never see again.

'Come on,' Ben repeated, sliding his arm away from her. 'Let's go and find your hotel. What's the name again?'

Chapter Two

———

The exit from the noisy, crowded station in the north of Paris and her subsequent senses were far different from how Helen had previously imagined. The excitement, apprehension and physical nausea of arriving and starting a new life in a foreign capital were very much in evidence but added to these was another, very different excitement that was totally unexpected, the furthest thing from her already jumbled mind. She had got on the train at Waterloo an independent if slightly nervous woman, with no other thoughts than trying to make a success of her new life in Paris. She'd expected to get off the train with these ideas even more in evidence, with the added incentive of arrival. She was still an independent if nervous woman, but during a very short time had become attached to another human being, a man who was, for several reasons, totally unavailable. She'd expected that man to help her with her luggage again, maybe kiss her one more time then walk out of the station, never to be seen again. But he didn't.

Ben carried his own holdall and pulled her suitcase behind him and Helen followed him down the platform, out of the station and into the busy street.

'This isn't the most salubrious part of the city,' Ben told her, 'so I don't think you'll be staying in a five star. Let's hope that it has at least the minimal comfort. Rue ... what was it? Right ... Okay, follow me.'

They crossed a busy boulevard, turned right and eventually arrived at a crossroads where Ben checked a convenient map of the neighbourhood and pointed to a short, narrow street on their left.

'There's the street. Let's go.'

The Hotel de la Gare was a tall, narrow building, the paint peeling off the walls, its sign battered and rusty, blowing in the fresh November breeze. Ben and Helen looked at each other. Ben shrugged and pushed open the door, which led to a short corridor and a crooked, worse-for-wear steep staircase. Helen and Ben exchanged another bemused glance before he took the heaviest bags and noisily heaved them upstairs to the equally antiquated and none-too-clean reception desk on the first floor. There was no one to welcome them. Ben pressed a bell on the untidy counter and the raucous clang echoed through the building.

'I wouldn't say your future employer's gone bankrupt with your expenses,' Ben remarked but before Helen could despondently agree with him, the receptionist appeared, a young North African man. He grinned at the couple, displaying a set of decayed and discoloured teeth and eyeing them up and down in a somewhat salacious manner. Ben quickly and in fluent French introduced the new hotel guest and the receptionist checked an outdated computer. He pointed to a sombre, narrow corridor on their right. Room number three. Ben led the way, wrinkling his nose at the fusty smell and 'kitsch' decorations, as he described them. Helen avoided his eyes, her enthusiasm and anticipation for her new life melting with every step. Ben turned the key in the lock and nothing happened. He pushed and pulled and shook and finally the door gave way but Helen knew her own fingers would never be able to perform that complicated ritual. She wondered if Ben would ever be able to play the piano again ... He stood back and Helen walked into the room.

Whatever optimism had remained now completely disappeared. The room was tiny; a single bed monopolised the space, sporting a faded grey, threadbare and stained candlewick bedspread haphazardly thrown across. A matching (at least it was matching) candlewick bedspread hung at the dirty and cracked window in place of a curtain. A dingy brown curtain hung in the corner of the room, behind which Ben found a rusty railing, supposedly from which to hang clothes, as there was no wardrobe. A cracked and stained wash basin stood in the opposite corner displaying a dripping tap and above it hung a lopsided and cracked mirror.

Helen's eyes clouded over in dismay and then blinked several times before opening in horror as they focused on the unclean washbasin. She pointed a trembling finger.

'Ben ... look.'

'Cockroaches. That doesn't surprise me. You're not staying here. Come on.'

He took charge of the luggage yet again, left the room and Helen listened as he said a less than fond farewell to the indifferent receptionist. He put the key on the desk and headed for the stairs.

It seemed to be getting colder. They stood on the narrow uneven pavement in front of the Hotel de la Gare and shivered. If my employer expects me to stay in a place like that, Helen was thinking, what on earth is she going to be like to work for? Oh God. She saw that Ben was grinning at her and then he bent and touched her frozen lips with his.

'You look exhausted and we both need to warm up and freshen up. This, my dear Miss Hartnell, is a typical Parisian hotel of a certain kind. Now, please allow me to introduce you to a typical Parisian hotel of a very different kind.'

14

It was four o'clock when Helen and Ben climbed out of the taxi on the already illuminated rue du Faubourg Saint Honoré and looked up at the elegant and obviously very expensive hotel that dominated the street. Ben asked the driver to wait for them 'just in case'.

'Ben,' Helen grabbed his arm, panicking, stammering. 'I ... I can't possibly stay in a place like this. I can't expect my employer to pay and there's no way I can ...'

'Sshh, I'm just going to make enquiries. You wait in the taxi and if the news is good, I'll come and grab you.'

He came back ten minutes later with the news that, unfortunately, there were no vacancies. Relief and, at the same time, a wild panic surged through Helen's veins.

'But what am I going to do, Ben?' She looked up at him, shivering, her voice small and almost indistinct. 'Look ... I think I'd better take the taxi back to the Hotel de la Gare ... at least I'll have a room for tonight and ...'

'Your room there is already occupied, remember? Leave it to the cockroaches, my love, they'll appreciate it much more than you will. Le douzième arrondissement, monsieur, avenue Daumesnil.'

'Where are we going now?'

'Wait and see.'

***

Ben and Kimberley Beaulac's apartment was on the top floor of a nineteenth-century building on a busy street in the south east of Paris. When they walked into the hall Helen wondered if their homes in New York and the Alps were as comfortably luxurious, as quietly exquisite as this. Ben took her coat and showed her into the living room where huge brick-red sofas and armchairs piled with cushions were scattered around; the walls were lined with books and what looked like original paintings; fresh flowers had been arranged in crystal vases and a majestic, shining black Steinway piano monopolised one corner. The room was warm and, in spite of its grandeur, very cosy.

'Sit down and make yourself comfortable,' Ben said, 'I'll make some coffee. Black and strong, isn't it? The CDs are over there if you'd like to put some music on. Fortunately, our garrulous but very efficient cleaning lady was expecting me and has done her job properly. Oh ... the bathroom's at the end of the corridor if you'd like to freshen up. And if you find any cockroaches, believe me, they weren't there before I left.'

Helen, feeling more than a little intimidated in spite of Ben's insouciance,

15

smiled shyly and went to find the cockroach-less bathroom. She gasped when she stepped into the pale grey, blue and pink tiled room with its double washbasins, ample shower stall and deep, pale grey bath. She suddenly had a deep desire to feel her tired, aching body pummelled by scalding hot water.

'Ben,' she dared to call. 'Do you think I could have a shower?'

'Be my guest. You'll find soaps and gels and creams and shampoos and whatever else women need on the shelves. Oh, and towels are in the blue cupboard.'

It was a dream, it had to be. A few hours previously Helen had been on the coach travelling down from Yorkshire to London, despondent having just said goodbye to her best friend and having just left a life behind her. Right now, she was taking a much-needed, very hot shower in the plush bathroom of a luxurious apartment belonging to an internationally famous musician … a married musician who had two wonderful children. She was spending the evening … maybe even the weekend … with a stranger, a man she'd only just met and purely by chance. A man with a curious but attractive accent, a man who obviously cared about her welfare, a man who'd called his wife on his mobile and lied to her, delayed his trip to the Alps because he wanted to spend some time with *her*, Helen Hartnell … a famous, talented man. A man she'd never see, probably never hear from again. She stepped out of the shower and wrapped one of the thick, soft blue towels around her – as far as she was concerned – uninspiring body. Her wet hair dripped on to the grey tiles and she patted it dry and pulled it back off her face. She unlocked the bathroom door, walked into the corridor and straight into Ben's arms.

***

He had at least the delicacy not to take her into his and Kimberley's bedroom. He carried her, dripping hair and all, into what was obviously the guest room. One of the many guest rooms, more than likely. He lay her gently on the pink duvet that covered the double bed and switched on the lamp with its matching shade. As he slowly pulled the towels from her still-damp body he nuzzled her neck and she clung to him and he whispered, 'What did the wife say who found her husband in bed with a Yorkshire-woman?'

'Oh Ben, don't … please don't …'

'That's quite possible. But, actually, she told him he really was a lucky guy …'

***

After making love, dozing, making love again, taking a shower together and making love under the gushing, foaming water, Helen opened her case and took out what she thought was her most beautiful garment. The height of fashion it definitely was not, nor was it chic or elegant. It was a plain beige jersey dress with three quarter sleeves and a discreetly plunging neckline, quite inappropriate for her, she thought, as she didn't have much to plunge. Her mother had never missed an opportunity to tease her about her 'pinpricks', as she'd always referred to Helen's breasts. Why should she waste 'er 'ard-earned brass on buying 32As for a kid who obviously didn't need a brassière? Who did she think she was, Elizabeth bloody Taylor? Jill definitely 'ad one up on 'er in that department; probably 'er top 'alf were all that Tom saw in 'er, anyway ... But, small breasts or no small breasts, she had always felt reasonably dressed up in the garment that she'd bought in a small boutique in London, and the girls on the training course there had paid her compliments when she wore it.

Ben threw on a pair of black trousers and a pale blue shirt, over which he pulled a navy-blue sweater. They left the apartment and walked a few streets to a quiet and, as Ben insisted, typical French restaurant. They were shown to a table in a dimly-lit corner and Helen wondered if Ben was known there and he had previously reserved the suitably located table. He ordered a bottle of Bollinger and the waiter also placed a bowl of olives and small dishes of various nuts on the table when he served the champagne. He solemnly handed them menus and Helen was pleased to see that the dishes had been translated into ...

'A kind of English,' Ben grinned. 'For example, take a look at the entrées ... third one down.'

'Third ... one ... down ... okay. Egg mayonnaise on a bed of salad with cherry tomatoes and raped carrots. Oh Ben ... what on earth ...?'

'Carottes rapées ... grated carrots to you and the rest of the Anglophone world ... But I do think that raped carrots has a certain "je ne sais quoi", don't you? I don't know who translates the menus in these places but I reckon they should switch jobs and try writing comedy scripts. I was once tempted into ordering stuffed shrimp's balls, just for the hell of it ...'

'Oh Ben!' Helen wiped her eyes, not knowing if the tears were from laughter or the misery of knowing that she'd wake up from this dream far too soon and no doubt be delivered into a very different nightmare.

'Now, let's order. I can recommend the veal blanket. Excellent on a bed of lettuce ... no, don't laugh. Or, how about the cock in wine sauce? No? Well,

I'm going to settle for the snails followed by a juicy steak. How about you, my love?'

Helen looked at Ben mischievously over the top of her huge and entertaining menu and grinned.

'What did the man say who found his wife in bed with a Swede?' she asked him.

'Nothing to do with raped carrots, I hope?'

'Certainly not. That's a turnip for the books!'

'And so is this.'

Ben stood up, leaned across the table and kissed Helen on the lips, almost taking her breath away. The approaching waiter discreetly kept his distance until Ben had sat down again and nodded in his direction.

'Monsieur,' he said, 'on est pret. Les oeufs mayonnaises et carottes rapées pour Madame et, moi, je prends les escargots. Après, Madame, elle va prendre la blanquette de veau et moi le biftek – à point – et une bouteille de Châteauneuf. Merci.'

He stretched his arm across the table and took hold of Helen's left hand.

'Now, my lovely lady, you know all about me and my claim to fame and you know all you need to know about my family. You've visited my home and made rather a mess of the sheets in the guest room – in the nicest possible way, of course. Now I want to know all about you.'

No, you don't, Helen thought and looked away from him. This was where Ben Beaulac began to realise his big mistake in getting involved with Helen Hartnell, the Nondescript. This was where she would start to notice signs of boredom creeping in; barely disguised yawns behind those oh-so-sensitive hands; not-so-discreet glances at the Baume et Mercier watch on his left wrist. The silence lasted quite a while.

'Let's begin at the beginning,' Ben finally said, picking up a handful of pistachios. 'When and where were you born?'

'You should never ask a lady her age,' Helen almost giggled but blushing.

'I'm not asking your age, I'm asking when you were born. Okay, we'll come back to that later. *Where* were you born?'

Helen sighed and looked away from him. The waiter hovered over their table and asked if everything was okay. Ben nodded, smiled briefly and waved him away.

'I was born in Firley; it's a village on the edge of the Pennines. In Yorkshire, as you know. I should have been born in Bradford but I took my mother by surprise.'

'You were a premature baby?' Ben was chewing pistachio nuts and dropping their shells into the bowl provided for that purpose. Helen watched the fingers that fascinated her.

'Only a few days.'

'And did you grow up in ... Firley?'

Helen examined Ben's face for premature signs of boredom, forced attentiveness, but for some inexplicable reason he appeared to be genuinely interested in her childhood. Well, he was certainly unique in that aspect. She helped herself to an olive and concentrated on the bitter but pleasant taste and how to get rid of the stone.

'Yeah,' she nodded her head. 'I lived in, went to school in and grew up in Firley. With my parents – and after my dad died of heart disease – with my ... my mother.'

Ben asked Helen about her mother and Helen told him and by the time she finished, the aperitif and the entrée had both been consumed and enjoyed, and two flutes of champagne happily consumed. Ben merely listened, nodded occasionally and then said, 'And friends. I imagine – and sincerely hope – that you had friends, or at least one good friend in Firley?'

And so she told him about Jill, the best friend anyone could hope to have, and her super family; in spite of Caroline, her eldest daughter, who was starting to cause serious problems. Ben continued to listen in silence, and when she finally came to a full stop and he didn't offer to speak, Helen started to panic. She could imagine the headline in a national newspaper the following morning: 'Nondescript Yorkshire-woman bores celebrated composer to death. Body found under table in chic Parisian restaurant.'

'You know, you have the most beautiful eyes I've ever seen,' Ben suddenly said, 'and a very beguiling smile, and I have a feeling that both are reflecting your thoughts. Are you going to tell me what they are?'

Helen smiled; *beguilingly* she doubted very much.

'Leave me some secrets, please.'

'Absolutely not. That smile makes La Gioconda look like the village gossip. Tell me, what are you thinking about?'

Helen's fork played with the veal on her plate and she avoided Ben's gaze. She told him that she was thinking how dull her life must seem to him and how his bored-to-death stiff body would be discovered the next morning and that she'd probably be found guilty of murder ...

'Manslaughter, perhaps, not murder. It wouldn't be wilful, remember. At least, I hope not.'

Manslaughter. Helen jumped and felt the blood drain from her face. She looked around the warm, comfortable, plush restaurant and watched the cortège moving slowly to the small church on the edge of the moor in Firley.

Her mother's final and only mute outing in the village. That hadn't been wilful ... not at all.

Ben sipped his wine and gently placed the long-stemmed crystal glass on the table. He covered Helen's right hand with his own.

'Helen, if you knew how much you don't bore me, you'd obviously be very surprised.'

They walked slowly back to the apartment, arm in arm, their breath visible in the cold air. Once inside his home Ben pulled Helen into his arms, ripping off the only decent dress she possessed and heedlessly flinging it on to the parquet floor. Their lovemaking was, if possible, even more passionate, more urgent. It wasn't until much later, when they lay in each other's arms, legs entwined and hands clasped, that Helen realised they were not in the guest room. This bed was wider, higher, with a kind of canopy over the top; a four-poster, for God's sake. The sheets were silky beige and the furniture in the room was sparse. There was a single mahogany chest of drawers, on top of which stood a Tiffany lamp, a crystal vase empty of flowers now, and a display of photographs. She tried not to look at them when Ben suddenly got up and told her he was going to 'take a leak'. After he left the room, however, her curiosity took over. She slid out of the bed and tiptoed across the beige carpet to the chest of drawers and her eyes skimmed over the framed faces. Ben and Kimberley sitting on a beach; Ben and Kimberley in ski-suits, laughing into each other's faces, snow-capped mountains in the background; two adolescents – obviously Jeremy and Amy in what looked like New York; Ben sitting at his piano; Ben and Kimberley ... no, not Kimberley. Ben and another, very beautiful woman, standing in front of another piano in what looked like a night club. The toilet flushed. Water ran into the basin; a raucous, out-of-tune singing. Come to think of it, Helen thought, which woman was his wife?

'Excuse me, monsieur,' Helen smiled at him from under the sheets when he loped back into the bedroom and perched on the bed. 'Can you by any chance play the piano?'

'It has been said, madame. Why do you ask?'

'Because you certainly can't sing.' Unoriginal maybe but Ben didn't seem to notice.

The next second Helen was in his arms again and his fingers were creating a beautiful melody on her skin. She clung to him, wanting him to make love to her all afternoon, all evening, all night ... and her mind shut out the smiling, beautiful women who also shared Ben's evidently complicated life.

Much later, when their bodies were replete and they were dozing in each other's arms, Ben suddenly murmured, 'I've just thought of another one. What did the guy say who found his wife in bed with a Turk?'

'Oh Ben. Not now ... I'm too exhausted to even think ...' Helen yawned.

'Don't be a killjoy. Just answer the question. What did the guy say who found his wife in bed with a Turk?'

'I don't know.'

'She's wild, man, you'd better Ankara to the bed. Ankara to the bed ... anchor her ... Do you get it?'

'Yes, Ben, I get it. I'd like to get some sleep, too, if that's okay.'

'That's okay. But first, what did the guy say ...'

'I've no idea, I don't care and I'm saying goodnight.'

'Killjoy. Goodnight.'

**

They slept late the following morning. Ben was still sleeping when Helen woke up, panicking at first because she had no idea where she was, and then because she knew exactly where she was. She heard, felt and saw the man lying beside her; shame and regrets kaleidoscoped around inside her head and slowly disappeared. But the panic stayed because the man would be leaving her the following day. Going to the French Alps to his wife and later his children and hard work; and where would she be going? She didn't have a bloody clue. She had no home to go to and now no hotel, either. She had to go see her future employer, introduce herself and find out more details about her employment at the beauty salon ... And that suddenly became something to be dreaded, too. She had quickly got used to having a man around her in the last few hours, a man to help her, take over in her time of need. But once Ben was on that train tomorrow, she'd be completely alone. She shivered in the warm bed and felt the tears squeeze out of her eyes. She wiped them on the silky beige sheet and felt Ben stir beside her. His right arm reached out and his hand worked its way around her waist.

'Okay, my love?' he asked

'Hmm.'

Ben looked at the small brass alarm clock at his side of the bed.

'Christ, do you know what time it is? Eleven-thirty. Do you realise, madame, that it's never been known for Benjamin Beaulac to stay in bed later than eight a.m., Sundays included?'

'There's a first time for everything.'

Ben yawned loudly, stretched and sat up. Looking down at her he said,

'What do you say we take a long hot shower together, have a long, hot coffee together and then go in search of a small, warm restaurant for lunch?'

'Is it lunchtime already?'

'No, but you're in Paris, and by the time we're ready it'll be time for aperitif. We'll find a quiet bar first and then I'll take you out to lunch.'

'You mean you don't want me to cook Yorkshire pudding for your Sunday lunch?'

'Okay. We'll eat in a restaurant and you can make dessert when we get back. Sounds good.'

Helen rolled her eyes heavenward and poked him in the ribs.

'Yorkshire pudding is *not* a dessert. You've been to Yorkshire; you should know that. I'm really not impressed, monsieur. By the way, why did you go there, how long did you stay and will you be going back? I want to know all your connections with my beautiful county.'

Ben disentangled himself from her embrace, got out of bed and rubbed both hands across his face, which was turned away from her. For a long time there was silence. Helen suddenly began to feel her flesh crawl and wanted to bite back her words. She looked at his back as he walked out of the bedroom.

'I didn't spend long enough time in Yorkshire to get acquainted with its culinary delights. Or any other delights, for that matter.'

***

They ate brunch in a large and lively brasserie in Saint Germain-des-Prés and Helen asked Ben about his work. He told her about his studies at the Conservatoire de Paris and his early failures and later successes that led to his fame and fortune. Helen told him that she had most, if not all, his CDs tucked somewhere inside her suitcase. Didn't she have anything better to squash inside her suitcase? he wanted to know.

'Well, there's my poetry.'

'Ah, and whose poetry is that? Philip Larkin? John Betjeman? TS Eliot . . . he's my favourite . . .'

'I told you. *My* poetry.'

Ben looked at her for a long time, his mouth slightly open.

'You mean you write poetry?' His fork stood upright in his left hand. 'Well, that's not bad at all for a boring Yorkshire lady. Tell me about it, Helen. What kind of poetry do you write?'

Suddenly, Helen regretted this small confidence. It had been foolish. And when was the last time she had written anything worthwhile? When was the last time she'd written?

22

'I used to ... scribble. A long time ago. Just for me. Nobody ever read my ... my poetry. Except ... well, my mother. And my best friend, Jill.'

Ben remembered the stories about Helen's mother that hadn't bored him at all and he could well imagine the woman's reaction to her young daughter's literary leanings. He smiled at Helen.

'And what was your mother's verdict?'

Helen pulled her eyes away from his gaze and cursed herself for having mentioned her damn poems – not to mention her mother. Ben Beaulac's music was the best thing that she'd squashed inside her suitcase. Full stop.

'She told the neighbours she was fed up of seeing me with a bloody pen in my hand – instead o' doin' summat useful.'

After a few moments, Ben lifted her chin with his right hand and smiled into her eyes.

'And your father? Did he read your poetry?'

Helen managed a smile and a slight shrug.

'I was a second Emily Dickinson as far as my dad was concerned. Bless him.'

'And maybe your dad was right. You should continue ... scribbling, Helen.'

She nodded and wrinkled her nose at him.

'Maybe Paris will give me some inspiration.'

'If Paris doesn't, nothing will.'

***

When they left the brasserie, the freezing air nipped and tugged at their faces. Ben pulled up the collar of his heavy raincoat and Helen shivered and hugged herself.

'Do you like Impressionist paintings?' Ben suddenly asked.

'Oh, I *love* them.'

'Okay. Come on.'

Helen didn't ask any questions, she only accepted and followed. They clattered down the stairs of the nearest metro station, Ben bought two tickets and they emerged at Place de la Concorde.

'Just imagine,' Ben said, 'you could have been living in the lap of luxury in the hotel a few hundred yards from here ... snug and warm, well-fed and your every wish catered for. Instead, you're standing in the freezing cold with a guy who can't sing and who didn't even know that Yorkshire pudding wasn't a dessert. What is Yorkshire pudding, by the way?'

'You honestly don't know? Well ... it's a kind of pancake that's cooked in the oven and rises ...'

'That reminds me. What did the guy say who found his wife in bed with a Yorkshireman?'

'I haven't the foggiest idea.' Helen's teeth were chattering.

'Neither have I but I'll think of something.'

'There's no rush. Be like the other American and take your time ... and did you bring me here to gaze adoringly at the hotel where I'm not staying?'

'Patience is a virtue, my love. Follow me.'

He took her to the Musée de l'Orangerie, a small but exquisite museum in the Tuileries gardens, packed with, amongst other masterpieces, Impressionist paintings by Renoir and Monet, including the latter's famous water lilies. Helen was captivated and Ben proved an excellent guide; he obviously knew a lot about Impressionism and the art world in general. Helen asked if he had ever studied art as well as music and he said no, but ... no, he hadn't. Before they reluctantly (at least as far as Helen was concerned) left the museum, Ben bought her a reproduction of Renoir's 'Filles au Piano' and later, sitting frozen stiff by the equally frozen Tuileries' lake, she asked Ben to sign the painting on the back. He looked at her with raised eyebrows, his nose bright red, his teeth making music.

'Are you asking me to forge Renoir's signature, madame?'

'No, idiot,' Helen laughed, 'I'm asking you to write a message on the back ... I want to have *your* signature.'

'My autograph, you mean.'

Helen nodded, her teeth chattering along with his.

'Aye, lad, then I can sell it when I'm a down-an'-out in Paris, wi' nowhere to live.'

***

It was getting dark when they left the park and went back to the apartment. When Ben unlocked the door, warmth and the fragrance of pine enveloped them. Helen, standing in the entrance hall, suddenly felt gauche and shy again; out of place in her married lover's home. He took hold of her hand and guided her into the living room, gently pushed her on to one of the deep, comfortable sofas and told her he was going to make a hot drink. She merely nodded and watched his agile body leave the room. She looked at the simple, black leather-strapped watch on her left wrist. It was six-thirty. In a few hours Ben would be getting ready to go to the station and take the train to his home in the Alps. And then, she had no doubts whatsoever, he would completely forget her. But what about her? What was she supposed to do tomorrow? Go back to the Hotel de la Gare? Beg in the boulevards? Go back to Firley? Neither of them had brought the subject up, crucial as it was. Ben obviously hadn't given it a thought, but then why should he? It wasn't his problem. He'd done his bit for her, hadn't he? When he came back a few minutes later, carrying a tray laden with mugs and a huge coffeepot, she avoided his gaze. He sat beside her, told her he'd be mother (That was the right British expression, wasn't it, Helen?) and handed her a steaming mug. They sipped the hot liquid in silence for a while and Ben didn't seem to notice either Helen's silence or her facial expression. He stood up and went to find the Renoir reproduction that Helen had left on the table in the hall. He sat down, carefully pulled the picture out of its wrapping and scrutinised it.

'It's beautiful, isn't it?' he finally said. 'Renoir is by far my favourite French artist. I also admire Monet, of course, and I like the English Turner's work … and, for my money, the most talented American painter is Norman Rockwell. Do you know Rockwell's work, Helen?'

After a while he turned to face her.

'Helen?'

'I've heard of him.' Her voice was barely audible. 'But I don't know his work at all.'

'You do realise you've just committed a gross criminal offence, don't you? Not know Rockwell's work …'

'Personally, I'm a great admirer of Atkinson Grimshaw.'

'Who the hell is … Atkinson who?'

'Touché.'

Ben threw his head back and laughed.

'Okay. You win. Now, do you still want me to write on the back of this?'

Helen didn't reply. She was still thinking about the following day and all the following days to come and her new life and terrible loneliness, a loneliness she hadn't really thought about until she thought about Ben Beaulac leaving her to join his wife at their chalet near Chamonix.

'Helen?'

'Oh … please yourself.'

Ben turned round and faced her on the sofa.

'Helen?'

'Write something on the back if you'd like to; if you don't, it doesn't matter.'

'Okay. What's wrong?'

She allowed the tears to come then and they gushed out of her eyes and down her cheeks and she hiccupped loudly.

'Everything's wrong, Ben. For me, I mean. Soon I'm going to start working for a woman I've never met in a place I've never seen. I don't know

25

anyone in this city and now, thanks to you and ... and your hot-headedness yesterday, I don't even have anywhere to stay.'

She breathed in deeply and wiped her face on the back of her hand. She didn't care how inelegant or gauche and childish she seemed. That wasn't her problem.

'Okay, so the Hotel de la Gare was a pigsty, but at least I had a place to go back to at night.'

'Along with the roaches.' Ben was smiling.

'Ben, for God's sake, I've got nowhere to live! I'm in a real bloody mess, don't you understand?'

And tomorrow you'll be leaving me and I'll never see you again and the solitude will be twice as bad than if I'd got off that train alone. But she kept those thoughts to herself.

'Go to the bathroom,' Ben said, 'dry your eyes and freshen up and then we'll have a long talk. Okay?'

When she came out of the bathroom twenty minutes later, Ben went in. The Renoir reproduction was lying face down on the otherwise empty coffee table. A long, black and spidery scrawl crawled across the paper.

My darling Helen,

Please don't sell my autograph, it won't be necessary. And don't worry, you're not going to be a down-and-out in Paris. You can stay here for as long as you like. Call Monsieur Henri Parisot on this number tomorrow 01.43.75.01.95 and you'll soon find a suitable apartment.

I can't tell you how glad I am that we met.

With my love,

Ben

'Who's Monsieur Henri Parisot?'

'A very good friend of mine. He owns an excellent music shop in Saint Germain-des-Prés – not far from where we had lunch – and he also owns a lot of property in Paris. Decent property; not cheap but not excessively expensive, either. Tell him you're ... an acquaintance of mine. He'll soon fix you up.'

Helen was putting the finishing touches to her simple makeup. They looked at each other over her handbag mirror.

'And I can stay here for as long as I want?'

Ben dragged his eyes away from her gaze and ran his right hand through his hair.

'Yeah. Well, at least until Henri fixes you up ... and, of course, you will have to be very discreet, Helen. For God's sake, don't be around when Madame Masson, our cleaning lady, comes, for example. She's here three

mornings a week, Monday, Wednesday and Friday, from nine till twelve.
And try to avoid the concierge, if you can. She's an inquisitive old ...
Anyway, I'll give you a key so you can come and go. Just be discreet, that's all
I ask. Well, you don't need me to tell you ...' He shrugged. 'So, Helen,
accommodation isn't your principal worry.'

Helen didn't reply at first, simply because she had to refuse. It would be
impossible for her to make use of Ben and Kimberley's flat, under the
circumstances.

'I don't think I can stay here on my own, Ben ...'

'Quite honestly, you don't have the choice, Helen. And it won't be more
than a few days if I know Henri Parisot, believe me. Call him first thing
tomorrow and make an appointment to see him.'

'Okay,' she nodded slowly. 'Well, thanks. Thank you, Ben.'

'Now. Let's go eat.'

'Actually, I'm not very hungry.'

'Well, I am. You can sit and watch me devour chicken in mustard sauce
and ...'

'No, I can't,' Helen laughed. 'But I'll blame you when I can't get into my
clothes.'

'Suits me. I prefer to see you get out of your clothes.'

***

They ate a light supper in a bistro a couple of streets away and over the meal
Helen shyly asked Ben more questions about his family. She couldn't help
but notice the fleeting look of irritation on his face.

'I've already told you about my family, haven't I? I have a wife, Kimberley
– Kim, on a good day – and two great kids, Jeremy and Amy.'

'I saw their photos in ... in the bedroom. They're gorgeous kids. You're
really lucky, Ben. But don't you have any brothers and sisters? Cousins twice
removed? Famous aunts and uncles?'

She tried to make light of the questions but her eagerness to hear his
answers was obvious in both her voice and her eyes. Families, especially big,
happy families, intrigued her. It was something she knew nothing about.

'Yeah, sure I have a family. I have ... I have a brother and sister-in-law and
God knows how many cousins.'

'In France or America?'

'France, the States. All over the globe. I've lost track.'

Helen, the childless, sibling-less, cousin-less orphan warmed quickly to
her subject, encouraged by Ben's frivolous but frank response.

'Oh, I think that's wonderful. You're *so* lucky, you know. Do you see them all? Do you manage to keep in touch with your family all over the globe?'

'Some of them, yes.'

Ben spoke quietly and his fingers crept to the cruet on the table and he knocked out a kind of tune with the salt and pepper pots. Some salt spilled on to the red and green checked tablecloth.

'Those whom I want to keep in touch with.'

'How come you were born in India, Ben?'

He dropped the cruet on the table and his right index finger slowly formed patterns with the salt. He laughed, a strange, dry sound that came from deep in his throat, a new sound to Helen and one she knew she didn't want to hear again.

'So, you know that much about me, do you? I'm afraid the media doesn't leave many stones unturned ... Anyway, it's a good question. How come I was born in India? Because my crazy, rather irresponsible and egotistical mother, very much against the advice of her obstetrician, insisted on travelling during a – I won't go into details – difficult pregnancy. It's a long, complicated story that's had permanent and damaging repercussions.' He paused. 'I have ...'

Helen's cheeks burned scarlet and she cursed herself for having touched a sensitive spot and her own out of place curiosity. What must he be thinking of her now?

'Did you live in India for a long time?' she interrupted. 'I mean, did you grow up in India or New York?'

'I grew up in New York and France – I've no memories of India at all. It's a pity. Maybe I'll go back there someday.'

Questions tumbled around inside Helen's head, her interest in Ben's family and their seemingly best-forgotten past exciting her interest but she knew she had to let the subject drop. There were a few moments' silence when she would have loved to be able to read her companion's thoughts, and then Ben said, 'Let's go back to the apartment, Helen. I want to hold you.'

Ben held her tightly most of the night and Helen rubbed her silent tears into his skin. Something to remember her by, she thought. *Her* autograph would be worth nothing, there was no point in offering that. And then she reprimanded herself for being immature and very unfair. They talked and made love and talked again, mostly about Helen's future, and Ben did his best to give her good advice. She listened but hardly heard his advice or anything else he said; she only wished he would be there, with her, part of her future. Before they drifted into a very short but deep sleep, Ben, his lips in her hair, whispered, 'What did the guy say who found his wife in bed with an Indian?'

Helen cursed him for his frivolity and total lack of sensitivity at such a time but said nothing.

'He said, "What a curry on."'

'Or maybe he said, "Rajah you than me."'

'I'm going to miss you, Helen Hartnell.'

Helen didn't, or rather couldn't, reply.

Chapter Three

———

'The only men *you're* capable of attractin' are either idiots or bastards.'
Her mother had said those words to her sometime after Malcolm, her precious and previously puppy-faithful Malcolm, had shown his true colours with Jill's undeniably alluring penfriend; and after Alan, the infatuated farmer's son, had literally swept her off her feet during one of their hikes and almost dropped her – accidentally, but even so – down a rocky ravine. It had started out as a laugh, just a bit of fun. It took a long time for Helen to get over that and she never spoke to Alan again. In retrospect her mother had been right. Malcolm Jones had turned out to be a right bastard and Alan Dakers the biggest idiot she'd ever had the misfortune to meet. And both of them, in their callow, shallow, short-sighted youth, had been attracted to her.

Benjamin Beaulac obviously found her very attractive. So, if Dorothy Hartnell's pessimistic pronouncement was correct, she now had to ask herself; was he a bastard or was he an idiot?

Well, he was no idiot. The world could testify to that.

Ben didn't need to pack very much; as he told her, most of his winter clothes and other daily necessities were in permanent residence at his chalet in Chamonix. He merely threw a few items into his medium-sized, dark green holdall while Helen sat in the living room trying to make her mind a blank. She had never believed in love at first sight, it was the stuff of corny novels and women's cheap magazines, but she had fallen head over heels in love with Benjamin Beaulac in a very short time and he had overturned her life. She already felt dependent on a man whom she couldn't depend on at all, for a number of reasons. She'd behaved totally out of character (the character that her mother had oh-so-carefully carved) and she hardly recognised herself, sitting here in the 'salon' of a plush apartment in Paris, ready to say goodbye to a man who would never give her another thought once he was on that train. And how was she supposed to cope alone and anonymous and completely out of place in his apartment? She couldn't stay here for any length of time, and what if Henri What's-his-name had no property available? Helen had never really felt very secure in her life, but she'd never felt as insecure as she did now. She listened to Ben's quiet humming and drawers being opened and shut and suddenly she could stand the silence of the room and her thoughts no longer. She tapped on the bedroom door and walked in.

'Ben.'

'Hmm?'

He was obviously preoccupied, his family-man thoughts probably being already in the mountains with his wife (Kim-on-a-good-day) and two wonderful children, who'd be arriving at Christmas. Maybe he was already preparing his first ski-jump of the season, or the musical, or the theme tune for the film that would be released next year. How could she, Helen Hartnell, compare with all that?

'I ... I'd like to go with you to the station. Stand on the platform and wave you off until the train is a mere speck on the horizon ...'

She tried to make her voice light, frivolous but her request was very serious.

'That's impossible, my love.'

Helen's heart plummeted and she swallowed loudly.

'Why? Why is it impossible, Ben?'

She hoped that she wasn't whining, although she knew that she was.

'For the simple reason that I'm not going to the station,' he grinned at her, zipping up his bag. 'I'm flying to Geneva – the nearest airport to Chamonix – and my wife will be picking me up there. No ... no, Helen, you can't come to the airport with me. It's too far out of Paris for you to return alone without getting lost or ... or something.'

'I'm not three years old, for God's sake.'

She looked into his eyes and Ben cleared his throat and turned away.

'It's better that you don't go to the airport with me, Helen.'

Of course. Ben Beaulac was too well known for him to arrive for his flight with a woman who wasn't his wife. Helen also turned away and walked back into the living room. Ben followed her.

'I'm sorry, my love.'

I'm not your 'love', Helen wanted to scream at him.

'It's far better that we say goodbye here and that you stay here. Don't go out at all today, Helen. There's everything you need in the apartment; food, drink, bed, music ... Just make yourself at home. And remember to leave everything as you found it – when you move into Henri Parisot's apartment.'

The entry-phone suddenly buzzed loudly and insistently. 'That's all I ask. Look ... I'm sorry, Helen ... I'll have to go. That's my taxi. I'll call you from the airport, okay? In about an hour, give or take. If the phone rings at any other time, please don't answer it. And don't forget to call Henri Parisot tomorrow.'

'I won't. Forget, I mean.'

Helen's voice was almost inaudible as she tried not to let her emotions show. Ben, it was quite obvious, had no emotions. The entry-phone rang again.

'I'll have to go.' Ben pulled Helen into his arms, kissed her for a long time and she clung to the body that she'd grown to know and love in such a short time. 'Take care of yourself, Helen.'

'I will. You too.'

'And enjoy Paris.'

Yeah, sure. He hugged her one last time, kissed her cheek and headed towards the door and, she imagined, out of her life.

'Oh Ben ... a key?'

'Oh God, yeah. Look ... there's a spare one in the kitchen. On a hook next to the window. On a teddy-bear key ring. It belongs to Amy. Bye, Helen.'

'Bye ... Ben.'

And he was gone.

***

Helen turned back into the salon but saw none of its luxury because of the tears that swam in her eyes and gushed down her cheeks. She had never felt so alone in her life and asked herself what the hell she had done and why had she done it. If she'd stayed in Firley and not taken that training course in London; if her mother hadn't ... died; if Jill had discouraged her from launching herself on this crazy venture, told her she needed her there, in Firley ... if ... if ... if. She walked into the bedroom ... Ben and Kimberley's bedroom ... and lay back down on the big double, unmade bed. She closed her eyes and, from sheer stress and lack of sleep, fell into a deep slumber. The telephone ringing about an hour later woke her.

'Ben!'

'You sound sleepy. Did I wake you?'

'No ... yes. But it doesn't matter. Where are you?'

'I'm in a very crowded and noisy departure lounge, I'll be getting on the plane very soon so I can't stay long. This is going to sound ridiculous, Helen, but I'm really missing you.'

In her confusion and sudden, unexpected joy, Helen attempted humour.

'Oh? And why should it sound ridiculous?'

He was missing her? Helen looked around the bedroom that was all too redolent of Benjamin Beaulac. The good-looking, the talented, the famous. She heard his laughter and then a lot of background noise and whatever he replied was unintelligible.

'I'm missing you, too!' she almost screamed, wanting him to hear her, understand her, not to go away from her. 'Ben ... Ben ... What did the man say who found his wife in bed with a... with a Swiss bloke? He said ... "Chalet tell you what to do?" Shall I tell you ... Do you get it, Ben? Do you get it ...?'

And she burst into tears. When, finally, she stopped crying, the drowsiness and lassitude came crawling back, along with a deeper feeling of regret. He should never have phoned her. He should have just gone, closed the door behind him and forgotten her. Left her at the Gare du Nord to fend for herself and never contacted her again. It would have been so much easier for her that way.

***

Ben hadn't told Helen if Henri Parisot spoke English or not and she hadn't thought to ask. She hadn't thought about Mr Parisot or anything at all while Ben had been there. But now Ben wasn't there and the unknown Henri Parisot was suddenly the most important person in Helen's life. On Monday morning at about ten o'clock, she dialled the number in front of her, written in Ben's spidery black scrawl, and a man's rather high-pitched voice spoke after the second ring.

'Allo?'

Emotion and nerves prevented Helen from remembering the simplest French phrase and she suddenly felt like a babbling idiot.

'Ah, Madame Hart-nell? You are the English friend of Mr Beaulac?'

'Yes. Oui, monsieur.'

'And you are looking for accommodation in Paris, I believe? Well, maybe I can help you. I have three properties available at the moment, madame, two in the city centre and one in the banlieue ... the suburbs. But I think for you, in the city centre, perhaps?'

'Oh yes ... yes, I think so, monsieur.'

'Exact. So, if you can come to my shop this evening, to discuss?'

'This evening?' Helen suddenly felt revived, alert. 'Oh ... oh, yes, of course. What time would you like me to come?'

'Let us say seven o'clock. Do you have the address of my shop, madame?'

He enunciated 'my shop' as though it were the Elysée Palace and Helen, smiling through her sadness and anxiety, told Monsieur Parisot that she didn't know the address. He provided her with the information plus the nearest metro station – Saint Sulpice – and Helen made a note. She thanked the owner of the music shop and property in Paris. The owner of her eternal gratitude if he could find her somewhere to live. Immediately. She wanted to phone Ben to tell him, to thank him, but she couldn't. He hadn't even given her his mobile number. Of course. After freshening up, arming herself with a metro plan and tentatively asking for directions in abysmal French, Helen arrived at the 'Parisot Marché de la Musique' on rue de Rennes five minutes before the appointed time. A bell tinkled as she pushed open the door and she found herself surrounded by Steinways and saxophones, clarinets and electronic keyboards. A short, almost perfectly round, bald and bespectacled man, probably in his late fifties, suddenly appeared in front of her and beamed, displaying a set of obviously very false teeth.

'Madame Hart-nell?' he said, again emphasising the second syllable.

'Oui, monsieur.'

'And I am Henri Parisot.'

He held out a soft, chubby and rather hairy hand which Helen took hold of and then he asked her to follow him into a back room. Once settled at the long, wooden, paper-filled table, Henri Parisot placed two of the papers in front of her, explaining that they were descriptions of two studios – single room apartments – he had available. Both were furnished, very basically; one was in the north of Paris with easy access to the Gare du Nord (he beamed knowledgeably at her, no doubt thinking of the Eurostar) and Helen shuddered, visions of cracked washbasins and cockroaches sailing in front of her. The second one was on the Left Bank, not too far from rue de Rennes, a lively, busy district but the street was quiet and the rent reasonable. After telling her the price – 2,500 francs a month – he added that the building was more than one hundred years old, typically Parisian, but he had refurbished it with a new bathroom and kitchenette. He thought she would find the studio comfortable.

'When can I have a look at it?' Helen asked, the excitement she was beginning to feel evident in her voice.

'Why not now, madame?' Henri suggested, smiling with his big white teeth and playing with his thick, grey moustache.

The accommodation was everything that Henri had described, and more. Typically Parisian it was; a winding, wooden staircase led to the first floor and the hall smelt of wax. Inside the studio, a highly polished parquet floor supported a simple but sufficient kitchenette and a living/bedroom with a sofa-bed, one armchair, a chest of drawers and a cupboard-cum-wardrobe. The new bathroom was small, modern, clean and free of cockroaches. This had suddenly become a priority. Half an hour later, Helen Hartnell had an address in Paris.

'But you won't be able to move in until your official papers are in order,'

Henri Parisot told her. 'You must have your resident's permit and salary slip before anything else may happen. But please don't worry, madame, the studio is yours.'

As they were getting ready to leave and Helen was having a final look at the place, Monsieur Parisot told her that if she wanted to decorate or change anything, she was free to do so. He winked at her as he locked the door and slipped the key into his briefcase.

'For example, I think a grand piano ... a beautiful, elegant, highly polished Steinway against the wall ... would look ... well, wonderful in your room, madame. And you?'

His salesman's eyes twinkled at her from behind his rimless spectacles and Helen smiled.

'Well, I don't play the piano, Monsieur Parisot, and I think it might be a bit of a tight squeeze ...' Henri Parisot frowned. 'The studio is a little too small,' Helen explained. 'I think I'll hang a picture on the wall instead.'

'Ah well, tant pis pour moi.' The Frenchman pretended to look heartbroken and then beamed at her again. 'And do you have a nice painting to hang on your wall, Madame Hart-nell?'

'Yes,' Helen managed to smile at him. 'Yes, actually, I do.'

Once outside, Henri Parisot asked Helen to let him know when her papers had been sorted out; hinting that it would probably be quite a complicated affair.

'Ah, l'administration française!' he exclaimed, rolling his eyes but offering no explanation.

They shook hands and before they parted Helen asked Mr Parisot to thank Mr Beaulac on her behalf, the next time he spoke to him. And then she disappeared before the little Frenchman had time to ask why she didn't thank Mr Beaulac herself.

***

As soon as she got back to the apartment-where-she-shouldn't-have-been, Helen felt Ben's presence all around her. His ridiculous jokes almost made her smile as she locked the door behind her; his hands touched hers when she spread honey on her 'biscottes' the following morning; his tuneless singing rang in her ears while she lathered her body in the shower; and his body covered hers in the too-big-for-a-lonely-lady double bed. She slept fitfully in the guest room, a thousand answerless questions turning around inside her head. Instead of thinking forward and of what the future held for her in the most fascinating city in the world, she could think only of the past few days and wonder why fate had dictated that she meet such a man at such a critical time in her life.

She got up at seven-thirty on Tuesday morning, her head heavy with lack of sleep, apprehension and remorse. Benjamin Beaulac was still with her, still inside her; she had to get rid of him. Mentally thank him for all that he'd done for her – a lot – and then totally and absolutely forget him. The only contact she would have with him in the future would be when she slipped his music on to whatever CD player she happened to have. Maybe much later in the future that would be quite an easy thing to do, but right now Helen had to indulge in a few tears before she was able to think about the day ahead.

She planned to pay a courtesy call on Madame Chantal Gauthier, her employer-to-be, who was still an unknown entity.

⁎

After a year's training at a beautician's school in London and passing the final theoretical and practical exams with flying colours, Helen realised that finding actual employment was going to be a very different kettle of fish. She had thoroughly enjoyed her year in London, in spite of the great age difference between her and her fellow students, girls fresh from school, inexperienced in any kind of work in adult life. Her mother had had a beano with that one; started calling her 'granny' every time she phoned home, until Dorothy realised it was like water off a duck's back to Helen. Then she'd started on a different tack. 'Aren't beauticians supposed to be beautiful?' A postscript of her 'You'll never be a beautician. These beauty salons only take on glamorous types. Some 'opes you'll 'ave.' Did all dentists have magnificent molars? Did all gynaecologists have faultless fallopian tubes? Was there no such thing as a corn-crippled chiropodist? Well, maybe not. But her retorts only added fuel to Dorothy Hartnell's inextinguishable fire and, in the end, Helen gave up. She also gave up calling home so often, and the fuel continued to ignite.

When she first arrived in London in September, 1996, the training school found accommodation for her in a residence for young women in Finsbury Park where other students were also staying. It was a soulless modern building but comfortable and with a warm, friendly atmosphere, and for the first time in her life Helen knew a certain amount of independence. At first the big city scared her but gradually she found her way around and she took advantage of a lot of what London had to offer. She also appreciated the domestic arrangements; sharing the kitchen and bathroom with other women wasn't a problem for her; it was fun because they cooked together, exchanged recipes and culinary tips and advice on table etiquette and Helen learned a lot. In other circumstances Helen, being by far the eldest, found herself in the unusual and rather touching position of maternal figure, agony aunt. Not feeling adequate to deal with this kind of relationship, she at first shied away from intimate contact with the girls, but little by little grew to appreciate their respect for her and reacted more positively. It was impossible for her to become close friends with any of them because of the age difference and also because of their often very different backgrounds, but that wasn't what Helen was looking for at the time. Her only target was to do well in her training and find a reasonable job at the end of it. She did, in fact, shine in her studies and grew interested in the human body in general; the way it functioned, nutrition, exercise and how to maintain its well-being. She came to understand the importance of a sensible diet and a healthy lifestyle and knew she'd have difficulty in swallowing Dorothy's mediocre and unappetising meals in the future. She was glad that she'd never been tempted to smoke or over-indulge in alcohol (at least not very often) and tried to get at least seven hours' sleep every night. That wasn't too difficult as her social life in London was less than exciting. She was invited to spend time with 'the girls' but their ideas of a good night out didn't really run on the same lines, which was normal. So, Helen concentrated on her studies, the theory and later the practice, and took more of an interest in clothes than she'd ever done, or been allowed to do, in the past.

When the final exams had been taken and passed, of course, Helen had to start looking for work. She would have liked to stay in the capital, at least for a while, have some work experience there so it would look good on her CV, but she very quickly realised that there was too much competition. After her third interview and subsequent rejection, Helen started to accept that maybe London wasn't the best place to start in her new career. She was being too ambitious. Working in and around Bradford, however, wasn't an exciting prospect. Beauty salons were few and far between and after a year living in London, Helen wanted to move on and away. Away from Firley and its very few happy memories – her dad, Jill, Tom and, of course, Malcolm. Away from its bitter memories, too; there were certainly more of those. But most of all she wanted to move finally and permanently away from her mother.

She found temporary work selling perfume in a department store in Bradford, to put her on until 'something better came along'. At least that's what she told everyone who wanted to know why she was 'wasting her time serving behind a counter when she were qualified to do better things'. But for Helen the few months she spent selling perfume and beauty products weren't a waste of time at all because she was still learning, stacking away bits of information that she'd be able to put to use later. How much later, she'd no idea. The temporary job lasted longer than she'd anticipated and she was still selling perfume in the department store long after Dorothy Hartnell had been buried in the small, untidy graveyard that surrounded Firley church.

One afternoon, standing idle behind the counter, Helen was flicking through a trade publication when her eye was caught by a large advertisement that stood out from the rest. Chantal Gauthier of the Institut de Beauté, rue du Faubourg Poissoniere, Paris, was looking for an English-speaking beautician to start in November of that year. There were few other details, but there was a telephone number to ring. Helen, on the spur of the moment, jotted the number down and that evening rang Jill. Caroline, the daughter who'd recently started to rock the Hopkins' domestic boat, answered the phone and Helen (Caroline refused to call her Auntie Helen any more) as usual, tried to chat to her before Jill took the receiver. Chatting to her mother's boring, middle-aged friends, including the erstwhile 'Auntie' Helen, wasn't exactly on Caroline's list of priorities, however, and Jill – tired, run-down, exasperated Jill – was soon on the line.

'Go for it,' she said.

'Do you think I should? Honestly? I mean, Jill, it's a bit like a dream, isn't it? I mean, can you imagine me ... working in Paris ... *living* in Paris? I sound like an excited kid on a school trip, don't I? I feel like an excited kid ... I don't speak French. You could give me lessons.'

'Oh, aye! You must be joking. When was the last time I spoke any French? But you could take lessons, Helen. There are evening classes in Bradford ... Oh, I know you; you'll sit and think about all the reasons not to do it and then it'll be too late. Helen, you can at least apply for the job. See what happens. Have a go.'

'Are you trying to get rid of me?' Helen laughed. She could imagine her friend raising her eyebrows heavenward on the other side of the village.

'Look, Helen, just do it.'

So, Helen took her best friend's advice and did it. But she couldn't summon up the courage to phone; instead, she wrote a rather lengthy letter to Chantal Gauthier, introducing herself and her qualifications, and wondered how she'd cope if Madame Gauthier invited her to Paris for an interview. Madame Gauthier did invite her, but not for an interview. The job was hers if she still wanted it, starting in November. The reply from Paris took Helen's and Jill's breath away. They sat and scrutinised its contents – In execrable English – over lunch one Saturday in the department store's self-service café.

'It's all your fault.' Helen grinned as she sat opposite her friend at the badly-stained Formica topped table. Jill didn't ask why the bloody hell it was her fault, as Helen expected her to. She only sort of semi-smiled and concentrated on her empty cup as though she were reading the leaves. Helen understood then and a little lump came into her throat; but she wasn't going to turn back now.

Helen put her mother's small, cramped terraced house on the edge of the moor on the market, took a short and very intensive French course with a non-native speaker – a highly competent, sari-clad Indian lady, in fact – and handed in her notice at the department store. She was going to Paris to wax legs and armpits, paint faces and massage overweight bodies … but whose faces and bodies would she be making beautiful in Paris? That was the titillating question that haunted her days and nights.

Helen's last meeting with Jill before she left for London and the Eurostar was a bittersweet affair. Tom stayed at home to keep an eye on the kids while they had a drink at the local Bay Horse Pub and dinner at their favourite Chinese restaurant in the new, too-modern-for-their-taste district of Firley.

'You will come and see me, won't you?' Helen urged for the umpteenth time. And Jill confirmed for the umpteenth time that of course she'd come and visit, as soon as Helen was settled. Helen said she felt she ought to invite the whole family.

'You must be joking.'

Jill looked her straight in the eye and said that if – or rather when – she came to France, she'd come alone. And, she added, pulling a face and sort of laughing, I might just stay there. They reminisced then, about their past, their childhood together, their adolescence. Especially their adolescence.

'Do you remember when …?'

'And do you remember what …?'

'Wouldn't it be funny if …?' Jill began and then bit her tongue.

'If what?' Helen prompted.

Jill looked away from her friend's eyes and slightly shrugged her plump shoulders.

'Well, if you bumped into … Well, you know …'

Jill's fingers played with the bill that the Chinese waiter had placed on the table, folding and unfolding it and absently screwing it up. Oh yes, Helen knew all right. She could think of nothing to reply and the silence lingered. When Jill finally abandoned the piece of paper and placed her credit card on top, she looked into Helen's eyes and there was an apology there.

'She's probably moved away from Paris by now, anyway. She'll be married with half a dozen snotty nosed kids and living in some suburb.'

Helen didn't offer to reply, looked at her watch and suggested they make a move. She was spending the night at Jill's home before the coach took her to London the following morning. She wanted to have a reasonably early night, she said. They said their goodbyes at the large and busy coach station in Bradford the following morning. They kissed and hugged each other but, fortunately, there wasn't too much time for sentiment; the puffing, perspiring and bad-tempered driver threw Helen's luggage into the compartment and checked her ticket.

'Victoria or Golders Green?'

'Golders Green,' Helen replied to the driver's back and when she turned round Jill had receded into the crowd of see-ers-off. She waved furiously as the London-bound coach steadily pulled out of the station, grinning like a Cheshire cat and failing to control her tears. Thank God she's not coming to Waterloo, Helen thought, scrabbling for tissues in her overloaded handbag.

**

The Chantal Gauthier Institut de Beauté was situated in the north east of Paris, rue du Faubourg Poissonnière. After consulting her street and metro maps, Helen was able to locate the road immediately. An obviously busy street that seemed to specialise in wholesale clothes shops. There was no shortage of cafés, restaurants, bars either. Helen, not having made an appointment and having all the time in the world, slowly made her way down the left side of the street, taking in everything, not missing a trick and at the same time thinking about her first formidable weeks in London. A prologue to *this*, she couldn't help thinking now. Although still feeling homesick, or rather Jill-sick, and Ben's sudden disappearance having left an ache where her heart had been, she was still capable of noticing the new life that was going on around her. However, the lethal mixture of homesickness, heartsickness and a feeling of total anonymity suddenly made her feel nauseous, tearful and she slowed down her steps as she approached the number she was looking for.

She walked past it. The number on the stonework high above the heavy wooden door had disappeared with time and Helen didn't notice the equally worn plaque on the wall that announced CH T L GA TH E IN T T T DE B AUT. When she eventually retraced her steps and discovered the shabby insignia, her heart and hopes tumbled at the same time. She pushed the 'Porte' button, and the door clicked open. Helen pushed it and peered round it and found herself in a small, cobbled courtyard. The four stone walls surrounding her belonged to estate agents, wholesale clothiers and Chantal Gauthier's salon.

It stood at the far end of the yard, a small, unremarkable place tucked into a corner. Helen stood in the November cold, in the middle of the yard, her disappointed eyes gazing at the exterior of her future place of work. Was this the Parisian beauty salon that advertised in a British trade journal because some of its clients were Anglophone? Helen's pre-conceived ideas of luxury and elegance in prosperous Paris plummeted away. A cockroach suddenly crawled across her thoughts.

***

She ambled across the cobbles and stood, several feet away, gazing at Chantal Gauthier's establishment. There were two small windows both with grimy and discoloured metal shutters. What once had been a bright orange awning but was now bird shit stained and tattered, hung above both windows, displaying the name of the salon – like the plaque outside, half the letters had worn away. The windows themselves were in need of a good wash. How long she stood and contemplated the uninspiring edifice, Helen couldn't have told anybody.

Some kind of siren heralded her arrival as she tentatively pushed open the door and stepped inside. Initially, there was no sign of life, only a low plastic white coffee table and two matching chairs greeted her, together with an unidentifiable odour that made her retch. To the left of the tiny waiting room – she supposed – was a frosted glass door, in better condition than its external counterpart. To the right, a dark narrow staircase led to who knew what horrors and at the foot stood a rubber plant badly in need of a drink. Dead yellow leaves carpeted the otherwise bare tiled floor. A full-length mirror hung on the back wall and a crack in the top left-hand corner created an aggressive pattern. As Helen gazed at her own disillusioned countenance, the door on the left flew open.

The woman who emerged from the salon was of more than middle age, quite elderly in fact, although she had tried to hide her years with practised artifice. Of medium height, her copper-tinted and tightly permed hair and mask-like makeup were grotesque to witness. Heavily black pencilled-in eyebrows tapered to a thin point, giving the effect of permanent surprise; the crêpey lids beneath hung low over rheumy and bloodshot eyes, surrounded by false lashes, top and bottom. The face had no cheeks, only jowls, and these were heavily rouged; bright red lipstick had been painted on to enlarge the thin lips which, when opened, revealed capped and too-white teeth which then monopolised the face. The hands that were being wiped on a grubby pink towel were flecked with large brown spots and raised blue veins, from which the immaculately painted red nails could not remove the signs of age. Helen inadvertently recoiled.

'Bonjour ... madame.'

She hoped that the caricature standing in front of her and waiting for her to speak was not Chantal Gauthier but she somehow knew that it was.

'Bonjour,' Helen faltered and continued in English. 'My name is Helen Hartnell and I ... erm ... I've just arrived from England. I'll be ... erm ... starting to work for you ... here ... next week.'

The large-toothed and artificial smile immediately fell off the beautician's face and she put out her right hand, waving the filthy towel at the same time.

'Stop!' she cried. 'Stop. Slowly ... slowly. Please speak slowly. Alors ... qu'est-ce-que ... what can I do for you?'

Helen's limited optimism was by now completely diminished. She fixed her unhappy gaze on Madame's three-quarter-length stained and frayed pink nylon overall that clung tightly to her ample figure. She began to speak again in halting French and, when the penny finally dropped, the seen-better-days towel began to move furiously and Madame's agile tongue clicked frantically on the roof of her mouth. She quickly did an about-turn and indicated for Helen to sit on one of the white plastic chairs. Helen did so, trying to discourage the disillusioned and dismayed tears that were threatening to show her up. She reminded herself that she wasn't a sixteen-year-old starting out in life. She was getting on for forty and she'd come a long way for this job, changed her whole bloody life, for God's sake. And what for? Visions of the sordid hotel room where Madame Gauthier had intended her to stay came flooding back to her, together with Ben's taking over and improving one hundred per cent her undignified situation. But now there was no Ben to wave a magic wand and transport her from squalor to luxury. Helen Hartnell was on her own and under the circumstances there was no turning back. Back to what? England and no home, no job, no family?

To try to take her mind off the situation Helen tried leafing through one of the outdated magazines and listened to the drone of French conversation in the adjoining room. Suddenly, the frosted door opened again and this time a pretty young woman walked out, opening her purse. Madame Gauthier, the professional smile slapped back on her face, relieved her client of a two-hundred franc note, slipped it into the till and politely escorted the woman to the door. The smile had obviously accompanied the woman to wherever she was going and, in its place, Helen noticed the two ravines that ran from Madame Gauthier's nose to her chin.

'Now. Why do you come here today? I don't understand. You will start ... You will start your work next week. Isn't it?'

She took a few strides across the room, back to the counter. Helen stood up and watched Chantal Gauthier open an olive green 1998 diary.

'Yes. I write here ... lundi seize novembre. Next week. And you must pass this week to get your official papers in order and ... find you permanent accommodation.'

'Yes. Yes, I know. I do understand all that.' Helen tried to smile her explanation. 'I just wanted to ... well, introduce myself and ... and have a look at the salon where ...'

'What? You speak too fastly. Speak slowly. S-l-o-w-l-y. What do you say, hein? Do you speak French?'

'Only a little. I ...'

The door opened then and a young woman, well wrapped up in winter woollies, almost skipped into the room.

'Ah, bonjour! Bonjour, Mademoiselle Dutot! Comment allez-vous? Installez-vous, mademoiselle, je vous en prie, j'arrive ...'

The girl all but danced into the salon, a room that Helen now felt rather ambivalent about investigating, and closed the door. Helen could make out the silhouette undressing behind the frosted glass. The beautician looked at Helen and, in faulty English, told her that she had no time for her that day, nor the rest of the week. They would – discuss – next week. If she had anything special to say to Helen in the meantime, she would contact her at the hotel. Or words to that effect; that was what Helen understood. She also understood she was being dismissed.

'But you can't contact me at the Hotel de la Gare, Madame Gauthier. I'm ... I'm not staying there,' Helen confessed as Madame made her way to her client, leaving Helen to make her own way out, she noticed. The beautician slowly turned back to her.

'Hein? What do you say?'

The fire burned in Helen's cheeks but she made her voice as calm as possible as she told her future employer that she'd made alternative arrangements for her accommodation.

'But I don't understand. I reserve you a room at the Hotel de la Gare. I know this hotel, it is absolutely ... suffisant.'

'There were cockroaches, Madame Gauthier.'

The filthy word hung in the air between them and it was impossible to tell by Madame's expression whether or not she understood.

43

'Hein? What do you say?'

Chantal Gauthier was frowning, her unbeautiful hands flapping at nothing in the air. It was at that precise moment that Helen spied a distant cousin of the hotel room's occupants crawling towards the deep crack on the mirror. She felt ice running in her veins and pointed with a trembling finger.

'Cockroach,' she said. 'There were cockroaches in my room at the Hotel de la Gare.'

Chantal Gauthier was evidently apathetic towards the creature crawling across her mirror; her thoughts were on higher planes.

'And where do you stay now, hein? You move into the Ritz, perhaps? Or the George V? If that is the case you cannot expect me to pay ...'

Did she honestly look as though she'd be staying at the Ritz or the bloody George V, for God's sake? Helen tried to smile.

'Don't worry, Madame Gauthier,' she said, 'I've actually found a studio on the Left Bank. I'll be moving in as soon as my papers are in order. In the meantime, I'm staying ... at a friend's home.'

Helen walked through the cobbled courtyard, her head held high, but as soon as she was on the street she wanted to collapse. She fell into the nearest reasonable-looking café, ordered a black coffee and tried to come to terms with her thoughts.

'Trust you, you can't do owt right, can you? Nob'dy with an ounce o' gumption would take a job like that without weighin' up all the pros an' bloody cons. Who in their right mind would take a job – in a foreign country to boot – without meetin' their boss first? Only *you* could do a mindless trick like that. Not an ounce o' gumption in yer 'ead, lass.'

Well, Mam, you never had the chance to say it but you sure as hell would have said it, wouldn't you, and this time you'd have been right.

What the devil could I have been thinking of? I ought to have known that something like this would happen, my own common sense should have told me. Or maybe my mam was right and I haven't got any common sense. What am I going to do? How am I going to work for this dreadful woman in such a squalid, so-called beauty salon? But she had to; she had no choice. At least for the time being – until she had the opportunity to change the professional life that she hadn't even started yet – and she hoped that would be sooner rather than later. Oh Ben, if only you were still here to advise me, to take over, to transport me from undesirable A to more-than-desirable B. But there was no Ben any more, there never would be. It had been her fate to meet him, to fall in love at first sight, more or less, for him to take charge of her, take her to his home and help her find a home of her own. A cute, if small, homely home. And then it was fate for him to disappear; never to be heard of again. Helen felt the lonely, frustrated, self-pitying tears pricking at the back of her eyes. If only Ben had stayed a little longer; if only he'd stayed forever. Well, looking on the bright side she'd discovered love at first sight for the first time in her life. And she had a home to go to once she'd sorted out her official papers.

And she had a job.

Chapter Four

———

The rest of the week was swallowed up in long hours at the Préfecture de Police, trying to get official papers in order and to obtain her essential resident's permit. There were complications: papers missing, photocopies to be made, endless queues to be tagged on to; efforts in making herself understood and diminishing confidence in the French way of doing things. However, at the end of the week she left the beautiful old building on the Ile de la Cité brandishing her precious resident's permit. No, not quite brandishing; her state of mind wasn't quite up to brandishing. She felt mentally drained, demoralised, wondering if it was all going to be worth it, hardly optimistic about the future the much-coveted permit guaranteed her. On Friday afternoon she once again took the metro to Saint Germain-des-Prés and pushed open the door leading into the Marché de la Musique. Unlike Chantal Gauthier, Henri Parisot was more than pleased to see her.

After he had heartily shaken her hand and taken her through to his office, Helen gave photocopies of her passport and resident's permit to her future landlord.

'Excéllent! Excéllent! Now we are in business, my dear Miss Hart-nell.'

He picked up a rather shabby briefcase off the floor, placed it on his untidy desk and snapped it open. His plump hand stayed inside the bag for some time and his small eyes blinked and twinkled at Helen across the desk. He finally pulled out two keys on a ring and handed them to his new tenant.

'And I hope you'll be very happy in my little studio, Madame Hart-nell. I hope you and I will have a happy and satisfactory relationship.'

Helen studied Henri's face when he expressed this wish with such fervour, but there was no sign of any ulterior motive in his words. She was being paranoid and, no doubt, downright daft. Henri Parisot expected her to be the ideal tenant and intended to be a good landlord, nothing more, nothing less. If only her employer had declared a similar sentiment. She happily took hold of the two keys – and in turn opened her own bag and took out her purse. Henri Parisot had previously informed her that he would expect three months' rent deposit when they both signed the lease. She counted several two-hundred franc notes on to the desk.

'Stop!'

Helen nearly jumped out of her skin and her startled eyes gazed at

Henri's right hand that was held in mid-air, palm forward, in front of her. His small eyes began their twinkling act again.

'Please return the money to your ... your wallet, chère madame.'

Helen stared at the suspended hand.

'Your *caution* – your deposit of three months' rent in advance is already in my bank account, Madame Hart-nell.'

He still put emphasis on the second syllable. Helen rather liked it. She blinked at him, wondering if there was some misunderstanding, some problem of language.

'I'm sorry? What did you say, Monsieur Parisot?'

Monsieur Parisot slowly lowered his right hand, took hold of his briefcase and gently placed it back on the floor, his amused eyes never leaving her bewildered face.

'Yesterday, I received a cheque from Monsieur Beaulac; a small gift, he indicated, for a good friend.' His perfectly round head dropped in a kind of reverential bow. 'That is you, Madame Hart-nell. A good friend. Voilà.'

Helen continued to stare at the music shop owner, her landlord. For a while she was incapable of speech, in a kind of shock. She didn't know if she felt dumb gratitude or humiliation and anger. Maybe a mixture of all three.

'A gift from Mr Beaulac? My deposit? I don't understand. Did he explain?'

Henri Parisot treated her to a superb Gallic shrug of the shoulders, his eyes darting towards the ceiling and down to the floor, both hands now arresting the air in front of him.

'Yesterday I received a cheque and a "mot" ... a note ... from my dear friend Monsieur Beaulac. He instructed me to deposit the cheque into my account immediately and to tell Madame Hart-nell – to tell *you*, madame, that it was a gift. For a good friend. Voilà. C'est tout.'

'Men only spend their money on women when they're after summat. You want to be careful, young lady, you'll be gettin' a name for yerself.' Malcolm had bought her a simple but pretty silver bracelet that year. Not for her birthday, not for Christmas, 'just because', he'd said. 'Yer dad never bought me owt like that, an' if 'e 'ad, I wouldn't 'ave thanked 'im for it. Just a load o' bloody show, if you ask me. I'm tellin' you, lass, you'd better watch out, there's a name for girls like you who take owt that's given an' don't ask questions ...'

'But I can't let Mr Beaulac pay my rent. It's not on. I mean ... well, it's not necessary.'

'It is too late, madame, he has paid your rent. You are "tranquille" for three months. After that, I shall be obliged to accept all the cheques you will to give me.'

47

Henri Parisot giggled at his grammatically incorrect little joke but Helen's mind was racing, not concentrating on the Frenchman's conversation and his enjoyment of the little drama. Why had Ben done this? What was his motive? Okay, so he'd installed her into his rather luxurious home and she'd gladly accepted that piece of charity and, under the circumstances, hadn't had much choice. He'd helped her to find suitable accommodation and for that, too, she'd be eternally grateful. But to pay her rent for three months? That was going too far. Did he want or expect her to be eternally beholden to him? Did he think the naïve, unworldly Yorkshire-woman had come to Paris unable to pay her rent, for God's sake? Or was this his final Ben-evolent act of friendship, passion or whatever it was he felt for her? It was kind of him but Helen didn't appreciate it. She felt belittled in the eyes of her landlord.

'Monsieur Parisot, do you ... I mean, could you let me have Mr Beaulac's telephone number in the Alps? I ... erm ... I don't happen to have it.'

'And neither do I, madame.'

'Oh. I see. Well ... do you have his mobile number?'

'I don't know if Monsieur Beaulac has a mobile phone.'

Oh, but he does, he does. He just never gave me the number. I didn't ask for it, he wouldn't have given it to me if I had (I'm sure of that) and I didn't give him my mobile number because I haven't got one. Maybe I'll get round to it one day, if mobile phones are still around in a few months ...

'And I am not able to give you – or anyone else – his private number. Excuse me, but ... well, I'm sure you understand.'

He was looking at her with his perfectly round head on one side, his hands folded in front of his equally round belly. The picture of inquisitiveness. And yet he was right; of course he couldn't give the pianist-composer's private number to anyone who asked for it. Even if that 'anyone' were a good friend. So, she would never be able to get in touch with Benjamin Beaulac, musician, composer, family man. Mr Bountiful. Cheat. The man she was so foolishly in love with.

**

Helen left the large and comfortable but taboo apartment in the twelfth district and moved into the small but cute and cosy bedsit at eleven o'clock on Saturday morning. She had nothing to take with her but the suitcase that had been the means of her meeting Benjamin Beaulac. She arrived at her own front door quite exhausted and took a few deep breaths before she inserted the brand-new key in the lock. Then she dragged her case through

48

the small kitchen and into the bedroom/living room. The flat was warm, she was pleased to notice, the heating being a collective system for the building. She looked at the sofa-bed and the cupboards and drawers in the kitchenette and spent a happy afternoon deciding where to put things when she had things to put. She had a painting for her wall; she would eventually buy more pictures and some plants; she would frame some photos and buy a couple of vases and ... and candles. She hung up her few clothes in the just-about-adequate wardrobe and made herself a light lunch with the few provisions she'd brought with her. She looked for electric sockets and found plenty and she also found a plug for the phone, another priority; she must have a phone. In the meantime, she would become adept at letter-writing.

She wrote a letter to Jill that afternoon, sitting at her tiny kitchen table and drinking endless cups of instant coffee. She told Jill everything that had happened to her since their tearful goodbyes in Bradford and wondered if her best friend would think she'd lost her marbles since their parting or that she'd suddenly become a very imaginative liar. Her meeting with the celebrated musician and subsequent events seemed more the stuff of farfetched romantic fiction than the humdrum life of Helen Hartnell the Nondescript, as she'd long ago baptised herself. She told Jill to keep all this to herself; she didn't want any tongues wagging on her behalf in Firley. Her name associated with Benjamin Beaulac was incongruous in the extreme and she could imagine the incredulous and uncomplimentary comments.

But she wasn't making it up; every scribbled word was fact and as she wrote Helen's mind drifted towards the meeting she'd had with her landlord and the surprising disclosure he'd made. Ben had paid her first three months' rent. And then she thought of their brief and blissful (well, as far as she was concerned) weekend and she thought about her mother's opinion; or at least what her mother's opinion would have been. Helen Hartnell had prostituted herself. Would Jill think on the same lines?

The bakery on the corner of Helen's short street stayed open until late on Sunday afternoon, she was delighted to discover when she went for a walk later when writer's cramp had well and truly made its presence felt. She ventured into the warm and welcoming 'boulangerie' and bought half a baguette and a difficult-to-resist pastry and was pleased that the plump and jolly assistant had been able to understand her. Later, she heated a can of tomato soup and poured it into a large, cracked bowl that she'd found in one of the cupboards. She would have to make a shopping list but not until the writer's cramp had taken its leave; crockery and cutlery would be a priority, she decided, when trying to cut the bread with a seriously blunt knife. But it would be fun. She was thirty-nine years old and for the first time in her life shopping for her own home.

The letter-writing, hot soup and the sheer novelty of things had made her drowsy and at nine-thirty she took a hot bath before wishing herself a goodnight on the not very comfortable sofa-bed. In spite of the 'novelty of things' and her more than cold feet about the following day, Helen slept soundly and awoke at six-thirty refreshed and ready to tackle the day. Ready to tackle Chantal Gauthier. Maybe even ready to tackle the cockroaches.

***

Chantal Gauthier, dressed in a long, synthetic grey fur coat and matching hat, black boots and scarf, was opening the shutters of her 'Institut' when Helen arrived. She heard Helen's steps on the cobbles behind her, briefly turned round but obviously thought her new employee merited no more than a curt nod. She stepped indoors, switched on the lights and Helen, trying very hard not to feel intimidated, followed her. As Helen entered the waiting room, Madame Gauthier was taking off her coat and hanging it on a plastic peg behind the counter. She looked up and frowned as Helen approached, evidently feigning non-recognition.

'Bonjour, madame. Puis-je vous … ah, it's you. Well, come in and close the door, close the door, there is running air in 'ere.'

Helen frowned at the Frenchwoman, and then realised there was a terrible draught coming in through the door. Better not correct her, Helen told herself, it's probably not the best way to win her over. She obediently closed the door but noticed that the 'running air' continued to invade the salon. The place was freezing. When she looked at her employer again, she was sitting on a plastic stool behind the counter, her right leg held out in front of her.

'Come 'ere … come 'ere. Voilà. Please take my boot … my boot.'

A red-varnished nail stabbed at her outstretched leg and her grotesquely made-up eyes travelled over Helen's inert body.

'Now … please. Before my client is arriving.'

Helen choked back an indignant reply and bent to tug off the plastic boot. She would have liked to pull off the malodorous foot at the same time. She certainly hadn't expected red-carpet treatment on her arrival but she hadn't imagined anything as base as this, either. And as her hands wrenched off the cheap pair of boots and the stench greeted her unprepared nostrils, Helen nauseously wondered how long she'd be able to tolerate life as Chantal Gauthier's employee.

The Institut's owner started her day by turning on the machine to heat the wax for epilation. The machine, Helen noticed, was old and dirty, unlike the machine she'd practised on during her training. Everything and everyone at the school in London had been spotless, spic and span, one hundred percent hygienic, unlike anything and anyone here. The couch where the clients lay for their treatments still bore the paper sheet from the last day's work. Helen wondered whether Madame Gauthier changed the sheet with every new client – a golden rule. She sincerely hoped so but seriously doubted it and it looked as though Saturday's sheet was to be Monday's, too. She suddenly felt very nauseous and when she saw a thick covering of dust on tables and shelves, she tentatively asked Madame Gauthier if she employed a cleaning lady. Madame Gauthier eyed her, warily.

'Non!' she finally snapped. 'I occupy me with everything. Clients, accounts, cleaning. I need no person to clean.'

Oh yes, you do, Helen mentally told her. Maybe this was why Chantal Gauthier had advertised for help in her salon; someone to dust and sweep the floor, clean the machines, help with the accounts. Exterminate the cockroaches. A member of that undesirable race was just making its way across the floor to who knew what delights under the clients' couch. Maybe this was why Madame Gauthier (surely there couldn't be a Monsieur Gauthier?) had advertised for an Anglophone beautician; a woman miles away from home and less likely to complain; less likely to flee.

'Bon,' the salon owner suddenly announced, looking around the imperfect room and seeming satisfied. 'My first client will come at ten forty-five, a leg epilation … you may occupy that. First, I propose to 'ave coffee, okay? The … cafetière … is upstairs.'

Helen was astonished, foolishly she later admitted, that her employer had shown absolutely no interest in her, Helen, as a human being, newly arrived in a foreign country. No questions had been asked, no welcoming gestures made. She despondently climbed the dim flight of winding stairs and found the coffee percolator in a tiny annexe off the toilet. When she saw both, Helen almost threw up. There was no door on the toilet, the loo itself was exposed to the short landing, the lid non-existent, the bowl cracked and stained. There was a tiny sink opposite, from which a cockroach was now escaping and from which a filthy towel hung. Tears sprang into Helen's horrified eyes – the eyes that she'd oh-so-carefully and discreetly made up that morning. It was no wonder Chantal Gauthier had booked her into the inhospitable Hotel de la Gare; she would have been totally oblivious to its squalor. Fortunately, she'd written and posted her letter to Jill; it was too late to inflict and worry her with a description of this. She would only relish details of the romantic encounter and Helen's delightful little bedsit; she wouldn't have to suffer this. Helen turned away from the smallest room and turned her reluctant attention to the coffee percolator that stood on a coffee-stained and sugar-splattered shelf. She pulled out a used filter and looked for a convenient bin. She didn't find one. There were no kitchen facilities other than a packet of coffee, a packet of filters and two unwashed cups. Helen queasily balanced the soiled articles in both hands and made her way down the dim and dangerous staircase.

'Qu'est-ce-que ... what are you doing? Where are you going with those things?'

'The percolator and the cups,' Helen faltered, deciding to avoid the word 'dirty', 'I'm going to wash them.'

'Yes, but not 'ere. Not in my salon. You can do that in the lavabo upstairs.'

The outer door suddenly opening took her exasperated attention away from Helen, who stood on the bottom step, speechless. Was she supposed to wash up in that filthy washbasin in the toilet? It wasn't only unhygienic, it was illegal. In England, anyway. Maybe in France ... Her thoughts flashed back to the impeccable training school in London. She didn't move. She opened her mouth but the first client of the day – her leg wax, probably – was walking into the salon. To lie down on the unchanged paper sheet? Helen closed her mouth, shuddered and made her way back upstairs. She almost threw the cups into the washbasin and turned on the tap – only cold water spurted out. And, of course, there was no washing up liquid. She made coffee for her employer and none for herself; she decided that dire thirst and a desperate need for caffeine were far preferable.

Helen's first client, she later discovered, was a 'putain', a prostitute. Helen had no idea while she was doing her job, daubing the hot brown wax on to the girl's shapely but, at the moment, hairy legs with the well-used spatula, and ripping it off. She felt quite nervous; her first real client, and what if she was a chatterbox and Helen didn't understand her? But she wasn't a chatterbox, she was quite taciturn, her thin but glossy lips firmly sealed, her expressionless eyes showing no inclination of the mild pain she must be suffering. Helen glanced at her client's face several times but the pretty, worn-out looking girl obviously wanted to avoid eye contact. Helen's curious gaze fell on the black lambswool sweater and the too-short-for-the-season skirt and the suspenders that now hung loosely on her fleshy thighs. It was later, when Madame Gauthier shut shop and invited Helen for a quick bite to eat at a local café, that she learned of her first client's profession.

Chantal Gauthier ordered two croque-monsieurs and beer for their lunch and, while Helen attacked the delicious toasted ham and cheese, she listened to Madame Gauthier's account of their clientele.

'Des putains,' she said, matter-of-factly. 'You do know, of course, that I ... enfin ... we ... work in a red light district? Of course, some of my clients are businesswomen, house-women ('wives' Helen wanted to correct but didn't), schoolgirls.' She shrugged her shoulders as she took her last gulp of cold beer.

'But the most of my clients are prostitutes.'

The ice-cold beer that Helen hadn't ordered and didn't really want seemed to be travelling through her veins and she shivered. Chantal noticed and caught her eye across the small, round and rather wobbly table. Helen saw wry amusement there.

'Are you shocking?'

Yes, she had to admit she was a bit shocked but she knew that if she was going to survive working for this woman, even only for a short while, she was going to have to be strong. Hard, even. Or at least, seem that way. She managed a smile that didn't reach her eyes.

'No, of course I'm not shocked. Not at all,' she replied, adding, 'Pas du tout,' to show off her limited French. Maybe I'll have the opportunity to ask a client if she thinks I prostituted myself with Benjamin Beaulac, she thought, irrelevantly. But when she thought of Ben, she suddenly didn't feel quite so flippant. Fortunately, he wasn't able to see her place of work.

Helen had two more customers during the afternoon, both epilations, one leg, the other bikini line, and she couldn't help but wonder what their profession might be. She spent the rest of the time watching Chantal performing a massage and facial ... Her boss had made it clear that Helen wouldn't be given that kind of work for quite some time. Leg waxing and sweeping the floor would be her lot for the time being. Helen bit her lip and said nothing. The last customer left at six o'clock and Chantal decided to close early. She normally didn't leave before eight o'clock. She invited Helen to help force the too-small boots back on her still-malodorous feet and the two women tiredly stepped across the cobbled yard together. They parted company on the busy street, Chantal with a curt nod and a brief 'A demain' and Helen with a dread of tomorrow and all the tomorrows to come.

Chapter Five

——

The tomorrows that came very much resembled the first disagreeable day. There were few clients at the Institut and the ones whom Helen was permitted to work with were the ritualistic and uninspiring waxings. She was allowed to observe her employer, ostensibly to 'learn', doing her best to make a plain face beautiful, obese bodies sylph-like, or as near as dammit. But Helen learned more about the detached and totally indifferent attitude of her boss towards sanitation in all its aspects than about her business. Chantal Gauthier had her regular clients, who seemed oblivious to the lack of hygiene. But there were other clients, first timers whose first time was also their last. Occasionally, the door would open, a prospective customer would step into the salon and make an appointment that she didn't keep. Sometimes she would take a look at the interior and head straight for the door. Helen wasn't surprised by this reaction; she was amazed it happened so infrequently. She was, however, also embarrassed, ashamed and wanted to run after the disgusted woman and say, 'It's not me. I've only just arrived. I hate it as much as you do.' Chantal Gauthier, on the other hand, turned a very blind eye to the women who walked in and as quickly walked out of her squalid establishment. She never asked herself any questions, or if she did, the silent replies were of no consequence, either to herself or the 'good' name of her business.

At the end of the first week Helen had performed countless leg waxes, welcomed as best she could the clientele, made numerous cups of coffee that she never drank and counted half a dozen cockroaches. She'd tried very hard to show enthusiasm for her work and to befriend, to a certain extent, her employer, having no other friends of any description in the big city. Her enthusiasm for both her work and her employer were not very high, however, and she went home most evenings feeling depressed and ready to pack it all in.

The first couple of evenings she battled with the far from pleasant rush-hour metro and then she discovered a bus that stopped not far from the Institut and dropped her off at the end of her street. Although it was still the frantic Parisian peak-hour the bus seemed to encourage a more congenial atmosphere where strangers, if not exactly friendly, were rather less hostile than in the underground train. It better suited Helen's friendly

Yorkshire temperament. She was also treated to Paris by night and delighted in the lively boulevards, old-fashioned shops, arcades, lamps and flood-lit fountains in the autumn dusk. Delighted may be too strong a word; but Paris by night and by bus was a pleasant sight for her very sore and tired eyes.

As soon as she got home. she closed her shutters against the world outside, made herself a simple but nourishing meal and read for a while, her temper beginning to melt along with her frozen bones. If she'd had a particularly bad day, once at home she'd allow herself the luxury of a few tears, after which she'd reprimand herself, yet knowing that she really did have the right. Most women in her position would have turned tail and fled back to Yorkshire, or wherever, of that she was sure. A single woman completely alone in a foreign capital, no family, no friends. An employer who was totally indifferent to her and a workplace that nauseated her. With no immediate prospect of any improvement. And the idea did cross her deeply disillusioned mind during that first week or so. When she was struggling to work on the miserable metro in the morning, slapping hot wax on hot prostitutes' legs and counting cockroaches during the day, and sitting in her cosy but solitary studio in the evening, with nothing to look forward to but an identical tomorrow, oh yes, she did think about giving up and going home. But she didn't have a 'home'; her home was, in fact, the cosy but solitary bedsit. At least she had a decent place to live. But if she went 'home'? There was nobody, not even a second cousin twice removed, who could put her up in England. Jill would gladly have adopted her, of course, but there was simply no room. Maybe Theresa and Jack Mooney, Jill's mam and dad ... but they were getting on in years and she certainly didn't want to be an inconvenience. In Paris she had a landlord. She didn't even have that much in England.

The Friday of Helen's first week was reasonably quiet, the lull before the Saturday storm, Chantal informed her. The three clients whom Helen looked after were all quite chatty young women, all regulars apparently, all whores. One of them had dirty toenails, another wasn't particular about body odour, the third needed the services of a good dentist. As they prattled to Helen in their native tongue, she was relieved to have an excuse not to encourage them. She hardly understood what they were saying and wasn't yet capable of making conversation. She managed the odd smile but behind the pleasant gesture she was retching. At the same time, she questioned herself; did she have the right to feel so negative about these young women? She didn't know what had led them to follow their insalubrious professional path. She knew nothing of their backgrounds and personal lives, their upbringings. And who was she to criticise, question, condemn? If they'd been anonymous women with questionable personal hygiene, would she have been so quick to criticise and condemn? Probably not. So, Helen felt uncomfortable with her own reactions while at the same time unable, at least for the moment, to change. Chantal's pronouncement of a busy tomorrow didn't bring her any joy; she prayed for cancellations and in doing so realised she was digging her own financial grave.

In spite of the lack of interesting work Helen felt exhausted when she stepped into her building at seven-thirty that evening. Exhausted, or rather weary. Worn out and despondent. She switched on the light and unlocked the chipped wooden letterbox that bore her name. A long white envelope was lying there. Her heart gave a leap of optimism – Jill must have written back immediately, bless her. It would be great when she had a telephone installed, or even if, one of these days, she treated herself to a mobile phone? They weren't going to go away, she'd been told, they were *the* thing of the future ... In the meantime, she'd take great pleasure in devouring Jill's letter. But the handwriting was in black ink and wasn't Jill's. It was long and spidery and Helen had only seen it once in her life before. She locked the letterbox and, her heart suddenly hammering in her chest, she ran upstairs with her treasure.

As soon as she unlocked her door and turned on the light Helen's trembling fingers ripped open the envelope. Then she took a deep breath, put the piece of totally unexpected correspondence on the sofa-bed and filled the electric kettle. She put a herbal tea sachet into a mug and poured the boiling water on to it, allowing it to brew for quite a while. She wanted to read Ben's letter slowly, taking her time, devouring every full stop and comma.

Chamonix
18.11.1998

My dear Helen,

I'm happy that Henri found you a place to live so quickly. Wasn't I right? He tells me your studio is small but furnished, near Montparnasse, a lively and interesting district of Paris. I do hope you'll be happy there. If you have any problems at all don't hesitate to get in touch with Henri. He's not only a good and honest landlord, he's one of my best friends. And the job? How's it going? Well, I hope. My wife has gone skiing with friends but I played tired in order to be able to write you. It was a need, Helen. I not only wanted but needed to write to you. I can't explain but over a very short time you somehow managed to creep right into my heart and soul. You left your mark and it won't go away. I fell in love with you but, very sadly, there's absolutely nothing I can do about it. I must be satisfied with my memories. Enjoy your new life in France, Helen. If I asked you to forget me, I'd be a hypocrite because I very selfishly don't want you to forget me. I want you to remember me with pleasure, if possible, as I remember you. Take good care of yourself. You're a very special lady.

With my love,
Ben

It was more and it was less than she expected. She'd expected nothing, therefore it was more. When she'd torn open the envelope, she'd expected to be able to reply to him therefore it was less. He was in love with her and he'd taken the time to write and tell her so. Therefore, it was oh so much more than she'd expected.

***

Helen read Ben's letter so often over the next few days that she knew it by heart. She thought about it and him constantly and wanted desperately to contact him. But if Ben had wanted her to reply, he'd have given her either his mobile number or address or both. At least thinking about Ben, knowing that he was thinking about her, took her mind off less pleasant subjects and people. In fact, she dreamed her days away.

Jill's letter arrived the following week, chatty, comical, very Jill, and Helen felt that her best friend was talking to her, not writing. Her astonishment about Ben was quite hilarious and the main subject of her letter, of course. She asked three times if Helen wasn't pulling her leg for some obscure reason. She hadn't breathed a word of the exciting and illicit romance to anyone, not even Tom. Well, there was no point; Tom probably wouldn't know who Benjamin Beaulac was, anyway. But Helen would let her know the next episode, wouldn't she, and there was bound to be a next episode; it was obvious the bloke was keen. And was Helen still keen on him? How did she think it would all turn out? She couldn't wait to hear from her again … And when was she going to get herself a phone, for God's sake? Preferably a mobile … They needed to *speak* about this, have a good heart-to-heart, a good old natter … She mentioned Helen's new home and thought it sounded charming and typically Parisian and she really envied her … And, of course, she wrote about the kids and what they were up to and how Caroline was upsetting the whole family in one way or another, and who in their right mind would have a teenager in the house? And write back soon, Helen, I want to know all the sordid details. I'm missing you so much already.

***

It was a cold, wet and very miserable Sunday at the beginning of December. A couple of weeks previously, Helen had discovered a lively Sunday morning market a few streets away from her home and that day decided to investigate. She mingled with the crowd, stopping at the stalls, trying to order food whose French name she didn't know but, through necessity, learned very quickly. She bought herself a piece of fish and giggled with the poissonnier, although she didn't have a clue what he was saying. She was proud when she made herself understood, frustrated when she didn't, but felt she was learning anyway, so what the hell. She was drawn to the window of a tempting looking pâtisserie and treated herself to a chocolate éclair. She watched in wonder as the fastidious young assistant placed the dessert very carefully in a fancy box and tied it with ribbon. There's no point, Helen wanted to tell her, you're wasting your time, it's only for me and I'll be eating it alone. She arrived home shivering but happy with both her short expedition and her purchases. Maybe she was totally alone in Paris but at least she was able to make herself a good lunch.

After the good lunch she made coffee and looked out of the window at the almost deserted wintry street. Suddenly, being able to buy food in a foreign language, treating herself to a beautifully wrapped cake and drinking freshly-percolated coffee wasn't enough. She would have liked to share her shopping trips, her Sunday lunch, her coffee. She wondered whether Ben was sitting at a much bigger dining table with his family, eating a delicious gourmet meal cooked by his (delicious?) wife, prior to taking the ski lift and zooming down Mont Blanc or whatever. Or maybe he was sitting at a piano keyboard, his sensitive fingers that had oh so beautifully brought her to orgasm creating a tune that would be played, hummed, whistled around the world. Or maybe he was thinking about her and composing another letter.

Later that afternoon, she wrote a very long letter to Jill to enclose with her Christmas card. Not wanting her friend to worry about her, she made light of the filthy beauty salon with its orthopterous residents and unsavoury clientele and she sketched an amusing caricature of Madame. She went on to tell her best friend of the purchases she'd made for her bedsit and her slow but sure progress in speaking the language. And, of course, she wrote about Ben and his unanticipated letter. As Helen sealed and addressed the envelope, she couldn't help but think how strange life was, how unexpectedly topsy-turvy things often turned out.

In her student days, Helen had never really been interested in languages, geography – anything related to travel. Encouraged only by her father to study for a worthwhile career, her interest in all things academic came to an abrupt end after his death. Or rather, her own slowly budding ambitions were nipped in the bud by a mother who saw no interest in a girl goin' in for exams and all that stuff and nonsense. What were point when all she'd end up doin' were gettin' wed, 'aving kids and spending rest of 'er life in a bloody kitchen? Look at 'erself, for example, that's all she'd ended up doin'. And for what, she'd like to know? Her 'usband, 'im what she'd slaved and scrimped an' saved for all them years, what 'ad 'e gone and done? He'd gone and died on 'er, that's what. Well, she'd never taken no exams and even if she 'ad, what good would they 'ave done 'er? None whatsoever. That were a girl's lot in life, so 'er Helen'd better start learnin' fast – there were no point in learnin'.

Jill had been the academic one, the one who was interested in languages and wanted to see the world. She'd always excelled in French and her mum and dad didn't hesitate in inviting her penfriend to stay one year. She'd stayed with Jill's family for almost a month that summer. The summer that Helen would never forget; the summer that had quickly changed her young life. She abruptly pushed the small pile of Christmas cards away from her, or rather she pushed Jill's card away from her as though she could push that summer – the very hot summer of 1976 – away and all that it implied. But that was impossible. She'd never blamed Jill. Jill was and always would be her best friend. And Jill had had no control over the situation. Helen poured herself another cup of strong coffee and knew she'd have problems sleeping that night.

***

During the most of December the beauty salon was exceptionally busy and the two women worked from early morning until late in the evening. Helen was finally allowed to give facials and manicures but, although she'd been craving to perform those tasks since her first day, once her hands touched the unknown skin, she instantly questioned her previous impatience. As soon as she got home, she had a shower and scrubbed every inch of her body. Only when her skin was dry and she was wrapped in her old, comfy dressing gown and sipping hot herbal tea did she feel the guilt. She had no right; no right whatsoever. There but for the grace of God, so to speak ...

At the end of every week Helen was exhausted. One Saturday evening she got on the already full-to-capacity bus shivering and almost falling asleep, squashed between Christmas shoppers and early revellers. There was an occasional guffaw from somewhere down the aisle but most of the passengers were silent, grim, poker-faced. Suddenly, as she felt herself nodding off, Helen was thrown sideways into the copious bags of the woman standing next to her, who had been hurled across the lap of the man sitting in front of her. There was a shriek of brakes, another lurch, more bodies slipping and sliding and then raised, violent voices. Helen picked herself up and watched the driver leap off the bus, arms flailing, face beetroot as he verbally attacked the faulty learner driver in front. It was obviously going to be some time before the bus got mobile again and Helen recognised a lot of French curses as passengers made their way to the exits. She decided to follow suit and walk the rest of the way home. It wasn't very far; she was already in her own neighbourhood. Instead of taking the main, hectic boulevard, she decided to wander through the labyrinth of narrow, as yet unknown streets, killing two birds with one stone. She'd avoid the festive, noisy boulevard and get to know her district better. The streets were old, quaint with interesting nineteenth-century architecture and bookshops, bistros, florists, craft shops and small 'épiceries'. As she crossed a particularly narrow street, she noticed an elegant and beautifully decorated restaurant on one corner and on the other, an Institut de Beauté. Like the restaurant it looked extremely elegant. The salon's name, 'Au Bonheur des Dames', was printed in silver on a dark blue awning. The salon was getting ready to close. Helen stood on the pavement outside next to a huge Christmas tree, glittering with gold ribbons, fairy lights and artificial snow. She moved towards the window and peered inside. The large, pine reception desk stood in the corner, complete with modern, compact computer. Silk-shaded lamps stood at various angles in the reception area and Christmas garlands hung from the bright chrome ceiling. The floor was tiled in a blue and white pattern and the bright white walls boasted, alongside the tinsel and fairy lights, framed pictures of beautiful women.

A white-overalled receptionist was turning off the computer and preparing to leave when a tall woman with long black hair and dark eyes came out of a room marked 'Salon No. 1'. Stifling a yawn, she said something to the receptionist and they both laughed. The dark-eyed and very beautiful woman was holding a spotless white towel and drying her perfectly manicured hands. She suddenly caught sight of Helen standing there, gaping, half in and half out of the establishment. She looked at Helen enquiringly, her head tilted to one side. Helen blushed, smiled briefly and shook her head. The receptionist then pressed a button and the metal shutters started to descend. It was then that Helen noticed, along with advertisements for perfume and beauty products, an advert for a qualified beautician, preferably with a knowledge of English and some experience, to start work in January the following year.

Chapter Six

Helen was more than surprised when she received a visit from her landlord on Tuesday, 22 December. She was getting ready for an early night when her entry-phone rang. There was someone downstairs who wanted to see her. Someone who knew the code and had got into the building. At first a mild panic struck her – it was getting late, for God's sake – and then she remembered the entry-phone was her protection. She didn't have to let whoever it was in if she didn't want to. She warily lifted the earpiece.

'Bonsoir, madame,' Henri Parisot's cheerful voice crackled down the line. 'Excuse me to disturb you.'

Henri Parisot, well wrapped up in a heavy grey overcoat, scarf and trilby, stepped into her tiny home and heartily shook her hand. His glasses were a little steamed up and he laughed as he wiped them on a piece of chamois leather.

'I do not wish to regard you through a big fog, madame,' he beamed.

Helen stood watching the quick movements he made with the beige cloth and wondered what on earth he'd come to see her about. Was he increasing her rent already? No, he didn't have the right. Not until the three-year lease had expired. Was he going to throw her out? Of course not – ditto. Was he about to make a physical nuisance of himself? No, she was flattering herself, being ridiculous. Maybe it was something to do with Ben. Of course! But what, for goodness' sake? She felt her heart beating a little faster. She watched as he meticulously folded the cleaning cloth, placed it inside his glasses case, snapped the case shut and slipped it into his inside pocket. Her heart had started to hammer by the time he looked at her and grinned.

'Please sit down, Monsieur Parisot. Would you like anything to drink?'

'No, no, no, madame, please don't occupy yourself with me. Please – have a seat.'

Instead of joining him on the sofa-bed Helen discreetly sat on a dark green wicker chair that she'd previously placed in front of the window and smiled, shyly, across the small room at him. Henri Parisot then started to talk about the weather, his work, the price of Christmas purchases, and Helen mentally willed him to get to the point. Why on earth had he come? Apart from anything else, she was desperate for her bed.

'And what are your plans for Christmas, Madame Hart-nell? Will you go back to England?'

Helen jumped at the unexpected question. Christmas was something she was trying not to think about. The beauty salon would be open until eight o'clock on Christmas Eve so she knew she'd be collapsing into bed before ten. And on Christmas morning she planned to have a long lie-in and then try not to feel sorry for herself the rest of the day.

'No, I'm not going back to England,' Helen forced herself to smile. 'Actually, I've got no plans. None at all.'

'That's what I imagined would probably be the case. So, madame, my wife and I would like to invite you for lunch on Christmas Day.'

Helen stared for what seemed a long time at her landlord.

'Well, that's really kind of you, Monsieur Parisot, but ...'

The short round man held up his right hand, wrinkled his stubby nose and grinned.

'It will be a great pleasure for us, madame. We will spend the twenty-fourth with my wife's family but will be alone on the twenty-fifth. Please don't refuse our invitation.'

'How could I?' Helen smiled at him. 'It's really kind of you both. Thanks ... thank you.'

Henri Parisot also informed her that he'd arranged for France Telecom to fix the telephone line a couple of days later, at ten o'clock in the morning, and if Helen were at work, then Madame Parisot would quite happily 'deplace herself to receive the engineer'.

Before her landlord took his leave, telling Helen that he and his wife would expect her at noon on Christmas Day at their apartment above the music shop, she tentatively asked if he had any news from Ben.

'No news exactly, madame, only our usual Christmas card from the Haute Savoie. The French Alps.'

Helen's card from the Haute Savoie arrived the next day. It was waiting for her when she arrived home feeling shattered and unclean, as usual. The envelope was pale blue, the card a magnificent view of the Mont Blanc range and 'Meilleurs Voeux' embossed in gold letters. Ben had written, 'I wish we could be together over the festive season. In Paris. On Mont Blanc. In a prison cell. Wherever. But together. Ben.'

***

Helen was surprised to find Paris as busy and bustling on Christmas Day as any Sunday. Certain food shops were open, public transport was quite regular and the streets filled with people. Well, that's not right, is it? she could hear her mam saying. I mean, Christmas i'n't Christmas when you can go out and buy bloody spuds like any other day. I don't like that idea. It's not right.

She stepped out of the metro station at Saint Sulpice clutching an enormous bright red poinsettia and a box of Belgian chocolates. She hadn't really had a clue what to give them, not knowing Madame Parisot at all and her husband very little. It was monsieur who greeted her at the door and invited her into the spacious, soberly-decorated but stylish apartment. A rich aroma of spices and something roasting wafted from the kitchen on her right as she stood in the hall while Henri Parisot helped her out of her well-worn grey woollen coat. And then a female version of Henri emerged from the kitchen: a short, plump, smiling woman with grey curls and gold-rimmed glasses. She and her husband looked so alike they could have been siblings. After the coat had been dispensed with Henri ceremoniously put his arm around Helen's shoulder and pulled her towards madame.

'Amandine, this is my favourite tenant, Helen Hart-nell. Helen, I'd like you to meet Amandine – my favourite wife.'

Amandine Parisot wore a pink plastic pinafore over a turquoise silk two-piece and wielded a plastic spoon in her left hand while shaking hands with her right. After an 'Enchantée' she apologised for her appearance, disappeared into the kitchen and Helen wondered if she'd arrived too early. Henri fussily ushered her into an elegant but comfortable living room where a gleaming Steinway was the predominant feature. Amandine was pinafore-less when she joined them five minutes later; Henri poured the champagne aperitif and Amandine generously served a variety of nuts and nibbles. There was a brief silence after the clinking of champagne flutes and a hearty 'Tchin'. Helen surprised herself by breaking that silence.

'Thank you so much for coming to the studio for the telephone engineer, Madame Parisot ...'

'Amandine, please ... I insist. Oh, it was my pleasure, Helen. He was a pleasant and very beautiful young man. And I hope your telephone is now working well?'

Helen nodded and smiled, thinking about her far-too-long conversation with Jill that morning and the many more that would follow.

'Yes, it is, thank you, Mad ... Amandine.'

Henri crunched loudly on a handful of peanuts then led the conversation, chatting about his work, his clients, the 'chaotique and fatiguing' pre-Christmas period. Amandine looked at Helen, rolled her eyes behind their lenses and gently thumped her husband on his ample left thigh.

'And who would be very sorry if there was no chaos and no fatiguing customers before Christmas, hein? Would we be drinking champagne and eating oysters today, may I ask you that, hein?'

Henri adjusted his glasses that his wife had knocked slightly askew, and in his turn looked at Helen and rolled his eyes.

'I'm not complaining, my chérie amour, I am merely stating a fact.'

Amandine put her empty glass on the table, wiped her hands on the seasonally-decorated serviette and slowly stood up.

'He states exactly the same fact every year, Helen.' She looked at her gold Rolex watch in an exaggerated gesture. 'At exactly this time on the twenty-fifth of December.' And she left the room.

The other two followed her into the dining room where they spent the rest of the day. They ate oysters – the first time for Helen and she couldn't help but think it would be the last – foie gras, roast turkey stuffed with mushrooms and chestnuts with a variety of vegetables followed by a variety of cheeses and a choice of dessert. They drank a different wine with each course and Helen, unused to so much alcohol, made sure she drank as much mineral water. Contrary to her previous misgivings the conversation was lively, thanks mainly to her landlord who had many anecdotes to tell. His wife became more talkative after a couple of glasses of wine and told Helen about her childhood in the north of France. They both asked Helen discreet questions about her background, but they didn't know Yorkshire at all, only London.

'And what about family?' asked Amandine. 'Your family is still in the Yorksheeer?'

Her hostess's delightful pronunciation eliminated all nostalgic thoughts and Helen smiled at her.

'I ... don't have any family,' she said, simply.

'No family? But that's so sad, Helen. Henri, did you hear that? Helen has no family. Your parents?' Her voice had lowered.

'They're both dead,' Helen replied.

'I'm so sorry. How sad.'

A rather embarrassed silence followed and the three people concentrated on the food in front of them. Henri suddenly raised his eyes from his plate and beamed at his guest across the table.

'And your job? I hope you are enjoy with your job, Helen?'

She decided not to say too much about her work while they were eating and they rightly guessed that all wasn't well there, either. Helen suddenly smiled, however, and holding up her crossed fingers said,

'Actually, I have an interview for a new job in the new year.'

'Ah bon? And where is that?'

An Institut de Beauté not fifteen minutes away from her bedsit, but the owner was away from Paris until the first week in January. Helen had made an appointment – her first telephone call, in fact – for the fourth.

'There are hundreds of beauty salons in Paris,' Amandine informed her, unnecessarily. 'If you are not lucky with this one, there will be another ... By the way, chéri, isn't Marie-Laure's salon somewhere in that district?'

Henri, shovelling yet another spoonful of Christmas log into his mouth, merely nodded, and when the coffee percolator's distant glug-glugging came to a halt, Amandine left the table. Her husband concentrated on his dessert in his wife's absence and Helen wondered who Marie-Laure was and if she could be the same beautician. If so, Helen wanted to ask at least thirty-six questions about her and her salon, but when Amandine started to pour the coffee, she also started another conversation.

Towards the end of the afternoon, after Amandine had lit the softly shaded lamps, she asked her husband to play the piano for a while. Henri was only too happy to oblige and the two women sat silently side by side while he tinkled a few Christmas tunes on the keyboard, tunes that made Helen remember her childhood and her father's glorious carolling in Firley church and later the silly party games that even her mother enjoyed. There had been quite a lot of parties when her dad was alive. And much later, Jill and Tom and she and Malcolm singing (excruciatingly out of tune) at the youth club Christmas party and at each other's homely Yorkshire houses. The same melodies seemed incongruous somehow in this opulent Parisian apartment. Suddenly, Henri Parisot gave a resounding crescendo to 'Silent Night' and swivelled round on the red-velvet padded stool.

'Helen,' he beamed, 'here is my grande finale. Tell me who is the composer of this beautiful Christmas tune.'

His seemingly unsuitable chubby fingers moved slowly across the keys, creating a haunting melody that had been in everyone's ears and hearts two Christmases before. A beautiful, unforgettable piece of music composed by Benjamin Beaulac, the theme tune of a seasonal film. Helen suddenly felt the tears squeezing into her eyes. And as she listened and watched the composer's friend playing, the short but adequate fingers became the long, perfect fingers of her lover; the shiny bald pate with its ridiculous fringe became the thick, lustrous grey hair that just touched her lover's collar. Her lover who composed beautiful, haunting Christmas melodies. Her lover who had sent her a Christmas card and who wished he could have spent the festive season with her.

***

Wednesday was normally Helen's day off – or parole, as she'd come to think of it – but she had managed to convince her usually inflexible boss that she desperately needed to be free on the first Tuesday of 1999.

She'd walked by the 'Au Bonheur des Dames' salon many times since that first Saturday and her subsequent telephone call. She had stood on the pavement outside looking in, observing the bright lights, elegant displays, seemingly genuine smiles on the staff's faces. And most important of all, the almost antiseptic cleanliness. There appeared to be two receptionists who worked shifts: one a smart, bespectacled middle-aged woman, the other a young girl, both impeccable, neither of whom was the owner who was away from Paris until January.

***

'Bonjour, madame. Qu'est-ce-que je peux faire pour vous?'

The older receptionist, wearing the ubiquitous white overall, immaculate makeup and a welcoming smile, addressed Helen as she walked into the pleasant establishment. It was very cold but dry that morning and Helen wore the newly dry-cleaned grey woollen coat over a simple black skirt and a bright brick-red polo-neck sweater. She'd tied Jill's Christmas gift, an even brighter red and black scarf, around her neck, which added a touch of elegance, she couldn't help thinking – thanks a lot, Jill. Her black ankle-boots were newly heeled and she carried an as-near-as-dammit matching handbag. She returned the receptionist's smile and introduced herself.

'Ah oui, Madame Hartnell. Installez-vous là-bas. Madame Colombe sera avec vous dans quelques minutes.'

Helen smiled, congratulated herself on understanding every word and sat on one of the dark blue leather chairs that surrounded a smoky-glass coffee table, piled with glossy magazines. She was flicking through one of them when the salon's owner slowly came out of Salon No. 1 and walked towards her. Helen put down the magazine, stood up and took hold of the outstretched hand. She looked into the large, probing brown eyes and noticed that the black hair was swept into a chignon and held in place with a glittering comb. Luminous, fashionable stockings clung to the long, shapely legs and the hand that held hers was small, soft and perfectly manicured. The two women eyed each other, taking each other in. After a while, Helen had the impression that she was being examined, professionally scrutinised, but there was something else in those dark, searching eyes that she couldn't quite put her finger on. She felt a quiver of apprehension as she followed her interviewer into Salon No. 1.

The room was large and contained a variety of modern, gleaming equipment, soft clean towels, an abundance of lotions and potions. Highly polished mirrors and soft pink lights adorned the walls. Helen was invited to sit in yet another blue leather chair while her companion organised two cups of coffee to be brought by the receptionist. After finally sitting down in the chair opposite Helen, she continued her physical scrutiny, her inspection and Helen almost flinched at the unfathomable expression in the other woman's eyes. After what seemed an age, she spoke.

'Alors, vous êtes anglaise. Do you prefer to speak English or French, madame?'

Helen jumped and smiled in relief.

'Oh, English. Please. If you don't mind. My French isn't very fluent ... yet ... to say the least.'

She knew she was gabbling and quickly stopped herself. The coffee cup was shaking in her hand and she steadied it, her head bent. It seemed a while before the beautician spoke again, although the dark eyes never left Helen's face. Helen wondered if she was supposed to speak first, say something, maybe ask a question, but she felt rather intimidated and didn't know how to begin. As she lifted the small porcelain cup to her lips and sipped, the other woman spoke.

'Where do you come from, Madame Hartnell?'

She was studying Helen, the same strange expression still in her eyes. If Helen had been forced to describe it, she'd have said there was curiosity and discomfort in that look, with a touch of panic and maybe ... vice. Helen took a deep gulp of her own coffee and put the cup and saucer on the table, managing to spill some of the black liquid into the saucer. She pulled a face and inwardly cursed.

'I come from the north of England ... Yorkshire. I ... I don't know if you know it. I'm actually from a village called Firley, on the Pennines ... near Bradford. Maybe you've heard of Bradford? Or Leeds? Leeds is ...'

The other woman also put down her empty cup, crossed her legs and smiled slowly at her interviewee.

'I certainly have heard of Bradford and Leeds, Madame Hartnell. I've even heard of Firley. Believe it or not but I've actually been there ... to Firley.' She paused and narrowed her beautiful dark eyes. 'Tell me – Madame Hartnell – how is Jill? Does she still live in Firley? Or has she moved away from the village, too?'

Their eyes met and Helen felt the blood flowing cold in her veins. She swallowed the saliva that was threatening to choke her and tried to calm her trembling limbs. Their facial expressions and general demeanour, magnified around the salon by the omnipresent mirrors, were identical.

'My God, Marie-Laure. Marie-Laure Colombe,' Helen eventually whispered. 'I'd completely forgotten your real name. But I remember it now. Marie-Laure Colombe – Turtle Dove.'

She sank further back into the soft leather chair, her initial eagerness and desire to impress now giving way to more negative thoughts and best-forgotten memories. For quite some time the two women continued to gaze at each other while their coffee and their hopes for a shared professional future both turned cold.

Chapter Seven

'Well, you just think on. Don't you be gettin' any o' them fancy ideas, Helen Hartnell. I'm 'avin' no foreigners stayin' 'ere. An' don't you be invitin' her for any meals, either. I don't want to 'ave to start cookin' owt fancy.'

Dorothy Hartnell finished her uncalled-for and unnecessary harangue by picking up her cup of tea, cradling it fondly (far more fondly than Helen could ever remember being cradled) and quickly swivelled in her chair to look out of the sash window. It wasn't a sudden need to gaze on to the incomparable view of the Yorkshire Pennines that caused her to do this. The house she'd lived in since her wedding had the most enviable view in the whole village and Dorothy spent most of her idle afternoons drinking it in, along with the endless cups of sweet, milky tea. Her mornings, over the past ten years, had been spent cleaning the bookies' office in Firley, nine-thirty till twelve. No, it was the sudden need to avoid eye contact with her daughter, having settled her point and wanting no contradictions, thank you very much, young lady. Not that she'd ever had to contend with contradictions from Helen. Her daughter had been trained from a very young age never to contradict, disagree or argue with her mother for whatever reason, and certainly never to express an opinion of her own.

'Don't contradict me', 'What I say goes', 'Because I say so, that's why', were but a few of her mother's rejoinders that echoed down the years of her repressed childhood, often accompanied by a well-aimed slap. So now it would be unthinkable to suddenly question Dorothy Hartnell's discipline and so-called edification in the formidable period of Helen's adolescence. She'd been indoctrinated at a very early age, with the help of a well-meaning but basically weak and anything-for-a-quiet-life father, that her mam's word was always final.

'I'm only telling you 'cos I'm pleased for Jill, Mam, that's all.'

Dorothy sipped her tea, continued to look out of the window and didn't offer to reply.

'Her name's ... oh, blimey, I can't remember. Anyway, she's coming next month. The first of August.'

Helen had long since realised that she was talking to herself but carried on anyway.

'Her plane'll be arriving at Leeds and Bradford airport and Jill and her mam and dad are going to pick her up. She's seventeen, I think ... about the same age as us, anyway. Jill doesn't even know what she looks like, you know, she's never seen a photo or anything. I think she's expecting a Brigitte Bardot look-alike. Blimey, Mam, that'll liven this place up a bit if she is, won't it?'

Without turning round Dorothy pushed her tea-stained mug away and drummed her fingers with their grubby nails on the plastic tablecloth.

'*This place*, as you so nicely call it, doesn't need any livenin' up, young lady, and certainly not from any fancy French piece. Now, let's change the subject, shall we?'

She finally looked at her daughter and a deep frown furrowed her already prematurely lined face. Dorothy Hartnell wasn't yet forty-eight but looked ten years older.

'And for God's sake, lass, will you stop fiddlin' with that bloody 'air ... the rate you're goin' you'll be bald by time yer thirty. Just stop if off.'

She stood up and let go a long, rumbly fart that went ignored by both of them. Helen stopped 'fiddling' with her long and resplendent chestnut tresses and swept them down her back with a slow toss of her head – yet another mannerism that got her mother's much-maligned goat. If she put an end to all her habits and little pleasures that, for some unknown reason drove her mother up the wall, she'd very quickly become a mental and physical paralytic.

'Now, is young feller-me-lad comin' for tea tonight?'

Helen looked up at her mother, who was on her way to the stairs. As usual, she didn't question her mother's choice of vocabulary; she was used to it by now, but she still recoiled when Dorothy mentioned Malcolm, which was never by name. Always His Nibs, Feller-me-Lad, Yon Swain (Evelyn Myers, their hard-of-hearing next door neighbour had understood 'John Wayne' and had been tickled to death. Dorothy, as usual, hadn't seen the funny side and Helen's hopes of her mam finally calling Malcolm by the name he'd been baptised were thwarted), and even Himself.

'Mam,' Helen had always wanted to say, 'his name's Malcolm. Why don't you just call him Malcolm?'

But she saved her breath, knowing there was absolutely no point whatsoever.

'Yeah, Malcolm's coming for tea. About six, if that's okay. And then we're going for a drink with Jill and Tom.'

'Well, at least pair of you won't be under me feet all evening. Right then, you'd best get yerself down to supermarket and decide what you want to feed Himself on tonight. An' while you're there you can get me some chocolates or summat, seein' as 'ow I'll be stuck in on me own all night.'

***

July 1976 was in the middle of a heatwave that had started in mid-June and was to last all summer. Helen dashed up to the village's small supermarket wearing a sleeveless cotton blouse and a not-quite-mini denim skirt. She wore flip-flops on her feet and her very (as far as she was concerned) average legs were already lightly tanned. At the moment she was unemployed and able to take advantage of the unprecedented scorching summer. She would have preferred to be working and earning or studying hard for A levels like Jill, but still. She was in a 'lather', as her mam described it, when she got home but there wasn't any hot water for a necessary shower. Her mam hadn't switched on the immersion heater that day; she was 'careful' with the electricity, it ran away wi' yer brass.

'But, Mam, I'm sweating like the proverbial pig. I must stink. I'll have a cold shower, then.'

Dorothy, who was still sitting at the table, her fleshy chin tucked into her equally fleshy right hand, glared at her daughter as though she'd suggested walking across the moor stark naked.

'You'll do no such thing, young lady. What d'you want to do, give yerself pneumonia? I've never 'eard owt so daft; a cold bloody shower. That's what they give bitches on 'eat. 'Ave a swill, that'll do. Anyway, if you do stink, maybe Himself'll keep his 'ands to 'imself for a change. Right then, if he's comin' at six, you'd best get a move on wi' that ham and lettuce. I'll butter some bread ... 'alf a loaf, I reckon – I know 'ow much that bugger can go through.'

Malcolm Jones was also 'lathered' when he rang the doorbell five minutes before six o'clock. In spite of the visible sweat and accompanying malodour, Helen's young heart gave its usual little leap when he followed her into the kitchen and discreetly pecked her cheek. Malcolm, at nineteen years old, was almost six inches taller than Helen and, thanks to a healthy appetite, had 'plenty o' meat on 'im' as Dorothy said. But the meat was firm, muscular. His thick fair hair flopped into his blue eyes in a way that sent Helen's heart to the moon and back (she'd actually written that in one of the poems that were hidden away in her chest of drawers upstairs) and sent Dorothy round the bend.

'Why don't you do summat wi' that bloody 'air o' yours?' was a frequent greeting, if she had the doubtful pleasure of opening the door to him. 'You look like a bloody Yorkshire terrier. Or terror, more like it.'

Malcolm had long ago stopped trying to think of original quips to this reception and Dorothy's worn-out and unappreciated repartee unfortunately persisted.

She was standing at the sink wiping some dishes when 'Himself' walked in and didn't see the fond exchange of kisses and hugs. Her copious body being wedged between the sink and the already set table, she didn't turn round to greet her guest, only called, 'Is it 'ot enough for you, Romeo?'

Helen pulled a weary face and turned her unnecessary attention to the table.

'Not really, Mrs Hartnell,' Malcolm genially replied, risking a pat at Helen's handy bottom, 'to be honest, I could do with a bowl o' soup to warm me up.'

Dorothy could never cope with her future son-in-law's (or so she and everyone else supposed) quips and bloody quirks and always responded with more antagonism.

'Right, well, park yerself then, young feller-me-lad. And you'll 'ave to make do with 'am salad and a hot drink. There is no bloody soup.'

They all took their usual seats at the table: Dorothy nearest the sink; Helen with the best view in the world opposite the window; and Malcolm on her left with the worst view in the world, facing his future mother-in-law. There was a more or less happy silence for a short time while they tucked into their tea and Helen was the first to break it.

'I saw Jill this morning. Her penfriend's coming over on the first of August. She's getting right excited.'

Malcolm swallowed some tomato, flicked his hair out of his eyes and grinned at the table.

'Does she look like Brigitte Bardot?'

'Oh, don't *you* bloody start.' Dorothy scraped her chair away from the table and stood up. 'Who wants some tea? I'm gaggin'.'

They both nodded, their mouths full.

'Why should *you* be so interested in what she looks like, any road?' Dorothy's voice rasped over the cold water filling the kettle. 'You should only 'ave eyes for my lass.'

'I might have finished me meal, Mrs Hartnell, but there's nothing to stop me reading the menu.'

Helen giggled and tapped the tanned arm that was resting on the table. Dorothy's silent exasperation was audible; her future son-in-law was the only person on God's earth who could leave her speechless.

'What's her name?' Malcolm asked.

'Don't know. Jill told me but I couldn't pronounce it if I tried. I think we'll have to give her a nickname.'

'Frog wouldn't be a bad idea …'

'Oh Mam, honestly! That's really awful …'

'And I've told 'er this afternoon not to get any ideas about invitin' any foreigners 'ere. I'm not standin' for that. Yer 'ome isn't yer own. Theresa Mooney'll 'ave a few tales to tell in September, I'll be bound.'

'They might be nice ones, Mam.'

Dorothy Hartnell made an incomprehensible clicking noise with her tongue and badly decayed teeth and banged the brown teapot on the table.

'Aye, an' they might not, an'all.'

'When are we going to meet her, then?' Malcolm asked.

'Next Sunday, I suppose. I hope her English'll be good enough for us to communicate …'

'If not, old Malcolm might have to be called upon to give a few lessons!'

He grinned and looked at Dorothy through a number of stray fair hairs … She made a show of collecting the empty plates accompanied by the musical clicking of her tongue; a skill she seemed to have just acquired.

***

The Bay Horse Inn stood at the top of a particularly steep and stony road that overlooked almost the whole village, with spectacular views from the front windows and the beer garden. Built over a hundred years ago, the pub was the oldest of the village's four, a home to the oldest locals who liked to sit in the bar and chatter to anyone and everyone. It was also home to the youth of Firley, who organised snooker and darts tournaments in the tap room, and there was the occasional social reception, particularly weddings. The décor was dark wood, red corduroy and brass, and heavily-framed pictures of local scenes hung on the walls. Jill and Tom were sitting near the open door – the beer garden being full – when Helen and Malcolm arrived. Jill's short, light brown hair had been cropped even shorter to cope with the unusually hot summer and framed her flawless complexion and bright, hazel eyes. She grinned and waved when she saw her friends and Tom stood up and ambled to the bar. Without asking for their order, he came back with the usual pint of lager and a Coke.

'Cheers!'

After their initial greeting, the subject that occupied most of the evening was the forthcoming visit from the unknown and therefore intriguing penfriend.

'Marie-Laure Colombe,' Jill replied when Helen asked the girl's name again.

74

'Come again?' Malcolm frowned.

'If you can get your tongue round that one an' come out the other side, you're a better man than I am.'

Tom's dry and often unsmiling humour was always a refreshing contrast to Malcolm's sometimes tiring exuberance.

'That goes without saying,' Malcolm thumped his mate on his shoulder. 'But I still can't get my tongue round this name. Repeat, Jill, please, s-l-o-w-l-y ...'

'Marie-Laure Colombe. It's dead easy, repeat after me,' Jill giggled.

'Well, I think we should give her a nickname,' suggested Helen, 'one that we can all pronounce. It'll be fun.'

'That's easy then,' Jill said. 'Colombe means dove. So, let's call her Dove.'

'Turtle Dove's even better,' Malcolm murmured thoughtfully and received a punch in the ribs from his pal.

'The trouble with you,' Tom said, 'is that you always have to bring sex into everything.'

'Me? Sex? What's that?'

'Summat that coal used to come in,' Tom offered, and picked up his quickly diminishing pint. 'Now, hurry up and sup up 'cos it's your round next.'

'Well, I just hope you two are going to be on your best behaviour next week. I don't want you embarrassing the poor girl on her first day. Helen, you and Malc will come over to meet her on Sunday, won't you? I expect she'll want to meet my friends and she ...'

'*She*? Who's *she*?' Malcolm flicked his hair out of his eyes and looked enquiringly round the table. '*She* is the cat's mother, according to Helen's mam.'

'*She* is Turtle Dove,' Jill glared at him, stifling a grin as she threw a beer mat in his direction.

Marie-Laure Colombe was baptised Turtle Dove on that Saturday evening in the Bay Horse Inn, a week before she arrived on British soil. And during her short but devastating stay in Firley, she was never called anything else.

***

'Don't you be traipsin' up there, Helen Hartnell. I've told you before, it's just not seemly.'

'Why not, Mam? Malcolm's mam's invited me to tea and ...'

'I don't care if the Queen Mother's invited you to bloody tea, lass, let 'Imself come and fetch you ... call for you, as is good and proper ...'

'Mam, it's only fifteen minutes' walk away. I'm not likely to get molested between here and there.'

'I'm not talkin' about you getting' molested, Helen, and let's 'ave less o' your damn cheek. I'm talkin' about ... well, it's just not right, not proper ... a young lass makin' her own way to 'er chap's 'ouse. If yer dad 'ad any idea ... Well, I suppose you'd best be off this time but tell 'im from me that in future 'e comes and collects you.'

That conversation, for want of a better word, had taken place the previous summer, in July 1975, when the Helen-Malcolm romance was beginning to bud and Dorothy's outmoded and rather comical ideas had first come to light. Helen had tried to protest but Malcolm, in his new-found ardour, had curiously accepted Dorothy's absurd wishes and always 'came to collect' his girlfriend, no matter what their plans were. Helen frequently wondered how long his odd acquiescence would last but a year later Malcolm was still dancing to Dorothy Hartnell's often illogical tunes.

On Saturday, 1 August, 1976, Malcolm called for Helen at two-thirty p.m. Dorothy was settled for the afternoon on the front step, a large mug of tea at her side, a pile of old magazines in her lap and the 'best view in the world' in front of her. Malcolm raised his right hand in greeting as he climbed the steps towards her and brushed the undisciplined hair out of his eyes.

'You look nice and comfortable there, Mrs Hartnell,' he grinned, mounting the steep stone steps two at a time, 'but mind you don't get sun-burned. Have you got plenty of cream on?'

'I think I'm old enough to look after meself, lad.'

Dorothy took the edge out of her voice with the addition of a thin smile and the oblique instruction to 'elp 'imself from the fridge if 'e were gaspin'. Malcolm didn't need to be asked twice and took a can of Coke off the top shelf. He played for time looking for a glass, not wanting to spend time alone in his future mother-in-law's company. Not that that relationship was official yet. And not that Malcolm would have particularly chosen Dorothy Hartnell as his mother-in-law. But he couldn't imagine life without her daughter now.

'Helen's upstairs, primpin', though God knows what for. Any mush she puts on 'er face today'll soon slide off in this 'eat. So, you'd best park yerself next to me, lad, yer probably in for a long wait.'

In contradiction to Dorothy's unwelcome prediction, Helen suddenly appeared behind them, closing the door to the bedroom stairs. She wore a strappy blue sun dress that she'd found in a closing down sale in Bradford, and had tied her hair in a pony tail that fell down her back, revealing a makeup-free but still pretty face. Malcolm slowly smiled at the vision in front of him and felt the familiar aching in his groin. Oh Jesus, if only ... He held out his hand to her and Helen almost skipped towards him, her pleasure at seeing him evident in her every movement. Dorothy visibly flinched in front of them but managed to keep quiet for once, and went back to her magazine.

'Right, we'll be off, then!'

'Will you be back for tea?'

'No,' Malcolm called, taking the steps two at a time, 'we'll either eat something out or back at Mum's. See you, Mrs Hartnell.'

'Bye, Mam.'

At the bottom of the uneven, cobbled street and on the path that led across the moor, Helen breathed a sigh of relief. At the same time, she felt Malcolm's hand slide into her own. He had often, in the earlier months of their relationship, attempted to put his arm round her shoulder, hold her hand, kiss her on the lips even, all in the presence of her mother. But he'd soon learned the folly of his ways. Dorothy let him know in no uncertain terms that that sort of exhibition just wasn't on. But this is 1976, not 1876; I'm not raping her, Mrs Hartnell, I'm just being affectionate ... But in view of Helen's embarrassed compliance with, rather than defiance of, her mother's wishes, Malcolm eventually gave up on physical demonstration of his affection. At least in front of Mrs Hartnell. He often wondered what Helen's dad had been like and wished he could have known him. He must have been quite something to live with that old battle-axe for any length of time. It was pretty obvious that his daughter took after him and not her mother, and Malcolm could only be grateful for that.

They followed the narrow, gently rising path for about a mile across the parched moor until the heat got the better of them and they finally sank down on the harsh, prickly grass, almost yellow now through lack of moisture. Helen had stocked up on soft drinks and they happily gorged themselves now while the unrelenting sun continued to scorch their skin.

'She'll be here by now.'

Helen wiped her sticky mouth on the back of her hand and screwed the top back on an empty bottle.

'Who will?' Malcolm closed his eyes and offered his face to the sun.

'You know very well who. Turtle Dove. Or whatever her real name is. They should be back at Jill's by now.'

Malcolm grunted something unintelligible and slowly lay back on the warm but uncomfortable grass.

'Don't forget we're going to see her ... we're going to Jill's tomorrow afternoon.'

'I haven't forgotten. But in the meantime …'

Helen was sitting cross-legged in the grass, her back now turned to her boyfriend, who was lying beside her, his chest naked. For a while they didn't speak but Malcolm silently squinted at the girl's sun-kissed back and slowly his hand reached out, slipped one of the straps down her arm and kissed her pink shoulder. For a while there was no response; Helen almost indifferently allowed him to stroke her skin. And then Malcolm suddenly pulled down the zip on the back of her dress and in the same movement pulled Helen on top of him. The ribbon attaching the pony tail came loose and Malcolm was surrounded by chestnut hair, soft pink arms and responding lips on top of his. He slipped his shaking hand inside her now-loose dress and slowly began to caress Helen's small breasts. She moaned with mounting excitement and Malcolm thrust his tongue inside her mouth. She kissed him back, caressed him with equal passion, equal longing, and Malcolm's hands began to play with the bottom half of her dress. He slowly, cautiously, pulled it up, his hand lingering on Helen's slim thigh and then he hesitated … Helen's arms were round him now, squeezing, caressing, her moans becoming louder and her kisses more passionate, more urgent. Malcolm held his breath, hardly daring to believe, to hope … and then it was over.

Helen sat in her original position at his side, slightly in front of him, the only difference being her rather dishevelled appearance. She struggled silently with her straps and Malcolm silently watched. He let several minutes go by before he touched Helen's trembling hand and said, 'What's up, love?'

'You know what's up, Malcolm. I can't. I want to … you know that, but I just can't. And especially not here.'

Malcolm sat up abruptly, frustration and anger visible in his movements, on his face.

'Why not here? We're miles from anywhere, Helen, we left the path behind and we're off the beaten track. Nobody ever comes this way. Not from Firley … and the hiker's trail's miles away. How many times have we been over this? I want you and I'm sure you want me and if not here, then where? Shall we ask your mother if we can borrow her bedroom? I'm sure she'd oblige if we asked her nicely and gave her a couple of quid to have a night on the tiles. Or – an even better idea – we'll give me mum and dad a floor show and do it on their rug while they're watching Coronation Street.'

'Don't be vulgar, Malcolm, I can't stand that.'

'Look, love, I've suggested going away for a weekend – Scarborough or somewhere – but you won't hear of that, either.'

'Of course I won't! How would I explain that to me mam? Don't be daft.'

'You're over sixteen, Helen.'

'Aye, I know. What difference does that make to *my* mother?'

Suddenly, Malcolm laughed, a mirthless, self-pitying jeer that was unlike him and Helen turned to face him. He was leaning on one elbow chewing a freshly-plucked blade of grass, his naked chest gleaming in the sunshine, the fair hairs glistening with sweat. Helen wanted to reach out and touch him but, of course, she didn't.

'We could take her to Scarborough with us.'

Helen ignored the silly remark and said nothing.

'Why not here?'

He was obviously not going to give up that easily and Helen sighed. He threw away the chewed stalk and flung out his right arm to encompass their sequestered surroundings.

'Look, we're miles from anywhere!'

At that moment, a German shepherd puppy came bounding towards them, seemingly from nowhere, followed by a harsh, 'Prince! Here! Come here, this minute!' and a middle-aged couple in summer hiking gear walked steadily by. Prince, tongue hanging and tail wagging, gambolled away, barking happily and Helen laughed. She jumped up, quickly zipped up her dress and put her hands on her hips, looking down at Malcolm.

'I rest my case,' she giggled.

But Malcolm didn't appear to see the joke.

***

'Who needs Brigitte Bardot?' had been Tom's first mental – fortunately not verbal – reaction. He hadn't been to the airport with Jill and her parents. He'd decided it would be better to let the French visitor meet her host family first and the rest of the entourage later. Besides, Mandy, his elder sister, had just come home from university after finishing her studies in Psychology and he'd promised to run her into Bradford for much-needed shopping and lunch. The only car owner in the family, Tom was used to chauffeuring people around but he didn't mind at all. And he certainly didn't mind spending Saturday morning with his sister. Malcolm Jones was his best mate, Jill the best girlfriend in the world; and after them Mandy was the only other person he could have long, interesting conversations with. A person he saw only too rarely. Okay, so her studies at Cardiff University were now over, but she'd be looking for work very soon and he doubted very much that she'd do her hunting on home ground. So, he was going to make the most of her while he could.

Finally, Mandy had insisted on doing her shopping alone. She didn't want to bore the pants off her brother; so once in Bradford he went to a quiet pub for a solitary pint and met his sister for lunch at one of the better Indian restaurants in the city. Mandy had arrived and was sitting at a table for two and nibbling poppadums when Tom put his appearance in.

'You'll be late for your own funeral,' Mandy smiled up at her brother.

'Better late than never. Or then again, maybe not.'

They chatted eagerly about their respective lives and Mandy was as interested in Tom's computer programming studies in Leeds as he was in her future career as a psychologist. When she'd first announced her professional intentions several years before, everyone had been a little bit shocked and highly amused. A psychologist in the family? Well, bugger me! Anyhow, there were plenty o' nutters in Firley so the lass'd never be out o' work ... It had all been a bit of a joke and there had been a lot of leg-pulling in the beginning, but nobody was laughing now or making inappropriate remarks ... The whole clan was as proud as Punch.

Replete after their vindaloo with basmati rice, Mandy looked at her brother across the table and said, 'And after your studies, Tom, what are you thinking of doing? Will you stay in Yorkshire or look for work a bit further afield?'

Tom suddenly looked a little bit abashed and shuffled about on his chair, offering his sister an impish grin at the same time.

'I suppose that depends on Jill ... a bit.'

'Aha! Do I hear the sordid sound of wedding bells?'

Mandy's sisterly smile slowly disappeared and she gently touched Tom's lightly tanned hand. Tom didn't respond.

'Look, don't rush into anything, Tom. I like Jill a lot, you know that, but you're both so young ... kids, really. I know people still tend to get engaged and married young in this part of the world but ... well, you're a bright lad and it'd be a shame to throw away a future on ...'

'I wouldn't be throwing my future away on Jill.'

'That's not what I'm saying, Tom. Just ... well, just don't rush into things, that's all. You've got all your lives ahead of you. See a bit of the world, or at least a bit of Britain before you tie yourselves down with a mortgage and half a dozen kids. It'll be too late then and ...'

'Thanks for your advice, big sister.'

Mandy, a female replica of her brother with short blonde hair, blue eyes and good skin, shrugged her shoulders and pulled a face at him.

'I suppose I'm wasting my time, aren't I? Anyway, after this French girl's influenced your Jill, she might be off to live in gay Paree.'

'Over my dead body.'

'Ah well, we'll see. And how's Helen, Jill's inseparable? Has she found a proper job yet?'

Tom pulled a few pound-notes out of his pocket and beckoned the young Indian waiter.

'*She'll* never find a decent job; she's one of life's drifters. Nothing much'll become of our Helen. I reckon that mother of hers is to blame, but I don't know. And before you ask, aye, Malcolm is still besotted. I tell you what, the best thing that could ever happen to her is to get married and raise a big family ... although I'm not sure I wish that fate on me mate. One thing's for sure though, old Malc'd never run out of mother-in-law jokes.'

Tom checked his watch as they left the restaurant.

'I'll be seeing them both round at Jill's tomorrow afternoon, to meet the Frenchie. Are you sure you don't want to come round there, just to say hello?'

'Don't you mean "bonjour"?' Mandy grinned and shook her head. 'Not this time, Tom. I've too much to do, too many of my own friends to see. I'll say bonjour another time.' She gave him a dig in the ribs. 'What do you think of my accent?'

Tom didn't acknowledge the dig and his expression was the usual deadpan.

'I've always put a great store by your Yorkshire accent, sis. I'd have been right upset if you'd come home talking Taffy.'

***

Who needs Brigitte Bardot?

'Marie-Laure, this is my boyfriend, Tom. Tom, this is Marie-Laure Colombe.'

She was seventeen, the same age as Jill but somehow managed to look older and years younger at the same time. She was pencil-thin and so tanned that Tom thought she must have some Indian blood or something – or maybe that was because he'd enjoyed a vindaloo the day before. Her black-as-night hair was cut short but looked soft and feminine and enhanced her huge, almond-shaped dark brown eyes. She wore no makeup; she didn't need a scrap of it. Silver bangles jangled on her right arm as she held out her hand to Tom.

That Sunday afternoon the five of them – Theresa and Jack Mooney, Jill, Tom and Turtle Dove – sat in the front garden under the hideously ostentatious red and white checked parasol and drank gallons of liquids, trying to keep cool and trying to keep a reasonable conversation going. Although Turtle Dove had problems understanding the local accent she spoke well and obviously wanted to learn and was therefore interesting. She was also the epitome of charm and courtesy.

'Ah, here comes Helen,' Theresa Mooney suddenly smiled and waved, 'and Malcolm.'

Chapter Eight

The only real advantage that the Hartnell's terraced house had over all others was its position on the very edge of the village, with a sweeping view of the moor. At least, the view would have been sweeping if the sash windows had been that bit wider – and that was another of Dorothy's domestic grouses. The disadvantages were numerous. There was no proper road in front of the house, only a wide expanse of rubble and stone which made driving impossible and walking a hazardous business. The house was also quite small. The rooms, including a cellar and attic, lacked space and furnishing them had been no pleasure at all for Mrs Frank Hartnell, newly-wed in the mid-fifties. Frank Hartnell had promised her the world when he'd placed that plain gold ring on her finger, which to her way of thinking meant decent furniture and a home she could stretch in. So, she always thought she'd been a little bit cheated on the material side of her marriage when Frank bought their small dwelling because of its position and fine view, without a thought to living conditions and any kids that might come along. She'd kept quiet at the time but over the years gradually gave vent to her frustration and dissatisfaction until Frank, who was more than content in his little homestead with its magnificent view, finally agreed to look for something bigger. Grander. A place where Dorothy could lounge on an elegant three-piece suite and not have to dry the washing round the fire, making the place damp and steaming up the windows. (There were no views at all, then, were there?) But there was no garden for drying washing. The back door led straight on to the pavement and the front door on to the rubbly road and the moor. And the cellar was damp and a bit spooky so Dorothy couldn't dry her washing down there, either. It had to be done in front of the fire, there were no two ways about it. That was why their Helen was always snufflin' and chesty.

And speakin' of Helen, how could she bring friends 'ome; 'ave anybody to stay? The lass couldn't, there weren't any room. Not that 'the lass' was encouraged or ever would be encouraged to bring a lot of friends home, even less have anyone to stay; but that was another arrow that Dorothy fired at Frank in their private domestic war. All her arguments included Helen in one way or another because she knew it were the only way to get George to listen, an' if she were lucky, react. Ever since the birth of their only child

Dorothy knew that her own desires, needs, simple requests would perhaps be granted provided their daughter's desires and needs had already been satisfied. It didn't take long for the seeds of jealousy and resentment to grow from this realisation. By the time Frank Hartnell finally came round to her way of thinking and took it into his head to look for a bigger and better place for his family – without leaving Firley, mind – he went and kicked the bucket. So that were that. And Dorothy and Helen stayed put. Because Dorothy, quite honestly, couldn't be bothered to finish what her husband had started.

The advantage of the Mooney's house was its situation right in the middle of Firley, in a long row of semis with a decent garden (back and front) and ample sized rooms where you could bring your family up properly. There were no view, of course, but who needed a view when you 'ad a garden?

At the beginning of the girls' friendship, when Helen and Jill were still attending Firley's Victorian primary school, Dorothy and Frank were often invited to the Mooney's, along with their daughter, for Sunday tea or beer and a game of cards on Friday evenings while the girls played (and later played records) up in Jill's room. That soon dropped off, Dorothy noticed, after Frank's untimely demise. They still kept in touch with Jill's best friend's mother – Christmas and birthday cards and the odd invitation to tea – but it weren't a regular thing anymore and Dorothy felt let down and felt she couldn't count on them; couldn't call them 'er friends. And she never invited them back, of course. Her invites to anybody had been few an' far between when Frank were alive an' kickin', but after he'd gone they stopped altogether. She had neither the room nor the inclination to entertain Helen's friends after she became a widow. It weren't the same when you weren't part of a couple. What could she offer them, anyway? A good view if they strained their necks a bit and they didn't need that, they 'ad a garden.

***

The Mooneys were in their garden now. In spite of having a flair for and thoroughly enjoying 'entertaining', Theresa Mooney seemed a bit out of her depth that afternoon, not quite sure how to deal with the unprecedented event of the summer. The arrival of Helen and Malcolm sent her scurrying back to the kitchen, eager to be in the wings, backstage and busy.

Theresa Mooney was an older, plumper version of her daughter. Short, brown hair framed a perpetually laughing face, twinkling eyes, an exterior that revealed a genuinely warm, caring and cheerful personality. The complete antithesis of her neighbour and acquaintance – she could never

84

call Dorothy Hartnell a friend even after all these years. And if the French girl's visit had put her, Theresa Mooney, in such an unheard-of panic and 'tiz-woz', how on earth would Helen's mother have coped? She wouldn't, there were nowt surer. And with that little thought to boost her morale, Theresa was soon bouncing back across the lawn, balancing a tray of various refreshments in her fleshy hands.

Turtle Dove accepted and seemed to delight in the nickname bestowed on her and happily fell into her new role as Star of the Month. Theresa's misplaced feelings of inadequacy were quick to disappear when she began to think of Turtle Dove as her second, very temporary, daughter. All was new and mysterious to the French visitor and she seemed to be taking an interest in everything and everyone – starting that Sunday afternoon when she was surrounded by the Mooney's friends and neighbours. Neighbours who 'just happened to be passing' and were invited to have a glass of something and meet Jill's penfriend, Turtle Dove ...

''Ow d'yer come by a name like that, then?'

'What do you think o' Yorkshire, then? Wait till you get up on them moors, lass – that'll blow all them Paris cobwebs off you!'

'She's a bonny lass, Theresa. I'd keep an eye on your Jack, if I were you!'

But the central characters that afternoon were Jack and Theresa Mooney, Jill and Tom and Helen and Malcolm. And, needless to stay, Turtle Dove. After Tom's initial 'Who needs Brigitte Bardot?' he quickly slipped into his role of interested but poker-faced looker-on. Alert to everything, asking pertinent questions and providing unasked for droll comments. Jill, however, did most of the talking, dragging her friends into the stilted conversation and sometimes bringing a very reluctant Helen into the limelight. Although Helen had been looking forward to the penfriend's visit, now that the girl was here in flesh and blood she could think of nothing to say to her. Turtle Dove, however, was the first to break the ice. After a short lull in the conversation, she turned her soft, dark brown eyes and slow smile on Helen.

'I suppose you are at school with Jill?'

Helen blushed and tried to smile back but it was difficult. She took a long drink of Coke, hiding her embarrassment behind the tall glass.

'No, actually, I'm not,' she finally said. 'I left school last year. Actually, I'm ... I'm looking for a job ...'

Turtle Dove nodded at her, turning the foreign words over in her mind, making sure that she'd understood correctly.

'And what ... what kind of a job are you looking for?'

The innocent question only caused more embarrassment. Helen wasn't really looking for a job; she wanted to study and pass exams, do something interesting with her life, not ... but her mother had decided on a different route. Helen decided not to tell her pretty interlocutor that she'd already lost two menial jobs in the last six months.

'Oh ... anything, really.' She shrugged her shoulders dismissively, conveying an idea she was really far from feeling. 'I'm not like Jill,' she went on in a kind of self-defence. 'I'm not really academic. I just want to ... find a job ... really. Work.'

There was a brief silence after this hesitant and, as everyone knew, inaccurate speech. Helen concentrated on her drink and felt Theresa Mooney's gentle, sympathetic and maternal eyes fixed on her. She's as academic as me own, if not more so, Theresa was thinking; she'd be as successful as any of 'em, given half the chance. But that one back there won't give her that chance, has never encouraged her to get on and never will. Since her dad died, she's had nobody to believe in her, make her believe in herself. If he'd lived, he wouldn't have dragged her out of school to make a living for him ... doing any unsuitable thing that came up. And then there were the lovely poems she sometimes wrote; Jill had told her mum about Helen's flair for writing poetry but the girl kept that particular light well hidden under a bushel, for reasons best known to herself.

'Helen writes lovely poetry, Turtle Dove. I'm telling you because *she* never will.'

Although Theresa wasn't looking at Helen, she knew that the girl was blushing furiously and cursed herself for opening her mouth – Helen would never thank her and neither would Jill, needless to say. But she'd just had to say *something*. Stick up for the lass ... anyway, her words seemed to fly away in mid-air because nobody had responded, least of all Turtle Dove, who had suddenly turned her attention to Malcolm. He seemed to find a little difficulty in looking the girl in the eye but apart from that he answered questions about himself and his new job at the photographic shop and studio in Keighley.

'And do you take photographies (no one corrected her) or do you ...'

'Develop and print them? I do both. I'm training to do everything. I'm going to buy the studio next year and my name will be in lights over the shop door!'

Turtle Dove squinted at him across the white wrought-iron table, weighing up both him and his words. Even the female members of the party couldn't help but think how fetching she looked.

'He's having you on, love,' Jill's dad said, laughing. 'Don't take in everything yon Malcolm says or you'll end up as a dustbin.'

The look of sheer bewilderment on Turtle Dove's face was even cuter, even more fetching ... even the female members of the party thought so.

∗∗∗

Malcolm, although at work during the day, had plenty of opportunities for taking photographs that hot month of August. The Mooneys, on holiday the first two weeks, took Turtle Dove on excursions in the car every day, visiting interesting sights in Yorkshire and occasionally crossing the Pennines into Lancashire. They visited Leeds, Harrogate and Manchester for shopping; York and Haworth for culture; and picnics at the seaside and on the moors for physical pleasure. Turtle Dove loved everything and hinted more than once that she hoped this wouldn't be her last visit to Yorkshire. The unemployed Helen often joined them on their trips and spent many a happy hour in the Mooney's garden that month, but she always paid for it one way or another when she got home.

'And what would you prefer me to do?' she dared to retort one evening, drained but at the same time exhilarated after a walk across the moor with the Mooneys and their guest. Her mother had been waiting for her in her usual position on the doorstep.

'I'd prefer you, you impudent young bugger, to be goin' out lookin for a job, that's what I'd prefer. It's not normal a young lass like you ...'

Helen trudged past her mother's inert figure into the kitchen and poured herself a glass of tap water. She didn't reply to her mother's verbal assault; there was nothing to say.

'Did you 'ear what I said, young lady?'

Helen drained the glass, rolled her blue eyes heavenward (probably towards her dad, she couldn't help thinking) and, after putting her glass into the sink, muttered that yes, of course she'd heard.

'Well, in case you're interested, they're lookin' for somebody at Farnham's.'

No, Helen wasn't interested but knew better than to say so.

'Farnham's? What's Farnham's?'

Dorothy Hartnell twisted her plumpness round on the top step in order to observe her daughter in the kitchen.

'Eeh, our Helen, I think this sun's addled yer 'ead. Bloody Farnham's! That fancy new chemist that's opened on Main Street. I saw an advert for a sales assistant in their winder this mornin'. So, I reckon you'd best get yerself up there.'

Helen leaned on the door jamb slightly behind and to the left of her mother, looking out at the slowly sinking sun on the lilac horizon. Well, she'd been a sales assistant in a newsagent's and a sales assistant in a haberdasher's and had lost both jobs on account of 'lack of enthusiasm for the job', or something like that. So, why not a sales assistant in a chemist's? Maybe she would have enthusiasm for the job and get the sack for something else? Giving lethal prescriptions to the wrong customers and causing multiple deaths in Firley; or blowing up condoms and handing them out as balloons to the village kids? The possibilities were endless.

'The job'll probably be taken by now.'

Dorothy, still sitting on the top step in her twisted and uncomfortable position, glared up at her daughter.

'Well, I'm glad yer father's not alive to 'ear you say things like that, our 'Elen. 'E always thought you 'ad more oil in your lamp.'

***

Harold Watts Photographic Studio and Shop in Keighley, where Malcolm had been employed for two months, was located in a small, modern shopping centre near the town's bus station. Harold Watts employed four people: his wife Marjorie, who helped out on a part-time basis; his eighteen-year- old son, Danny, who was to inherit the business; Valerie, a gormless but willing Saturday assistant; and Malcolm. Although Malcolm was learning all aspects of the business, he was particularly interested in taking photographs in the small studio behind the shop and then developing and printing them. Harold Watts was a patient teacher and both Danny and Malcolm benefited from his tireless instruction. Danny would inherit the business on his father's retirement but Malcolm was going to use his years there as a stepping stone to greater things. He intended to become a professional photographer, maybe even work in journalism, or the police, so he took every advantage he could of Harold's experience and tuition in those early days of his career. And he wanted to get a move on quickly; his wages at Watts were minimal with little prospect of improvement. He'd never be able to get a mortgage and keep a wife and family on his earnings there, so he'd have to look a bit sharp and better himself a bit sooner rather than later. It didn't look as though his lovely Helen would ever make anything of herself, professionally at least, so earning the bread and butter would definitely be up to him. And anyway, the only way he was ever going to get inside her knickers was if he put a ring on her finger and bought a home of their own. So, Malcolm intended getting ahead fast.

***

It was almost a quarter to six on Monday evening and Malcolm was alone in the shop, thinking about getting ready to lock up for the day. Harold was in the studio putting some equipment away, Danny was at day release school and Mrs Watts never put her appearance in on Mondays. It was her day off, as Friday was Malcolm's. Malcolm looked at his watch again and poked his blonde head round the studio's door.

'It's a quarter to six, Mr Watts. No sign of any customers – shall I start putting the shutters up?'

'Aye, lad, you might as well.'

Malcolm stepped into the small display window and took the more expensive photographic equipment off the shelves and carefully placed it inside the shop's safe, in the office next to the studio. Harold Watts, who in spite of the heat was dressed in shirt, collar and tie, came out of the studio and offered to give his young assistant a hand with the heavy steel shutters. He did this without fail. Every evening he offered to help Malcolm put the shutters up and every evening Malcolm had to bite his tongue and tell his boss he could manage, thanks. Did the old geezer think he wasn't capable of putting shutters up, for God's sake? He struggled outside with the steel grille and carefully leaned it against the now almost empty window before attempting to hoist it into position.

'Hello, Malcolm. Are you finishing your work now?'

At first, he thought he was hearing things. The voice was soft, throaty and barely audible and the name had definitely been 'Malcolm'. He slowly turned round, wiping a sweaty hand across an equally sweaty brow.

'Oh! Oh ... erm ... hello. Hi!'

Turtle Dove was a couple of inches shorter than he but she seemed very tall in beige shorts and white sleeveless tee-shirt and tanned limbs. A pair of gold-framed sunglasses were propped on top of her short, black hair and makeup-free dark eyes twinkled up at him. Her teeth shone white in her bronzed face. Her very photogenic face, Malcolm couldn't help thinking every time he laid eyes on her. The shutters were temporarily forgotten and Malcolm looked down into the still-smiling, he could have sworn teasing, face, and he searched in vain for something to say.

'Are you finishing your work now?'

Malcolm nodded, his professional eyes fixed on that photogenic face.

'Malcolm! Have you got them shutters fixed yet, lad? Come on, get a move on or we'll be here all night.'

Malcolm tried to turn his attention to the shutters while keeping his eyes

89

on the French girl in front of him. It proved too difficult, however, so he pulled himself away and grasped the heavy piece of metal in both hands, putting it in place before Harold Watts locked up.

'We thought about taking you next door for a drink if you were just finishing, Malcolm.'

Next door was a newly opened snack bar whose chief clientele were too-early passengers for the bus station, and the new voice belonged to Jack Mooney.

'We're on our way back from Haworth – Turtle Dove's been following the Brontës' footsteps and now we're ready for summat to sup. So, we stopped in Keighley and thought we might just catch you before you shut shop. D'you want to come with us for a glass o' summat cold?'

Sweat poured out of Malcolm's every pore as he strived to put the shutters in place in the still steaming heat, feeling the French girl's eyes boring into him. I'm making a right pig's ear of this, he cursed himself, and had to put the grille down, wipe his hands on his trouser leg and take a deep breath. He didn't look at Turtle Dove but he felt her twinkling, mocking eyes and could almost feel those too-white teeth biting into his sticky flesh.

'Here, lad, let me give you a hand.'

Harold Watts, impatient to leave his own premises for once, had stepped outside and picked up the recalcitrant grille, hoisting and clicking it into place in one swift and easy movement. He turned to Jack Mooney, whom he'd never seen in his life before and grunted,

'I don't know, these young 'uns, they can't 'old a candle to the likes of us, can they? All right, lad, you'd best be on your way, I'll see to the other one. And don't be late tomorrow morning.'

He winked at Theresa and Jack Mooney and his fifty-five-year-old eyes slithered over their young companion. Malcolm reddened and sweated even more. Shit, he thought and almost said, then realised with inexplicable relief that Turtle Dove wouldn't have understood a single pejorative word his boss had said.

'Let's go next door, shall we?' Theresa Mooney suggested. 'If I don't swallow summat cold and sharp soon, I'll collapse.'

'How about a razor blade in a glass of cold water, Mrs Mooney?' Malcolm grinned.

'I knew you'd say that.' Jack rolled his eyes and gave Turtle Dove a gentle push forward in the direction of the café.

'Where's Jill?' Malcolm asked when they were seated at a less than clean Formica topped table in front of the self-service counter.

'Oh, she had a dentist appointment this afternoon,' Theresa told him.

'That wisdom tooth that's been botherin' her, you know. I wanted to go with her but she wouldn't let me; she's so damned independent, that one. So, we took Turtle Dove to Haworth for the day. We've been to the Brontë Parsonage and Turtle Dove bought some books and … what else was it? Oh, aye, some bookmarks and a Cathy and Heathcliff tea-towel to take home. Then we 'ad a stroll across the moor but it were too hot to go far so we decided to have a rest an' a drink on the way home. An' then I thought about takin' you with us and droppin' you off at 'ome. Well, it'll save you waiting for the bus, love, won't it?'

'Thanks a lot. I appreciate it.'

Malcolm looked at Turtle Dove, who was looking in her shoulder bag, and he wasn't too sure what it was exactly that he appreciated …

'So … she's having it out, then?'

'Who's havin' what out?' asked Jack, putting a large tray of various cold drinks on the table.

'Our Jill. I've just been tellin' Malcolm that she's gone to the dentist … 'Ere you are, Turtle Dove, that's your orange juice … and a straw if you want one. I tell you what, kids, I'm going to finish this Coke in one big gulp.'

'As long as you do it quietly,' said Jack and winked at his French protegée. His French protegée had understood nothing, of course, and looked helplessly at Malcolm. He grinned at her and suddenly realised that he was blushing and he wanted to say something nice, funny and … and *understandable*.

All he could think of was, 'How's your orange juice? Does it taste better through a straw?' and immediately wanted the none-too-clean floor to swallow him up.

Theresa put her almost empty glass on the table, licked her lips and looked at Malcolm.

'By the way, love,' she said, 'I hope you and Helen 'aven't made any plans for this Saturday evenin'.'

'Why?' he asked and the single word came out as a little croak; he had to clear his throat. Turtle Dove had taken the sunglasses off her head and was cleaning them. He watched her blowing little puffs of hot breath from her soft, moist mouth on to the black lenses and the quick movement of her chamois-covered fingers as they stroked and rubbed. He moved restlessly in his sticky, plastic seat. He had to ask Mrs Mooney to repeat what she'd just started to say.

'We've decided to 'ave a barbecue in our garden on Saturday evening. We thought it'd be a great opportunity to get together with a few people before Turtle Dove goes home. Tom and 'is sister – if she's still in Yorkshire – you and Helen, that goes without saying. 'Er mother, if she likes. Some of the girls' old schoolfriends, neighbours ... What do you think?'

Malcolm nodded, his eyes still fastened on the moving fingers.

'Yeah, it's a great idea, Mrs Mooney. Great.'

Turtle Dove stopped cleaning the sunglasses and slid them into a red-velvet case. Malcolm noticed the name of a well-known French designer printed at the corner; at the same time, he felt her leg lightly brush against his. She was looking around the now empty snack bar with its cheap plastic furniture and tasteless pictures on the walls and taking everything in, as usual. He wondered how much of her stay in Yorkshire she'd remember; what places would be printed like photographs on her memory; which people she'd recall in later life and think of with pleasure and who she'd immediately forget. The latter thought gave him a sudden, unexpected pang and he watched her, now playing with her empty glass, her almond eyes still travelling, taking in, summing up. He mentally pleaded with her to turn those eyes back on him. And she did.

'Right then, gang, shall we be makin' a move?'

Jack Mooney stood up and moved away from the table, rubbing his large hands together as though in expectation of something. He had parked the rust-coloured Ford Granada just outside the bus station. He opened the back door for Turtle Dove to climb in, followed by Malcolm. Turtle Dove giggled when his leg got stuck between the front and back seats. He pretended to thump her and while Jack and Theresa prattled about mundane things on the short journey home, Malcolm and Turtle Dove held a kind of English lesson-cum-wrestling-match which dissolved into silence and physical distance when either of their escorts looked through the rear-view mirror.

***

'Well? 'Ow did it go? When will you be startin'?'

Helen slipped out of a pair of hollow, platform-soled shoes that had been killing her, and into her well-worn but comfortable slippers. She stretched her aching feet and the relief showed on her face.

'I told you not to buy them shoes but, as usual, you wouldn't listen. You'll be cripplin' yerself one o' these days – an' don't come cryin' to me when you do. Well, answer me question – when will you be startin'?'

Helen fell into her usual chair at the table in front of the window and leaned her chin on her right hand. With her left one, she played with the cutlery.

'It wasn't an interview, Mam. I told you, I've got an interview on Friday. Two o'clock…'

'Did they seem all right?'

Oh, they always seem all right, Helen thought, till I start working for them. But then, they probably think the same about me.

'I spoke to the chemist, Mr Farnham. Yeah, he seemed all right.'

'Well, I 'ope you show a bit more enthusiasm at yer interview else you'll get nowhere. By the way, is 'Imself coming tonight? You didn't say if he were coming for 'is tea or not, so I didn't…'

'No – he's not coming tonight, Mam.'

'Oh? I thought he'd 'ave shown a bit of interest in yer interview, at least…'

Helen took a deep breath and closed her eyes.

'I didn't tell him anything about it, Mam. I only went to apply for this job in person. And I'm not going to tell him I have an interview on Friday, either. There's no point till I know I've got the job.'

'Sounds daft to me. I thought he'd be interested.'

'He would be interested if he knew, but he doesn't know.'

'That's what I mean. *Why* doesn't he know? 'E's yer boyfriend, I'n't 'e? 'E ought to be interested in you lookin' for a job. I don't reckon much to a bloke who's not interested in—'

'Mam … I'm not telling him about my interview until I'm sure I've got the job. If I don't get it, he'll never know I had an interview. There's no point. Okay?'

Dorothy heaved her capacious shoulders and pulled her thin lips into a pout as she placed a sardine salad on the table.

'Sounds daft to me but I suppose you know what yer doin'. When's yer interview, did you say?'

Helen picked up her knife and fork and sucked in her breath.

'Friday. Two o'clock.'

'That's Romeo's day off, isn't it? 'E could go with you.'

Helen gaped at her mother.

'Go with me? To an interview for a job? Mam, why on earth would I want Malcolm to go with me to an interview in a chemist's shop?'

Dorothy shrugged and pouted and attacked the simple fare on her plate. There was a minute's silence that Helen prayed would last a lot longer.

'Friday at two o'clock, did you say? Well, they can't be in much of an 'urry. They've probably got somebody already an' it's their way o' fobbin' you off. I wouldn't build me 'opes up, if I were you.'

There was another minute's silence but Helen had stopped praying.

'Is 'e comin' down later? After tea?'

'I don't know. He's supposed to be phoning me.'

'What time?'

'I don't know. He just said he'd phone.'

Helen waited until eleven o'clock but Malcolm didn't phone that evening. Theresa Mooney called to tell her about Jill's visit to the dentist, the extraction of the wisdom tooth and her subsequent pain and inability to either eat or speak. She'd be out of sorts for a couple of days. And she also told Helen that she was planning a barbecue in the garden that Saturday evening ... depending on the state of Jill's mouth, of course!

But Malcolm didn't phone.

Chapter Nine

———

Between Monday and Friday that week Helen found herself very much alone. Jill suffered with an infection for two days after the extraction of her wisdom tooth and stayed at home while her parents looked after her guest. Helen wanted to see her friend, be with her when she was feeling a bit poorly, but Jill gently put her off. She wasn't really in the mood for company and she couldn't talk anyway. So Helen, in order to get away from her mother's tongue, often went walking on the moor, alone with her thoughts.

She and Malcolm were too young to get married, of course. She knew that he'd marry her next Saturday if she said yes. If only to get her into bed at long last. She drove that thought quickly out of her mind along with thoughts of her own unsatisfied needs. Oh, she knew that he loved her and wanted to spend the rest of his life with her, but unlike her he also had professional ambition, other goals in life. He enjoyed his job at Watts but it was only temporary, as he kept telling her. Malcolm was going to be a professional photographer working in journalism, something glamorous, and he'd have to move away from Firley to achieve that objective. And he'd more likely succeed as a single bloke than a too-young husband and father. And Helen didn't want to stand in his way. On the other hand, she loved him and wanted to marry him, create a life with him. Since she'd met him at Firley youth club the year before, he'd become the most important person in her life.

Jill had been dancing the last smooch of the evening with Tom and, rather than look like the wilting wallflower that she obviously was, the lone looker-on at the edge of the dance floor, Helen had wandered into the other, smaller room of the Firley youth club pre-fab building that was reserved for snooker and darts and other predominantly masculine games. The 'bar', an area that served soft drinks to the under-eighteens who frequented the place, stood against one wall, and the other window-less walls sported coloured photographs, local landscapes of the Pennines. Suddenly conscious that she was the only female in the room and aware of teasing eyes and ribald comments, Helen shuffled towards the first photograph that caught her eye, in order to hide her blushes. It was a beautiful picture of the moors in early autumn, purple with heather, and two Labrador puppies frolicking in the foreground. Her feigned interest gradually became genuine and she stood staring at the image in front of her for a long time, long after the last smooch had finished playing in the adjoining room.

'What do you think to it, then?'

Helen jumped at the unexpected voice behind her. She'd neither seen nor heard the fair-haired, smiling boy with a snooker cue in his hand approach her. She smiled back at him, shyly.

'I ... well, I think it's lovely. Those ... those puppies look so real.'

'That's because they were real. I didn't invent them.'

Helen blushed again.

'No, I didn't mean that. I meant ...'

She shrugged her shoulders and her fingers played with the long, lustrous hair that surrounded her face.

'Did you take the photo, then?'

The boy hadn't moved and she had to say something.

'Yeah. I took all of 'em. That's what I'm going to do when I leave college next year – I want to be a photographer. A professional.'

Helen's big blue eyes scanned the other exhibits and came back to rest on the original.

'What do you think, then?' the boy, obviously proud of his work, asked her again.

'They're all ... really good.' Helen smiled. 'But I think this one's the best. It's ... it's lovely. I love these puppies; they look so real.'

She sucked in her breath, blushed yet again and the young photographer threw back his head and laughed. His mates at the snooker table were starting to shout rude remarks, the older boy serving behind the alcohol-free bar was yelling 'Time!' exactly like they did in the pubs and Helen was aware of Jill and Tom hovering together in the doorway, watching.

'Anyway, it's yours if you want it.'

'What is?'

'This ... masterpiece. They're all coming down next Friday ... so, if you like it, I'll give it to you.'

You can't go takin' presents off a lad you've only just met. Eeh lass, I thought we'd brought you up better than that. You just give it right back to 'im ...

'You can't do that!'

'Why not? I've got the negative, I can print another one. Will you be here next Friday?'

Jill and Tom were walking towards her, Tom making foolish, inquisitive grimaces in the boy's direction.

'I ... I don't know. Probably not. We don't come every week.'

'Well, in that case, you'd better give me your address and I'll bring it round. I suppose you live in Firley?'

'Yes, but ...' Helen's sudden panic was written all over her face. 'Jill, let's go, shall we?'

She turned away from the boy who took lovely photographs and threw a quick 'Bye' over her shoulder.

'What's your name?' he called after her.

'Helen. Helen Hartnell.'

He only just caught her name because her voice was little more than a whisper and her head was bent.

'I'm Malcolm Jones. What's your address? Your phone number?'

Helen pretended not to have heard him and quickly disappeared through the main door. Jill, dawdling behind her best friend, turned round and smiled at Malcolm Jones.

'Don't worry about her address and phone number. We'll be here next Friday ... I'll make sure of that.'

The following Friday evening Helen became the proud possessor of a beautiful framed photograph and a deep and lasting friendship was formed between four young people. And that evening, the photograph tucked safely away at the bottom of her bottom drawer, Helen curled up on her single bed and wrote her first love poem.

Long fair hair and laughing eyes
That look at me as if I was
Well, special.
A cheeky grin that can't disguise
The fact that
He maybe thinks that
Well, I'm special.
Am I being stupid,
Am I being vain?
Maybe ... I'll call Cupid
And he can explain
Why I'm sure that this boy
Is going to be
Well ... special.

***

Malcolm and Jill were the only two people she really loved. And they both had better prospects in life than she did; she sometimes wondered what the pair of them saw in her. Jill being so academic, so clever so ... well, capable. And Malcolm so boyishly good-looking, so ambitious, so ... so capable. There was that formidable word again. And her, so ... so bloody incapable. Hopeless; gormless, as her mother never stopped pointing out.

And Malcolm was so sexy. Maybe Jill was sexy too, Helen didn't know about that. But she did know about Malcolm. His very masculine physique, cheeky eyes and disobedient hair all sent electric signals through Helen's nubile young body. Very natural signals that Helen knew from years of Dorothy-indoctrination should never be satisfied until after the ring was safely shoved on to her third finger. She wanted Malcolm as much as he wanted her but she also knew, from the same source of Dorothy-nation (as she'd come to think of it), that if she let him know her feelings, her needs, he'd never respect her. He'd discard her as easily as he'd discard a pair of old, soiled underpants. That's what her mam had drilled into her, only she hadn't said 'soiled'; she used a different, Dorothy Hartnell-type adjective, that she'd probably made up. Helen wanted Malcolm as much as he wanted her. Now. Not after they were married in the dim and distant future. But, better than any professional brain-washer, Dorothy had persuaded her that to make love with Malcolm (or anybody else for that matter) would immediately label her a slut and earn his eternal contempt. And there'd never be a wedding ring after that, would there?

***

She sat in the same spot where she and Malcolm had lain a few weeks before, when he'd stroked and kissed her and wanted her and she'd wanted him and had had to let him believe that she didn't. She plucked the course dry grass and gazed at the magnificent horizon and couldn't help but wonder why Malcolm hadn't phoned her for two days. It just wasn't like him. Maybe he was ill. She ought to phone him, of course, but while her mam was around – and wasn't her mam always around? – she couldn't phone her boyfriend because she'd be accused of 'throwing herself at him'. Making herself cheap. And the subject wouldn't be dropped for days. No, she was being generous. The subject wouldn't be dropped for weeks, months. The rest of her life. She'd thought about ringing him at Watts while her mam was out cleaning the bookies in the morning, but she didn't really like the idea of phoning him at work. She didn't want to get him into bother. Suddenly, however, the anguish of not knowing why he hadn't been in touch, the need to speak to him and the fact that she had change in her purse, all got the better of her. She'd call him from a phone box in the village.

On her third attempt she found a phone box that hadn't been vandalised and it happened to be two minutes away from Jill's house. So, she'd kill two birds with one stone and call to see the invalid on her way home.

'Good afternoon, Watts photographers. How can I help you?'

'Oh … erm … good afternoon,' Helen stammered. She supposed the man she was speaking to was Malcolm's boss, Mr Watts. 'Could you tell me if Malcolm's at work today, please?'

'Malcolm? Aye, he is. D'you want to speak to him?'

'Oh yes, please, if I can.'

''Old on a minute, he's in winder.'

Helen hoped she wouldn't have to hold on too long, she didn't have that much change.

'Hello?'

'Malcolm, it's me. Are you all right?'

There was a pause and then Malcolm said, 'Me? Who's … oh … yeah. Hello, Helen.'

There was something in Malcolm's voice that she'd never heard before and that she didn't like.

'What's up?'

'Nothing's up, Malcolm. I … well, I haven't heard from you and …'

Don't you be ringin' 'im up, chasin' after 'im and makin' a fool o' yerself. 'E'll never respect you, you know.

'… and I wondered if you were all right.'

'Of course I'm all right.'

Pause.

'Look … I can't talk now. I'm busy. You know you shouldn't ring me at work, don't you? Look … I'll phone you. Maybe tonight. Or tomorrow. Okay? See you … Helen.'

The line went dead and Helen was left with moths crawling around her stomach and blood pounding in her head. Her mam had been right, after all. She pushed open the heavy red and glass door and stumbled out of the confined, suddenly claustrophobic space. She stood quite still for a while, in the middle of the street, taking deep breaths and trying to choke back the hot tears that were threatening. And then she made her wobbly way to the Mooney's house.

Jill was sitting in a low red and white striped deckchair in the garden and her mother sat by her side, reading a woman's weekly magazine. They both beamed when Helen pushed open the small iron gate.

'Well, this is a nice surprise!' called Theresa Mooney. 'Sit down with your pal, sunshine, and I'll get you something to drink. You look as though you could do with one.'

'Don't bother yourself, Mrs Mooney, I'm all right.'

'I know you're all right, love. In fact, you're smashing! And now I'll get you that drink.'

She pulled herself out of the deckchair and headed towards the back door that led into the kitchen.

'How are you feeling now?' Helen asked her best friend, dropping on the grass at her feet and trying to look as though all was well with her world. She'd never, ever admit to Jill that she'd phoned Malcolm at work. She studied her friend's swollen cheek and lopsided smile.

'A bit better, thanks. Sorry I haven't been very sociable but, honestly, I couldn't speak for two days ... Dad said he'd never had so much peace ... and I felt lousy. But I'm sure I'll be all right by Saturday.' She held up her fingers and crossed them. 'I hope.'

'Oh yeah, the barbecue.'

There was very little, if any, enthusiasm in Helen's voice. Theresa was heading back across the lawn, a glass in one hand, a folding chair in the other and the omnipresent smile on her face.

'There you are, sunshine. You might as well be comfy, love.'

'Thanks, Mrs Mooney.'

It was then that Helen realised that something, or rather someone, was missing. She looked around the garden but there was no sign of the French girl.

'Where's Turtle Dove?'

Jill tried to pull a sympathetic face, difficult with the swelling.

'Well, the poor thing's been at a loose end since I've been like this ...'

'She's been like a cat on a hot tin roof ... rarin' to go!' Theresa put in.

'I feel really guilty but ... honestly, Helen, I haven't been able to move for two days. Have I, Mam?

Anyway, she must have been feeling a bit cheesed off because this morning she said she'd go off by herself for the day.'

'I didn't like that idea at all,' Theresa interrupted. 'But Jack's back at work now and he's got the car, of course, so I couldn't take her out. I'm worried about her being on her own, though. We are responsible for her safety, after all.'

'Oh, she'll be all right, Mam. She's no fool and she speaks English well enough to find her way around.'

'Where's she gone?' Helen asked, admiring the French girl's autonomy, her obviously independent spirit.

'She wanted to go back to Haworth,' said Theresa. 'She fell in love with the place and said she wanted to find out more about the Brontës. She can't find out much more ... we drained 'em dry.'

'I suppose your dad'll be picking her up this evening?'

'No,' Jill suddenly winced and rubbed her bloated cheek. 'Turtle Dove insisted she'd be able to find her way home from Keighley and not to worry about her.'

'I do worry, though,' Theresa frowned, 'I mean, she's still young and a foreigner and she doesn't know the place. And we are responsible for 'er, Jill. What time did she say she'd be back?'

'She didn't. Oh, she'll be all right, Mam. If I didn't think so I wouldn't have let her go by herself. Now, we were talking about the barbecue just before you came, Helen, so you can help us to organise it. Mam's made a guest list and the only Firley residents who won't be coming are in the graveyard.'

Malcolm didn't phone that evening, either.

***

When Helen woke up at six o'clock on Friday morning her first thought was the phone call she'd received from Malcolm the previous evening. The phone call she'd been waiting for all week and that had come when she least expected it. She'd been in the bath, preparing for her interview the next day, so Dorothy had taken the call. She didn't shout for her daughter immediately so Helen guessed she'd had something to say to the disappeared-from-the-face-of-the-earth-for-the-past-few-days boyfriend. When Helen, wrapped in a pink and white checked bath towel, finally picked up the receiver, Malcolm had that edge to his voice that she had heard for the first time on Monday. But this time with good reason, she thought, watching her mother watching her. There were no pre-conversation niceties and endearments from the other end of the line.

'I'm phoning about the barbecue tomorrow.'

'Oh. Yeah. The barbecue. I'm ... I'm looking forward to it.'

After a while. 'So am I. What time shall I call for you?'

Helen's heart leaped into her throat, the phone felt clammy in her hand. This wasn't her Malcolm speaking; she didn't know this boy at the other end of the line. She cursed her mother's attentive eyes and ears.

'Well, it'll be starting about seven-thirty.' She waited but there was no response. 'So ... about seven o'clock, I suppose. Malcolm?'

'What?'

'Nothing. It's okay.' She wanted to apologise for phoning him at work, hoped she hadn't got him into trouble. But she couldn't because she wasn't alone. 'Are you all right?'

She heard the sigh before Malcolm replied, ''Course I'm all right. Why wouldn't I be? See you tomorrow, then. Seven-ish. Okay?'

'Yeah. Yeah, okay, Malcolm.'

Helen hurried out of the room and back upstairs before her mother had time to verbally assault her and before she had time to accuse her mother of interfering. That was one road she'd never been down, much as she'd often wanted to.

I love him and
I want to marry him, be his partner in this wretched life.
I want to share his home
His table, his bed, his life
I want to be his wife.
But I don't think he wants me
Any more
In his life.

***

She wore a simple yellow cotton dress and tied back her hair with an almost matching ribbon, in order to feel and appear cool in the still-blazing heat. Dorothy mumbled something inaudible as she left the house but Helen didn't ask her to repeat it. It probably wasn't worth hearing, anyway. The way to Main Street and Farnham's chemist was uphill and Helen had left home well in advance so that she wouldn't have to hurry and arrive at her interview panting and perspiring and probably smelling not quite nice. Dorothy had no doubt passed a remark about that when she was leaving; nothing more interesting or encouraging.

She arrived at Farnham's at five minutes to two and slapped a smile on her face as she stepped over the threshold into the busy chemist's shop. A pristine, white-overalled young assistant smiled back at her.

'Hello. Can I help you?'

'Hello.' Helen coughed. 'I have an interview at two o'clock. My name's Helen Hartnell.'

'Oh yes. Well … Mr Farnham's making up a prescription at the moment and it could take quite a while.'

The assistant nodded discreetly to a very old, very large lady seated by the window who was having difficulty breathing.

'Would you like to come through and wait?'

The friendly young woman invited Helen to follow her behind the counter and through a curtain of plastic ribbons to a small ante-room next to the prescription room. She invited Helen to sit on a wooden stool behind the array of ribbons. From where she was sitting, she could see the middle-aged, grey-haired and bespectacled chemist at work with his drugs on her right; in front of her was a panoramic view of the shop. The assistant was back behind the counter, busy putting price tickets on boxes and bottles and keeping an eye on the infirm customer at the same time. The elderly patient's condition seemed to be worsening and Helen was suddenly overcome with a sense of foreboding. It hadn't struck her before, but what if she'd be expected to cope with and help diseased and disabled people who came into the shop? She could never have been a nurse, she was too squeamish – her mam had once split her sides when, as a little girl, Helen had announced her intention to become Yorkshire's answer to Florence Nightingale. 'You a nurse? Don't make me laugh; you'd be killin' 'em off instead o' makin' 'em better. You'd pass out at first sight o' blood.' She'd been ten years old at the time and had quickly given up that idea. Until now she'd never thought of a chemist's shop as a place where people may need physical help ... and just supposing ... someone walked into the shop.

'Good afternoon. Can I help you?' the assistant asked and Helen was snapped out of her pessimistic reverie. The customer didn't answer immediately. Helen's eyes drifted away from the old lady and moved to Malcolm, who was standing in front of the counter. Her first reaction was to leap off the stool, pull the ribbons aside and shout his name. On reflection, she realised how silly and unprofessional she'd look and how ridiculous the situation would seem, so she kept quiet and moved away from the aperture. If she did get the job then she'd obviously tell him about her interview at Farnham's and her first experience of espionage.

Malcolm was looking along the shelves at the various displays but it was obvious he couldn't find what he was looking for. He moved from the shelves back to the counter and the assistant asked once again in a pleasant voice if he needed any help. Helen had the impression that, for once in his life, and for no apparent reason, Malcolm was struck dumb. His eyes, now travelling along the array of painkillers on the counter, finally looked directly at the girl who'd addressed him.

'Yeah. I ... erm ... I ...' His cheeks were a deep fuchsia and, like the old lady, he was having difficulty breathing. What on earth was wrong with him? Was he really ill? Was that why ...

'I'd like … erm … apacketofcondomsplease.'

Helen couldn't see the girl's face but there was a smile and a relax-I've-done-this-before manner in her words.

'Yes, of course. A packet of three, six or nine?'

She had opened a well-concealed drawer at the back of the counter. Malcolm's mouth opened and closed two or three times and his eyes looked everywhere but at the young woman who was serving him.

'A packet of … three. Yeah. That'll … be enough. I think. Please.'

She dropped the packet of three condoms into a small plastic bag that boasted FARNHAM'S in blue letters, placed it on the counter and told her ridiculous customer the price. He pulled the wallet that Dorothy, in one of her rare moments of generosity, had given him the previous Christmas, out of his pocket and pulled out a pound note. Helen heard the till ring loudly and the tinkle of change. A muffled 'Thanks' and Malcolm was gone.

Mr Farnham, the chemist, stepped out of the prescription room, briefly smiled and nodded at Helen and handed the large bag of drugs to his assistant. He turned back to Helen, sitting like stone on the uncomfortable stool, and held out his hand.

'Good afternoon, Miss Hartnell. Sorry to keep you waiting. Would you come this way, please?'

Helen looked up at the middle-aged, grey-haired, bespectacled and absolutely *wonderful* chemist, stood up and grinned at him.

'Hello, Mr Farnham.'

'It's another hot one, isn't it?' he chatted. 'I'm beginning to wonder if this summer is ever going to end.'

Helen followed him into yet another room and she answered his questions and asked some of her own. But in spite of sailing through the interview on a golden vessel, Helen's thoughts were actually elsewhere. He still wanted her then, still loved her and was obviously determined to have her. And protect her at the same time. No unwanted babies in the Hartnell household. Perish the bloody thought. And this time she wouldn't refuse him. Oh no, she'd learned her lesson and this time she'd give herself, every nook and cranny of her aching, frustrated young body to Malcolm Jones. Because he wanted her and she wanted him. And soon, finally, they were going to have each other. And they'd have each other for ever. Her thoughts trailed towards the moor and the dry, parched grass and the gentle, skin-kissing breeze, where Helen was now convinced their first time would take place. *Their* place. Their piece of earth. Their own very private part of that vast and lonely, lovely moor. And when Mr Farnham asked her when she'd be able to start, she said, 'Tomorrow!' without really thinking about it.

Mr Farnham laughed and said he didn't employ new staff on Saturdays, it would have to be Monday. And Helen laughed with him.

***

Mandy Hopkins had rented a small but adequate bedsit in the university area of Leeds, on a temporary basis. It would do nicely until she found permanent work and moved away from Yorkshire. That probably wasn't going to be easy. She had enjoyed and excelled in her studies in Psychology in Cardiff but she knew she would actually learn more when she started practising her chosen career; but she wasn't sure when that would be and in what capacity. Of course, ultimately, she wanted to have her own practice, but she'd have to work damned hard for that and getting there would probably be tough. Still, she had youth on her side; all her life in front of her.

In the meantime, Mandy enjoyed merely studying people in general. Their personalities, defects, their reasons for behaving in certain ways. Analysing. In fact, she had to admit, normal relationships with anyone could probably be difficult to establish now. Even her close relatives whom she knew so well and loved dearly were unsuspecting victims of her unspoken psychoanalysis. And that was one reason why she'd opted to live alone. Coming back to Yorkshire she could, of course, have lived with her parents and her brother, Tom. They'd expected her to do that and had been mystified when she chose to live in a cramped (as far as they were concerned), incommodious bedsit in Leeds. But psychoanalysis apart, Mandy needed her independence. It was important to her. Very important. And she'd find it easier to leave Yorkshire later when she wasn't in the bosom of her family and friends.

Nonetheless, Mandy was happy to have been invited, along with Tom and her mum and dad, to the Mooney's barbecue. It had been kind of them to think of her but that wasn't surprising, really. They were a kind family and Tom was lucky to have met Jill and be part of that family. On the other hand, as she'd already made clear to him, she didn't want him rushing into a young marriage no matter how suitable Jill was. Tom had a lot to offer the world and vice versa, and Mandy hated to think he'd be straining at the leash when it was too late. She mentally shrugged and reminded herself that she couldn't live her baby brother's life for him. She had her own life to put in perspective first.

Mandy looked at her reflection in the crooked mirror over the shabby washbasin. She liked what she saw. Clear, pink-tinted skin (she was too fair to tan), huge eyes that alternated between blue and sea-green depending on the light, and short blonde hair that waved around her face. She applied a minimum of makeup – a little eyeshadow and mascara to enhance her best feature and a lip gloss more for protection than aesthetic purposes. She ran a comb through her newly washed hair and swung it into shape. Then she pulled a grotesque face at herself and left the bathroom. She wore a strapless pink tee-shirt on top of white shorts and pink mules on her feet. She picked up a pink shoulder bag and the obligatory bottle of wine and left and locked the bedsit. She felt happy with herself. Inside and out.

***

I do as I'm told and Harry turns to the woman who's smiling (a bit nervously, I reckon) across the table at him and picking up her mug of coffee. Pretty smile, gorgeous eyes. Beautiful, silky, touchable hair. Probably a she-wolf in women's clothing.

'This young lady's going to ask you some questions, lad,' Harry Tyler's saying, 'and I want you to answer – truthfully. Okay? Right, love, you can ask him whatever you want – feel free – don't be embarrassed. Okay, lad. Off you go, then, love.'

Harry doesn't tell me who she is and why she's going to ask me some questions. And it's not my place to ask. He settles back in his wooden chair; the keys, hanging at his side, jangle as he moves. He picks up his mug and his small grey eyes underneath thick grey brows move more slowly, slyly, between the good-looking she-wolf and me. She turns her pretty, nervous (I reckon it's nervous) smile on me and I'm all too aware that I haven't touched a female for four years.

'First of all,' she says, clearing her throat and looking a bit embarrassed, a bit wary. She has beautiful hair, beautiful ... God, how I'd love to touch that hair, feel it in my penal-chaste but erstwhile experienced fingers, touch that smile. 'What are you in prison for?'

I look straight into her wary, questioning eyes.

'Rape.'

Chapter Ten

'Well, get yerself in, lad, don't stand on me doorstep like a bloody sweepin' brush salesman.'

Dorothy Hartnell stood aside to let her daughter's boyfriend into the house. Malcolm walked past her, head bent, and stood in the middle of the living-kitchen, his hands stuffed deep inside the pockets of his navy shorts, his hair a cascade falling down his forehead. Dorothy eyed him up and down, her cynical mind working overtime.

'Well,' she repeated, a simple monosyllable that always portended doom to the auditor. 'I were beginning to think you'd emigrated, lad. Where've you been all week?'

Her advice to Helen of discretion and a certain amount of aloofness with 'Himself' obviously didn't apply to herself. She had the privilege, as her daughter's mother, to plunge in at the deep end, go for the jugular, no holds barred. Regardless of the consequences. Malcolm dragged his eyes from somewhere around his feet and attempted to look his adversary in the eye.

'I've been busy.'

'Oh aye? Too busy to see our 'Elen? Well, I don't reckon much to *that*. Anyway, I see yer not too busy to go to this barbecue ... or whatever it's supposed to be.'

A pink tinge touched Malcolm's already rosy cheeks.

'Of course not. It's Saturday night. I'm never busy on Saturday nights, am I?'

Impudent young bugger. Dorothy seethed inside but could think of no suitable reply. She clicked her acrimonious tongue – busy even on Saturday nights – against the roof of her mouth and headed towards the foot of the bedroom stairs.

''Elen!' she yelled. 'Are you out o' that bath yet or 'ave you drowned? 'Imself's 'ere so you'd best get a move on.'

Helen shouted a muffled, inaudible reply and at the sound of her voice Malcolm fidgeted and looked around the small room as though he'd never seen it before.

'You'd best park yerself, lad, I reckon 'er ladyship'll be a while.'

Malcolm obeyed and sat on the two-seater sofa in front of the tiled fireplace, but contrary to Dorothy's prediction Helen walked into the room a few minutes later. Even Dorothy had to admire her daughter, she looked that grand. But silently, of course; if she ever did admire Helen, for whatever reason it was always in silence. It wouldn't do to speak 'er thoughts aloud; she didn't want 'our Elen getting above 'erself. But that lilac sun dress did suit her, and that pair o' lilac and blue 'airslides just set it off. Yon Malcolm ought to take a page from his girlfriend's book ... and put a bloody 'airslide in 'is mop. She saw his eyes travel over Helen's body as she – a bit bashful, like, Dorothy noticed – walked across the room towards him. Dorothy frowned. She didn't like it, but she liked it even less when Helen actually pecked him on the cheek and got no response whatsoever. What 'ad she been drummin' into 'er all these years? Never show the bugger 'ow you feel; it's best way to send 'im running in opposite direction ... And what were Malcolm doin' right now? Provin' her bloody point, that's what. And that daft young lass didn't even seem to notice, standing there, gazin' up at him wi' them bloody cow eyes, as usual.

'Right then,' Dorothy stuck her chin out and bobbed her tightly permed head up and down. 'Shall we be off? 'Ave you taken everything out o' fridge? I don't know, we might as well 'ave 'ad this bloody barbecue 'ere, we're takin' that much stuff. I can't see any point being invited ...'

'Everybody's taking something, Mam, to help out. It's normal; it's what people do these days. Except the queen, perhaps. Shall we go?'

'Well, I'm damn sure if I gave a party, I wouldn't expect me guests to bring their own grub ...'

But you never do give parties, do you? Helen looked conspiratorially at her up to now silent boyfriend. But her boyfriend wasn't looking at her, conspiratorially or otherwise. He was heading down the steps and on to the street, his hands stuffed into his pockets, his head bent. Helen thought he probably hadn't heard her mam's grumblings and groanings; if he had he would certainly have responded, in his own, inimitable way. He always did.

'Well, aren't you goin' ... to tell Romeo ... yer good news?'

They were slowly and breathlessly mounting the hill that took them to the centre of the village and the Mooney's home. They advanced, more or less, in single file, Malcolm taking the lead in total silence and without changing his posture. Helen, vainly trying to keep up with him, turned and threw her mother a don't-let-the-cat-out-of-the-bag look but Dorothy was too hell bent on getting to the top of the hill to notice. Malcolm, however, seemed not to have heard his future mother-in-law's remark and Helen's lack of response brought no reiteration from Dorothy. Farnham's chemist and her daughter's successful interview were both forgotten in the unbearable heat and her current discomfort

'Hiya! We were just about to give you up. We thought you'd got lost!'

Jill, her dental problems a thing of the past, stood behind the gate waving cheerfully, her mother slightly behind her, brandishing a cooking implement and adding a greeting of her own. Jill kissed Helen and Malcolm briefly as they stepped into the garden but her physical welcome didn't extend to Dorothy Hartnell. She ushered her best friend's mother through the gate and led the small party through the house and into the larger back garden, which was choc-a-bloc with friends, family and neighbours. Groups stood around chatting on the long lawn and a few people acknowledged the new arrivals with a shout or a wave of the hand. They came to a standstill at the bottom of the garden. Jill suddenly hugged Helen for no reason at all, Malcolm stood slightly apart from the girls, his hands in his pockets, his eyes slowly scanning the crowd. He chewed his bottom lip and there was a line between his brows as he frowned at various faces. Dorothy had retreated behind Helen and, winded, made a show of trying to get her breath back. After several minutes had passed, she thrust the aluminium-covered ham and cheese into Theresa's hands.

'Ooh, thanks a lot, Dorothy. It's so nice of everyone to contribute but, really love, you shouldn't have brought so much.'

Dorothy took a handkerchief out of her large and cumbersome handbag and wiped her face.

'Well, if everybody else 'as brought as much, you won't need to go shoppin' for a fortnight.'

Theresa felt the blood rush to her plump cheeks. She hadn't asked her guests to chip in with the food, everybody had offered; most of them had brought beverages, which were well and truly doing the rounds, if the empties scattered on the lawn were anything to go by.

''Ey up, Helen, Malc, Mrs H. I've been recruited to resident barman. What's your pleasure?'

After bowing ludicrously to Helen and Dorothy, Tom took hold of Malcolm's naked arm and dragged him to join a group of young males who were sitting drinking beer on benches below the kitchen window. Chickens were sizzling nicely on the giant barbecue a few feet away and Jack Mooney, wearing a red plastic pinafore and not much else (not in this bloody 'eat), was in charge of the cooking; and obviously thoroughly enjoying this responsibility.

Helen watched Malcolm's eagerly disappearing back and then felt herself being tugged forward and into the bosom of another group, all girls, ex-schoolfriends giggling and delighted to be reunited at a social occasion. Someone pushed a glass into Helen's empty right hand, filled it with white wine and asked what she'd been doing since she left school. Helen smiled into the familiar face. Jane Gregson, top of the class in everything except French and Art, excelled herself at sport. Looked like Farrar Fawcett-Majors.

'Nothing special, really, Jane,' she hated to admit, 'this and that. Actually, I'm starting a new job on Monday ...'

But Farrar Fawcett-Majors had already turned her attention elsewhere and Helen realised that she was talking to thin air.

' ... starring in a film they're shooting on the Pennines. A remake of Wuthering Heights. Catherine Earnshaw ... that's me. And who knows to what dizzy, wuthering heights that will lead?'

'What did you say?'

Jill was pushing a plate of Cumberland sausage, chicken and piccalilli into Helen's free hand. Helen took a bite of the sausage and watched her mother hugging an overflowing plate and sloping off into a shady corner; ostensibly to cool off but Helen guessed she'd decided to have a miserable time and to carp about it afterwards.

'I was thinking aloud,' she said to Jill. 'About my new job. I start on Monday.'

'At Farnham's? Oh, Helen, that's great. I'm really pleased. I'm sorry, I was going to phone you last night but with all this to think about, I completely forgot ...'

Helen shrugged and swallowed a mouthful of sausage. It was delicious compensation.

'That's okay, Jill. It doesn't matter.'

Jill was called away and Helen's eyes travelled to where Malcolm was sitting cross-legged with the all-male group and amusing his mates with some anecdote. Out of the corner of her eye she saw her mother, alone and gorging and sitting in such a position to spurn any greeting.

'Hello, it's Helen, isn't it? It's nice to see you again after all this time. What have you been up to?'

Helen hadn't noticed the blonde girl approaching and looking ravishing in tight-fitting shorts and tee-shirt. Mandy Hopkins, who was the sort of woman other women loved to hate – but it was impossible to hate her; she was far too nice. At least, she used to be, and Helen saw no reason why she should have changed. She smiled at Tom's sister.

'I'm okay, Mandy, thanks. But I've not been up to anything exciting, unfortunately ... maybe next year!'

she ended on a laugh. 'What about you? You've finished your studies, haven't you?'

Mandy pulled a face.

'Yeah, and I'm taking a short break before I start looking for work. I've got a feeling it's not going to be easy to find.'

'At least it'll be interesting.' Helen smiled. 'Psychoanalysing people.'

You could start with me mam, she mentally added, or even me. That'd keep you busy for a couple of years but you wouldn't earn much. Her eyes wandered again to Malcolm and his band of cronies. He was drinking lager from a can and managing to laugh at the same time, and his fair hair flopped around his pink and happy face. She realised that Mandy had spoken to her, asked her a question.

'Sorry, Mandy. What did you say?'

'I said I haven't seen the French girl all evening – the star of the show. In fact, I haven't even met her yet and she's going home next weekend, isn't she? Mind you, I don't need an introduction, I'd recognise her immediately after listening to our Tom's vivid and, shall we say, lengthy and lascivious descriptions!'

'She's over there.'

Helen's finger, stained with charcoal and ketchup, pointed in the direction of the group of males, which was no longer a group of males; a female was invading their midst, lowering herself on to the grass, balancing a glass of something in her hand and not trying to hide the show of small, firm breasts as she flopped down.

'So, that's her, is it?' Mandy murmured. 'Well, she seems to have found her little niche, doesn't she?'

***

In future years Helen had very little recollection of the barbecue held at the Mooney's home on that sultry evening in August, 1976. She had blurred memories of ex-schoolfriends giggling and flirting and some neighbours making pigs of themselves on … whatever there had been to eat. Her clearest memory was of Mandy, Tom's too-pretty, too-sensual older sister, and the memories, for a reason she couldn't put her finger on, gave her immense pain. But Helen had no recollection at all of Malcolm that evening, or of Turtle Dove, in whose honour the barbecue had been given. She couldn't recall having seen her, looking ravishing in her typical French way, nor even of having heard her inimitable accent and laughter. And Malcolm, her Malcolm, whom she'd spied sheepishly buying contraceptives because he was determined to make love to her; Malcolm, whom she'd loved and trusted with all her naïve young heart, she certainly had no recollection of him at the Mooney's barbecue, either. In later years, looking back, it was as though Malcolm and Turtle Dove (and Helen could never for the life of her remember the French girl's real name; it had never been used) had both been absent. But the strangest paradox was the total blackout of her own feelings that night; in retrospect, they must have run very deep.

She did, however, clearly remember leaving the Mooney's with her mother, the first guests to depart. Thanks to Dorothy, of course, who'd stayed in her cool corner all evening, had barely spoken to anyone and complained that the sausage had given her heartburn. Anyway, she were tired, she'd 'ad enough, she wanted to be off.

'Oh Mam, it's early yet, it's only half past ten ...' and her eyes searching everywhere.

'It might be early for you, young lady, but I'm ready for me bed. Oh well, if you don't want to come wi' me, I'll be off on me own ... you stay 'ere and enjoy yerself...'

She would never have heard the last of it if she had. Anyway, she couldn't let her mam walk home on her own at that time, just as the pubs were closing.

Helen kissed Theresa and Jack Mooney and thanked them, on behalf of her mam, too, because she was already at the gate, her facial expression belying the friendly wave. And then Jill and Tom came over, looking a bit anxious, a bit on edge and wondering why she was leaving so early, but one look in the direction of the gate told all. Jill kissed her and even Tom gave her a hug, and that wasn't like him but she could never remember what horrors had been passing through her mind all the while. Jill kissed and squeezed her best friend again and wished her luck for Monday.

'Thanks, Jill. I think it'll be okay ... Well, it's a job.'

The half-open gate suddenly started to rattle and Dorothy's 'Are you comin', our 'Elen? I want to be off!' finally dragged her away from her friends. Dorothy managed to make her way homeward at a much brisker pace than her arrival and Helen stumbled behind her, every other second looking back, looking for something, or rather, someone, in vain.

***

Helen slept very little that night and when she got up early on Sunday morning Dorothy was already sitting at her usual place at the kitchen table, gazing out of the window. Helen, not wanting conversation, walked past her and switched on the electric kettle.

'I suppose you've got an 'angover?'

'Of course I haven't got a hangover, Mam. I hardly had anything to drink.'

'You must've been only one, then. They were all knockin' it back and not 'alf. That Tom can put back a few, I noticed. Your Jill'll 'ave 'er 'ands full if she ever marries 'im.'

Helen didn't attempt to reply. She fixed her weary gaze on the kettle and her fingers drummed on the draining board.

'Stop that bloody racket, 'Elen, will you, it grates ...'

'Why, Mam? Have *you* got a hangover?'

'Er, less o' yer lip, please, young lady an' stop that bloody racket, do you 'ear?'

The kettle then belched out a sudden spurt of steam and Helen switched it off. She slowly prepared a mug of coffee and reluctantly took her place at the table. She pulled the thin cotton summer dressing gown across her otherwise naked breasts and fastened the plastic buttons. Dorothy's eyes were fixed on the moving fingers and Helen waited for the next offensive. It wasn't long in coming.

'Did you notice 'ow much Theresa Mooney went through last night? I'm not surprised she's put all that weight on.'

'She hasn't put any weight on, Mam.'

'Well, she's no bantamweight, is she? She were wolfin' that chicken down like it were on ration. An' she 'ad two baked potatoes. *Two.*'

And you had three, Helen would have liked to remind her mother.

'An' that sister o' Tom's. What's 'er name, Marilyn Monroe?'

'Mandy. Her name's Mandy.'

'Aye, that's it, Mandy. She's a right bloody Mandy, she is. She'll be gettin' 'erself into trouble one o' these days, walkin' around lookin' like that.'

Helen put down her coffee mug and looked her mam right in the eye.

'What d'you mean, Mam?'

Dorothy dragged the big brown teapot towards her and poured herself a third cup.

'You know damn well what I mean. Shorts showin' nick of 'er arse and 'er tee-shirt that tight it ... oh, you know what I mean.'

'What do you mean, she'll be getting herself into trouble?'

Dorothy blinked several times and then her bloodshot eyes fixed on her daughter's face and her fleshy fist struck the table. Crockery and cutlery rattled and a jam-coated knife clattered to the floor.

'You weren't born yesterday, were you? She'll be findin' 'erself in family way will that one ... an' then so much for all 'er fancy studies when she's stuck at 'ome with a bairn to look after. An' no 'usband.'

'And whose bairn do you think it'll be, Mam?'

Dorothy's shoulders suddenly began to move up and down and she licked her lips, a fast, flicking movement of her tongue that was almost obscene.

''Ow the 'ell do I know? Your Malcolm's mebbe ... or Tom the Piper's son's. Nowt'd surprise me. Nowt.'

It was the first time Helen had heard her mam speak her boyfriend's name for a very long time. And as soon as that name was out of her mouth Helen knew her mother had found an anchor; an omnipresent subject on which she could pour her eternal venom.

'An' speakin' of 'Imself, where did 'e get to last night? I didn't see much of 'im now I come to think about it. 'E weren't 'anging around *your* skirts much, were 'e? 'E didn't even walk us 'ome. 'E didn't even say goodnight to us, did 'e ... now I come to think about it. Where were 'e?'

Helen didn't reply because she didn't have a leg to stand on. Dorothy slurped her tea and added more sugar.

'I tell you who else I didn't see much of last night, either. Yer fancy French friend. She made 'erself a bit scarce an'all. Now I come to think about it.'

Her mam had obviously been thinking about it all night. Helen, already feeling bilious, couldn't face her morning coffee and pushed the mug away. Dorothy watched the tell-tale action and Helen imagined she saw a fleeting look of compassion, pity almost, in her mam's eyes. Then Dorothy reached down to pick the forgotten knife off the floor and make a show of clearing the table as noisily as possible.

'Well, is 'e coming for 'is dinner today?'

Helen's heart gave a tiny leap and she felt the rush of blood to her cheeks. 'Is who coming to dinner?'

'Prince bloody Charles! Who d'you think?'

'I ... I don't know, Mam. Not as far as I know. He'll ... he'll be phoning me, I suppose.'

Dorothy stood up, noisily piled the dishes into the sink and turned on the hot tap. Over the racket, Helen heard her mutter, 'Aye, 'earing'll be believin'.'

Malcolm didn't telephone that Sunday; nor did he come to dinner.

***

Farnham's chemist shop opened at nine o'clock and Helen was standing on the pavement outside at eight-fifty when Gilbert Farnham arrived, blue shirtsleeves rolled up, puffing and panting.

'You're an early bird,' he nodded at her, 'that's what I like to see.'

Only because I haven't slept a wink all night. But Helen didn't tell her employer that; she only smiled, stifled a yawn and wished him good morning.

Janice Woodman, the pleasant young assistant who'd served Malcolm his pack of three condoms, arrived shortly after and was given the job of showing Helen round the shop, explaining where different articles were kept and their prices. Mr Farnham himself showed her all the pharmacy, out of bounds to her as far as prescriptions were concerned – she'd only be expected to pass the prescription to him and hand medicine to the customer, of course. Apart from getting to know her whereabouts she was also plunged in at the deep end serving, as it was quite a busy morning. Normally, Helen would have quite enjoyed the work, learning the trade and meeting people, but she felt drained through lack of sleep and her mind was on other things.

Why had Malcolm been acting so strangely over the past few days? He'd been in a funny mood at the barbecue – and she'd hardly seen him anyway, and why hadn't he phoned or called round to see her yesterday? He couldn't have 'gone off her' (she hated that expression, especially in connection with her and Malcolm) so quickly, could he? And then her young, inexperienced and very confused mind flew back to the previous Friday and the exact spot where she was standing now, a packet of price tickets in her hand ... where Malcolm had stood asking for contraceptives, nervously, shyly, because it was a novelty for him, a first time, and he'd been thinking of *her*; making love to her and not making her pregnant; caring about her. And sitting there, hidden behind the colourful plastic ribbons, she'd loved and wanted him even more. And now, standing in her smart green nylon overall in the exact spot where he'd stood, Helen felt only bewildered.

It was five minutes to midday when Helen looked up from the counter to see a familiar face mouthing at her through the open door. Helen cautiously smiled back at Jill and raised her hand in a small wave. Jill made a song and dance act of pointing at her watch, followed by a feeding motion with her lips and fingers. Helen shrugged and diffidently approached Mr Farnham, who was busy in the prescription room.

'Excuse me, Mr Farnham,' she almost whispered, 'what time is my lunch break, please?'

The chemist dragged his eyes away from his drugs and gazed at the plastic clock on the wall. He told her she could go now if she liked and not to take longer than an hour. Janice, busy serving a young mother with gripe-water, called from behind the counter.

'I usually go at twelve, Helen, but it's okay. I don't mind swopping. I can see you've got company.'

'Thanks a lot,' Helen smiled at her.

Five minutes later she was walking down sunny Main Street with her best friend; Turtle Dove was once more conspicuous by her absence. Jill suggested having lunch at the only fish and chip restaurant in Firley – her mam was treating them. The thought of greasy fish and chips (which she normally greedily devoured) made Helen's stomach churn even more but she didn't say anything. They had ordered their 'treat', as Jill referred to their meal, before Turtle Dove was even mentioned.

'So ... where's Turtle Dove today?' Helen grudgingly asked, her curiosity getting the better of her.

Jill seemed to concentrate more than necessary on her forkful of mushy peas, her eyes avoiding those of her friend. She took a long time in swallowing and her eyes wandered around the small, busy restaurant.

'Well, as she's off back to Paris at the weekend she wanted to go shopping today. You know, buy presents to take home ... so she's ... she's gone to Keighley for the day.'

Helen nibbled at her haddock and asked why Jill hadn't wanted to go with her penfriend to Keighley.

''Cos I have another dental appointment this afternoon ... Oh, don't worry, it's only a check-up. And this morning I helped Mam to finish cleaning after the barbecue. We were too jiggered yesterday to do much.'

Ah yes, the barbecue.

'What time did it finish?' Helen asked, pushing a cold chip around her greasy plate with an equally greasy fork.

Jill mumbled something about the last people leaving in the early hours of the morning; about two o'clock, something like that. She didn't get to bed till four o'clock. There was a short, previously unheard-of silence between the girls before Helen's small voice asked, 'What time did Malcolm leave?'

Jill shuffled in her seat and avoided Helen's gaze.

'I can't really remember.'

'He didn't phone me yesterday.'

Jill pulled a face that Helen had never seen before, something between embarrassment, confusion and deep love.

'Well ... I suppose he was in bed all day ... like me.'

'I bet Tom rang *you*. Didn't he?'

Jill nodded, her eyes examining the table.

'I think Malcolm's going off me, Jill.' There was a heart-breaking catch in Helen's plaintive and naïve voice. 'And it's so sudden ... Honestly, Jill, I can't understand it 'cos only last Friday ...'

But somehow Helen couldn't bring herself to tell even her best friend about Malcolm's furtive purchase. It seemed a bit grotesque now. She looked at her watch and told Jill it was time for her to go back to work. Jill, uncharacteristically, seemed relieved.

***

Like most people, there were two sides to Dorothy Hartnell's character. Unfortunately, because of the circumstances and events of her life, the negative traits in her personality were more often in evidence. The only surviving child of strict and penniless parents whose daily struggle for survival gave little time or inclination for tenderness, she married the first man who asked her in order to escape parental tyranny and eternal hardship. After the wedding, she expected her lot to change and improve drastically. To know love, sensitivity and material comfort. If she'd wandered a little away from her immediate environment and sampled a few more specimens of the opposite sex, maybe her dreams would have materialised. Maybe. But Dorothy Clayton jumped from the proverbial frying pan into the fire and, although there was no austerity, no despotism in her marital home, neither was there the tenderness nor the luxury that she craved.

Dorothy Hartnell did, in fact, have a heart, but kept it well concealed under a whining, critical and often vicious tongue. It was hard to visualise Dorothy Hartnell, young Helen's mother, being a humorous, generous, warm-hearted woman. The woman she may have become if her life had taken a different turn. If Mandy Hopkins, in her capacity as professional psychologist, had spent time listening to and analysing Dorothy Hartnell, she would have immediately connected the cynical character to her difficult childhood and thwarted ambitions. And maybe Mandy would have been able to help and to change that character for the better. Unfortunately, however, the laymen of Firley didn't have that professional advantage. And in spite of Dorothy's membership of the village gossip circle, her reputation wasn't one to be envied.

Dorothy's latent compassion for her daughter saw the light of day the week following the barbecue in Theresa Mooney's garden. Helen hadn't been herself for a while and Dorothy had put it down to the girl's laziness, lack of work and moping after that long-'aired nincompoop she'd taken up with, far too young. If she'd listened to 'er mother she wouldn't 'ave just stuck to one, not at 'er age, she'd 'ave sifted them out, enjoyed 'erself, without doing owt wrong, but she'd 'ave sorted out the corn from the bloody chaff. Malcolm Jones were right enough and 'e might make a good 'usband one day, but they were far too young and 'Elen 'ad done nowt with 'er life.

Dorothy didn't want 'er daughter to end up like 'erself, cleaning a bookies office every morning an' sittin' on a kitchen doorstep, suppin' tea and chewin' the rag with 'er neighbours. She wanted 'er daughter to get more out of 'er life. But 'Elen 'ad nowt about 'er, no gumption. That's what Dorothy kept drilling into 'er but she wouldn't listen, never took no notice. No, 'Elen 'ad no gumption and she'd spend rest of 'er life in a small terraced 'ouse surrounded by a load o' bloody kids that she didn't really want. That Malcolm Jones were a randy young bugger an' Dorothy kept 'er eye on 'im; she didn't want 'er name dragged through village mud because of 'im, thank you very much. Dorothy were convinced, in 'er own way, that 'er seventeen-year-old daughter could 'ave done a lot better for 'erself. But she 'ad no gumption; none at all. She were 'opeless, were lass, always 'ad been and probably always would be. But no matter 'ow many times Dorothy told 'er that it didn't make an 'apeth o' difference.

Over the last few days Dorothy had watched her daughter's heartache and she'd cursed that bloody young Malcolm. 'E were 'going off' 'Elen, as they said these days. Keepin' 'is distance, taking coward's way out, probably 'oping that 'Elen would eventually take the hint an' just disappear out of 'is life, leave 'im be. An' then he'd leave 'er 'ere in Firley wi' no 'usband, no kids of course, and still no bloody gumption. It nearly broke Dorothy's 'eart to see 'Elen's 'eart being broken and sometimes she wanted to sit 'er down and give 'er a cuddle and a good talkin' to. But there were no point. Kisses an' cuddles and all that 'ow-do-you-do would only make 'er softer than she already were. An' she didn't need that, 'er 'Elen, she didn't need that at all. She needed a bit o' gumption.

Dorothy wasn't very good at showing that her heart was torn in two for her daughter.

***

The sun was slowly setting on that Monday evening in late August. Helen had come home shattered after her first day at Farnham's but the dark circles under her eyes were evidence of lack of sleep, not hard work. Dorothy had her tea ready and on the table when she walked into the kitchen at six-thirty.

'Hi.'

'So, 'ow did it go? 'Ave you been promoted yet?'

'Not yet, Mam. What's for tea?'

''Am and eggs. Come and get it while it's 'ot; and tell me about your day. 'Ave you 'ad many customers? What's 'e like to work for – Mr Farnham, I mean? What's 'is other assistant like?'

Helen quietly answered her mother's machine-gun questioning with little enthusiasm, adding that she'd had a fish and chip lunch with Jill, a treat from Mrs Mooney.

'An' What's-'er-Name, an'all, I suppose?'

'No. Turtle Dove went to Keighley today. Shopping.'

'Shoppin'? To Keighley? What for?'

'Presents to take back to France.'

'From Keighley? Wouldn't she 'ave been better goin' to Bradford or Leeds? If I were goin' to France – or anywhere else – I wouldn't buy me presents in Keighley. Bloody 'ell. What did she want to go to Keighley for?'

Helen studied her plate.

'I really don't know, Mam. Why don't you send her a questionnaire?'

Dorothy had stood up and turned her attention to the kettle.

'Eh? What did you say?'

'I said I don't know, Mam. I really don't know.'

Helen washed up, dried the dishes, put them away and looked at her mother sitting on the top step by the open door, struggling with the large pages of the 'Yorkshire Evening Post'.

'I think I'll go for a walk, Mam.'

Dorothy turned round so abruptly she knocked her plastic-framed glasses on the door frame and they fell onto the newspaper.

'Oh, bloody 'ell, now look what … go for a walk? Where d'you think you're goin' for a walk at this time? An' what about 'Imself? Aren't you seein' 'im tonight?'

Helen ignored the last question and told her mother she was going for a quick stroll on the moor, a bit of fresh air after being cooped up in the shop all day; she wouldn't be long.

'No, lass, you'd better not be. Goin' for a walk at this bloody time. I never 'eard owt so daft.'

It was turning seven-thirty and the sun was slowly setting over the western Pennines. Helen stumbled along the stony road, not having changed into her good walking shoes before she left home. A group of young people frolicked in front of her and she quickly overtook them. An elderly couple with a West Highland terrier were coming towards her and the little dog stopped in its tracks, its ears perked up, its sharp black eyes inquisitive.

'Evening!' the man said and the woman smiled and nodded.

'Hi.' Helen tried to smile and watched the Westie scamper off into the heather. The moor lay before her, parched brown grass, purple heather stretching miles ahead; dry-stone walls and the odd cottage. And then the cottages became fewer and there was nothing except the setting sun, the dry grass and the heather purpling the horizon. Helen continued to walk, to stumble, to move toward their piece of earth where Malcolm had wanted to make love to her, where she'd refused him and had later regretted it. Their little piece of earth where Helen had imagined lying with Malcolm after she'd witnessed him buying condoms from Farnham's chemist.

***

Dorothy answered the telephone on the third ring.
"'Ello?'
'Dorothy, it's Theresa. Is your Helen there?'
'No, she's not. She's gone out for a walk, of all things. Is there summat up?' There was a slight pause.
'Well, we were all wondering if Helen had seen Turtle Dove by any chance this evening.'
'Turtle Dove? Who the … oh aye, you mean yon French girl. I thought she'd been shoppin' in Keighley?'
'Aye, she had. And we haven't seen her since. It's nearly eight o'clock and she hasn't phoned or anything. The shops closed two hours ago and it's only a half-hour's bus ride. We're all going frantic here, Dorothy.'
'I'm not surprised yer goin' frantic; well, there's nowt I can do an' I'm sure our 'Elen's not seen 'er or she'd 'ave said. Anyway, I'll get 'er to ring you when she gets back. Let me know if you 'ear owt though, won't you?'

***

Helen's awkward stumbling gradually increased into a jog, a canter, as though she were running away from something when she was actually running towards something, although she was totally unaware of that. The land began to gently rise and Helen knew that when she arrived at the summit and over the grey, dry-stone wall, she'd be there – on their piece of earth – where she wanted to be. It was getting quite dark and … suddenly, low voices and a strange gurgling, childlike laughter blew towards her on the evening breeze. Helen began to slow down, began to walk and then almost prowl in the grass.

They were sitting there in the almost-dark, cross-legged and facing each other, Malcolm's chest naked, his undisciplined mane of hair blowing wildly around his laughing face. Turtle Dove, lovely in her own semi-nakedness, her silk panties shining pink in the darkness, her small firm breasts displayed to their best advantage, the nipples visible even in the decreasing

120

light. Malcolm's fingers suddenly reached out and worked a slow pattern along Turtle Dove's left shoulder, down the bronzed arm until they reached her left hand and rested there.

'Don't move. I'm going to take your photograph.'

'No.'

'Yes. Don't move.'

But Malcolm moved. He suddenly leaped up and the sweat sparkled on his chest and he raked the blonde locks out of his eyes. His Pentax stood on his discarded shirt beside him and, once more instructing the French girl not to move, he put the expensive camera in front of his face and the familiar click floated towards Helen on the breeze.

'And another! Now, turn your head slightly to the left ... yeah, just like that. Perfect.'

Malcolm's instructions that Helen had heard oh-so-often when the camera was pointing at her were followed by a loud but giggly 'Non! N-o-n!' and then an exquisite pose lying on the parched grass, the head turned slightly away from the photographer in a tantalising smile, the small, hard nipples pointing straight at the camera.

'That was great,' Malcolm said and dropped back on to the earth that should have been theirs. 'And I won't show them to anybody. I promise. These beauties are for me.'

It started in the pit of her abdomen, a gradual convulsion, a rising, almost audible grinding away of her insides that developed into an overwhelming nausea; and while she witnessed the scene in front of her, she retched and vomited on the thirsty grass. She'd subconsciously dropped to the ground, her head between her thighs, her hair falling like a final curtain over her livid face. When she raised her head, after she knew not how many minutes, the two totally unaware bodies were blurred by hair and hot tears and she heard rather than saw the regal golden pheasant as it flapped its wings behind the traitors and took off into the Yorkshire skies. Her heart was hammering behind her small breasts and Helen was afraid to stand, afraid of collapsing. After a while, however, when the hammering decreased to a melancholy thud, she took a deep breath, allowing her masochistic gaze to loiter on the erotic tableau that was taking place on their piece of land, and dragged herself up. Then, when she was satisfied that she'd been spotted, heaving great sobs she turned and ran, slipping, sliding, tumbling on the land she loved, unaware of the mixture of tears and hiccups, aware only of the great and sudden loss, the double treachery and her own naïveté. After running a while, when the pains in her legs and side were too severe, she stopped for breath and to listen for voices behind her; to listen for voices calling her name, she hoped, in guilt, regret and desperation. But there were no voices, only the cry of the pheasants in the heather, as though they knew that they had no future, either.

When Helen knew and accepted that she wasn't being pursued, she only wanted her mother.

***

'What on earth's up wi' you, lass?'

Dorothy had shifted from the step into her secondary position in the armchair opposite the television. Her curious, bespectacled eyes roamed from the soap opera she never missed, to the ancient clock on the fireplace, to her daughter standing in the doorway, trembling and staring in front of her with wild eyes.

'Well, don't just stand there like a bloody zombie, lass, get yourself in … an' lock that door, it's gettin' late. Where've you been till this bloody time and what on earth's up with you?'

'Oh, M-a-a-m …'

Helen didn't try to curb the hysteria that had been rising like bile inside her as she had stumbled back across the moor. Nor did she try to disguise the pain, the distress that had gripped her young, tender and naïve heart, and for the first time in many years Dorothy went to her daughter and laid the distressed head on her shoulder and rocked her and murmured nonsense and choked back her own maternal heartache. And later, when the tears had dried and cups of tea had been made and drunk and recriminations and subsequent apologies had been exchanged, Dorothy Hartnell said, 'I'll put kettle on for another cup o' tea an' I reckon you'd best phone Theresa Mooney. Or would you rather it were t'other road round? Go on, then, make a good strong pot o' tea … an' I'll 'ave a couple o' biscuits wi' mine. I'm feelin' a bit peckish; I don't know about you.'

No, Helen wasn't feeling peckish at all.

***

122

She was baptised one evening
Turtle Dove
In a pub called the Bay Horse, in Firley
She landed later
From the skies above
She was French, she was gorgeous and girly.
She was small and slim and
Very French
And all the silly village fell in love
The boys at the barbecue sat on a bench
And opened their arms to Turtle Dove.

I saw them together on our piece of land
Turtle Dove
Almost naked and encouraging the hand
Of the boy I love
I watched until no more I could stand.

I thought it was me he wanted
But – not surprising – I wasn't enough
How could I hope to compare with
The beautiful Turtle Dove?

The very clumsy but heartfelt poem was written many weeks later when Helen, although no less distraught or disillusioned, could at last come to terms with her emotions and was capable of concentration. The poem, scribbled in black ink on a sheet of lined writing paper, was carefully folded and placed with its predecessors in the bottom drawer of Helen's dressing table.

***

Turtle Dove returned to France without fanfare the following weekend and Malcolm, for the first time in his life, learned the meaning of ostracism. The only person in his immediate community to contact him was Tom.

'What the fuck have you been playing at, you prat? How to ruin your own and everybody else's lives in one easy lesson? I can't believe you've done this, Malc ... You know you've let us all down badly, don't you?'

'Give us a break, Tom ... Jealousy gets you nowhere and I bet you ...'

'You bet wrong, Malc. I know what side me bread's buttered and no French trollop ...'

'She's not ...'

'Have it your own way. See ya.'

After Tom had hung up on him Malcolm realised that it was really Jill who'd been speaking, but he also realised that Jill would probably always speak for Tom. That winter Malcolm moved away from Firley, found accommodation and photographic work in London and word eventually trickled round that he was doing very well for himself. He was 'getting on in life'. Jill ceased to correspond with her French penfriend, of course, passed all her A levels with flying colours and went on to study librarianship. Shortly after obtaining a post in a small Bradford library, she married Tom, and Helen, of course, was her chief bridesmaid. Two years after the wedding Jill was a mother and, as Dorothy insisted on repeating, all them studies an' fancy certificates were all for nowt – weren't they?

Helen worked at Farnham's chemist shop for five years and quite enjoyed the job. She learned a lot and found the work quite interesting – well, in comparison with other jobs she'd done – and at least she felt as if she was doing something useful. Even the poorly patients she'd dreaded proved to be a perverse kind of pleasure, made her think she was doing something worthwhile. Until she got home, jiggered, every evening and her mother told her she ought to find a better job than workin' in a chemist's every day, on 'er feet an' kow-towin' to people. She'd never make owt of 'erself, she'd not enough gumption. Helen and Janice became friends after a fashion and often went out together on Saturday evenings. Janice lived in Keighley so they usually went to pubs there and finished the evening either in an Indian restaurant or a noisy disco. That was how Janice met her future husband. She and Helen had gone to a new discotheque one Saturday evening and a tall, dark and handsome young man asked Janice to dance and that, as they say, was that. Helen had to find her own way home that night, her last night out with her colleague. You just can't trust folk, Dorothy said, yer their best friend one minute and next they don't give you time o' day. So, what are you goin' to do wi' yerself now, on Saturday nights?

She stayed at home on Saturday nights, in fact, and kept her mother company. They usually watched television and read the newspaper, sitting on the top step, and occasionally gossiped with the neighbours, especially Evelyn next door who always had something to 'report'. Evelyn, a retired ward sister and spinster, always insisted that she liked to 'keep 'erself to 'erself' but she seemed to know more about the village goings-on than anybody. And between her and Dorothy Hartnell, many a teapot was emptied, re-filled and emptied again. Helen was beginning to reluctantly accept that this was the regular and eternal pattern of her tedious life when, one morning, Alan Dakers walked into Farnham's chemist shop.

Alan was a local farmer's son and worked in his father's fields. One morning, while operating one of the many tractors, he injured his hand; not seriously enough to bother the doctor with, perhaps, but his father insisted he take a short walk into Firley and ask Mr Farnham to have a look at it. And he did. But while Gilbert Farnham was looking at his hand, Alan was looking at Mr Farnham's assistant and that evening he and Helen were sitting in the Bay Horse together – him nursing a heavily bandaged right hand and feeling totally tongue tied. It was Helen's first date since Malcolm had deceived and disillusioned her three years before. Alan sat next to her on the banquette and talked about the farm where he'd lived all his life, and alternated between making her laugh and making her stifle yawns. She tried telling him amusing stories about her days at Farnham's but he didn't seem very interested and kept interrupting with anecdotes of his own. In the end, Helen resigned herself to just listening. When they left the Bay Horse at eleven o'clock and Alan walked her all the way home, Helen thought he was just being gentlemanly and never expected – or really wanted – to see him again. So, she was surprised when he asked for her phone number and stunned when he rang. Stunned but not excited. Helen didn't think she'd ever get excited about a man again. Malcolm had been her excitement, her first love and probably her last. She'd trusted him with all her young heart, given him everything except her body and he'd betrayed her. No, Helen would never, could never love, or trust, another man again.

She never actually loved the scruffy, earthy Alan, but after a while she did quite enjoy going out with him. He could often be very boring but he made her laugh, too, and he was kind in a rustic, diamond-in-the-rough kind of way. He started coming to the house and her mother made him welcome in her own inimitable, take-me-as-you-find-me fashion. She didn't call him Himself, Yon Swain or Feller-me-Lad, but she didn't call him Alan either. Dorothy, for reasons best known to herself, couldn't bring herself to call her daughter's boyfriends by the name they'd been baptised. 'Aystack 'Arry, Farmer Giles, and Tractor Ted were the gems she bestowed on 'this one', and in spite of Helen's blushes and apologetic glances, Alan always took it in good part. He always had a cheery word for Dorothy Hartnell. He never got angry, was easy-going, easy to be with, very funny in a basic, unsophisticated kind of way. And he wasn't physical. Helen couldn't have stood that, if he'd been physical. The only man she could have been physical with, the only man she could have lain on the moors with, was Malcolm Jones and Malcolm had betrayed her. But Alan, thank goodness, wasn't Malcolm; he didn't seem to want to lie on the moors or anywhere else with Helen and it suited her. And she thought, after several months of an easy, if odd, courtship with 'Haystack Harry' (that was his favourite of Dorothy's sobriquets) that she was, in fact, falling a little bit in love with him. Maybe she could make her life with another man, after all ... eventually. Given a lot of time. And after a while she even found herself willing him to kiss her properly, for God's sake, instead of the half-hearted peck he always gave her when they said goodnight. He was a farmer, a man of the land, surely he needed more than that, too? And Helen realised that if she were desperate for him to ... to get physical, as her mam would have said, then she must be falling in love with him.

***

One Sunday, in the autumn of 1980, when the Pennines were at their most resplendent, Alan suggested taking a hike across the border and into Lancashire. He came to call for her early in the morning, bringing a cooked chicken from the farm, some fresh salad vegetables and homemade bread, and Helen took some fruit from the bowl and crammed it into Alan's large, bulging rucksack. It also contained various other articles as Alan hadn't bothered to empty it before leaving home. He threw the rucksack across his broad shoulders and staggered under the weight. He took several unintentional trips across the kitchen and Helen giggled.

'It's going to be too heavy for you,' she said. 'Why don't I carry some of the stuff in another bag?'

'Nah,' Alan grinned, 'it'll be reet. It'll be lighter when we've supped some o' this beer. Right then,' he looked at his watch. It was nine-fifteen. 'Shall we be off? It doesn't look as though your ma's getting up to see us off.'

Helen nodded and watched him stagger down the steps and onto the road that led across the moor.

'Are you sure you don't want me to carry anything?'

'I'll let you carry the whole bloody lot if you don't pipe down ... Come on, let's get crackin.'

They set off at a stroll, Alan stooping every now and then to readjust his burden and for both of them to have a drink. Although the morning was cool, hiking was thirsty work, as Alan said. Eventually, they arrived at and crossed 'their piece of earth', grotesque and morbid now, and Helen kept her head high and her eyes straight ahead. They walked and talked, too, and it was getting near lunchtime. The hike and the fresh, clean air had given Helen an appetite, and as they approached a well-known, deep and dangerous ravine, she suggested stopping and having a bite to eat before going any further. Alan, whose stomach had started to rumble loudly, agreed. He moved slowly towards the precipice, shaded his eyes with his right hand and looked across the horizon.

'After we've 'ad summat to eat we'll tackle this ravine,' he told Helen.

She stood slightly behind him and her own eyes scanned the drop. The Death Trap it had been labelled, after several hikers had lost their grip and their lives there, over the years. Her heart came into her mouth and the vertigo she occasionally suffered from was making its presence felt. There was absolutely no way she could or would 'tackle' that ravine. Anyway, it wasn't necessary; there was another, perhaps longer but much easier and safer route to the Lancashire border. Alan abruptly turned round and grinned at her.

'Come on,' he said, 'We'll 'ave us dinner when we get down there ... We'll really be ready for it by then. Follow me ...'

'Alan ... I'm ... I'm ready for something to eat now. I'm starving ... let's ...'

Alan turned away from her and peered again over the precipice, obviously not inconvenienced by vertigo. The steep rocks and lack of any tracks were a welcome challenge to him. He straightened, stretched and beckoned her with his left hand.

'Come on, lass,' he called. 'Just come and look at this view. There's nowt like it anywhere ... Unbelievable. Come on ... what's up wi' you?'

Helen put one foot in front of the other and wiped her sweating hand across her brow. Alan was smiling at her now, his booted foot slightly over the edge of the land, his left hand still held out to her. Helen smiled back at him, not wanting him to witness her nervousness, her psychological weakness, not wanting to let him down, and she slowly took hold of the outstretched hand. And then, without warning, she felt herself being hoisted up, swung into the air and both Alan's big hands clutching her waist from behind. He was laughing, chortling, and he held her away from his body, held her at arms-length, swinging her over the deep ravine, the Death Trap, shouting at her to look at the beautiful view ...

'Make most of it, lass, you might never see owt like it again ... Hold on tight ...' and he swung her from left to right, right to left, slowly then faster and faster and ... His jovial words were lost on the breeze and Helen's screams and she saw nothing because her eyes were shut tight and hot tears were streaming down her livid face.

'Put me down ... put me down ... PUT ME DOWN ...'

And then, because the rucksack, only a little lighter thanks to fewer beer cans, was still fastened to Alan's back, he suddenly stumbled under its weight. His grasp on Helen slackened and she felt herself sliding and then being hauled back again and Alan's legs doing some kind of primeval dance step. And then he was very still and panting and laughing again and, without warning, he threw her up in the air and miraculously caught her and dangled her, like a baby, over the precipice. Helen felt the bile rising in her throat and then she was being swung around and around and dropped on the ground. It was a long time before she either opened her eyes or was capable of speech. When finally she was, she looked up at the big, earthy, grinning buffoon in front of her and said, 'Yes, that's right, Alan Dakers, you get a really good look at me now, *make the most of it*, because after today you're never going to see me again.'

They never did reach the Lancashire border.

'The only men *you're* capable of attracting are either idiots or bastards,' her mother told her that evening.

And Helen believed her.

***

Helen stayed at Farnham's for five years, finally got fed up and did a series of menial, insignificant jobs that neither interested her nor paid well. She asked herself many times what really did interest her, what she really wanted out of life, what she could commit herself to. But the answers never came, only inadequate suggestions that her own lack of confidence or her mother's increasingly bitter tongue put an end to. Her friendship with Jill continued, although naturally they saw each other less often. Jill's commitment was to her husband and her rapidly growing family. Jill's sister-in-law, Mandy, had found employment in a Bradford hospital and seemed to be enjoying her work there, as well as counselling private patients. Her busy professional life and erratic hours dictated that she saw little of her family, although they regularly kept in touch by phone. And Helen kept in touch with Theresa and Jack Mooney, calling on them occasionally, but she knew they felt sorry for her and ever since – that evening – things had never been the same. But Helen liked and appreciated Jill's parents a lot. She indulged in Theresa's motherliness and was determined not to lose contact. She was determined not to lose contact with the world, either, something that would have been so easy to do, tucked away there in a small, cramped house on the edge of the moor – with a mother whose only interests were the neighbours' goings-on and television soaps. Helen joined the Bradford library where Jill had worked briefly several years before and also bought books when she could afford them.

'She's always got 'er bloody 'ead in a book,' Dorothy complained to the neighbours, especially Evelyn. ''Er eyesight'll be packin' in.'

One day, in the autumn of 1992, while shopping in Bradford, Helen found a cheap, second-hand cassette and cd player and managed to carry it home on the bus, speakers and all.

'An' what d'you think yer goin' to do wi' *that*?' Dorothy asked.

'Cook egg and chips on it.'

The remark merited a withering look from her mother and the request not to be so bloody sarcastic.

'I'm going to play music on it, Mam.'

'Oh aye, an' where d'you think yer goin' to put it? If you think ...'

Up your bum, Mam, if you don't pipe down.

'I'll fix it up in my room, if you like, and then we can both have a bit of peace and quiet and do what we enjoy doing.'

'Not on your nelly. If you think I'm goin' to put up wi' that racket comin' through bloody ceilin' while I'm tryin' to watch ...'

'What racket, Mam?'

'I don't know. What's that rubbish you've been buyin'? There – in yer bag.'

'Cassettes and CDs.'

'All right, don't be so bloody clever. I can see they're cassettes an' CDs. Give us 'em 'ere, let's 'ave a look. Benjamin Bewlac ... who's 'e when 'e's at 'ome?'

Helen picked up the cassette player and made her difficult way to the foot of the stairs.

'He's a composer, Mam. And a pianist. I'll put some of his music on now. I think you'll like it.'

'I'm sure I won't. An' if it interferes wi' me serial yer'll know about it ... You just make sure that volume's turned right down ... d'you 'ear?'

Helen liked to keep up with the news and always read the local evening paper from front to back, top to bottom. However, that evening, listening to Benjamin Beaulac's beautiful renderings of his own compositions, her eyes barely skimmed the printed word in front of her, and her brain failed to register what her eyes actually saw. The usual crises in the world: war, famine, fatal accidents and, of course, the all-important local gossip. She sat cross-legged on her single bed, the newspaper laid open on the eiderdown, her body swaying in time to the music as her fingers turned the pages. She briefly read an article about an accident on a motorway and her uninterested eyes travelled across the headline below: 'Rapist Jailed for Four

Years', but she didn't read the two columns, nor did she read the articles on the following pages. For the first time in a long time, she didn't read the newspaper from front to back, top to bottom. Her senses were focused on the sublime music of Benjamin Beaulac coming from her second-hand but well-functioning cassette player; there was little room for other business.

∗∗∗

'Please. Don't move.'

'Sorry.' A long yawn. 'I needed that. I'm tired.'

'This won't take much longer. Okay. Perfect. Now ... please don't move.'

'Can I move now?'

'Yeah. Sure.'

The slim body pulled itself up into a sitting position, stretched and slipped its naked feet into a pair of sandals. A big square hand suddenly reached out and, taking the smaller, feminine hand, pulled the amateur model to her feet. The woman smiled; so did the man. Blonde hair fell forward into bright eyes and a big hand pushed the hair away. The woman's body, without clothes, in its model's nudity, moved away from the man, her eyes searching for the discarded garments, her hands reaching out for underwear, a blouse, a skirt.

'You know, you're a very beautiful woman. Very beautiful.'

A soft, slightly embarrassed smile. Soft, busy hands fumbling quickly with cotton against skin. Quick movements of limbs, a stumble, a straightening of an almost flawless body.

'So I've been told. I wish I could believe you all.'

'All?'

'Yes, all. Do you think that's immodest?'

A soft, throaty laugh, a half-dressed torso. Distorted breathing and blonde hair falling into glazed eyes.

The woman moved again. She took a few steps across the room to pick up a beige blouse and she turned to face the man. But the man moved at the same time and while the woman tried to cover the top half of her body, the man brushed blonde hair out of blinking eyes and with his free hand, his left hand, he pulled the blouse away, bent forward and tried to kiss the soft, pink lips that had pouted and posed for him. The woman was in front of him now, facing him, her incredible eyes looking up at him, her lips re-forming into the pout, trying to say 'No' at the same time, but he knew her body was saying yes. He threw the discarded garment onto the sofa where the model had oh so provocatively lain and now her eyes followed the blouse. She was

130

free to move now; neither his hands nor his vocal cords prevented her. But she didn't move; she stood in front of him, raw and remaining; waiting, her eyes looking at and through him, the lips parted and pouting. Waiting and wanting. He kissed her and although she didn't move away, neither did she respond. He pulled away, they stood and stared at each other, breathing heavily yet almost breathless and then blonde hair fell forward again and an impatient, trembling hand pulled it and pushed it, well out of the way. The staring stopped, eyes moved now seemingly in all directions and then the woman moved, turned away from the man, but her eyes stayed with him and the lips kept their pout ... their promise? Only the body changed its posture and moved. It moved towards the sofa and twice-discarded blouse.

'Don't move. Don't leave me.'

A deep mocking laugh, but the eyes stayed the same after the laugh, the pout again ...

'I have to leave. I have to ...'

'Please. Don't move. Don't leave me. I won't allow you to leave me.'

The woman bent to pick up the blouse and turned her head towards him. Their eyes met.

'Now, you're being very silly, Ma ...'

Blonde hair fell forward, a big hand brushed it away and the other hand pulled the woman into his body and the model's pouting lips bled as teeth bit into them. Red nails clawed at hot, wet skin and screams were muffled by big hands and a mouth and a busy, probing tongue. Eventually, the screams gave way to moans and hopeless whimpering and when the blonde hair fell for the final time into glazed eyes, no hand brushed it away.

***

I didn't do it. How many times has that short, necessary sentence gone round in my head, along with the other one that means exactly the same? I'm not guilty.

Not this time.

Chapter Eleven

—————

'I haven't heard that name for a very long time.'
Marie-Laure Colombe had not taken her eyes off her English interviewee; their eyes, in fact, were locked together.

'Turtle Dove. I really liked that name, you know. I don't remember who thought of it. Do you?'

Helen finally tore her eyes away and they wandered around the pristine salon while her brain furiously tried to get things into perspective. Marie-Laure Colombe, alias Turtle Dove, was now smiling at her and she'd asked her a question. A totally different question from any that Helen had anticipated before entering the salon.

'No. No, I don't.'

Marie-Laure suddenly cleared her throat and stood up, her eyes also travelling around her domain, anywhere now but at the woman who had applied to her for a job.

'And ... Jill. How is she?'

Helen cursed her own voice; unnaturally high-pitched, audible evidence of her discomfiture.

'She's married to Tom and they have three children.'

'Ah. Très bien. That's nice.'

Their eyes met again and a thousand questions hung in the air between them but went unasked. Marie-Laure finally thumped her left palm with her right fist and sat down again, looking Helen straight in the eye.

'Look, Madame Hartnell – Helen – I have to know if you're still interested in working here. In my salon. Working for me.'

Helen's eyes met the other woman's gaze and she swallowed loudly. She blinked and briefly looked around the room; the clean bed, the shining, modern equipment, the tasteful decorations and twinkling lights. Her nose sniffed the delicate floral perfume in the air and for the first time her ears tuned in to the low, melodious music that came from she knew not where. Relaxing, soothing music that seemed vaguely familiar. And she remembered the filth and stench of Chantal Gauthier's workplace; the cockroaches, the questionable clients, the mutual lack of respect between employer and employee. Marie-Laure's question hung in the air for several moments and then their eyes met again. Helen knew that she really had no choice. This opportunity might never come again, or at least not for a very long time. She licked her dry lips and slowly nodded.

'Yes, I'm still interested in working for ... in the job.'

A small smile – Helen would have described it as a victorious little smile – flickered over Marie-Laure's face and she merely nodded.

'Good,' she murmured and then there was a pause. Helen watched the relief flooding across her face and what she thought of as the victorious little smile playing on her lips. Or maybe that was only her imagination.

'Okay, Helen. So ... tell me about your studies and your experience so far. I imagine you do have some professional experience?'

Helen told her about the training course in London and her brief but never to be forgotten experience in Chantal Gauthier's establishment. Marie-Laure, Helen had to give her credit, was suitably horrified.

'I don't understand how she's got away with it. I'm surprised she hasn't been reported to the hygiene authorities ... Maybe you should do that if you'd like to have your ... revenge.'

The word hung uncomfortably between them and once more their eyes met and locked. Marie-Laure briskly continued.

'Okay, Helen. When will you be able to start?'

It was then the first doubts crept in. Suddenly, Helen wasn't at all sure she was doing the right thing; she needed time. Would it be preferable to continue working with dirty equipment, cockroaches and prostitutes or working for the woman who'd maliciously ruined her young life?

'Will ... will next week be okay?'

'Yes, Helen, that will be fine. We open at ten o'clock on Tuesday morning. We are closed all day Monday, of course. I'll expect to see you then.'

After discussing all essentials, including salary, which was superior to her current one, Marie-Laure smiled her inimitable smile and held out a long, slim, perfectly manicured hand which Helen hesitantly took in her own. Marie-Laure's hand was cool, the grasp light but firm.

'I think you and I will work well together, Helen,' she murmured. 'I'm ... I'm looking forward to it.'

Helen could think of no other reply but 'Thank you. Au revoir.'

She walked the few streets back to her bedsit slowly, cocooned in her thoughts. She was about to put herself in the inferior position of Marie-Laure's – Turtle Dove's – employ. In the Frenchwoman's beautiful eyes, she had already been in the inferior positions of unemployed, unacademic and unqualified, under her mother's thumb and finally in the inferior position of deceived party – to Marie-Laure's superior position of usurper. The situation was crazy, unreal and totally unliveable. How could she hope to have the necessary respect from her boss? Helen mentally choked on the word. She phoned Jill that evening.

'Hi Tom, it's me. C'est moi! How is everyone?'

'All the better for hearing from you, me love. And you? Are you settling down any better?'

'Look, Tom, I can't stay on the phone too long, it's too expensive. I'll explain everything to Jill and then she can entertain you for hours this evening – that's a promise. Are you all right, Tom?'

'As right as I'll ever be, luv. Right then, I'll pass you to She Who Is Pulling Faces at Her Husband and Telling Him to Get off the Phone. Look after yourself, Helen.'

'Hi, Helen. God, I thought he was going to monopolise you till next week. How are you doing?'

'Are you sitting comfortably, Jill, with a cup of strong tea in your hand? Well, sit down and get Tom to make you one … either that or a stiff brandy, you're going to need one. I've got a new job. In another beauty salon.'

'Well, that's *great*, Helen. God, I thought you were going to announce some disaster or tragedy or something. Caroline, for goodness' sake, turn that music down, I can't hear Auntie Helen. Caroline! Did you hear what I said? Tom … go see to her, will you? That's better. I can hear you now. God, who'd have an adolescent? So … tell me about it. Where's the salon? Is it clean? And who will you be working for this time?'

'Turtle Dove.'

There was silence at the other end of the line.

'What did you say?' Jill's voice was a whisper.

'I said I'll be working for Turtle Dove. Marie-Laure Colombe. Your old penfriend. Malcolm's ex-paramour.'

'Okay, I'm sitting down now and I've sent Tom to the drinks cabinet. Stiff brandy about to appear. Are you having me on, Helen, 'cos if you are …'

'No, Jill, unfortunately I'm not having you on.'

She gave a summary of the course of events since before Christmas and listened to the silence after she'd finished speaking.

'How do you feel about it?' Jill eventually asked, quietly and with obvious sympathy. Helen mentally shrugged and swallowed loudly before replying.

'I honestly don't know. Well, let's put it this way. If I wasn't so desperate to get away from the cockroaches and filthy loo – not to mention Chantal Gauthier – I'd never have accepted the job. Never. But I weighed up the pros and cons and decided that Marie-Laure Colombe was the better of two evils. At least she and her salon are clean and I suppose her clients are the same.'

'Yes, but … oh honestly, Helen, I don't know what to say. Do you think …

134

well, do you think you'll be able to work with her every day knowing ... well, you know? I can't imagine how you'll feel, how you'll cope. God.'

'I won't only be working *with* her, Jill. I'll be working *for* her and that's what's really getting my goat. But I'll just have to try and forget what happened – it was a long time ago, after all – and just get on with things. Anyway, I don't suppose the subject'll ever be brought up and if it is ... well, it's all water under the bridge, isn't it?'

'Helen, she ruined your life. At the time. She behaved like a perfect slut, to say the least. And I for one know you've never really got over what happened ... Oh, you will keep me informed, won't you? Let me know how you get on? I'll be worried ... I'll be thinking about you ...'

'Of course I will, Jill. You don't have to ask. I can't believe all this is happening ...'

'Neither can I, and that's putting it mildly. I do admire you, Helen, I really do. I don't think I could have reacted the same way at all. God, you've got guts, you really have. Anyway, speaking of men and romance and things like that, (which we weren't but never mind), have you heard any more from ...' a pause, '*him?*'

'Not since his Christmas card, and I told you about that.'

'You'll be hearing soon, I bet you anything. Helen Hartnell, your life seems to have become the stuff of novels since you moved to Paris. I can't wait for the next episode ... But seriously, love, if things get difficult with Turtle Dove ... Marie-Laure ... don't stay. Promise me you'll look for something else if things get out of hand? By the way, what does she look like now? Has she changed much?'

'Well, her hair's really long now and she wears quite a lot of makeup. And she's still bloody gorgeous. And charming. And sophisticated.'

'And remember, you're both doing exactly the same job. The only difference is it's her own salon and you're her employee.'

'Exactly. That's exactly what's getting up my nose. Look, I'll have to go, Jill, this call's costing me the skin off my backside – as they say here. Love to everyone, Jill, and I'll call again very soon.'

'I'll call you next. Take good care of yourself, Helen ... and keep your chin up.'

After a meagre dinner, Helen prepared and rehearsed her resignation to Chantal Gauthier the following day. Her apprehension rose to such heights that finally she had to reprimand herself for blowing her own trumpet. Chantal Gauthier neither valued her as an employee nor liked her as a human being and would no doubt be totally indifferent to her resignation. In fact, Helen told herself, Madame would probably not even notice if her assistant never put in her appearance again. She could probably just pick up the phone or write a note. But she knew she'd never do that. It was cowardly and incorrect and she'd feel guilty. And Helen didn't want to start working for Marie-Laure Colombe bearing the burden of yet more self-abasement. Already she had to try to elevate herself in her own eyes before she could hope to work for Turtle Dove on an equal footing.

A light snow was beginning to fall the next morning when Helen left home and the pavement was slippery. She took short, careful steps to the metro station and when she arrived discovered there was a strike because a driver had been physically attacked the previous evening. She trundled out of the station along with what seemed like half of Paris and made her slow way to the nearest bus stop. The bus also took its time in arriving at the rue du Faubourg Poissonnière, which meant that Helen was almost an hour late for work. Which meant that Chantal Gauthier wasn't in the best of spirits.

'Two clients leave already. This is no good. You leave home early when there is snow – and grève de metro.'

'I didn't know there was a metro strike,' Helen replied, quietly.

'Hein? Listen … you help me with my boots.'

Madame Gauthier was sitting on the chair behind the counter and Helen watched the by now familiar leg as it stretched towards her, displaying a ladder in the black tights. Helen didn't move, she only watched the booted foot wriggling in anticipation of freedom. The salon was cold and Helen also watched her own breath making patterns in the air.

'I'm afraid I won't be able to work for you any longer, Madame Gauthier.'

'Hein?' The foot stopped moving.

'I'm … I'm resigning. I've found another job. In a beauty salon nearer my home. I'm … resigning.'

Chantal Gauthier stood up and the un-freed foot stamped the floor.

'I don't understand "I'm resigning". What does this mean?'

Oh yes, you do understand. Helen almost smiled to herself.

'I can't work for you any more, Madame Gauthier. I've found another job. Nearer my home.' She spoke slowly, very distinctly. 'I'm resigning. Leaving your salon.'

'Ah, les Anglaises! Qu'elles sont chiantes! Insupportables! Des vraies connes! Allez-vous en … illico … allez-vous en.'

It was Helen's turn not to fully understand; she only understood that her employer had not taken the news well.

'What did you say, Madame Gauthier?'

The older woman suddenly lashed out with her foot but fortunately she was too far away from Helen for the kick to hit its mark. Helen flinched and flushed in humiliation and anger. Chantal Gauthier was obviously telling her to leave the salon and she didn't need telling twice.

'And what about my salary?' she plucked up the courage to say.

'Salaire? Quel salaire? Vous ne meritez pas de salaire, vous.'

'Madame Gauthier, I insist that you pay me for the work I've done.'

'Jamais!'

'Madame Gauthier.' Helen choked back the nervous bile and tried to stop her limbs from shaking, knowing that, no matter how difficult, she had to defend her rights. 'You have to pay me for the work I've done.' She swallowed hard and coughed before adding, 'I refuse to leave the premises until you pay me.'

The two women eyed each other like boxers in their respective corners of the ring. Chantal Gauthier was the first to look away.

'Merde ... I ... send you a cheque.'

Helen felt the fight against the vile, unsanitary and unprincipled woman seeping out of her but she knew she had to stand up for herself. There was no one else to do it for her. She was on her own.

'No, Madame Gauthier, I insist that you give me the cheque now. I ... I won't leave the premises until you pay me.'

The beautician had blanched and beads of perspiration were beginning to form on her face. She turned to the counter and snatched up her handbag, pulled it open and a series of empty cigarette packets, used tissues and a throwaway lighter fell out, amongst other debris. Even her handbag was a shambles. She took a nibbled pen and on a notepad scribbled some sums before scrawling a cheque payable to Helen Hartnell. Helen accepted it with a quiet 'Merci' but without looking it over. She knew that her employer's sums were probably incorrect and the amount unjust but she didn't care. She'd won a substantial part of the battle and now just wanted to get away.

'Au revoir,' she muttered and ignored Chantal Gauthier's expletive because she didn't understand it. If she had understood it, she'd still have ignored it. She was only grateful to escape and to liberate herself from the woman's insalubrious business. Whatever happened under Turtle Dove's employment could only be an improvement. And then she corrected herself. Marie-Laure's employment. Turtle Dove was a person of the past; she had to keep reminding herself of that.

***

In spite of her limited funds Helen was determined to make the most of her unexpected week of freedom. It wasn't the ideal season and certainly not the ideal weather but she wasn't going to allow those two niggling circumstances to prevent her from enjoying herself. She spent hours ambling around the district she lived in and the more she saw the more she was grateful for having found a bedsit there. Shops of all kinds were in abundance; outdoor markets a couple of days a week and she found the tradespeople polite and friendly. There were multi-national restaurants, very French cafés and brasseries, cinemas and small, shabby theatres. Helen sampled several cafés, tasted many different beverages and eavesdropped on the conversations around her – for linguistic purposes, she told herself. She swanned around on the metro and visited a couple of museums. Her days were busy and, she felt, gainful in many ways, but her evenings were spent at home, alone and usually drenched in thoughts of Ben. Wondering whether he'd given her another thought since joining his family, and then reprimanding herself for the unfair thought. She knew damn well he'd thought of her; but was he still thinking about her, surrounded as he now surely was by family, old friends, old love. Her solitary, unguided tour around Paris that week brought her idyllic weekend with Ben back to her with a vengeance. She missed him. She missed his quirky humour, his authority in the big, foreign city, his physical presence. Oh, how she missed his physical presence.

One morning, after Helen had been visiting St Germain-des-Prés, she found herself walking on the rue de Rennes and within a few metres of her landlord's music shop. Mr Parisot didn't even know she'd found a new job and had already left her old one and she suddenly decided to pay him a call. She hadn't seen him since Christmas and she felt it would be a courtesy call. The shop was empty when she arrived and when the little bell tinkled her entrance Henri Parisot's smiling round face appeared behind the counter.

'Ah, mais voilà mon petit locataire préferé! How are you, Helen? I hope you have not problems with the studio?'

Helen grinned back at the pleasant little man.

'No, no, Mr Parisot, don't worry. I'm really happy in my little studio. I've just come to let you know that I've found a new job.'

And she recounted her adventures of the past week, omitting her previous, unsavoury and best-forgotten relationship with her future employer. Marie-Laure Colombe was a beautician in the fifteenth arrondissement of Paris and, as far as Helen was concerned, the woman had no past at all. While she was talking, a small questioning frown began to form on her landlord's wide, shiny forehead.

'One moment, Helen. Please repeat me the name of this beau … beau … esthétiticienne.'

'Marie-Laure Colombe,' Helen smiled.

'Ah, tiens! Oui, d'accord. Marie-Laure Colombe. Bien sûr. She is …'

The tinkling bell suddenly announced a customer, a cold draught blew into the shop and a deep, masculine voice said, 'Bonjour, monsieur. Madame.'

Henri Parisot's small, alert eyes moved from Helen, his 'petit locataire préferé', to the prospective customer. Helen was temporarily forgotten.

'Bonjour, monsieur. Qu'est-ce-que je peux faire pour vous?'

'Les saxophones …'

Helen made room for the customer and as the two men discussed saxophones and moved to a display of those instruments, she thought about Mr Parisot's reaction to the Marie-Laure Colombe. It had been impossible for her to tell whether it was positive or negative, it was somewhere in between and Helen mentally wished the client gone so they could continue their conversation. Unfortunately, the purchase of a saxophone – or any other musical instrument, no doubt – was not performed with any haste and Helen was frustrated to hear the bell proclaiming the arrival of yet another customer. She turned to the door and was dismayed to see a group of young men looking at a display of drumkits. Her eyes met those of Henri Parisot behind his glasses and they silently said, 'Au revoir'. Helen quickly left the shop and she neither saw nor heard from her landlord again before starting her new job as Marie-Laure's assistant the following Tuesday.

***

The following Tuesday arrived all too quickly and six o'clock found Helen wide awake, not having slept half the night. She was tired, felt worn-out, her new job was going to start off on the wrong foot, it was already doomed, that seemed obvious now. In spite of Marie-Laure's enthusiasm in hiring Helen and her own acceptance, their history couldn't be changed and, no matter how well they worked together, their pasts would always be their present. Before Marie-Laure came, however briefly, into Helen Hartnell's young life, her future had been reasonably secure. She'd felt safe, cocooned, as well as deeply loved and she had thought it would last for ever. But the coming of Marie-Laure had irrevocably changed all that; and a solid professional relationship between the two women could never totally annihilate the past. No matter how many times Helen tried to convince herself otherwise.

She got up and went through the motions of getting ready for work and trying to ignore the nauseous feeling deep in her abdomen. She pushed open the door of the 'Au Bonheur des Dames' at five minutes to ten and Nathalie, the young receptionist, smiled and held out her hand.

'Bonjour, Madame Hartnell. Helen?'

Nathalie spoke very little English and continued to address her new colleague in her mother tongue.

'Marie-Laure hasn't arrived yet; she'll be here about ten-thirty. Let me show you where to put your coat and I'll make us a cup of coffee. The first client will be here at ten-fifteen, a leg wax. You'll like Madame Lamy, she's friendly and talkative and has a wonderful sense of humour. They're not all like her, unfortunately.'

Nathalie's chatter suddenly stopped as she handed Helen a velvet-padded coat hanger.

'Vous me comprenez bien, hein?'

Helen smiled at the pretty and immaculate young woman.

'Yes, don't worry. I understand more than I speak ... But I hope my French will improve quickly ...'

Nathalie laughed and handed her a cup of coffee in one of the sparkling porcelain cups.

'You probably won't get much chance to speak here,' she told her. 'You're better off being a very good listener. The clients like to chat while the beauticians do strange things to their bodies. Marie-Laure always says a beautician's bed is the equivalent of a psychiatrist's couch.'

Helen laughed. She had the impression that Nathalie was fond of her boss and this pleased and reassured her, at least a bit. As they were drinking the hot, strong liquid, the outer door opened, a bell tinkled and Helen was reminded of Henri Parisot's shop and his final words that had been so frustratingly interrupted.

'Bonjour, Madame Lamy.'

Nathalie smiled at the middle-aged, chic and over-made-up woman who was walking towards the reception desk.

'Comment allez-vous? Il fait très froid, hein? Bon, c'est la saison. Aujourd'hui vous êtes avec Madame Hartnell – Hélène. Hélène, je vous présente Madame Lamy.'

While Helen was waxing her client's legs and her client was waxing lyrical, the bell chimed again and Helen heard Marie-Laure's voice in reception. Her voice and Nathalie's laughter. The pouring of coffee and clinking of porcelain. She suddenly realised that Madame Lamy had asked her a question and apologised for not having heard ... or understood, she white-lied. Madame Lamy asked her how long had been in Paris and went on to recount her own frequent trips to London.

'With Eurostar, the train, it's so easy now, isn't it? So quick, so efficient.'

Helen felt a warm flush tinge her cheeks and goosebumps tingle her skin and she merely smiled in reply. After the leg waxing was completed and Madame Lamy totally satisfied, Helen left her to put on her stockings and walked into reception. Nathalie was speaking on the telephone and Marie-Laure's head was bent over the salon's diary. She looked up as her new employee approached. Their eyes met and briefly blinked at each other and Marie-Laure smiled warmly, and it seemed quite genuinely.

'Bonjour, Helen. So, you've met your first client. Was everything okay?'

Helen cleared her throat and nodded. As far as she was concerned, everything was okay. She'd done a perfect job and Madame Lamy was a satisfied customer. But her formative years under Dorothy's doctrine had left their mark, together with her early years in the world of work. She'd often thought everything was okay in the various shops she'd worked in, only to find herself in the dole office queue the following week. So she could hardly be expected to be brimming with confidence at this very early stage in her new position, especially in view of the far-from-normal circumstances, now could she? The day progressed slowly. Clients were few in this post-Christmas and New Year period which meant there was plenty of time for coffee-drinking and chit-chat. Helen spent more time listening than chatting; listening and taking mental notes: Marie-Laure's attitude to her underlings, the way the women spoke and behaved to each other. Helen looked for animosity, jealousy, backbiting but she found none. She found only amiability and mutual respect between the employer and employees of the exquisite salon, and slowly but surely her own inhibitions and apprehension began to fade.

The weeks progressed too, and Helen quickly began to feel like an important and well-respected member of the 'Au Bonheur des Dames' team. Her clients valued her and, eventually, began to request her as their beautician. And as Helen began to feel her professional worth, her knowledge of the language she was obliged to communicate in improved and at the same time she received verbal approbation from her boss. Helen felt the unprecedented burgeoning of pride but beneath her smile and simple 'Merci, Marie-Laure' lay the guilty suspicion that the kindly, appreciative worm would eventually turn. She wasn't sure whether her scepticism stemmed from the fatal summer of 1976 or her series of professional catastrophes; whichever, the lack of trust, both in herself and Marie-Laure, was there and seemingly for good.

***

'Why don't I go with you? I can show you the best places to shop and maybe … if you'd like me to, give you some advice about … well, style, what's fashionable and what definitely isn't. Things like that.'

Helen had told her colleagues that she wanted to look around the local shops in her lunch break. They had all just been paid and, although she knew she had to be careful, Helen also knew she badly needed to spend a bit of money on her appearance. The last time she'd treated herself to new clothes had been during her training in London and she hadn't exactly been able to go on a spree then. But she hadn't expected her boss to volunteer her services as companion and fashion consultant and she certainly didn't want to encourage her. She gazed at Marie-Laure across the room where she'd just given a facial and was tidying up her tools. She almost dropped a pair of tweezers.

'Well, it's … it's kind of you, Marie-Laure. Thanks. But … well, I want to eat as well and I won't have much time …'

'I tell you what,' Marie-Laure grinned at her as she reached for her black leather and false-fur lined coat. 'We'll take an extended lunch break together. We're not going to be busy till later this afternoon. What time's your next client?'

'Three o'clock,' Helen reluctantly muttered.

'There you are. So, we'll have a quick look round the shops … some sales are still on so it's a good time … and then I'll take you to a lovely little restaurant I know where the chef is an absolute gem. He's Egyptian by birth but very French by cuisine! I'll reserve us a table now. What time? Shall we say about one-thirty? It'll give us time to go shopping and give ourselves an appetite.'

Without waiting for Helen to reply she went to the reception desk and reserved a table for two in the name of Colombe.

'Non,' Helen heard her laughing before she hung up. 'You know I never have lunch with my husband during the week. I'll be with one of my staff.'

It was the beginning of February and still very cold. Marie-Laure guided Helen through some narrow streets and on to the rue de Vaugirard and then to the place de la Convention; two very lively districts. She pointed out what she thought to be the most interesting and least expensive clothes shops and suggested one or two that they might try. Helen silently fell in with her spontaneous plans, merely replying to her questions, passing banal remarks and hating every minute. She agreed with Marie-Laure that the shops were wonderful but felt too inhibited and humiliated to try clothes on and parade in front of her boss, awaiting her approval or otherwise. She was determined not to put herself in that ignominious position. Finally, disappointed with her and obviously exasperated, Marie-Laure looked at her watch and said they ought to make their way to the restaurant; they'd be early but she didn't suppose it mattered. Helen felt she was expected to apologise but merely smiled and nodded and followed her hostess.

'Le Royaume' was a small restaurant with only six tables. Two of them were occupied when Marie-Laure pushed open the heavy glass and chrome door. As soon as the pair of them set foot inside, a small, slim and smiling middle-aged woman approached them – or rather Marie-Laure – and kissed her on both cheeks.

'Madame Colombe! How nice to see you again! Are you well? Excellent. Your usual table is ready for you in the corner. Let me take your coat.'

The leather coat was gently taken off Marie-Laure's back and then the woman turned to Helen and, with a brief nod, she held out her hand to take hers. Helen followed her boss to the table in the corner, taking in the bright white tablecloths, the silver cutlery, the china and the flowers on every table. No sooner were they seated than a man appeared from seemingly nowhere and, almost bowing to Marie-Laure, took both her hands in his and kissed them.

'Welcome, Madame Colombe, welcome! How nice to see you again! How are you? You are looking so well ... so well and so beautiful, as always.'

'Thank you, Pierre, I'm fine. May we have a dry martini, please?'

'Of course, Nadia will bring it immediately. May I recommend the sole today ... it's excellent. And perhaps a green salad with walnuts for entrée?'

'Thank you, Pierre. We'll have a look at the menu.'

After Pierre had disappeared Marie-Laure told her guest that he was the chef and owner of Le Royaume.

'But I thought he was Egyptian,' Helen frowned. 'You called him Pierre.'

Marie-Laure shrugged her shoulders and smiled.

'Egyptian by birth but French by cuisine. Pierre in the restaurant and God knows what elsewhere. I don't know his real name. Oh, and Nadia, the waitress, is his wife. She's Algerian. They're a sweet couple, aren't they? Thank you, Nadia, we'll have the à la carte menu today. Pierre said the sole was excellent ...'

'Pierre is right!'

'Do you like fish, Helen?'

Helen, who wouldn't have known sole from eel, nodded, feeling herself being swept away on Marie-Laure's imperious tide. She listened while Marie-Laure ordered the entrée followed by sole with brown rice and beans and half a bottle of Sancerre. She gently took the white linen napkin out of the crystal glass in front of her and placed it on her lap. The martinis arrived and Marie-Laure raised her glass and gently clinked it with Helen's.

'Cheers,' she said. 'Here's to a happy working relationship and eventual friendship.'

She sipped her drink and looked at Helen, who had not replied, a smile playing on her glossy lips.

'I don't usually drink during the day,' she confided, 'but this is rather a special event, isn't it? Our first meal together. That's why I wanted to bring you somewhere special.' She paused, fingered her glass and looked at Helen again. 'Tell me, Helen. You don't feel ... well, I hope you're not feeling a little bit self-conscious here. I'd hate you to feel uncomfortable but I did so want to bring you somewhere nice.'

Helen felt the blood rush to her cheeks and her mouth dry up. Oh, the bitch. The mean, unfeeling bitch. If only she'd been blessed with a wittier tongue, a quicker brain. If only, in her formative years, she'd been encouraged, even allowed, to express her feelings, her thoughts, her anger ... She picked up her own glass and, instead of flinging its contents at the beautiful face opposite hers, she took a swig of her aperitif and hoped she looked like the rustic plebian that Marie-Laure obviously thought she was. She was sorely tempted to wipe her mouth on her frayed brown sleeve but delicately used her napkin instead. She waited for the fury to subside and then created a smile.

'Yeah, actually I do feel a bit uncomfortable, Marie-Laure; I'm dying for a pee. Where are the toilets?'

'Over there, on the right.'

'Keep your fingers crossed that I don't wet myself before I get there.'

'Helen!'

The first half of the meal was eaten in almost total silence and, although Helen knew she should really apologise for her crass behaviour, she didn't. She avoided looking into the eyes which she knew were probing her face and cursed having accepted Marie-Laure's obviously malicious invitation. It was after the smiling, sycophantic Nadia had served the sole that Marie-Laure spoke again.

'You know, it's a shame we didn't spend more time looking round the shops, Helen. There are some real bargains at the moment; the boutiques in Paris are very expensive, you know – and you could have taken advantage today. You really need to treat yourself to some new clothes, Helen, I'm sure you don't mind me saying. You always look so ...'

Helen raised her eyes and felt the blood rush to her cheeks again.

'I always look so *what*, Marie-Laure?'

'Oh, don't misunderstand me, for goodness' sake, Helen. I'm not criticising ...'

Helen raised her already arched eyebrows.

'No ... of course I'm not criticising. I'm advising. I've been working in the beauty business for many years and I know what I'm talking about. It's all very well having a perfect face and body but clothes, you know, are the icing on the cake. They're a part of you; they speak for you; they're the first thing people notice about you. Believe me, Helen, you may have gorgeous eyes, lustrous hair and a stunning figure but clothes ... they're just as important, if not more so and ...'

Helen put down her knife and fork, picked up her napkin and wiped her mouth again. She waited for what she knew was coming next.

'Please don't be offended, chérie, but you don't have "le look". You don't make the best of yourself. People notice, you know. I hope I'm not upsetting you because I don't want to do that but ... think about what I'm saying. Have another look around the shops while the sales are still on, and for goodness' sake, treat yourself. You really need to do that, Helen.'

Deeply stung, Helen could find no words to fight back with, only her thoughts, her opinions, which she knew would be scathingly laughed at. Finally, she retaliated with, 'But we always wear white overalls at the salon, I don't understand what the problem is ...'

Marie-Laure sighed and raised her right hand to catch Nadia's attention.

'I'm not talking about work, Helen, although ... well, never mind. But if you want to have any kind of social life; and especially if you want men to find you attractive, take my advice and do something about your appearance. Buy new clothes, smarten yourself up ... get fashionable. It's the only way to be socially – and romantically – successful in Paris. I'm telling you for your own good. Chérie.'

The words battered and bruised Helen's brain and she felt the unwanted tears threatening at the back of her eyes. And then she thought of lying in Benjamin Beaulac's arms and the Christmas card she'd received and the tears somehow disappeared and she was able to look the other, beautiful, impeccably turned out woman straight in the eye.

'Some men care more about what's inside than what a woman wears,' she murmured, somehow managing not to stammer and fall over her words, 'and that's the only kind of man – person – I'm interested in.'

'Then I'm afraid, Helen ...'

'And I think real men care more about what a woman looks like when he takes her clothes off. That's why I enjoy being in the beauty business; otherwise, I'd probably work in a boutique.'

Marie-Laure's almond eyes widened and she opened her mouth but no words came. One round to me, Helen couldn't help thinking.

They refused the dessert and coffee, Marie-Laure paid the bill and they walked in total silence back to Au Bonheur des Dames.

The sales didn't finish until mid-February and during those brief weeks Helen spent a lot of her free time reluctantly wandering around the local boutiques. Reluctantly, because she didn't have money to throw away and she preferred to spend her hard-earned cash on other, more urgent, things. Necessities for her new home, for example. But Marie-Laure's harsh words still rang in her ears and, if Marie-Laure were right, then Helen knew she'd have to make an effort with the 'icing on the cake'. She bought herself a couple of sweaters, a skirt and a pair of trousers that had to be taken up, all of which went unnoticed by her boss. Or if Marie-Laure did notice Helen's recent purchases, she made no comment.

***

'So ... has she invited you to lunch again or did you show her up so much last time that she's never bothered since?'

Helen laughed.

'Oh, Jill, she's invited me a few times since then and it's getting embarrassing. Sometimes she suggests we have an aperitif together after work, or go to a café during our lunch break ... She's even suggested dragging me round a few more shops. I can't always find an excuse so I go along with her plans.'

'It's peculiar, don't you think so? If I were in her shoes, I'd avoid you like the plague ... if you know what I mean. She's either still got no scruples or she's trying to make amends in her own sweet way.'

'I don't know what her idea is but, quite honestly, I just wish she'd leave me alone.'

'Has she ever mentioned Malcolm – and what happened – or is she keeping schtum?'

'She behaves as if we'd never seen each other before in our lives. She's avoiding the subject as much as I am. In fact, if it weren't so stressful it'd be amusing ... When we're together outside the salon, she talks about work, shopping, clothes, of course ... anything but ... Like I said, Jill, it's as though we've only just met for the first time. She never even mentions you.'

'What about her family? You said she was married. Does she talk about her husband?'

Helen laughed.

'Oh, she sometimes mentions him, Monsieur Marie-Laure Colombe. I don't even remember his name. She's kept her maiden name for professional reasons like a lot of French women do. If she talks about him it's always 'My husband has a bad cold, I have to go to the chemist,' or 'My husband and I had dinner at such-and-such a restaurant,' or 'My husband likes to wear my bra and pants so I have to call at the lingerie shop.' (I've just made that one up) So, I've christened him Monsieur Marie-Laure Colombe.'

'Have you ever seen a photo of Monsieur Colombe?' Jill asked, giggling.
'No.'

'You don't think she's actually married to Malcolm, do you? We don't know what happened to him after he left Firley, do we? Only that he got on well professionally.'

There was humour in Jill's voice but Helen's heart gave a little flutter. She hadn't thought of that. Oh God, that was all she needed ...

'I never thought of that. Oh, Jill ...'

'Well, I was joking actually.' Jill paused. 'Look, Helen, for God's sake don't start worrying about that. Promise me?'

It was Helen's turn to pause.

'I'll do my best. But you have got me thinking. Why else would she be so secretive about her husband?'

'Can't you have a quiet word with your colleagues ... what's her name, Nathalie, for example?'

'Oh, I don't think so. Not just yet, anyway. French people are really reserved, you know, until you've known them a while. No, Jill, I'm not going to pry into her private life. But ... do you think ...?'

'Oh, Helen,' Jill sighed. 'I wish I'd never opened my big mouth. Look, forget what I said. It was a joke, okay? If she's as glamorous and sophisticated as you say, I can't see her being married to Malcolm.'

'Thanks.'

'You know what I mean.'

'He moved to London, remember, and became a professional photographer. As you said, we don't know what happened to him after that.'

'Okay, you're right. But I still don't think he's married to your boss. It would be too much of a coincidence and too cruel on her part.'

Helen didn't reply.

'Look, Helen, I'm sorry but I'll have to go – there's some kind of catastrophe in the kitchen. Can you hear the coyotes? I'd better go investigate.'

'Is everybody okay, Jill? Sorry, I've been too wrapped up in myself. I haven't asked about you.'

'Yeah, everyone's fine. Tom's just had a bit of a promotion and a raise and Caroline's staying over at a friend's tonight, so we'll have a bit of peace. But maybe I'm speaking too soon ... FOR CRYING OUT LOUD, WHAT'S GOING ON IN THERE? I'm sorry, Helen, I'll have to go. I'll phone next week, okay? And, look, for God's sake, don't worry about Marie-Laure's husband. She's probably married to a politician or a secret agent or something ...'

'Yeah, you're probably right, Jill; you usually are. Thank God I've got you to talk to. Give my love to everybody. Speak next week.'

'Lots of love to you, Helen. We all miss you. Say bonjour to Marie-Laure from me. Bye.'

Monsieur Marie-Laure Colombe. Madame Marie-Laure Jones. Mrs Malcolm Jones. Oh God.

***

It was late March, cold and very windy, and Marie-Laure had invited Helen to have lunch with her at a new pizzeria on the rue de Vaugirard. She had reserved a table for two by the window and as the waitress served their coffee, both women looked outside at the busy boutiques and the frozen passers-by. And then Marie-Laure made her totally unexpected announcement. After a long moment they looked at each other and Helen felt the familiar rush of blood to her cheeks while her companion unnecessarily stirred her sugarless black coffee.

'I'm sorry. What did you say?'

'I think you heard me, Helen.'

Marie-Laure placed the busy spoon in the saucer, folded her arms on the table and the usual, enigmatic smile played on her lips.

'Look, let's be honest. That summer in Yorkshire has been hanging over our heads like the sword of Damocles for two months and we can never become friends – real friends – until we clear the air. I like you, Helen, I like you a lot and I do so want us to be close; why not? I don't think you have many friends in Paris – if any at all – and I ... well, I ... I like you and I'd like us to become friends as well as employer/employee. Why do you think I like to spend time with you out of working hours? But I don't think we can ever be close until we clear the air.'

Helen sipped her coffee, unable for the moment to return the smile.

'No, I suppose not,' she finally murmured.

Marie-Laure suddenly leaned across the table, her beautiful, almond brown eyes boring into Helen's soul.

'Nothing happened between me and Malcolm, Helen. I remember that evening so well. I'd been to Keighley, shopping for presents, and we ...

148

Malcolm and I ... bumped into each other at the bus station. When we got off the bus in Firley it was still very hot; do you remember that summer, Helen? Malcolm suggested having a walk on the moor; he was a gentleman; he carried my bags, as well as all his photographic equipment. We walked and walked and eventually we were sticky and uncomfortable so we took off some of our ... our outer garments. Only to cool off, to be more comfortable. It was a natural thing to do. And we just talked and talked.'

'And Malcolm took photographs of you and told you he wouldn't show them to anybody. They were for him.'

There was a fraction of a pause and Marie-Laure's eyes travelled briefly to the street and back.

'Look,' she smiled again, 'maybe your Malcolm was ... ah, what's the expression in English? I don't remember and I used to like it so much ... ah yes ... maybe Malcolm had a crush on me? I was the visiting French penfriend, the foreigner, a little exotic perhaps to a boy who'd never travelled and who had ... Do you understand what I'm saying, Helen? Maybe he took photos of me as a souvenir, I really don't know. But I do know that he loved you. He wanted to marry you, one day. He told me all that. I promise you, Helen, nothing happened between your Malcolm and me.'

Stop saying 'your Malcolm'; he's not 'my Malcolm'; he hasn't been 'my Malcolm' since you put your appearance in.

'And ... and what about the barbecue?' Helen took a deep breath. 'Where were you and Malcolm that evening? Everyone noticed ...'

Marie-Laure's glossed lips curled into a smile and she gave a little shrug, picking up her spoon again.

'That was the evening I realised Malcolm had the crush. Of course everyone noticed, he was so obvious and it was very embarrassing for me. He followed me everywhere like a little puppy. I went into the garden hut to bring more chairs and he followed me ... I went into the kitchen and he followed me ... upstairs and he followed me. I tell you, Helen, he was embarrassing, a nuisance. But what could I do without causing a scene? I was thinking of you, too, Helen, and Jill ... I didn't want ... Nothing happened between your Malcolm and me. Okay?'

They looked at each other and drank their coffee in silence for a while and Helen turned Marie-Laure's speech over in her mind and she believed her. Maybe it was the expression in those dark eyes, the urgency in her voice, Helen didn't really know why, but she believed her. And suddenly she wanted to be close to Marie-Laure Colombe too, wanted to be her friend. Marie-Laure was right; Helen had no friends in Paris, she needed friends, friends were so important. Especially when you didn't have family. And then she remembered something else, something long forgotten, and all thoughts of intimacy and friendship with the Frenchwoman were forgotten.

'I'dlikeapacketofcondomsplease. A packet of three.'

Or something like that. Helen couldn't remember the exact words or even the exact expression on his face, not any more. Not after all these years. Well, maybe the bloody things got thrown in the wastepaper basket or blown away across the moor and lost in the heather, because she had never had the benefit of them and, according to Marie-Laure, neither had she. Helen closed her eyes and sighed. Hell, it was all water under the bridge now, it all happened (or rather didn't happen) so long ago. They had all been so young, teenagers starting out in life, now they were mature women heading for middle age with the possibility of close friendship as well as a good working relationship. And Helen wasn't in a position to deny that affinity.

'You do believe me, don't you, Helen?'

Helen pulled a face, something between a half smile and a grimace and she impulsively took hold of and squeezed her employer's hands.

'Of course I believe you ... Turtle Dove!'

The two women giggled, one more loudly and unnaturally than the other.

Two days later, on Helen's day off, she was about to leave her bedsit to go to the supermarket when her telephone rang.

'Allo?'

'Hello, Helen, it's Marie-Laure.'

Helen's greeting was a little less than enthusiastic, imagining that her boss was phoning to ask her to work; the salon was really busy or Nathalie was ill or ... but she was wrong.

'Tell me, do you have anything planned for this Sunday?'

Did she have anything planned for any Sunday?

'No. No, I haven't.'

'Good. Then I'd like you to come for lunch to my home and spend the day with us. Would you like that?'

Spend the day with US.

'Oh yes ... yes, of course I would. That'd be ... lovely. Thank you.'

'Great! Well, let's say about twelve-thirty – I'll give you details of metros, entry-codes for our building et cetera before then. Don't forget to write it in your diary!'

What diary? Helen thought as she hung up and opened the door. Maybe next year ... The invitation pleased her more than she liked to admit. She wasn't going to be alone the coming Sunday and she was finally going to meet Monsieur Marie-Laure Colombe. And maybe this would be the beginning of a social life in Paris?

Marie-Laure lived in the west of Paris, on the top floor of a nineteenth-century building with a view of the river Seine. Helen arrived a few minutes after the given time, wearing a plain dark blue, slightly flared skirt with a paler blue polo-necked sweater (bought in the sales) and she'd clipped two matching blue slides in her shoulder-length hair. She also wore the inevitable grey woollen coat and carried a small bouquet of pink and white tulips. She pressed the entry-code number, the door clicked open and she entered a large and majestic marbled hall, abundant with trailing plants, mirrors and soft lights. She took the old-fashioned and very slow lift to the fifth floor and stepped into a wide, red-carpeted corridor. She turned to the door on the right and pressed the bell, feeling suddenly overwhelmed and out of place. She hadn't expected such splendour. After a few moments she heard light, feminine footsteps tapping across uncarpeted floor and the door was pulled open. Marie-Laure stood smiling at her and looked stunning. She wore olive green trousers with a beige silk blouse and jade jewellery adorned her neck and wrists. Her hair was taken back off her face and arranged into an attractive knot on her head. Her makeup, as always, was light and immaculate and her perfume light and refreshing. She smiled and Helen stepped into the apartment. She stood in front of her hostess, clumsily clutching the flowers, feeling rather less than elegant, and suddenly wished herself as far away as possible. Marie-Laure, still smiling, kissed her on both cheeks.

'Bonjour, chérie … you're well wrapped up and quite right, too. It's freezing out there.'

Helen nodded wordlessly, smiled weakly and held out the bouquet.

'Thank you, they're lovely. But I told you not to bring anything and that included flowers. Save your money for new clothes, you need them more than I need tulips!'

Wham. Helen took a deep breath and forced a smile and a mild tone of voice.

'Oh, you know me,' she said, 'I never do as I'm told.' Helen followed her hostess into the first room on the left. The sensual fragrance of Marie-Laure's perfume mingled with the delicious aroma coming from the kitchen and the result was quite potent. Helen's olfactory senses weren't the only ones to be awakened, however. As they walked into the vast living room, decorated with antique furniture and original paintings, strains of a Benjamin Beaulac composition wafted towards her from the CD player in the corner. She felt her body stiffen, the flush bursting in her cheeks and the sudden dryness in her mouth. Marie-Laure smiled and invited her to sit down on one of the cream, multi-cushioned sofas either side of the marble fireplace. Helen sank into the one facing the living room door.

'Okay, I'm going to leave you for two minutes, I have to check lunch,' Marie-Laure chuckled. 'Cooking's not my speciality, you know, but I really do want to impress you!'

She left the room and Helen found herself alone with the haunting tones of Benjamin Beaulac's music. She wriggled deeper into the soft, brown and yellow cushions surrounding her, closed her eyes and allowed the music to take over, if only for a short time … After a while, she became aware of another presence in the room; she suddenly realised that she was no longer alone. She opened her eyes, pulled herself into a more elegant position and turned her eyes to the door.

A man was standing there and he'd just spoken to her. He'd said, 'Hello' or 'Hi', she wasn't sure which. He was smiling at her, moving towards her and holding out his hand to her and the blood drained out of her body as all reason drained out of her mind. She stood up but her legs weren't strong enough to support her and she fell back on the sofa, her bewildered eyes searching the man's face. Oh Ben, she silently pleaded, how could you do this to me? Did you know? Did she, Marie-Laure, Turtle Dove, know? Is this some kind of macabre play on your part, both your parts? Or is it only sheer, unbelievable coincidence? No, it can't be coincidence. Marie-Laure has talked to you about me, that I do know, she invited me to lunch, she wanted me to meet her husband. This is her idea of revenge. No, I was the one who should have looked for revenge, not her … She knew, somehow she knew, she found out about us and this is her morbid idea of a joke or … As the haunting music suddenly rose to a crescendo and then died away, Marie-Laure walked back into the room, the smile slapped on her face, her arms outstretched equally to the man on her right and the woman sitting on the sofa in front of her.

152

Chapter Twelve

Helen stood up again on more than unsteady legs and the man looked into her eyes, smiled and reached out to take her hand. She trembled visibly, tried to ignore the sudden nausea and dizziness and wondered about his terrible sang-froid under such painful circumstances.

'Helen,' said Marie-Laure, 'this is my husband. Adam, this is Helen Hartnell.'

They shook hands, they said hello, I'm pleased to meet you. Adam said he'd heard a lot about her and Helen mumbled some kind of reply. She was invited to sit down again and Adam asked her what she'd like for aperitif and Marie-Laure placed ceramic dishes filled with pistachio nuts and olives on the mosaic-topped coffee table. Adam repeated his question, asked her again what she'd like for aperitif, looking at her quizzically with his head slightly on one side. Helen really didn't know and Marie-Laure suggested a dry martini. Adam walked to the drinks' cabinet at the far end of the vast room and poured two dry martinis and a whisky on ice into crystal glasses. Marie-Laure was speaking to Helen but Helen heard not a word she said and therefore wasn't capable of replying. Of course it wasn't Ben; couldn't possibly have been. Ben had two children, Jeremy and Amy, and a wife called Kimberley – Kim-on-a-good day. Marie-Laure didn't have and didn't want children. So, Helen's confused thoughts hadn't been logical in her temporary disorientated dilemma, and to the background of Benjamin Beaulac, who could have blamed her for thinking ...? And Adam, of course. Even after blinking several times and gaping rudely at the man sitting opposite her, she could still accuse him of being Ben Beaulac, musician, composer and her very temporary lover. And when he spoke, as he was doing now, it was Ben's voice; Ben's strange but attractive accent addressing her.

'I'm ... I'm sorry. What did you say?'

'I asked you how long you've been in Paris.'

'Oh ... four months ... Yeah, about four months now.'

'And Marie-Laure tells me you have a studio in the fifteenth arrondissement, not far from the salon. That's great. Nice place?'

Helen nodded and tried to pull herself together in order to have a normal conversation with this very pleasant Ben Beaulac look-alike.

'It's very small but cosy. Yes, it's nice. I was lucky to find it, really.'

'Oh? And how did you find it? Do you have a fairy godmother who waved a magic wand? Accommodation – and especially good accommodation – isn't easy to come by in Paris, you know.'

Helen chewed her lip and tiptoed cautiously through her words, knowing that she had to be very careful. Knowing that Ben Beaulac was obviously no stranger to these people.

'Oh, I got it through an agency,' she lied. 'I was really lucky, I suppose.'

'And your studio's decent ... clean and well-maintained, I mean? It's not always the case in Paris, I'm afraid. Hey, don't I sound negative about this great city?'

Helen accepted a handful of pistachio nuts.

'Yes, actually, it's perfect. For me.'

Marie-Laure sat down next to her husband, squeezed his right hand and blinked at her guest. There was a slight frown between her otherwise unfaultable eyes.

'Are you okay, Helen? You're not feeling ill, are you? You look ...'

'Oh no ... no, I'm fine, honestly. It was so cold outside and it's so lovely and warm in here. Change of temperature, probably. I'm fine.'

Helen knew she was waffling and she stuffed a few pistachios into her mouth as an excuse to stop talking. She looked away from Marie-Laure's curious gaze but could find nowhere to rest her eyes. Adam suddenly put down his glass and stood up. He moved towards the now silent CD player.

'And what about your landlord?' he threw over his shoulder. 'Is he decent, too? There are a lot of charlatans in Paris. You have to have your wits about you, dealing with these people. They're usually very happy to bank the rent every month but when it comes to maintenance, it's a different story. If you ever want to move or your landlord gives you any trouble, Helen, let Marie-Laure know. We have a friend who ...'

Helen decided to strike while the iron was hot.

'Oh, there's nothing wrong with my landlord. He's a love. So far, anyway.' She leaned forward and tapped the wooden edge of the coffee table. 'His name's Henri Parisot and he owns a music shop in St Germain-des-Prés.'

Helen watched as Marie-Laure and her husband exchanged a surprised glance.

'Henri Parisot! Well, I'll be darned! Well, you are the lucky one, Helen, you'll be fine with him. Old Henri is a friend of ours, the one I told you about. He's a gentleman and a decent landlord. You were fortunate to find him.'

The seemingly innocent subject was getting a little too dangerous and

Helen racked her brain for other channels to go down. She watched as Adam moved to the CD player and slipped the CD into its plastic cover.

'That was lovely music,' she began, but she had to cough and start again, searching for the right words that would induce the right information and satisfy her growing but painful curiosity. 'It was ... Benjamin Beaulac, wasn't it?'

Adam laughed and placed a different CD on the player.

'Sure was. So, you enjoy my brother's music, do you? That's good to know.'

Helen watched him striding back to the sofa, grinning at her, an unmistakeable look of pride in his eyes.

'Benjamin Beaulac's your brother?'

Adam nodded, sat down and playfully accused his wife for not telling her friend about her illustrious family. Marie-Laure stood up, patted her husband's cheek and replied, 'Don't you think we women have more important things to talk about than you, chéri, and your illustrious family? Anyway, I'm going in the kitchen now so you can have the pleasure of telling Helen everything you want her to know. But don't take too long ... lunch will be in five minutes.'

'I'll need five years to tell Helen everything I want her to know about my family.'

Adam's smile suddenly and fleetingly disappeared and he added, almost incoherently, 'or infamous, depending on ...'

But instead of finishing his tantalising sentence he turned his attention to his wealth of music at the other end of the room. In a little over five minutes, Helen learned that Ben and Adam were twins, that they had both wanted to become musicians and composers from a very early age and had both studied at the Conservatoire National de Paris. Benjamin was gifted at composing as well as playing but Adam had settled for life as a jazz club pianist while his twin went on to fame and fortune. Oh, was he a jazz pianist? Helen had no idea. So, Adam grinned the grin that inadvertently turned his guest's heart over, his wife hadn't told her anything about him? He'd have to have a severe word in Marie-Laure's ear.

'Can I fix you another martini?' Adam was already making his way to the drinks' cabinet.

'Oh no. No, thanks. Adam.'

'How about joining me in a glass of whisky?'

'Won't it be a bit of a tight squeeze?'

'What?'

Adam turned round and Helen managed to grin at him.

'Not to mention a bit on the damp side.'

Adam's puzzled expression transformed into a smile.

'My wife isn't a very communicative woman, is she? She didn't tell you about her celebrated family and she certainly didn't tell me what a wonderful sense of humour her new assistant has. She's definitely going to have to be punished. Okay, Miss Hartnell, would you like me to serve you with a whisky along with my own? Or maybe a cocktail or ...'

'Nothing, thanks.' Helen was blushing slightly and didn't really know why. 'I don't drink much alcohol apart from wine. And not much of that.'

'Excellent. You must encourage my wife to follow in your very sensible footsteps – it'll save me a fortune. How about an orange juice?'

'Nothing thanks. Really. But I will have some more of these. They're delicious.'

She picked up another handful of pistachio nuts and blushed again.

Adam came back to sit opposite her with his replenished glass and went on to tell her about his quartet that played around the jazz clubs of Paris, other major cities in France and occasionally abroad. He and his brother, Ben, had important contacts in the States and Adam's band, the Adam Beaulac Quartet, were regularly invited to play in New York, Chicago and California. Marie-Laure's voice suddenly called from the dining room and Adam stood up, reached out his hand to help Helen to her feet and a kind of electric shock ran through her at his Ben-like touch. Fortunately, the contact was short-lived and Helen, trying to control her thoughts, feelings and body movements, followed her host out of the room.

***

The dining room was large and long and Helen gazed at the mahogany table with its array of china, crystal and silver. Her tulips had been prettily arranged in a Baccarat vase and placed in the centre of the table. Reproductions of epicurean paintings graced the walls. Helen sat down, rather self-consciously, and Marie-Laure served a crab and avocado salad. Adam uncorked a chilled bottle of Sancerre and poured the liquid into Helen's glass.

'I've been telling Helen about my European and American tours,' Adam told his wife, 'and Helen asked if you ever tagged along.'

Marie-Laure shrugged her silk-clad shoulders and pulled an unfathomable face.

'If Ben's wife – Kim – is "tagging along", then I make a special effort. We keep each other company ...'

Her voice trailed away and Helen, holding her breath, saw the look that passed between the husband and wife. It was fleeting and a disinterested person certainly wouldn't have noticed; but Helen wasn't disinterested. She picked up her glass of wine and took a sip; she needed a distraction.

'But I have my own business to think of, of course, and can't get away as often as I'd like. So, Adam and his boys – and sometimes his brother – usually travel without me. Fortunately, I'm not a jealous wife.'

Adam leaned to his left and affectionately kissed his non-jealous wife on her cheek.

'But I am a jealous husband, Helen, and with very good reason, you know. When I think of all those semi-naked guys lying in the salon having their heaving, hairy chests waxed by my wife … Well, fortunately, I'm not there to witness it.'

Helen laughed and commented that, up to now, she'd never seen a man set foot in the salon, and looked enquiringly at Marie-Laure.

'Oh, it occasionally happens, not very often. But it's true that men take more care about their appearance than they used to. And good for them, I say. Except my husband, of course. He wouldn't be seen dead walking into a beauty salon.'

Marie-Laure pulled a face at Adam and he winked at Helen.

'There's one thing you're forgetting, chérie. I did offer to come and be massaged by your last delectable assistant – Helen's predecessor – and what was your answer to that?'

'Unrepeatable, probably,' said Marie-Laure.

Helen laughed at the badinage and couldn't help but think how not only was their physical appearance identical but Adam's sense of humour was so like his brother's, too. She tried not to think of Ben teasing Kimberley in the same way, and affectionately pecking her cheek. They went on to talk of other things but whatever subject came up, Ben's name always managed to be mentioned by Adam. And when he spoke of his twin there was always a note of respect, idolatry almost, and the love glowed on his face. Helen wondered why Ben hadn't mentioned his twin; he'd told her only that he had a 'brother', she remembered. But she supposed the time they'd spent together had been too short, dare she believe too precious, to spend on anything, or anyone, other than each other.

They were sitting in the living room drinking coffee when Adam asked Helen about her first meeting Marie-Laure so many years before; nearly twenty-three years ago. It's incredible! He asked if she was still Marie-Laure's penfriend's best friend. Helen, uncomfortable with the direction the conversation was taking and wanting to discourage awkward questions, simply smiled and nodded.

'And she's married now, I understand? With children?'

'Yes, she's married to Tom; Marie-Laure knew Tom. And they've got three children.'

'That's great. Nice kids, I hope?'

Helen said yes, Jill's kids were nice but the eldest, Caroline, was a bit of a worry. She'd started smoking heavily, drinking, going around with a 'bad lot' and, of course, not the slightest bit interested in her studies.

'Sounds quite serious,' Adam commented. 'How old is she?'

'Sixteen.'

'So ... Caroline must be about the same age as you two when you first met?'

Helen and Marie-Laure looked at each other across the coffee table, their eyes locked, but neither of them answered Adam's question. He sipped the last dregs of his coffee and put the china cup back in its saucer on the table. He leaned back on the sofa, crossed his long legs and placed a relaxed arm around his wife's shoulder.

'And did the pair of you have adolescent problems and give your mothers terrible headaches? Were the pair of you into a life of debauchery, drugs and illicit sex up on the Yorkshire moors?'

The two women's eyes remained unsmilingly locked across the room. Adam's second question was greeted with a dead silence and he was about to add something equally fatuous when his final words rang a faint bell in Helen's mind. Her curiosity was aroused in spite of the sudden awkwardness and it was a good excuse to put an end to the silence.

'Do you know the Yorkshire moors, Adam? Have you ever been there?'

The frivolous expression very quickly left Adam's face and the relaxed arm seemed to become rigid and moved away from Marie-Laure's shoulder. His eyes darted around the room, evidently not wanting contact with either his wife or his guest, and his fingers began to fiddle with a cushion. Helen noticed that Marie-Laure's initial discomfort at her husband's inane chatter had given way to a second embarrassment and one that was obviously shared. Helen felt her face reddening and the bile rising in her throat and she wished she could suck the words back into her mouth. Adam finally spoke.

'I've been there, yes. Well, I've been to Yorkshire. But not to the moors, unfortunately.' He paused and when he spoke again his voice was barely audible. 'My experience of that part of the world was, well, let's just say it was rather less idyllic than my wife's.'

Helen began to feel very uneasy. If her curiosity had got the better of sensitivity, she would definitely have asked him what on earth his experience of Yorkshire could have been to create such a negative reaction. She asked no such thing, of course, and was glad when Marie-Laure stood up, stretched and suggested a stroll by the Seine.

***

Marie-Laure insisted that Adam drive Helen home that evening. She tried to refuse. The metro was still running, she could even walk home, at a pinch. At a pinch ... Marie-Laure didn't understand, had no recollection of the English expression, but she got the general idea and refused to allow Helen to go home alone. As did Adam. His silver Renault was parked a little way down the street and as she slipped into the passenger seat, Helen noticed sheets of music lying on the back seat. She also noticed Adam's long, pianist, Ben-like fingers as he moved the car into action. An unwelcome nausea made its presence felt, not for the first time that day, and when Adam turned to smile at her, it was his brother who was sitting beside her in the French car. Why had fate dealt this unimaginable coincidence? Just when she was starting to settle down to her new life, to the city, to her work, just when her tricky relationship with her employer had started to blossom into friendship, the past more or less put in its place, this had to happen. She racked her brain for something to say to Adam Beaulac, now that she was completely alone with him. A safe, neutral subject for conversation on the short journey home. Adam, however, beat her to it.

'I'm so pleased that you're a music lover, Helen,' he said, his eyes concentrating on the busy road ahead. 'That means I can invite you to my concerts. Why don't you come with Marie-Laure to the next one?'

In spite of herself, Helen was genuinely pleased with the invitation.

'Oh thanks, Adam. I'd love to.'

'We're playing at the Cave Supérieure in a couple of weeks. Do you know it? It's a jazz club in the Latin Quarter ... been there since Charlemagne, I reckon! It's a great atmosphere, you'll love it. Write it in your diary.'

Helen thanked him again when he pulled up outside her building, and she also thanked him for the lift home. She turned to wave to him as she pressed the entry-code and pushed open the door. And as she was getting ready for bed, she couldn't help but wonder if Marie-Laure and Adam would ever mention their friendship with the English beautician, Marie-Laure's employee, to Ben. The thought kept her awake most of the night.

***

As usual, Henri Parisot was delighted to see his 'petit locataire preferé' and shook her hand with alacrity.

'Comment allez-vous, ma petite madame?' he cried, and after the month's rent had been handed over, Helen enthusiastically told him about her new job at Marie-Laure's salon. His reaction was as she'd expected. He told her what he'd been going to tell her the last time she was on his premises and had been interrupted by customers.

'But you know, Marie-Laure Colombe is married to Adam Beaulac, your friend's brother; a very famous jazz musician ... an excellent pianist! Not quite as famous as his twin, of course,' he gave a small, Gallic shrug, 'but ... quand même! What a charming coincidence, ma petite madame!'

Helen smiled patiently at the little man's enthusiasm and after he'd calmed down, she murmured, 'Look, Monsieur Parisot, I'd be ... I'd be really grateful if you didn't ... well, I mean, I don't want you to ... Look, Monsieur Parisot, when you see Adam or Marie-Laure, please don't mention ... please don't tell them that Ben and I are friends.'

Henri Parisot raised an eyebrow. His agitated hands had stopped wafting the air and his small eyes were now gazing at her, disappointed, perplexed and obviously very intrigued.

'Ah bon? Mais alors! Pourquoi?'

Helen didn't want her landlord to have a bad impression of her, nor did she want him to put two and two together and make seventy-six. She didn't want to explain her life, she didn't want to talk unnecessarily about Ben and she didn't want to lie. She only wanted her landlord to accept her request with good grace and to use his integrity. They stood looking at each other for a long moment and then the tinkling of the tiny bell signalled occupation for Henri Parisot.

'Thank you,' Helen smiled at him, as she headed towards the door. 'I ... erm ... I know I can count on you.'

'Your secret is safe with me, ma chère madame,' he called after her, pulling at his moustache and winking ridiculously. Helen cursed her burning cheeks and hurried out of the shop.

Chapter Thirteen

Paul Atkinson knocked out an unidentifiable tune on his two-year-old saxophone, lay it on the floor beside him, lit an umpteenth cigarette, promised himself for the umpteenth time to give up and settled back into the worse-for-wear imitation leather armchair. The rehearsal was due to begin at two o'clock; he had thirty minutes in which to smoke in peace and gather his thoughts together. He leaned forward to flick ash into the tin ashtray that stood, together with music-orientated magazines, old newspapers and the inevitable girlie magazines on a square piece of plastic that balanced on top of a less-than-immaculate drum. To complete the percussion effect a misshaped, dinted cymbal hung from a black cord over the table, a makeshift lightshade. Paul glanced at his watch, then at the door and picked up one of the non-girlie magazines and flicked through, killing time, evading his own thoughts. He was hoping that Adam would be the next one to arrive, in time for a bit of private conversation. He didn't relish the thought – in fact, he wouldn't be able to talk to him about what he wanted to talk to him about – in front of the others.

But Paul (if he'd been self-pitying, he'd have said it was the story of his life) was unlucky; Adam wasn't the next one to arrive. He was the last and ten minutes late. Before Paul had time to finish his cigarette, Philippe and Serge barged unceremoniously through the door, the former brandishing his double bass in its well-worn cover and almost falling over it as the door crashed shut behind him.

'Salut, l'Anglais! Quoi de neuf?'

At the same moment another door on the other side of the large but almost vacant room flew open and a small, plump and smiling elderly woman came through, carrying a tray of coffee. As Philippe propped his precious instrument carefully against the wall, the woman clumsily placed the tray on the so-called table and coffee predictably slopped out of the pot.

'Merde.'

Serge gave the cymbal a light tap with his professional fingers and told the rehearsal studio's long-suffering secretary that a tray of beer cans would have been more appropriate. But thanks anyway. The woman pulled a face at him, uttered a few choice words, chuckled and disappeared into her office. Philippe, having made sure his double bass wasn't about to keel over and crash to the floor in a thousand pieces, flopped onto the sofa near Paul and helped himself to some coffee. Serge tried, without much success, to create a tune on the cymbal and the others told him to wait until the rehearsal, for God's sake, and do everyone a favour.

'Where's Adam? He's late. Not like him.'

'Maybe he's paid his wife a visit and the wax has stuck indelibly to his armpits – or wherever.'

'Or maybe he couldn't find the right colour nail varnish to match his keyboard.'

'Arrêtez les conneries, les salauds!'

Maryse, the secretary, was not much of a lady, but the 'boys', as she called them, loved her.

'Don't worry, Maryse, we say exactly the same to his face. He's used to it. By the way, will Madam Adam be coming to the club tonight?'

Paul leaned forward again, stubbed out his cigarette and bent his head low over the magazine; he would have hated the other two men to witness his boyish blushes. It was the same, very important question he'd wanted to ask Adam himself. Although it wasn't Madam Adam he was interested in.

'Talk of the devil and in he walks.'

Serge moved towards the door to welcome his friend and fellow musician, Adam Beaulac, a man he'd worked with for a long time and whom he highly respected. Serge, shorter than Adam, and thin with a prematurely lined face and laughing south-of-France eyes, embraced the pianist, as did Philippe. Philippe was the complete antithesis of the drummer: tall, thin, blonde and blue-eyed. The men jostled each other and laughed and joked and finally it was Paul's turn to be acknowledged but in a more reserved way because of his Englishness and youth.

'Okay, are we ready for action?' Adam asked, rubbing his hands together, eager to attack the keyboard.

'There's coffee in the pot; it's still warm.'

'No, thanks. If you're ready, let's go.'

'You're in the basement today, boys!' Maryse called through her open doorway. 'I forgot to reserve the ground floor room for you.'

The 'boys' groaned in unison.

'You're more than useless, woman!'

'Thanks. I love all of you, too.'

The ground floor rehearsal room was the most coveted because the basement meant struggling down a narrow spiral staircase with double bass and saxophone and all other accoutrements. Adam led the way, followed by Serge – both instrument-free – while Paul came third and Philippe took up the rear, juggling with his instrument on the narrow steps. Once installed in the warm, soundproof room, all banter stopped. Adam strode to the far corner where a magnificent black grand piano stood and Serge settled himself behind a set of gleaming red and white drums. Philippe and Paul set up and tuned their own instruments and displayed their sheets of music. With mere glances at each other and without preamble, the four musicians burst into their first number, the piece of music they were to open their performance with that evening; a masterpiece by Miles Davis. Paul suddenly struck a false note and the music stopped while he re-tuned his keys. The other three ribbed him while continuing to tinker with their own instruments and Paul cursed both his blushes and his boyishness. He was almost thirty but looked much younger and felt years younger beside his friends. He didn't wish middle age on himself by any means, only maturity and fewer feminine traits … like bloody blushing, for God's sake. He wasn't the only one to strike a wrong note, however, and each one came in for his fair share of chaffing. Paul could never bring himself to tease the others, though, he felt it would have been disrespectful. It wasn't until they'd played several pieces perfectly and they were all satisfied with their work that they decided to take a break.

They left their instruments in the basement with as much loving care as a mother would have left her baby in its cot, and made their way back to the ground floor and more coffee. Paul prayed for Serge and Philippe to disappear for five minutes to give him chance to ask Adam the all-important question. Unbelievably, his prayer was answered. Serge went into the office to make a nuisance of himself with Maryse and get as much back, and Philippe badly needed the 'urinoir'. Paul quietly let out a long sigh of relief. Adam had sunk into the armchair that Paul had previously occupied, leaned back and closed his eyes.

'Adam?' Paul's voice was almost a squeak and he cursed himself again.

'Yeah?' He continued to lean back in the chair, his eyes firmly closed, his tongue making a circular movement around his lips.

'Do you think Marie-Laure will be … will be coming tonight? To the club … the concert?'

God, he was babbling. And blushing. He watched Adam's tongue make one more tour of his lips and then one eye slowly opened.

'Yes, Paul. I think she will.'

The eye closed again and an almost non-existent smile played on his moistened lips. There was a pause. Paul picked up the abandoned packet of cigarettes and fumbled with it for a while, not really wanting to smoke, only needing something to do. He finally pulled one out and threw the crushed packet on to the table. He accidentally knocked the cymbal in his clumsiness and pulled a throwaway lighter out of his jeans pocket.

'Next question!' Adam smiled, his eyes still shut.

Paul felt his cheeks burning. He flicked the pale blue lighter several times before it produced a flame.

'Next question,' he mumbled, feeling and no doubt sounding very foolish. 'I ... I don't suppose her friend ... what's-her-name ... will be coming with her again. Will she?'

'Her name is Helen Hartnell. And yes, I think she'll be coming, too.'

Adam's eyes were open and twinkling now and his grin was broad and mischievous. Paul turned his face away and blew smoke circles in the air. His otherwise blemish-free, round face was scarlet.

'Erm ... look, Adam ... I was wondering if ... well, do you think tonight ... at the club ... during one of the breaks or after the show ... well, what I mean is, would you mind ...'

'Sure, I'll affect an introduction,' Adam grinned up at the scarlet, smoke-surrounded face and added, 'If you were as skilful with the opposite sex as you are with your sax, mon petit bonhomme, you'd be a real Don Juan. But I've a strange idea that the ladies prefer you the way you are.'

***

Paul Atkinson had arrived in France five years previously, with his first saxophone, a few francs in his pocket and very little else. Disillusioned with both his domestic and musician's life in the west country, he'd impulsively and without any real background knowledge decided to try his luck in Europe, mentally vacillating between France and Spain. He finally settled on France, a country he knew not at all. At first, he avoided the capital. He disembarked off the ferry at Calais one cold evening in March and there he stayed for several months, busking in the streets by the port and using his feeble earnings to pay his bed and board expenses in a less than third-class hotel. He decided to move on to Paris when he realised that the small but lucrative success he'd had in the north of France would perhaps double in the capital.

At first, he thought he'd made the biggest mistake of his short life. At twenty-four, a graduate in Economics and Law at Exeter University, but with music in his blood, he couldn't help but wonder what his life would have been like if he'd taken the same straight and narrow path as his friends and fellow students. He often thought about their fat bank accounts, comfortable homes, pretty wives – their security – as he stood in draughty metro station corridors and inside malodorous, packed carriages playing his beloved but by now battered instrument to indifferent audiences. Totally alone and friendless in what appeared to be a hostile city.

Paul's first piece of luck came when a talent-spotter spotted his talent in the Bastille metro station and offered him work two nights a week in what turned out to be a more than sleazy 'jazz club' on the rue Saint Denis, whose main clientele were pimps, prostitutes and drunks looking for fights. 'Jazz club' was a musical euphemism for 'brothel cum gambling den'. However, Paul earned quite a lot of money and a certain reputation, and as long as he kept a low profile he felt he could put up with the squalor and bawdiness until something better came along. He was fortunate enough to meet other, equally amateur and ambitious musicians through the club and, in spite of his shy unworldliness, quickly made friends and improved his limited knowledge of the language. He formed a duet with a run-of-the-mill pianist from the east of France and together they applied for work in other, superior clubs in and around Paris. Their demand in other clubs was at first very limited, but their enthusiasm, ambition and tenacity paid off and they eventually found themselves hired by more desirable employers.

The pianist, for reasons known only to himself, suddenly decided to return to his native region and marry his childhood sweetheart, but before Paul had time to panic, he met another better-than-average pianist who introduced him to a drummer, and became part of a trio. The trio, who earned quite a name for themselves in the Parisian jazz world, fell apart after one year when the drummer collapsed and died on stage, the victim of a massive heart attack. The pianist subsequently decided to try his luck, solo, in the United States; New Orleans, to be precise. Paul was desperate, imagining his blossoming savings in a French bank whittling away to nothing, being thrown out of his small but adequate bedsit in the north of Paris and finding himself busking again in draughty metro stations.

And then he met Serge Vidal. They'd been chatting for a good half-hour before either of them knew the other was a musician. The party was boring for both of them up to the moment the two men discovered their mutual passion. Serge had made the acquaintance of Adam Beaulac, the incomparable Ben Beaulac's twin brother and pianist in his own right, several years before and they were at that time in the process of forming a professional partnership and on the look-out for two more talented people to make up a quartet. Paul and Serge left the boring party together and walked the few streets to Paul's bedsit where, in spite of the late hour and sleeping neighbours, he agreed to play a few pieces for Serge. A couple of days later he was introduced to Adam Beaulac (whose brother he greatly admired) and the duet became a trio. Philippe made the trio into a quartet two months later. The Adam Beaulac Quartet had been playing and gaining more acclaim around the leading jazz clubs of Paris for the past two years.

The Cave Supérieure was the Mecca of the Parisian jazz world and had attracted only the most coveted clientele for more than two decades. Uninspiring from the outside, a dark blue door opened onto a wide, blue-carpeted staircase that led to two large rooms in the cellar. Low, wooden tables surrounded by equally low, multi-coloured and comfortable chairs filled both rooms. The floor was stone with odd rugs thrown down here and there and the white walls sported black and white photographs of outstanding jazzmen. Soft shaded lamps stood in various nooks and crannies and a long, well-stocked bar filled one wall. The numerous barmen hardly had time to breathe and the white-jacketed, bow-tied waiters flitted like giant moths amongst the tables, smiles hardly leaving their – more often than not black – faces. And the music beautifully invaded and created magic in both rooms from a low stage in one corner. The Adam Beaulac Quartet had been playing there regularly every Saturday evening – and well into Sunday morning – for the past two years. Because of their increasing recognition and popularity in the well-respected club, Adam was hoping that finally he was about to taste the much-merited fame that his brother had known for many years.

Because of the quartet's fixed contract with the Cave Supérieure, Paul had the pleasure of seeing the English woman sitting in the audience with Adam's wife several times. She always seemed distant, somehow, unapproachable and very lovely. Her blue eyes shone like extra lights in the semi-darkness and her rare smile lit up her entire face. And Paul Atkinson had often wondered what personality lay behind the attractive exterior. He was intrigued, to say the least.

The Cave Supérieure didn't open its doors until nine o'clock and the musicians didn't start playing till nine-thirty. It was now about five minutes past nine and the Adam Beaulac Quartet were on stage, lovingly fondling and tuning their instruments, exchanging brief but necessary dialogue and throwing occasional glances at the rapidly-filling room.

Marie-Laure, Adam's beautiful wife, was sitting at one of the reserved tables directly below the stage. She was ordering a drink, smiling up at the obsequious waiter who eventually turned from her to her companion. Paul turned a little away from his fellow musicians to catch a glimpse of the face that had beguiled him for the past few weeks. Helen also smiled up at the waiter but with less flamboyance than her friend. In spite of her natural attractiveness, she was less striking than Adam's wife, less well dressed and

166

the waiter seemed to be less subservient when taking her order. But if Helen Hartnell noticed she obviously didn't care, didn't react. As soon as the waiter disappeared, she turned her attention back to Marie-Laure, who was explaining something to her with the help of extravagant physical gestures. Helen was smiling and nodding in response. Paul tried to concentrate on his instrument and the Miles Davis number that the Adam Beaulac Quartet were about to play. But he was looking forward to the half-hour break when Adam had promised to introduce him to the woman who'd haunted his dreams for so many nights.

***

The music, of course, was loud and conversation was impossible so Helen settled back in her seat, caressed her glass of dry white wine and concentrated on the quartet. And as she caressed her glass, the music that she'd come to love caressed her ears and her right foot began to move to the rhythm. Marie-Laure's eyes never left the white Steinway and the pianist, her husband, whose long, nimble fingers stroked the keys and whose face now and then smiled at the audience. The pianist, her husband, with whom, Helen had come to realise over the past few weeks, Marie-Laure was passionately, deliriously and very possessively in love. And the feelings were one hundred percent reciprocated. Sometimes it was achingly poignant and a little embarrassing to witness their mutual adoration.

Helen's eyes avoided the pianist, as usual, and darted from the drummer's tools-in-trade to the double bass player's grimaces and the saxophonist's equally fierce concentration. Helen not only loved their music but she admired them; they all made their beautiful art seem so simple, which made Ben's art as a composer seem sublime.

Helen had never met any of Adam's group in spite of her frequent attendances at the club. She had never thought about or even hoped to meet them; it wasn't something that particularly interested her. In fact, it was better perhaps if she didn't; she'd have felt too embarrassed, tongue tied, even with the young saxophonist who was English. She loved and appreciated their music and was more than happy to listen to them play – and that, as far as she was concerned, was that. She certainly had no great yearning to become part of their coterie, in spite of the pianist's wife being her close friend. Helen was content to be an anonymous and nondescript member of the audience.

But while Marie-Laure had been driving her small yellow Fiat through the narrow streets of the Left Bank that evening, she had very casually announced that, during the break at eleven-thirty, Adam was going to introduce Helen to the musicians. It was about time, he'd commented. Helen had turned her surprised gaze on Marie-Laure as she manoeuvred the Fiat through the heavy, noisy, Saturday evening traffic.

'There's one particular person who wants to meet you, Adam tells me.'

Helen stared at the driver whose eyes didn't leave the road.

'What?'

Marie-Laure braked at red traffic lights and threw an amused glance at her passenger.

'Don't you mean "Who", Helen?'

'Who on earth wants to meet me, Marie-Laure? And why?'

'Wait and see.'

'You're having me on.'

'Not at all. Why should I?' The car suddenly shot forward. 'You have an admirer, apparently, my little English rose. I'm so happy you're wearing that red dress, you look ... nice. It's so much prettier than that dreadful lilac thing you wore last Saturday.'

Marie-Laure's very personal comments about Helen's appearance were becoming much more frequent and without inhibition. Occasionally, Helen accepted and even appreciated her remarks and thought of them as quite normal coming from a Parisienne who knew more about style than she did or ever would. She was only offering advice, trying to help. Or was she? When the criticisms became more frequent and, quite honestly, without just cause, resentment began to creep in and Helen racked her brains to work out the best way to deal with it. Although Marie-Laure quite consciously rubbed salt into Helen's long-established wounds, it was impossible for her to strike back. She felt incapable of hurting anyone, even if that 'anyone' thoroughly deserved to be hurt. She was also, for the moment, financially dependent on Marie-Laure the boss so her fault-finding – with her clothes, hairstyle, makeup and sometimes even her behaviour – festered inside her. She could feel the festering now. The 'dreadful lilac thing' – that she'd paid the skin off her backside for – was the pride and joy of her limited wardrobe. And her mam had always said that lilac was one colour that *did* suit her.

'And your skin's looking much better since the facial I gave you yesterday. You were beginning to look rather ... well, fanée ... faded. Parisian pollution is terrible for the skin as you're beginning to find out. Unlike the clean, fresh air of the Yorkshire moors.'

A thousand images flashed through Helen's mind at Marie-Laure's last words and she found nothing to say in reply. Her now fresh-looking skin blushed scarlet and Helen could only think that, despite a blossoming, promising friendship, certain skeletons were still rattling in best-forgotten cupboards. And for the moment she forgot all about the mysterious musician who wanted to meet her.

***

'Hi! How are you enjoying the show?'

Adam Beaulac turned from his wife's embrace to Helen's embarrassed blushes as her gaze darted from Adam's grin to the shadowy presence behind him. Her clammy hand briefly took hold of the cool pianist-fingers and then Ben Beaulac's brother quickly moved aside and pushed his saxophonist, now minus saxophone, forward. The boy, as Helen couldn't help but think of him, was obviously as shy and maladroit and foolish as she was. So, this was her admirer, the young and baby-faced Englishman; and Helen felt a ridiculous pang of disappointment. Adam moved into an empty seat next to his wife and a split second later a beaming waiter put his appearance in. Paul rather clumsily lowered himself into the chair next to Helen, blushed furiously and made no conscious effort to untie his tongue. His light brown eyes flickered at Adam, who introduced him, very theatrically, to Helen, his wife's employee and very good friend. Helen, feeling herself in the limelight and hating every minute, took Paul's slightly shaking hand and whispered, 'Hello.' She could think of nothing witty, dynamic or even intelligent to add. There followed a long silence during which four pairs of eyes glanced at each other and danced around the smoky room. Adam had ordered drinks for everyone and when the waiter left, turned his attention to his wife, almost turning his back on Paul. Paul made a play of fidgeting with his chair, stood up, sat down again, glanced around him, coughed and pulled a crushed packet of cigarettes out of his pocket. With a still visibly shaking hand, he offered the packet to Helen and she smilingly shook her head.

'I don't smoke ... thanks.'

She watched as Paul lit a cigarette and almost burned his trembling fingers in the process. He swore under his breath, in French Helen noticed, put the cigarette into an otherwise empty ash tray and blew smoke circles into the air. Helen, in her own great discomfort, felt amused and sorry at the same time, but disappointed in her young admirer. They hazarded a benign smile at each other and Helen realised that if Paul had no intention of leaving his chair, she was going to have to be the first to speak. And she was going to sound banal, hackneyed and commonplace and then it would be her admirer's turn to be disappointed – unless he already was, of course. Now he'd viewed her close up.

'You play the saxophone very well, Paul,' she finally said. 'How long have you been playing?'

How many times must he have heard that unoriginal, lack-lustre question? He replied with equal vapidity and didn't offer to elaborate. Helen glanced at Marie-Laure deep in laughing conversation with her husband and continued to rack her brains. She wondered if her taciturn admirer was racking his, too. She supposed he had some hidden away inside that round, pink head.

'Whereabouts in England are you from?'

'The west country. Bath, to be precise.' A long pause. 'And you?'

'Yorkshire. The Pennines. Firley, to be precise.'

'I thought I recognised a slight northern accent.'

Helen could think of nothing else to say and concentrated on her too-quickly-diminishing glass of wine.

'How long have you been in Paris?'

Several seconds had passed and they both asked the same question at the same time which, at least, provoked a little laughter. Helen suddenly felt Marie-Laure's and Adam's eyes fixed on the pair of them, waiting for the farce to reach its finale. She was absolutely hating this unsolicited parody and wished she could have made herself disappear. Paul repeated the question, Helen replied and Paul took a long puff on his cigarette. He picked up his glass of beer, swallowed a mouthful and looked at the pianist, his current mentor, a soundless cry for help. Adam, however, ignored him. The silence continued until everyone finished their drinks and Paul finished his cigarette. He and Helen avoided each other's eyes. After an infinity, Paul looked at his watch, Adam looked at him and they both prepared to make a move. Spotlights were again fixed on the stage, as were Philippe and Serge. Helen saw the sudden panic on her admirer's face that led to a very unexpected paroxysm of words.

'Look … erm … Listen. Helen … erm … look. Look, I'd … erm … well, I'dreallyliketoseeyouagain. Erm … soon. In fact. Not here. I mean … erm … I'dliketoinviteyoutoarestaurant. Orthecinema. If you like. I'm sorry, I … erm … havetogonow. The break's over … too short. Well, wouldyougiveme … couldIhaveyourphonenumber. Please?'

Paul had stood up out of necessity and was looking down at her, anxious, fuchsia and unsmiling and she was looking up at him, amused, fuchsia, but smiling. Adam had left and Marie-Laure was relaxing in her chair, obviously enjoying the little scene. Helen scribbled down her number, folded the

170

paper and gave it to the now tardy saxophonist. He pushed it into his trouser pocket together with his packet of cigarettes, coughed a 'thank you', attempted a smile and stumbled over a chair on his way back to the stage.

The Adam Beaulac Quartet began to thump out the opening chords of a Ben Beaulac number, one of his earlier successes, a theme tune to a popular French film. Marie-Laure settled back into her chair but her voice, as clear as a bell, rang out across the table, implying Helen knew not what.

'Well, that boy's either an idiot of the first degree or your fatal charms have rendered him totally speechless. I wonder which one it is?'

The Adam Beaulac Quartet continued to play Ben Beaulac's music until the sleepy club closed its doors at four o'clock. And Helen knew that she'd been an idiot of the first degree to have given her phone number to such a man ... a boy, in fact. And a close acquaintance of Ben's brother.

Chapter Fourteen

Paris in the month of May was every bit as beautiful as Helen had heard and imagined. The prolonged and heavy showers of April had given way to warm, sunny days, abundant blossoms on the ubiquitous chestnut trees, café clientele spilling on to busy pavements and a general atmosphere of bonhomie. The good weather had brought with it good business at the 'Au Bonheur des Dames'. Winter-smothered flesh was now well and truly on display and women wanted hair-free, glowing, showable bodies. Nathalie's exhausted remark 'There aren't enough hours in the day' was repeated several times during that month and the beauticians and receptionists left work late every evening, thankfully hurrying home to their private lives and their beds.

Although Helen was as tired as everyone else, she was never in a hurry to go home in the evenings. During the winter months her small bedsit had been a haven, sheltering her from the cold outside and the unfriendly, alien city. But now it was warm and the city much more congenial. She had friends, or at least acquaintances, and after a while she began to be recognised and acknowledged by neighbours, shop assistants, the dry cleaner. Her small bedsit now felt a little claustrophobic and she welcomed the long days to take advantage of the outdoors; simply walking in Paris was a pleasure but she occasionally also sat in pavement cafés and read a book or people-watched. She once even tried writing a poem about the city she'd come to love. Sitting at her solitary table in her favourite café on Boulevard Saint Germain, watching and appreciating the life around her, she took a pen and a scruffy piece of paper out of her handbag. She sat and stared at the paper for a long time and then carefully smoothed out the creases before picking up her Bic. She continued to stare at the white sheet in front of her and the pen remained poised in mid-air. The city. The monuments. The parks and the people. The food. The wine. The language and the music. Paris. A poem in itself. But the perspiration and the slight trembling slowly came back, the pen became damp in her hand and her mind a complete blank. She screwed up the piece of paper and put it in the empty ashtray, put the pen back into her bag and finished her coffee. Although the evening was sultry, Helen shivered. It was no use even trying; Helen had written her last poem and had suffered the consequences in more ways than one.

She often returned home quite late in the evening. Little by little she had decorated her room to her own taste, buying lamps, a couple of bookshelves, cheap and cheerful vases, plants. She'd had Ben's gift, the Renoir reproduction, framed and it hung on the wall over her bed. It was the last thing she saw before she slept and the first thing she saw when she blinked her eyes awake. The bedsit was her home and to a certain extent it now felt like home, but she knew she couldn't stay there for ever. It was too tiny … too claustrophobic. As soon as she'd saved enough money, she intended asking Henri Parisot to find her a bigger place.

It had been three weeks since her meeting with Paul Atkinson. In spite of Marie-Laure's incessant and, she couldn't help thinking, supercilious teasing, Helen had thought of him very little since then. In fact, there was nothing to think of. He hadn't impressed her. Physically, she would have described him as 'cute', nothing more; he was much younger than she and his excessive shyness – almost to the point of ridicule – had embarrassed and confused her. He'd been too much like herself – or of what she thought was herself – to be attractive. Maybe too much unlike Ben Beaulac, as all future men in her life were unfortunately destined to be. Paul hadn't phoned in the last three weeks and she no longer expected him to. She felt only relief.

***

It was a Friday evening at the end of May and the fierce sun was beginning to set in the west of the capital, creating a pink glow on the elaborate architecture. Helen had finished work at seven-thirty and left the shop with Marie-Laure and Agnès, the older receptionist. Agnès had quickly gone her own way, leaving Marie-Laure and Helen chatting on the pavement.

'Listen,' Marie-Laure said, putting her long, slim hand on Helen's shoulder, 'leave next Sunday free. Adam and I would like you to come for lunch. Okay?'

Helen smiled and murmured her thanks. She enjoyed the odd Sunday or whenever spent at the Beaulac's home, but at the same time it wasn't easy for her. Adam's mere presence was always perplexing and she wondered if he ever noticed anything strange in her attitude towards him. And Ben's name was frequently mentioned, his compositions frequently played on the expensive and intricate CD player. She sometimes wondered if her hosts knew and they were performing some kind of persecution rite, and then she told herself she was being ridiculous. It was impossible for them to know. She trusted her landlord's integrity and Ben certainly wouldn't have disclosed his secret. And she also questioned – and then chastised herself – Marie-Laure's friendship. They got on well both professionally and socially and if Helen had met her for the first time in January, she would have accepted the woman at face value. But, under the circumstances, she couldn't help but wonder if Marie-Laure's often excessive overtures of affection and hospitality were a means of absolving her own guilt. After the one occasion when she'd strongly, and without provocation, denied having had a sexual relationship with Malcolm, she'd never mentioned either him or that short period in her life again. Many times, Helen tried to put herself in the other woman's position and work out how *she'd* behave but it wasn't easy. She was no woman of the world, had little experience of life and intricate human relationships but she was convinced that, if she'd been given an opportunity to get in touch with Jill again – and her lovely family – then she would have done so. But Marie-Laure had shown no interest whatsoever in contacting her old penfriend; nor had she shown any interest in Jill's phone calls and occasional letters to Helen. Marie-Laure had been an enigma twenty-odd years before and she was continuing to be so, in various ways. Her frequent negative remarks and unsubtle hints about Helen's clothes were also starting to niggle and humiliate, but Helen told herself that Marie-Laure's profession was getting the better of her courtesy. At least, that's what she told herself.

***

A letter was waiting for Helen when she arrived home late on that beautiful, balmy May evening. The long blue envelope was standing upright in her letterbox with a Paris postmark and writing that Helen didn't recognise. She didn't have time to think about that, however, as she heard her phone ringing on the first floor. She ran up the winding staircase two at a time, cursed when she dropped her key and managed to pick up the receiver before Jill gave up.

'You're out of breath, love. Have I interrupted anything... exciting?'

'Chance'd be ... a fine ... thing. I've just hurtled up a flight of slippery stairs and dropped my key, if you think that's exciting.'

'Only on a very boring day,' Jill laughed. 'I'm disappointed; I thought you might be having a grand old time with your cute saxophonist ... I thought maybe he'd livened up a bit.'

'If he has, I don't know anything about it 'cos I haven't heard from him since.'

'You're joking. I thought he sounded dead keen. Men; honestly. Mind

174

you, he did sound a bit of a weirdo, if you don't mind me saying. I know some blokes are shy but it sounds like he has a serious disorder. Like he needs some kind of treatment ... Maybe I should send Mandy over there, she'd sort him out. And what about Benjamin Beaulac? God, I still can't believe what happened between you and him, you know. You must admit, it sounds like farfetched romantic fiction ... and I'm dying to tell all Firley. But don't worry, I won't.' Jill finally paused for breath but there was no response from Helen. 'Oh no, don't tell me you haven't heard from him again, either ...'

'Not for a while.'

'Don't worry, I'm sure you will. And probably from the other one, too. His shyness is probably all a big act and he'll knock on your door one night, sweep you off your feet and have his wicked way with you. Hey, Helen, do you think they know each other? It's highly likely, don't you think? They're probably big buddies and ... hey, this is better than any telly serial, Helen Hartnell, I hope you realise that. I can't wait to hear the next episode ... And how's my old penfriend?'

Helen mentally shrugged and, pulling the phone closer to her, sat down on her sofa-bed.

'Oh, she's still the same. You know, nice, kind and cruelly critical. What I don't understand is that she never asks about you or offers to contact you. It's not normal.'

'She's probably feeling guilty and ...'

'But I told you, she denied that anything happened between her and Malcolm. I hadn't even brought the subject up.'

'Yeah, I know,' said Jill, 'but even if that's the case ... and I'm still not sure myself ... She still behaved badly to us ... her host family. Didn't she?'

Helen agreed.

'And to be honest,' Jill continued, 'after all you've said about her, I'm not sure I want to speak to her again. I don't think she's improved with age.'

Helen suddenly felt very drained and needed to change the subject.

'Anyway, enough of me and my entertaining life. How are you and the tribe?'

'Oh, not much news from this end,' Jill sighed, 'only the usual, I'm sorry to say. Caroline's still causing me a lot of headaches and sleepless nights ...'

'Oh no, I thought she was settling down a bit. What's she up to now, Jill?'

'Well, you know what she's like, so easily influenced; easily led. There's a big drug scare at the school at the moment, can you believe it? Tom and I've tried talking to her about it but you know how sullen and unresponsive she can be. Her interest in school is zero and her marks in every subject are

175

getting worse. All she thinks about is boys and more boys. Tom caught her necking with a real roughneck one evening last week, up on the moor, not far from your old street. He interfered, of course – you know what Tom's like – and the lad gave him a mouthful for his pains. Tom was sorely tempted to hit the young bugger but he didn't, thank God. Caroline caught it good and proper from her dad when she finally came home, though. Not that it did any good. She didn't come straight home from school the next day. I was worried sick ... she finally rolled in as large as life about ten o'clock. Cocky as you like. She wouldn't go to school the next morning and when I got home from work His Nibs was lying on the sofa, half undressed and drinking Tom's whisky. I daren't tell Tom about that. I honestly don't know how to deal with her, Helen, I'm at my wits' end and scared and it's going to get worse. If that's possible. I'm also scared that my other two'll follow in her footsteps.'

She came to a full stop and there was a short silence.

'I'm so sorry, Jill,' Helen finally murmured. 'I honestly don't know what to say, what to advise. She was such a lovely little girl; I can't believe she's turning out like this. Although I'm sure it's only temporary,' she added, quickly. 'She's an adolescent and she's not the only one to go off the rails but ...'

'... But she's my kid and I'm worried and fed up and ... oh, enough of that, Helen. I didn't phone to tell you all my troubles, far from it. I wanted to hear all your juicy news!'

'About as juicy as a black banana,' Helen laughed.

'Anyway, I do have a bit of good news,' said Jill.

'Let me guess – Tom's won the pools and you're all off to the Bahamas for six months.'

'Tom stopped doing the pools before Sharon was born, Helen. No, actually, Mandy phoned out of the blue the other day and she's got something exciting up her professional sleeve (hey – you could put that in one of your poems!) but she's not saying anything much until it actually takes off.'

'Well, didn't she give you a clue ...?'

'Not really, she's keeping very schtum until things have got off the ground. I can't tell you any more than that but she's bubbling over with enthusiasm and excitement so it must be something special. So, Tom and I are keeping our fingers crossed for her; Tom's feeling dead proud already and he doesn't know what for yet! Anyway, that's about it from my end. Over to you ... Parisian sexpot!'

Helen laughed.

'I'll try not to disappoint you but I'm not promising anything. So, it's my turn to phone you next and ...'

'Oh, before you go, I wanted to ask if you had anything planned for your summer holiday? If not, why don't you come and spend a couple of weeks with us? We'd love to have you ...'

'Oh, that'd be great, Jill, I'd love to come and it'll be something to look forward to.'

She went on to tell her best friend that holidays hadn't been mentioned yet at the salon, and she'd have to work there a year before paid holidays were due. And she didn't want to dig into her savings too much; she never knew when she'd need that money from the sale of the house.

'You know you don't have to worry about money when you're with us.'

'I know and I appreciate it, Jill. I'd love to come and I'll let you know. Have some fish and chips ready on the table.'

'And a bottle of Dom Perignon?'

'Actually, I'd prefer a bottle of Sarsons vinegar.'

'Ring me next week ... before, if you have any news.'

'Will do. Lots of love to you all – and try not to worry too much about Caroline. I'm sure it's only a phase she's going through.'

'It's a bloody long one, I can tell you. Lots of love to you, too. Bye now.'

'Bye, Jill. Lots of love ...'

'To you, too. Bye ...'

Helen sat on her sofa-bed for quite a while after she'd replaced the receiver, thinking about Caroline and the sweet, adorable little girl that she used to be. What a shame she'd turned out the way she had, even if it was only a glitch in her life; causing her parents so much worry and upset, not to mention the two younger kids. She hoped she'd grow out of it fast, for everyone's sake. Jill's invitation gave her food for thought, too. A couple of weeks on home ground with warm, wonderful and genuine (now, why did that adjective come into her head?) people would do her the world of good. She'd have to check up on her holiday rights and think about it.

Helen had placed her piece of correspondence on the sofa next to her and remembered it as she started to stand up. She opened the envelope and sat down again.

Dear Helen,

I was so happy to meet you at the Cave Supérieure and really did intend phoning you but time went by and ... well, after waiting so long I'm afraid I got cold feet. You must think I'm a real twerp and you're right. I am. Anyway, I thought I'd just drop you a quick line to let you know I haven't forgotten you. I'd still like to take you out to dinner one evening and I promise ... I will phone.

Take care of yourself,
Best wishes,
Paul Atkinson.

Helen read the letter three times but couldn't make head or tail of it. Either he wanted to see her or he didn't; and how did he find her address? Well, from Adam, obviously, it needed no Sherlock Holmes to work that out. But she was too tired to give it any thought, and although tempted to call Jill and cheer her up with the little titbit, instead she made herself a hot drink and slipped into bed and a deep sleep.

***

Paul didn't phone her but she received a second letter in much the same vein a few days later. At first, she was amused and then angry. Was he playing some kind of cranky game with her? It wasn't possible that a fairly well-known musician who played in packed Parisian clubs was so cripplingly shy. And then the awful thought crossed her confused mind that maybe Paul was in league with Marie-Laure ... and Adam ... in a kind of persecution game because they somehow knew about her and Ben and ... It was a gruesome idea and without thinking too much about it, Helen accused herself of being melodramatic, paranoid and completely ridiculous.

But young Paul Atkinson, the 'cute' saxophonist, was becoming a mystery and one that she didn't like at all.

***

During the course of the week the sun continued to shine and when on Thursday Marie-Laure reiterated her invitation for the following Sunday, she added that they would be able to have lunch on the balcony if the weather kept up, and maybe a 'sortie' in the afternoon. She and Helen were sitting in Salon No. 1 having a quick cup of coffee during a brief lull and, as Marie-Laure was talking on a personal level, Helen decided to show her the two baffling letters, or rather notes, from Paul Atkinson.

They were somewhere in her handbag along with other paraphernalia that she had to sort out.

Marie-Laure's eyes travelled over the enigmatic, stumbling words and an equally enigmatic smile played on her perfect lips.

'Quel con!' she murmured and Helen laughed at and agreed with the impolite expletive.

'Yes, well, even he admits he's a twerp, doesn't he?'

'He's not wrong,' Marie-Laure laughed. 'Look, leave this "twerp" to me, okay?'

'Oh, Marie-Laure, I don't want ...'

'Okay?'

'Look, I only showed you the letters because I'm ... well, I'm a bit confused. I don't give a damn about them, really ... or him. Anyway, if I don't respond he probably won't bother me anymore and I prefer it that way. Honestly.'

'Leave the twerp to me,' Marie-Laure repeated and the expression on her face, and especially in her eyes, encouraged no reply.

So, when Helen arrived at the Beaulac's home for lunch that Sunday, she wasn't at all surprised to find the table laid for four.

***

The table stood on the balcony that was bedecked with great earthenware plant pots and vases filled with tulips, daisies and freesias. The balcony looked on to a private garden with a small fountain at the back. Marie-Laure, immaculate in a short, body-clutching white dress, her long black hair tied up in a knot, told Helen that her husband was tied up on the phone.

'So, I'll see to the drinks. What would you like, Helen? A glass of wine as usual, or are you going to be a big girl and try something stronger?'

Helen ignored the knot that had already tightened in her stomach – the lunch was starting well – and forced herself to smile. She lowered herself into a wicker chair.

'A glass of dry white wine, as usual, please. I'll stay a little girl for the time being.'

'As you like.'

Marie-Laure was gone a good ten minutes and came back with a glass of chilled white wine and a dry martini clinking with ice and lemon. She placed the drinks on the low table filled with nuts and crackers and told Helen that Adam was still on the phone.

'Men say women can talk – but I promise you that Adam and his brother could put any woman to shame!'

Helen's hand, outstretched towards her glass, halted in mid-air. She wanted, out of politeness, to say something in reply to Marie-Laure's frivolous remark but could think of nothing appropriate. Instead, her inquisitive eyes moved to her left and to the exquisitely decorated table for four. She hadn't wanted to mention it; she'd wanted her hostess to explain the fourth place in her own good time, but now out of necessity to change the subject, she casually asked who the other guest was going to be. As if I don't know, she mentally added. Marie-Laure sank on to the chair opposite hers and the unique and mischievous dark brown eyes twinkled at her.

'Well, as the poor, dumb, inarticulate boy isn't capable of doing his own dirty work, I thought I'd make the way easier for him.'

'I suppose you mean Paul Atkinson?'

'Who else?'

Helen resented Marie-Laure's description of Paul, immediately taking the insult to him as an indirect one to herself – a reflection of her mother's manifesto echoing down the years. The only men you're capable of attracting are either idiots or bastards. She felt her cheeks flushing and hid her face in her drink. Why couldn't Marie-Laure mind her own damn business? Hadn't the woman – girl – caused enough catastrophe in Helen's romantic life? If the boy – man – if Paul really wanted to see her, he'd get round to it in his own good time. And, in any case, whether he did or not was a matter of pure indifference to her. And Helen couldn't help but wonder if Marie-Laure was being genuinely kind and helpful or maliciously meddling. She obviously had no high opinion of the 'cute' saxophonist. The doorbell rang.

'Et le voilà!'

Marie-Laure gaily put down her glass and skipped off the balcony towards the door. Helen took a deep, cringing breath. She shuddered involuntarily and then a terrible thought occurred to her: had Marie-Laure told Paul that Helen would be invited too or was this supposed to be a happy surprise for him? Marie-Laure had little enough respect for him to play such a mean trick.

'Paul, you've already met Helen, one of your compatriots, haven't you?'

Paul was clutching a bottle of Châteauneuf-du-Pape and a small bouquet of flowers which Marie-Laure relieved him of, while he gazed wordlessly at

Helen. So, she'd been right. Paul Atkinson hadn't expected to see her today.

'I'll go put my lovely flowers in a vase. What would you like to drink, Paul?'

'Oh … erm … could I … erm … could I have a whisky, please? With ice? Thanks … thank you.'

Helen had stood up to shake Paul's hand in the socially correct French manner and once more found his palm clammy, the fingers trembling. Oh, Marie-Laure, why couldn't you have minded your own business? Why the heck did I show you his letters? I must have been mad. They sat down, Paul taking Marie-Laure's vacated chair, and they quietly eyed each other across the table. Helen swallowed loudly and dragged her eyes away from his. Paul's appalling shyness and lack of self-confidence seemed such a contradiction to his lifestyle. It was intriguing really. And he was attractive in a boyish kind of way … well, cute, and he had a nice smile. Helen knew she would have to be the one to break the silence.

'Thank you … thanks a lot for … your letters.'

She watched the colour inflame his cheeks and his normally active fingers search for something to touch, to fiddle with. They found nothing and he began to wipe them up and down his thighs. After a long moment he managed to stammer, 'I … I hope you weren't offended.'

Helen frowned at him and her lips involuntarily parted.

'Offended?' She tried to smile at him. 'No, no, of course not. Why should I be offended?'

Paul didn't reply, only blinked at her and continued to wipe his trouser leg with his clammy fingers. Helen silently cursed Marie-Laure for the umpteenth time.

'Will you be coming back to the club?'

'Pardon?'

'La Cave Supérieure. Erm … do you think you'll ever come back? I mean … well, with Marie-Laure?'

Helen shrugged her shoulders and looked at the table. She loved going to the jazz club, it had become one of her favourite 'sorties', and something for her to look forward to; but now she wondered if she'd ever want to go there again.

'I don't know. I suppose so. Probably.'

'We … play there most Saturdays.'

'Yeah, I know.'

Maybe it would have to be her, Helen, who made the first move and put the young bloke out of his misery. But what was she thinking? She didn't want to make *any* move; she really had no desire to go out with this tongue-tied, abysmally shy … boy. Because that's how she thought of him; he was a boy. And any attraction she could possibly have felt for him had been squashed good and proper – as her mam would have said – and the thought of spending an entire evening alone with him put the fear of God in her. Well, maybe not fear but the idea wasn't a happy one. Her jumbled thoughts suddenly spun back to the previous November and the oh-so-different approach of Ben Beaulac, whose exuberance, charming self-confidence and quirky sense of humour had crushed her own timidity. Ben Beaulac who was speaking on the phone to his twin brother right now.

Adam suddenly appeared on the balcony behind them and Paul, obviously grateful for the diversion, quickly stood up and waited for the usual boisterous, hail-fellow-well-met greeting, but it was a long time in coming. Adam's sun-bronzed face was blanched and his eyebrows almost met in a deep frown. A thin sliver of saliva ran from the corner of his mouth down the side of his chin. His hands were thrust into his trouser pockets and when he pulled them out, he seemed not to know what to do with them; they moved and made strange patterns in the air. In spite of their mutual inhibitions Helen and Paul exchanged an anxious look. And then Adam remembered his social duties. He bent to kiss Helen on her cheek and briefly shook hands with Paul. He vaguely muttered a few mundane niceties and dropped into a third chair on Helen's left. He steepled his fingers, his elbows on his knees, and lowered his forehead onto his hands. Helen and Paul exchanged a now panic-stricken look and were both relieved when Marie-Laure arrived with the tray of aperitifs. Her polite hostess's smile disappeared when she looked at her husband.

'Chéri, what's the matter? What did Ben want? Why did he call?'

Helen's stomach turned a somersault and she stared at Adam, wanting and not wanting him to reply. Adam threw his wife an 'I'll speak to you later' look, wiggled his fingers, cracked his knuckles and offered his glass of champagne for a toast.

'Tchin.'

'Cheers!' Helen and Paul muttered in unison, although Helen was feeling far from cheerful. She could feel her cheeks burning, her curious eyes levelled on Adam's face, her ears preparing themselves for a blow. But the blow, whatever it was, didn't come. Adam, confirming what his eyes had communicated, told Marie-Laure they'd talk later, and added, 'Let's enjoy our lunch with our two delightful guests.'

He sipped his champagne and put his glass down.

'Now, Paul, you hopeless Englishman, are you going to invite this lovely lady or would you like me to do it for you?'

Adam's last words would have humiliated Helen if his first words hadn't sounded so pessimistic. But Helen wasn't in a position to ask questions. She didn't know Adam's twin brother, Ben, only by name and music, she had no right to be the slightest bit concerned about him. Any frustration she'd felt in her life before – and there had been plenty of that – paled into oblivion now. Surprisingly, Paul seemed motivated by Adam's tactless and crass comment and he suddenly turned a smiling, if embarrassed, face towards her. She had the impression that Paul accepted that his overt shyness was a source of mockery amongst his friends, and that it was the norm for them to help him along in life. Feeling rather irritated, she raised her eyes to him when he finally spoke to her.

'Okay. Look, Helen, I know it's taken me long enough to get round to it but ... well, will you have dinner with me ... erm ... next ... next Thursday evening?' He paused, chewed his moist lip and looked everywhere but at Helen. 'It's the only night we're not performing,' he quickly added, 'sorry.'

Both Marie-Laure and Adam grinned and applauded loudly. Paul, the performer, pulled a face and blushed at his audience and bowed his head. And as she listened and watched, Helen felt a rush of blood to her cheeks together with a rush of anger. Puppets; she and Paul Atkinson were puppets, pawns, being manipulated and ridiculed by people who should have known better. If she'd been in love with, or remotely attracted to the overly-shy musician, maybe she'd have felt differently, maybe she'd have been grateful for their concerned ministrations. But she wasn't the slightest bit interested in Paul Atkinson; she was in love with an unavailable man who'd caused his twin brother a lot of pain, for God's sake, but that was her secret and would stay that way. And as the three pairs of smiling eyes scrutinised her, Helen felt powerless to say no, to refuse Paul's invitation. How could she? She desperately wanted to say thanks but no thanks, but courtesy and other people's desires had to come before her own selfish ones. She'd learned that maxim at her mother's knee. Seconds, if not minutes, had gone by and although three pairs of eyes were still staring at her, the smiles had slipped away. Helen's mouth was dry and the words – right or wrong – wouldn't come. She wanted to say, 'No, I can't – won't – don't want to – have dinner with you next Thursday.' She wanted to ask, 'Adam, why are you so upset about Ben?' But she actually said, 'Yes, okay. Why not?' and the applause struck up again. She felt trapped, manoeuvred, lampooned, a pawn. She suddenly felt herself being swung high in the air over a deep, endless ravine on the Yorkshire Pennines. Powerless, trapped, at someone else's mercy. Afraid. But this time she wasn't afraid. The ravine was emotional, not physical, and she wasn't totally powerless. You've got no gumption, lass, that's your trouble ...

'But I'm really busy at the moment, Paul. We're working late at the salon every evening ... aren't we, Marie-Laure? And I'm ... well, I'm busy sprucing up my bedsit, trying to make it into a home. It's getting there, slowly but surely. So ... maybe just this once. Next Thursday.'

Her voice trailed away and an embarrassed silence hung over the table. Helen sensed she'd committed an unpardonable blunder and was furious that the whole, silly and unnecessary episode had grown so much out of proportion.

'That's okay,' Paul nodded his head and smiled rather sadly, otherwise the silence continued.

Adam stood up and handed out pistachio nuts with an air of, 'Well, I've done my bit', the frown forming around his eyes again. Helen had the feeling that if Ben's phone call had been a cheerful one, the entire silly scene would have taken place differently. She thought of Adam speaking to his brother somewhere in New York about something that was unpleasant, maybe to both of them. And she desperately wanted to know what that something was. And as her thoughts concentrated on Ben, she once again told herself that he'd probably forgotten all about her. He hadn't contacted her, tried to get in touch with her for a while. His life was another world away in more ways than one. She'd just been a woman he'd picked up on a train and whiled away a couple of days with. To kill time, perhaps, or to have good sex and plenty of it in his wife's absence. As an act of contrition, he'd helped to find her a home and paid a couple of month's rent – and, she had to admit, that was beginning to rankle. She should never have accepted. As far as Ben was probably concerned, it was the end of the sorry story. Helen had no right to, and she was foolish to wonder and worry about it now. But she did.

Adam's air of disquietude continued throughout the afternoon and, in spite of Paul's victory during the aperitif, his shyness in Helen's company showed no signs of diminishing. There were long and awkward gaps in the conversation that no one seemed mindful of or able to deal with effectively. Even Marie-Laure, usually the perfect hostess, seemed to have difficulty in keeping things on an even keel and her frequent glances of anxiety at her husband added to the general uneasy atmosphere.

During one of the interminable silences, Helen suddenly remembered her last phone conversation with Jill and eagerly announced to the table that she'd received an invitation to Yorkshire for the summer holiday.

'Will I be able to take a couple of weeks off in August?' she asked her hostess.

Marie-Laure was pouring the coffee and she and her husband exchanged a glance before she replied, 'The salon will be closed for the whole month of August, Helen. Parisians disappear from the capital then, they take their holiday for the whole month, so of course we have very few clients. Which means that we work like Trojans in July – so be prepared! But, you know, Helen, Adam and I have been making our holiday plans and we planned on inviting you to come away with us this summer. We have a chalet in the Alps, not a million miles away from Mont Blanc. We always spend Christmas there and this year we've decided to spend our summer holiday, too. The mountains are so beautiful in summer. And we'd like you to join us. To show you another corner of la belle France. And it'll be fun!'

Helen, sitting opposite Marie-Laure, gazed at her across the table. Adam plopped two sugar lumps into his coffee.

'The chalet actually belongs to my family,' he said, 'it's our vacation home. Ideal for skiing in winter, walking and relaxing in summer. Marie-Laure remembered how you used to love hiking in the Pennines and thought you'd really enjoy yourself in the mountains. There are some splendid walks ... as I'm sure you can imagine. We would love you to come with us this summer, Helen.'

Marie-Laure was smiling and nodding her beautiful head as her husband spoke.

'Please come, you'll love it. The scenery's out of this world, of course, and it's so peaceful ... after chaotic July in the salon you'll really appreciate that.' She laughed. 'Look, phone Jill and tell her you'll go to Yorkshire next summer ... or why not for Christmas? Honestly, Helen, you'll have a wonderful time in the Alps. Adam and I will make sure of that.'

The surprising invitation was more than tempting. Helen, who loved the hills, dales and the wild Pennines, had idyllic visions of snow-capped mountain peaks, pine forests, wooden chalets adorned with blood-red geraniums, cascading waterfalls ... The invitation was too good to turn down and she may not get a second chance. Yes, she'd phone Jill and ask if she go for Christmas instead ... and then she felt the heat rise in her cheeks. God, she was so *stupid*. How could she even consider going to the Beaulac family chalet? It was impossible for so many reasons and even more impossible to explain why.

'So, is it all settled then?' Adam grinned at her.

Helen cursed her burning cheeks, took hold of her coffee cup and stroked it, concentrating on her moving fingers.

'Can I think about it, Adam? It's a bit ... well ... unexpected. And, quite honestly, I don't like to let Jill down. She'll be really disappointed ...'

'And we'll be disappointed if you don't come to the Alps,' Marie-Laure interrupted. 'We thought you'd be pleased ... an opportunity to visit a lovely region of France, meet new people, lots of lovely walking ... and, of course, it won't cost you a centime. Only your spending money.'

For a while there was silence and Helen continued to stroke her now empty coffee cup. She was sorely tempted, it sounded wonderful, a place she'd always wanted to visit. If only she could be sure that ...

'Would there be just the three of us there? At the chalet in August?'

Her seemingly innocent question went unanswered for a while. Finally, Marie-Laure confirmed that there would be just the three of them, with lots of callers from the village; everyone was friendly, not to mention inquisitive.

'Unless you'd like your admirer to join us and make us an equal number?' Adam grinned and transferred his mischievous eyes from Helen to Paul. Helen physically jumped and the subsiding heat in her cheeks came back with a vengeance. She glanced at her admirer and he obviously hadn't taken the suggestion at all well; embarrassment was written all over him but there was something else there, too, something that Helen couldn't put her finger on. She suddenly began to feel sympathetic towards him and wondered why Adam took so much pleasure in making the young Englishman uncomfortable. It took a long time for Paul to reply and he looked at no one in particular when he said, 'That would be really great. Thanks a lot. But I ... I can't promise. I'm ... erm ... I'm supposed to be going to Antibes this summer with Serge, you know.'

Adam looked genuinely surprised.

'No, I didn't know. Well, you're a pair of dark horses.'

'We only talked about it a couple of weeks ago. It's all a bit up in the air. Nothing definite, yet. We'll see.'

Helen's thoughts were in a turmoil. Was this another silly and unforgivable ruse on the parts of Marie-Laure and Adam? Another move on the Beaulac chessboard, another means of making them feel inadequate and beholden? When she'd asked if there would be just the three of them, her apprehensive thoughts had been with Ben, but now they quickly shifted to Paul Atkinson.

'Paul spent three weeks at the chalet last spring,' Adam told Helen and she politely turned her attention to him. 'He had a great time, didn't you, mon petit Anglais?' He winked at the distinctly uncomfortable, obviously wretched, petit Anglais. 'That is until he did his famous disappearing act and confused everybody.'

Paul didn't attempt to give a rejoinder to this remark. He simply seemed to withdraw into himself and his eyes focused on nobody and nothing. They were vacant and the only part of him that moved was his fingers, which were screwing up the edge of the tablecloth. After yet another long silence, Marie-Laure was the first to speak and she told Paul that he'd be very welcome to join them if the holiday in Antibes fell through.

'And this time,' she winked at him, 'maybe you'll have a good reason to stay till the end of your holiday.'

Paul didn't reply.

It was the moment for Helen to withdraw her eager acceptance of the unexpected invitation. If Paul decided to accept, what nightmare would they be letting themselves in for? On the other hand, a chalet in the Alps near Mont Blanc; how could she refuse? Why should she deprive herself of what was probably the holiday of a lifetime? Why should she miss out on such an adventure because of this irksome and exasperating young bloke?

'And what about you, Helen?'

'I don't have to think about it, actually. I'd love to come.'

She felt Paul's eyes suddenly burning into her but didn't look at him. Marie-Laure stood up and her smile took in everyone.

'Now that's settled – more or less,' she added, 'shall we have a little sortie? A walk along the river, perhaps?'

'Look... erm ... if you don't mind, I'd like to get away now,' Paul said, hurriedly. 'I've got one or two things to do at home. It was a super meal as usual, Marie-Laure. Thanks a lot.' He looked at Helen. 'Well, I'll ... erm ... I'll see you on Thursday. Shall I come to your place or ...?'

Helen, aware that three pairs of eyes were scrutinising her, suggested they meet somewhere in Montparnasse; why not on the corner of Montparnasse and rue de Rennes? Paul's head was nodding and he was biting his lower lip as though making some great decision. Then he smiled, agreed and suggested eight o'clock.

After the door had closed behind him, Marie-Laure grinned at her remaining guest.

'Petit con! Now, let's go for a walk – and we can start making some holiday plans.'

***

'Hello, Helen. Thank you ... thank you for coming.'

'Hi, Paul. Sorry I'm a bit late. There was a problem in the metro – just by way of a change!'

They both smiled but avoided each other's eyes. Paul cleared his throat.

'Don't worry about it; you're here, that's all that matters. Shall we try this crêperie on the corner here? Do you like pancakes?'

'Love them!'

As soon as they walked through the door a waiter bustled towards them and showed them to a table for two in the middle of the busy little restaurant. The tables were made of dark wood and boasted jars of small flowers, red and white checked napkins and little ceramic pots instead of glasses for cider. The walls were filled with sepia photographs of old Brittany, its fishing villages, its countryside and Bretons in traditional dress.

'This is lovely,' Helen smiled, looking around as she sat down.

'Did you know that when a lot of Bretons came to Paris looking for work, they ... they settled here in Montparnasse? That's why there are so many crêperies here, the traditional Breton dish. That's why you're spoilt for choice. But this one's my favourite. Okay, let's start with a "galette", shall we? A savoury pancake with whatever filling you like, and then we'll have a sweet one for dessert. They're all delicious here, by the way. And I hope you like cider ... it's compulsory to drink cider with crêpes!'

Helen stared at her companion over her large menu. It was the longest speech she'd heard him make, without either stammering or blushing. He'd even more or less chosen her dinner for her and she felt slightly irritated.

'I do like cider, a lot,' she told Paul, 'but is it really compulsory to drink it with crêpes? I'm very thirsty and ... well, actually, I'd like a glass of water.'

Paul gave her a lopsided smile.

'I'll let you into a little secret, Helen,' he said, 'You can actually have both.'

Helen then reprimanded herself for being churlish and unfair. The poor bloke couldn't win. His appalling shyness drove her to distraction but when he showed some kind of authority it ruffled her feathers. She grinned at him.

'Thank you, kind sir. And as you're obviously the expert in Breton cuisine, you'd better order for me; I love pancakes – like my mam used to make on Shrove Tuesday when I was a kid – but I've never been to a real Breton crêperie before.'

Paul gave her a mock bow, beckoned the busy waiter and ordered two 'galettes' with smoked salmon and cream and a bottle of dry cider.

'Oh, and a large carafe of water, too,' he added and winked ... He actually *winked* at her. She stared at him, unable to identify this seemingly self-assured young man with the self-labelled twerp she'd come to know.

'So, tell me what you did before working for Marie-Laure. Have you always been a beautician?'

'Not always,' Helen smiled. 'In fact, it's my first job in ... no, I tell a lie. It's my second job in a beauty salon.'

'The first must have been *really* inspiring if you've forgotten about it.'

'Oh, it was inspiring all right,' Helen laughed and told him about her brief but unforgettable period working for Chantal Gauthier.

'Well, if I ever decide to have my chest waxed, I'll give that place a miss,' Paul said. 'How the hell did the woman manage to stay in business? But I'm intrigued … you must have thought about flying back to England on wings of speed while all that was going on?'

'No, actually, it never entered my head to go back to England. It would have been too defeatist. Anyway, I've got nothing to go back to.'

'But did you have anything to stay in Paris for? Friends … family …?'

Helen shook her head and smiled, rather wistfully.

'No family, no friends. All I had was my new bedsit.'

'Well, congratulations, Helen.'

'Congratulations?' she blinked at him. 'What for?'

The waiter came and carefully placed two plates in front of them and dextrously organised the huge, cold bottle of cider and plain carafe of water. He wished them 'Bon appetit' and waltzed away.

'Because I think most women in your circumstances would have given up and gone home,' Paul continued. 'Even if you have no family in Yorkshire, it's still your home … your roots. But you decided to stay and stick it out. Bravo. Congratulations.'

Helen felt a sudden rush of blood to her cheeks. She poured water into two glasses and took a long drink.

'Well. Thank you. And what about you, Paul? What did you do before you met Adam?'

'I was a penniless busker when I first came to France.'

And Paul told Helen about his earlier life in Calais and Paris and the circumstances that led to his membership of the Adam Beaulac Quartet. Helen was enchanted and she also marvelled that a bloke who'd done all that, who'd lived such an unusual and precarious lifestyle, could still be so painfully shy with women. Except this evening, apparently. He didn't seem to be at all shy with her this evening. It was strange; he was behaving like a completely different man. They went on to talk about other things. Films; they didn't have the same taste at all. Paul enthused about American action films, the more violent the better, and the subject didn't last long. They talked about books, art and of course music and, needless to say, Ben Beaulac's name came up so Helen made sure that subject didn't last long, either. They talked about travel and Paul asked Helen if she was looking forward to her holiday in the Alps. She cautiously told him that she was and even more cautiously asked him if he thought he'd be going there, too. For the first time that evening, Paul blushed and looked ill at ease. After a while, he moved his head in such a way that it could have been either a shake or a nod.

'I'd like to accept Adam's invitation,' he murmured, 'but ... well, I just don't think it would be a very good idea. Anyway, I'm supposed to be going to Antibes with Serge.'

'I've never been to the south of France,' Helen told him, hoping to divert the conversation to safer ground.

'You don't know what you've missed,' Paul told her.

Helen had to admit that she'd enjoyed Paul's company; he was attentive, polite and even entertaining. But by eleven o'clock she was very tired and ready to go home. She'd had a busy day. Nathalie had phoned in ill, so she'd helped out at the reception desk as well as in the salons. She'd spent a happy but exhausting day and now she just wanted her bed.

'Let's have a saunter up the boulevard,' Paul suggested, eagerly, taking her arm as they left the restaurant.

'Well, actually, I'm really tired, Paul,' Helen smiled weakly at him. 'I'd like to go home now.'

She could see the disappointment on his face and his hand slipped away from her arm.

'I'll come with you ... on the metro. I'm not allowing you to go home alone on the metro at this time.'

'It's not *that* late,' Helen tried to smile, 'and anyway, I'm used to it. Don't worry about me.'

'But I will worry. I'm taking you home.'

Helen, surprised by his sudden firmness, his almost aggression, resisted no more but mentally practised an assertive speech of her own once they arrived at her door. The carriage was crowded and they had to stand apart from each other and Helen avoided catching Paul's eye. After leaving the metro station, they walked in silence and without touching, through the few quiet streets to Helen's building. There they stopped and stood facing each other, wordlessly. Helen finally forced a smile and said,

'Thanks for a lovely evening, Paul. And for ... for seeing me home. Okay then ... goodnight.'

Paul didn't reply. He only stood gazing at her and then she saw his eyes glance at the entry-code box on the wall. The saliva crept into Helen's mouth and she forced back panic. He was going to be difficult.

'Can I ... erm ... Helen, do you mind if ...?'

Helen studied the strange mixture of male in front of her, alternating between the blathering, impotent youth and predictable macho man. The 'cute' saxophonist was turning out to be rather an enigma, a human conundrum, and Helen's feelings alternated between surprise, anger and apprehension.

'No, Paul, I've told you, I'm really tired. Not tonight.'

Not ever, Paul.

'I'll just see you safely into the building, Helen. I promise I don't want ... in fact, look, there's something I'd like to explain to you, to talk to you about. Maybe ask your advice ... and ... and ...'

Helen hardly heard his stammering as her fingers flitted, as adeptly as any pianist's, across the entry-code number. There was a sharp click and the heavy wooden door opened. Paul's eyes blinked and Helen moved. She muttered another 'Goodnight' and, pushing the door a fraction, slipped into the hall and slammed the door behind her. The image of Paul's stricken face stayed with her for a long time, although his final words hadn't registered with her at all.

Chapter Fifteen

Maryse Chopart shuffled across the spacious room and nodded to the saxophonist as she placed his coffee in front of him. The cymbal/lightshade swayed and dust spun in the warm June air as her ample figure straightened and stretched. Paul offered a quiet 'Merci' but continued to study the sheets of music in front of him. It was a new piece by an up-and-coming French composer and difficult to master. Paul Atkinson, however, was determined to master it. Maryse, her lonely lady's hope of brief conversation dashed, gave a loud 'Humph' and made her way back to the office. Paul's eyes didn't leave the black notes on the white paper as he picked up the cracked coffee cup and sipped. The door was already open because of the heat so he didn't hear the drummer enter a few minutes later, and pad across the floor. He jumped out of his skin when Serge's hand struck the cymbal. The merry south-of-France face burst into a myriad of tiny lines and his laughter echoed around the room.

'Un petit café?' an almost feminine voice called from the office.

'Bien sûr, ma puce!'

Paul's sheets of music had scattered across the floor and he was still cursing as Serge obligingly picked them up and slapped them on the table. They discussed and dissected the new and elaborate musical arrangement for several minutes while finishing their drinks and then Serge brought up a subject they'd purposely met to talk about.

'Okay, I've had confirmation this morning, the apartment in Antibes is ours for the whole of August. I phoned my cousin Mathieu and he's going to organise a boat; we'll be able to hire one without going totally bankrupt. It'll be at our disposal every day for the whole month.'

Serge paused.

'Well, you could at least try to show some enthusiasm, mon ami.'

Paul fiddled with his sheets of music and finally placed them on the coffee table, his eyes avoiding those of his 'ami'. There followed a few moments' silence when only Maryse's heavy movements in the office could be heard.

'What's up?' Serge finally asked. 'You're not having second thoughts, are you?'

Paul quickly glanced at the other man and wiped his June-moist hands up and down his thighs. He cleared his throat.

'It's all arranged, isn't it? The deposit's paid, I suppose?'

'Of course. We're lucky to find somewhere this late in the year. Okay, what's up?'

'Nothing's up, Serge. Except Adam's invited me to the chalet. You remember I went there alone last year. Great place. And ... you ... erm ... you remember Jacqueline ... don't you? Yeah, of course you do. I shouldn't have told anybody, least of all you, you old bastard.' He grinned, briefly. 'Anyway, let's just say Adam's offer was tempting.'

Serge's normal merry face was far from merry. The only time Paul had seen that expression before had been in the not-so-distant past during an altercation with a too-demanding club owner. He'd heard a lot about Serge's temper and certainly didn't want to be on the receiving end.

'Why didn't you mention this before?' Serge's voice was already several octaves higher than normal. 'We've had this holiday planned for weeks. You knew I was going to contact Mathieu last week and that there shouldn't be any problems. So ...' His practised hand bashed the cymbal and more dust floated around the stuffy room. 'Well ... let me know what you intend to do ... very soon. So that I can make other arrangements. But let me tell you, petit con, this is the last time I'll ever do anything other than work with you.'

He shoved his empty coffee cup so that it shot across the table; scraped his chair on the floor, stood up and paced around the room, his tanned hands thrust into his jean pockets. The expression on his face was one that Paul had hoped never to witness again. But he had to admit, he deserved Serge's Mediterranean wrath.

'Look, I'm not seriously thinking about accepting Adam's invitation. To be honest, I'm not even sure if *he* was serious; he just sort of mentioned me tagging along to make up a foursome ... nothing concrete.'

His voice trailed away. Serge was standing at the open door, his dark eyes gazing on the busy, late spring street, his hands still stubbornly, aggressively jabbed into his pockets. He slowly turned to face his temporary adversary, the deep lines of anger suddenly relaxing into curiosity.

'Make up a foursome?'

Paul picked up the music sheets, put them down again, picked up his saxophone that was lying on the floor beside him, lay it down again and his eyes avoided those of the drummer. He didn't want others to know about his abortive attempts at a relationship with Marie-Laure's friend, although he was convinced that somehow Serge and Philippe would have an inkling of what had already taken place. His crippling timidity with women and resulting disastrous affairs were a disagreeable and well-known fact and the others enjoyed ribbing him in a gentle, older brother kind of way. Until quite recently, he'd accepted it. The women he'd met and made a mess of things with had been anonymous and his feelings often fleeting and superficial. So, his lack of confidence and courage and the subsequent teasing he received were of no consequence; it didn't matter. Things had inevitably started to change the previous year, but he put all thoughts of Jacqueline and the memories she evoked to the back of his mind. She hadn't been anonymous and neither was Helen Hartnell; she was an employee and friend of Adam's wife, and his interest had at first been kindled by her apparent indifference. Over their meal at the crêperie, getting to know her a bit better, he knew that he could relax with and talk to her, that she was a good listener ... Not many people had been given that gift and that's what he needed right now, a damn good listener. Not a quick thrash around a bed as she'd obviously thought he needed, or rather wanted, but someone to talk to, to confide in, who'd listen to and advise him. Okay, so he'd been physically attracted to Helen; she had a lovely face and an okay body but ... well, she was quite a bit older than him, even if she didn't look it and ... well, Jacqueline's name had suddenly come up out of the blue and although Paul had buried, or at least tried to bury, his feelings for the girl, they were still there just under the surface, waiting to see the light of day again. And he desperately needed to talk about them – his feelings, and about her – he desperately needed to talk about Jacqueline.

'Yeah, Adam and Marie-Laure, her friend ... what's-her-name – Helen Hartnell and me.'

Serge's already modified expression now relaxed into a comprehending grin. He slowly took his hands out of his back pockets and moved towards the centre of the room and his no-longer adversary.

'Aha! Mon petit Anglais ... now I understand. It's another "histoire d'amour" and mon petit Anglais is willing to give up a summer on the Côte d'Azur (with a boat thrown in) and as many beautiful women as he wants, for summer in a chalet in the mountains and an English mademoiselle thrown in. Well ...'

Serge now stood over him, his arms folded, his expression only slightly amused.

'Well, you'd better let me know very soon so I can make alternative arrangements. There are plenty of others who'd give their eye teeth for a reasonably cheap holiday in Antibes ... with a boat thrown in. So, let me know.'

'I'm coming to Antibes with you, Serge. Of course I am. I wouldn't play that lousy trick on you ... you know me better than that. Anyway, like I said,

I'm not even sure if Adam's invitation was serious, he just kind of mentioned it, threw it into the conversation.'

Paul was gabbling and Serge cut dead his almost inarticulate excuses.

'Well, just in case Adam's invitation was serious, you think carefully about it, mon petit Anglais, and while you're thinking, remember that the petite Anglaise won't be in Antibes, she'll be in the Alps. And if you prefer to be where she is, there are plenty of others who'd prefer to be on the Côte d'Azur. With a boat thrown in.'

He whacked the cymbal with a clenched fist.

'Think about it. And let me know.'

He walked away from the table and headed towards a door behind and to the left of Paul's chair. Maryse had remembered to book the ground floor rehearsal room for them that day.

***

Paul's small flat in the north of Paris, tastefully furnished by his landlord, was cold and draughty in winter thanks to faulty glazing and an ancient heating system, and was totally airless in summer. He'd moved into the place three years before, settling for the first thing that came along; anything was better than third-class Parisian hotels. For the first twelve months he'd been reasonably happy; in comparison with his former domestic arrangements, the flat was a haven. And he spent so little time there he wasn't so demanding in his requirements. Over the years, though, the flat's faults and defects had become more evident, and as Paul grew older his needs began to change. He no longer felt settled in the tastefully furnished but less than comfortable flat; it was time to look for something else. Bigger, brighter certainly, and in a more salubrious district.

He walked into the living room and opened the window to let at least a little air into the stultifying room. He crossed the cracked, tiled floor and went into the kitchenette, pulled open the fridge door and peered inside. It badly needed de-frosting. Apart from polyunsaturated margarine, two eggs and a mouldy piece of brie, there were only cans of beer on the shelves. Paul took one out, pulled its metal ring and licked the foam that spilled over his fingers. He took a long gulp of the ice-cold liquid, finished the can while standing in front of the fridge and then took out a second one. He kicked the door shut, walked back into the living area and lay down on the red and black checked sofa. He propped his head on a threadbare cushion and his eyes trailed to a solitary, unevenly-hung picture above the fireplace. He was proud of that photograph. The background of the Mont Blanc range was magnificent against the flawless blue sky, and in the foreground the geranium-filled balcony formed a colourful frame. In spite of his lack of expertise and thanks to his new, expensive and efficient camera, Paul had taken a superb photo and was more than proud of it. He drank the second can of beer more slowly, his eyes riveted on the Mont Blanc range.

***

The loneliness of the chalet had got to him in the end. At first, he'd been happy there, needing the solitude and the calm to counteract the stress that had been building up over the past few months. The stress of playing every evening to enthusiastic but demanding audiences, lack of sleep, a bad diet, too much alcohol, too many cigarettes. A distinct lack of affection in his life. When Adam had offered him a month at the chalet (he and Marie-Laure had been spending time with Ben and Kim in the States), he'd jumped at the opportunity. A chalet in the mountains, far away from any major city, time to relax, to think, to know a different and stunning region of France. At first, the holiday had lived up to all his expectations. He revelled in the seclusion, slept a lot, walked a lot, thought a lot. If he'd only slept and walked maybe his holiday would have continued to satisfy him, but unfortunately the thinking took over. And his thoughts took on negative, unpleasant turns and caused some sleepless nights – and another excess of cigarettes and alcohol. He continued to appreciate the scenery – the view from the balcony of his bedroom was particularly breathtaking – but it wasn't enough. He'd been told about the neighbours, their friendliness that could sometimes be taken for nosiness, and at first he turned away from all overtures of affability. When the village residents stopped in their tracks to speak to him, he merely nodded, muttered a brief 'Bonjour' and continued on his way. Indifferent to the impression he was giving. After a few days the neighbours accepted his curt greeting and replied in kind and Paul realised that he'd probably got a name for himself and that it would no doubt get back to Adam. But he didn't really care. He hadn't gone to the chalet to make superficial friends, he'd gone to rest, think and sort out his young life. And then, one morning at the end of his first week, a loud rap on the front door woke him up, followed by a loud and merry, 'Bonjour, monsieur, c'est Bénédicte!'

Paul had been told about Bénédicte in particular and, although he would have liked to turn over between the sheets and ignore the unwelcome, early morning summons, his curiosity got the better of him. He yawned, cursed – both loudly – and slumped downstairs. He cautiously opened the door to the eccentric, elderly ex-nun, wearing only a towel wrapped around his waist and, as he'd expected, she didn't bat an eyelid. His was the mouth that dropped open.

Bénédicte stood in front of him wearing a pair of fashionable white leggings that stopped just below her otherwise naked knees. Bright yellow and white trainers graced her tiny feet and a pink broderie anglaise blouse with short puffed sleeves almost completed the ensemble. Almost but not quite. Because on her head of freshly-washed, short white hair, a red and white checked tea-towel was held firmly down with four brightly coloured clothes pegs.

'Bonjour, monsieur,' the old lady peered up at him through her thick lenses. 'I'm very happy to meet you. Yesterday, I baked a brioche ... I'd like you to have some for your breakfast.'

She thrust an aluminium-covered dish into his unprepared hands and before Paul could drag his eyes away from her rather unusual headgear, the old lady had skipped away down the steep and stony path. Before she headed back to her own chalet, a few metres up the mountain, she turned round, grinned and waved furiously.

The unexpected early morning visit put a spark of joy into Paul's up to then desultory state of mind. He ate with relish several slices of the delicious brioche, plastered with butter and cherry jam and washed down with several cups of strong black coffee. After his fortifying breakfast, he watered the many Alpine plants that occupied the wide, wooden balcony and then set off on his daily hike, heading down the mountain to the nearest village where he bought a newspaper and treated himself to a beer in the local bar. Later, he slowly climbed back up the mountain, passing the few and far between chalets until he reached a plateau where he sank on to a grassy mound and watched hang-gliders colourfully soaring into the sapphire skies. It was a breathtaking sight and he wondered if he'd ever have the courage to have a go himself ... He very much doubted it. It was late afternoon by the time he reluctantly dragged himself away. The descent was easier and more pleasant and as he approached his temporary home, he began to look forward to a quick dinner and a couple of cans of thirst-quenching beer while watching the sun set over Mont Blanc ... an unforgettable sight he'd quickly come to appreciate ... and a reasonably early night. The mountain air had well and truly knocked him out.

Bénédicte was in her garden when Paul approached her chalet on his way home, watering some thirsty plants. The leggings, pink top and yellow trainers were still in evidence but the tea-towel had disappeared and her short hair shone silver in the setting sun. Paul would have given anything to be invisible but the ex-nun seemed to have eyes in the back of her head ...

either that or particularly well-functioning aural organs that compensated for her short-sightedness.

'Bonsoir, monsieur!'

Paul slowed his heavy steps and grinned at the old lady. Her presence was something you couldn't ignore and was, in a strange way, a comfort and a delight.

'Thanks for the brioche. It was delicious.'

'I'm glad you enjoyed it. If you're still here next week I'll make another one. Will you still be here next week, monsieur?'

'Oh yes,' Paul nodded, still grinning. 'I will. I'll be here another couple of weeks and then I'll be back to the stress and strain of Paris.'

'Ah, Paris! The big city. I cannot imagine what Paris must be like.'

'You mean you've never been there, Bénédicte?'

The idea that any French person had never visited the capital was inconceivable to him.

'Never! And I never shall, monsieur! Chamonix is my idea of hell – too stressful.'

Paul laughed. Well, if she thought Chamonix was stressful, she did right to keep away from Paris.

'You're absolutely right.' He smiled at her. 'You live in the best place.'

'Don't I?' The old lady suddenly bent and picked a handful of small purple and yellow asters out of a basket that she'd just filled. 'Voilà, monsieur! Put those in a vase on your table and think of me while you're having dinner this evening. And maybe tomorrow evening you'll come and have dinner with me?'

Paul accepted the posy rather awkwardly; he'd never been given flowers by a lady before. And he'd never been able to pluck up enough courage to offer flowers to a lady, either, although many were the times he'd wanted to. He was also highly amused by the gift and nonplussed by the invitation. He opened his mouth to reply but nothing came out. He merely stared at his unconventional neighbour, foolishly clutching the flowers at his chest. In fact, they had been staring at each other for quite a while and the ex-nun was the first to break the awkward silence. Her steel-rimmed spectacles slipped down her shiny nose, she pushed them back up with an arthritic finger and squinted up at Paul.

'You have absolutely nothing to worry about, monsieur,' she assured him. 'You'll be perfectly safe with me. I'm still married to God in my heart.'

It took a moment for the words to sink in and when they did, Paul blushed violently and then he laughed with her. Adam and Marie-Laure had often spoken to him about their outlandish and lovable neighbour but even their lengthy and amusing anecdotes hadn't prepared him for this. He knew that Adam and Marie-Laure loved Bénédicte dearly and now he understood why. He could easily love the old dear himself. He was about to thank her and accept the invitation when her long, bony forefinger stabbed him in the stomach and, gazing up at him, she continued, 'If you really don't trust me, monsieur, if you really are afraid to be alone with me, let me invite you to the village restaurant instead ...'

She then crumpled up and her delighted laughter seemed to echo around the mountain. She took off her glasses, carelessly wiped them on the pink broderie anglaise blouse and planted them firmly back on her nose.

'In fact, I think that's a better idea.' She suddenly grabbed Paul's arm and she spun him round, her finger now pointing in a southerly direction.

'It's called "La Grange" because it used to be a barn. Do you like fondue? You don't know fondue? You haven't visited the Haute Savoie until you've tasted fondue ... I'll take you there tomorrow evening. We'll take my car – it's getting old and, like me, it needs some exercise. I'll pick you up at seven-thirty. Goodnight, monsieur. Sleep well.'

Paul didn't move, he stood staring at his temporary neighbour. Bénédicte had turned her attention back to her garden but, realising she still had company, looked up at him again.

'Do ... do you have a car, Bénédicte? Do you drive?'

Bénédicte planted her hands on her fleshless hips, shook her head at him and once again her glasses slipped down her nose.

'If I could afford to employ a chauffeur, monsieur, I would ... A Sean Connery look-alike, preferably. But that isn't the case so I have to drive myself. And let me tell you, monsieur, the entire Alpine inhabitants run for their lives when they see me coming. Oh, that reminds me.'

Her look suddenly turned serious and she moved forward and looked up into his face as though searching for something there. The heavy gold cross that hung on a chain around her neck gleamed in the weak rays of the disappearing sun and Paul had a deep sense of foreboding. Goosebumps invaded his warm flesh, he shivered and waited apprehensively for the ex-nun to continue.

'Do you like motor racing?' she asked. 'Formula One? There's a race on television on Sunday afternoon if you'd like to come and watch it with me. I'll make sure there's some beer in the fridge.'

The excitement in her myopic eyes then died away as she continued to gaze at him and then she shrugged her thin shoulders, ridiculous in the pink, puffed sleeves.

'No, I don't suppose you want to spend your holiday indoors with an old crone watching television … of course not. You'll be off hiking up the mountain … but I can tell you something for nothing, monsieur – my afternoon will be a lot more exciting than yours! See you tomorrow evening.'

Her merry laughter echoed down the garden as she made her way to her chalet and Paul, delighted and rooted to the spot, watched her go.

***

Paul was physically exhausted after the day's excursion but his enchanting conversation with Bénédicte had mentally aroused him. After a long soak in the green and white-tiled bathroom, he made a simple meal of salami salad with great chunks of crusty bread thickly spread with butter, two cans of beer and a slice of brioche to finish. What a character. He smiled to himself in the fading light of the old-fashioned pine kitchen and realised he was looking forward to dinner at La Grange the following evening. So long as she didn't wear a tea-towel and clothes pegs on her head, he reckoned it should be okay.

After his meal and the strong coffee that followed, Paul didn't feel quite so sleepy. Instead of heading for the bedroom stairs he ambled into the living room and idly looked around him, not for the first time. But for the first time he seemed aware of family life, or rather a family's life at the chalet in the Alps. The lid of the old cottage piano that stood against the wall on his right was raised and music sheets stood open above the keyboard, as though the piano had been played only yesterday. He walked towards the instrument and peered at the music in the growing gloom; 'Clair de Lune'. He sat on the piano stool and his inexpert fingers titillated the keys and the tune would have been faintly recognisable to a generous audience. His eyes slowly moved from the keyboard to the display of photographs on top of the piano. A picture of Marie-Laure, beautiful, immaculate, rather disdainful. A picture of Adam seated at his Steinway in the Paris apartment. A photo of Ben and his wife, the lovely Kimberley. At least, Paul presumed it was Ben, maybe it was Adam and Kimberley? He moved away from the piano, walked across the room and turned on a lamp that stood on top of a well-filled wooden book-case. There were more photographs on either side of the lamp. A photo of Adam and Marie-Laure together in their skiing outfits surrounded by snow. And a photo of Ben, Kimberley and their two kids, obviously taken in New York. And on every picture, smiling, happy faces. Happy families. Something that Paul knew absolutely nothing about. He sat down on the small sofa and, after glancing again at the array of faces, he picked up a couple of magazines that had evidently been left there since whoever's last holiday. Women's magazines. He idly flicked through them but his thoughts were still with the smiling, contented faces around him and he thought of the lack of family pictures in his own home in Bath.

***

Paul's mother had died of cervical cancer when he was a small, timid boy of three. His father, a headmaster in a highly-disciplined boys' school in Bristol, was too professionally preoccupied to care for his son, and Paul was therefore put into the care of and brought up by his elderly and no-nonsense maternal grandparents. Affection and displays of emotion of any kind were severely frowned upon in the unhappy household. John Atkinson was determined that his son grow up in the same way that he expected his schoolboys to grow: strong, phlegmatic, independent. The grandparents, mourning the early death of their only daughter, felt too numb, too resentful to provide the love and affection little Paul needed so much. Wherever he turned for comfort, praise, simple affection, he was emotionally kicked in his milk teeth and he quickly developed a sense of his own unworthiness, becoming an emotional cripple at a very early age. Incapable of self-expression, incapable of self-love. When he later began to show an interest in music, the family was totally indifferent; when that interest began to develop and Paul made noises about making music his career, the family – especially his father – became hostile. His son was either going to be an academic or a business tycoon. Paul tried to reason with the man who was more a headmaster than a father and never a dad, but it didn't take him long to realise he was banging his head against a brick wall. He finally bought a cheap, second-hand saxophone, paid for cloak-and-dagger private lessons in an ex-professional's basement flat a couple of evenings a week and studied Law and Economics during the day. When he became competent on the instrument he loved, he plucked up enough courage to give a private, unsolicited performance to his family, expecting them to fall in rapture at his sandal-clad feet. Needless to say, his family did no such thing and, after only a little reflection, he discarded his studies and booked a one-way ticket on the ferry to Calais.

Yes, there had always been a distinct shortage of family photographs in the home he'd grown up in. His grandparents had never owned a camera, never felt the need of one, and all school photos of Paul had either been thrown into the back of some drawer or thrown away, he never knew which. And photos, as far as his regimental father was concerned, were

201

synonymous with sentiment and therefore forbidden. Paul couldn't ever remember seeing a wedding picture of his parents, or even one of himself as a baby. He suddenly wondered what he'd looked like as a baby, a child. He choked back the threatening tears. Happy families. He put the magazines back where he'd found them and his eyes travelled again over the Beaulac family. Good-looking, successful, happy people. A close, happy, affectionate family. And because of his upbringing and his inadequacies as a human being – as a man – he knew that he'd never have a family of his own. A feeling of great inertia suddenly swept over him and he stood up, stretched, switched off the lamp and made his lachrymose way upstairs.

There were four bedrooms in the chalet. The master bedroom, occupied by either Adam and Marie-Laure or Ben and Kimberley, was at the far end of the landing, with a spectacular view of Mont Blanc on the horizon. The three smaller bedrooms each contained two single beds; the small but adequate bathroom separated the two sets of bedrooms. Paul still didn't feel as though he could sleep and knew he was going to have a difficult night, aggravated by his recent negative thoughts of so-called home. Whenever he felt like this, and it was quite often, the only release for his emotions was the saxophone. He played and played until there was no breath and no emotion left. But his instrument was safely locked inside his flat in Paris. He shuffled into his room, the first at the top of the stairs, on the left. Still not sleepy, he threw himself on to the single bed, thumped the deep soft pillow and lay there in the glow of the bedside lamp, the shutters open, gazing into the blackness of the Alpine night. His thoughts travelled to his neighbour and he wondered if she was asleep yet, and if not, what she might be doing. Saying her prayers, probably … or maybe she was watching some exciting motor race on television. Paul's introspection drifted from the old lady he'd quickly developed an affection for to the lady who'd supposedly brought him up, looked after him. And lying there, sleeplessly, it suddenly occurred to him that he'd never been kissed goodnight. Neither his grandmother nor his father had either kissed him goodnight or tucked him in. And he began to irrationally wonder whether Bénédicte had ever been kissed goodnight, tucked into bed by loving, maternal hands … His eyes slowly began to close and they fell, not for the first time, on more photographs that stood on the dressing table under the open window. A picture of either Adam or Ben, he didn't know which, as teenagers; good-looking, virile young blokes, and next to it, a large family photograph. There was that word again. Paul shivered as a mountain breeze blew into and across the room and touched his nakedness. He thought about the one thin summer sheet on the bed. He stood up, walked towards the window and leaned over the low dressing table in an effort to close the shutters. And then, his eyes caught the display of photos again. He grinned to himself and shook his head, giving in. Was it Adam or Ben? Ben or Adam? He'd no idea. He hadn't known either of them as adolescents so he'd no way of telling. Today, maybe ... maybe he'd be able to distinguish one from the other when they were together. He knew Adam and all his idiosyncrasies pretty well. And then he looked at the family picture taken when the brothers were infants. And then he looked again. He picked up the silver framed photograph and it was a long time before he put it down again.

As he'd predicted, he suffered a sleepless night and not without cause.

***

The weather had changed when Paul opened his unrested eyes the following morning. When he opened the shutters, instead of bright sunshine bathing the mountaintops, great grey clouds hung low and a high wind was making the fir trees perform a strange, ominous dance. He could hear the various pots and jars rattling like musical bones on the balcony outside. A storm was obviously on the menu today and therefore a day spent indoors. Paul cursed having left his sax at home and wondered how he could spend a whole day inside someone else's home alone. His eyes and thoughts fell on the display of photos beneath the window and they lingered there for a while. And then he went downstairs to devour a hearty breakfast.

While he was drinking his second mug of coffee and finishing a second slice of Bénédicte's brioche, the idea of how to fill at least part of his day crept into Paul's mind. He tried to push it away. The thunder was crashing now around the mountains and lightning like he'd never seen before was creating a silver screen across the black skies. The rain fell in torrential sheets, slicing the tiny windows and Paul, momentarily distracted from creeping, undesirable thoughts, wondered if he ought to close the shutters. He also wondered if his neighbour might be afraid and then told himself that the old dear would be used to such weather ... She'd probably be worried about him. He had a quick shower, dressed in jeans and a white tee-shirt and went back into the bedroom to make his bed; or so he told himself. That operation was very quickly carried out, of course, the bed having only one single cotton sheet ... and then he was standing once more in front of the dressing table and the display of Beaulac faces. The three deep drawers of the dressing table bore no lock. Paul opened the first one.

It contained a fragrant sachet of potpourri and nothing else. The other two drawers didn't even boast potpourri; they were empty. Paul's disappointment was disproportional and he asked what exactly he'd been expecting. A clue, that's what. His eyes glanced at the old wooden wardrobe but he knew its contents by heart – the few clothes he'd brought with him and a couple of ski-ing outfits covered in cellophane. His underwear lay on a couple of the shelves inside the wardrobe. There was no other furniture; no other cupboards, drawers or shelves in his bedroom.

But there were three other bedrooms.

When Paul arrived at the chalet, Marie-Laure and Adam had already been there a week, resting, making the place comfortable for their guest and preparing their own holiday. Marie-Laure had given Paul the pleasant bedroom at the top of the stairs, telling him that apart from theirs, this room had the best view. One of the others was decorated in too feminine a style for him and the fourth room, the one next to his, was really only a boxroom and used for storing old furniture and bric-a-brac. There was a bed that had belonged to some ancient Beaulac aunt and would probably collapse if anyone lay on it. Bed linen and guest towels were also kept there so Marie-Laure and Kimberley went in from time to time, but Adam and Ben had just about forgotten its existence. When Amy and Jeremy had been tiny, they pretended the unused room was haunted and dared each other to open the door and go inside – imagining the ancient aunt's ghost to be lying on the bed, perhaps. So, there were really only three bedrooms in the chalet, she'd joked, and one haunted boxroom. Paul thought about that room now.

He pushed open the door with some difficulty and switched on the light – a single bare bulb hung low from the ceiling. The ancient aunt's iron bed stood on his left, cluttered with old teddy-bears, dolls and other no longer used toys. A Victorian wardrobe stood on his right, its ornate key very rusty and its mirror cracked and stained. And in front of him an enormous and ugly matching chest of drawers. Old paintings and knick-knacks lay on top and cardboard boxes stood in front of it. Paul stared at the piece of furniture for a while and then attempted the obstacle course across the room.

After a brief frisson of guilt, Paul opened the top drawer. It shot out almost too easily and contained nothing but drawer liners. The second one was as disappointingly empty as the first. There were three more to investigate. Paul, feeling an odd mixture of guilt, curiosity and excitement, inhaled deeply and his hands tugged at two wooden knobs. The third drawer came away with much less ease. Reams of paper and heavy legal documents greeted his gaze. He felt his heart begin to beat a little faster. He stood up, stretched and listened to another crash of thunder and wondered if the chalet was about to collapse around him. He had no right to open these drawers and ferret through these papers, these documents, no right at all, but he thought about the photographs in the room next door and his curiosity rose to almost fever pitch. His long fingers touched the ageing yellow sheets and loitered, and then he slowly closed the drawer.

The next one's contents was much the same as the first two and Paul didn't bother to look inside the fifth and last. But his fingers finally clutched the two knobs and pulled but the drawer didn't move. He tugged but nothing happened; it was obviously crammed. Paul's excitement increased and he slightly reprimanded himself for being foolish and a bit feminine. He continued to wrench and the drawer finally gave way, revealing old photograph albums tied with frayed ribbons. Paul let out a long sigh, pulled them out one by one and slowly carried them back to his room. He sat on the bed, placed the first album on his lap and turned the pages, feasting his curious eyes on the old black and white photos and dated captions beneath each one. It took a long time to study the many pages and when he came to the last album, he found a large, bulky and sealed envelope that had obviously been pushed to the bottom and back of the drawer. There was no writing on the buff-coloured paper, no clue as to its contents. Paul knew he was trespassing and what he was doing would probably be considered a petty crime, but he'd come this far and had been rewarded and knew he had to go on. His lithe fingers gently pulled open the sealed paper. Yet more pictures fell out and spilled across the floor. Paul's greedy eyes slowly travelled over the exhibition and he shivered and felt the gooseflesh on his skin. He could feel his heart thudding in his chest and he suddenly felt like a peeping Tom, a voyeur. The large envelope was still in his hand, not yet empty. He pulled out some smaller envelopes, the edges yellowing, each bearing the same name and address, the same stamp. He took a deep breath and slowly exhaled, his fingers fondling the envelopes, his eyes studying the writing, the address, the stamps. And then a loud hammering on the door downstairs brought him back to the present. He quickly scraped up the pictures, slipped them back into the envelope together with the unopened letters, tiptoed back into the boxroom and shoved everything, rather haphazardly, back into the drawer. He left the small, untidy room, quietly closing the door behind him. Like young Amy and Jeremy, he too now believed the boxroom could well be haunted.

'Cou-cou!'

Bénédicte's inimitable voice rang through the chalet. Paul took a deep breath and skipped downstairs. Bénédicte, wearing a supermarket plastic carrier bag on her head, a trench coat three sizes too large and a pair of green Wellington boots, stood in the kitchen, her face a picture of concern.

'Monsieur! I've been so worried about you. I said to myself the storms in

Paris and England are only splashes compared with this and I guessed you would be afraid. Especially when I saw the shutters hadn't been opened, monsieur, when I drove down to the village this morning.'

Paul smiled at the delightful apparition in front of him, his dishonourable but revealing activities upstairs temporarily forgotten.

'You drove down to the village in the storm, Bénédicte? Wasn't that a bit dangerous?'

Bénédicte rolled her short-sighted eyes heavenward, tut-tutted at the silly young Englishman and asked, more to the point, was *he* okay? He confirmed that he was but added that Alpine storms were definitely impressive.

'Today is nothing, monsieur. A mere trickle to a musical background. Speaking of music, do you play the piano?'

'No, the saxophone's my instrument, but unfortunately I left ...'

'Ah, the saxophone! My favourite instrument. You know, there's a first-class jazz club in Chamonix and the saxophonist was imported – if you know what I mean – from New Orleans. Have you ever been to New Orleans, monsieur? No? And you play the saxophone? How can you play the saxophone if you've never been to New Orleans? The first time I went there ...'

'You've been to New Orleans, Bénédicte?'

'Twice, monsieur. The first time I lived there and did community work in the French district for a year.'

'Ah! And the second time?'

'The second time was for fun, monsieur! An extended holiday and I spent every evening in the jazz clubs – chatting up the players. Or did they chat me up? I don't remember now; it was a long time ago. Did you say you left your saxophone in Paris?'

Paul, enchanted, grinned at the old lady and nodded his head.

'Pity. But maybe you and I could go to Chamonix one evening? We'd have to get there early to get a good seat ...' The ex-nun was peering up at him through misted lenses, of which she seemed to be totally oblivious. 'But we still have a date this evening, don't we? I hope you haven't forgotten, monsieur? La Grange! Fondue! I can't wait!'

She suddenly turned as if to leave and then looked back at him, still trying to focus through non-functioning spectacles.

'And of course, monsieur, this evening you will meet Jacqueline.'

She giggled and, adjusting the plastic bag so that not a hair was liable to get wet, she scuttled away down the slippery stone path.

'Who ... who's Jacqueline?' Paul called after her.

But Bénédicte seemed to have suddenly developed a hearing complaint. Paul watched her heading back up the mountain and, smiling to himself, he quietly closed the door. Whoever Jacqueline was, she couldn't be more endearing or entertaining than this old dear.

Chapter Sixteen

The vicious storm gradually grumbled away towards the end of the morning and early afternoon saw the sun peeping from behind not-quite-white clouds and over mountaintops. Paul didn't venture out of doors all day; nor did he venture back into the boxroom. If he hadn't replaced his disturbing discoveries as impeccably as possible, then he'd do it another day. For the time being he didn't feel able to set foot in that room again. He did, however, wander back into his own bedroom in the early afternoon, out of both curiosity and necessity and his avaricious eyes once more examined the array of photographs. He took advantage of his whereabouts to take a nap but woke up two hours later feeling far from refreshed. The sun burst through the window and cast strange shadows around the room and Paul lay for a long time looking at the low ceiling and thinking about the coming evening in the company of his neighbour.

She had known the Beaulac family for a very long time and Paul wondered how he could broach the subject with her, discreetly and without fear of any repercussions. Well, he'd feel his way through the evening, see how the land lay ... Bénédicte was definitely very open, friendly, easy to talk to. On the other hand, he was sure she wasn't the kind of woman given to gossip. Paul hated the word ... it was meant for old women who had no better things to do than poke their noses exactly where their indiscreet noses weren't wanted. And that's exactly what he'd be doing if he started quizzing the old girl. He rolled off the bed and headed straight for the door, averting his eyes from the dressing table under the window.

***

Bénédicte tooted the horn at the precise time they had agreed upon and Paul gave a cheery wave as he left the chalet and locked the door behind him. The warm, fresh mountain air greeted him as he scrunched down the path and towards the waiting Deux Chevaux. The old lady pushed the passenger door open and Paul grinned, more to himself than at her, as he slipped into the seat beside her.

She wore a straw hat with a large floppy brim and a pink ribbon that floated down her almost fleshless back. She had attached a tiny posy of mountain flowers in the band. A pink and white gingham dress fell in feminine flounces over her knees, the short lacey sleeves barely covering the top of her skeletal arms.

'Bonsoir, monsieur; ça va?'

'Oui, ça va!' Paul grinned and was suddenly thrown back in his seat as the Deux Chevaux shot forward, screeched to a halt, shot backwards, veered precariously to the left and then hurtled over stone and rubble down the not quite perpendicular road. Paul silently thanked God for seat belts and ex-nuns like Bénédicte.

'You're looking very pretty this evening,' he hazarded, wondering if it was quite 'comme il faut' to pay compliments to an ex-wife of God, and surprising himself by the ease with which he'd paid her that compliment.

'You're very kind, monsieur. And I agree with you!'

The car suddenly came to another noisy halt and Bénédicte leaned out of her window to enquire about the health of a fellow-driver who was heading in the opposite direction. Paul's eyes avoided the sheer drop to his right and he surreptitiously gripped his seat. Bénédicte, satisfied that the driver was in tip-top condition, put the car none too gently into motion again and turned her attention to her passenger. Paul let go of his seat and wiped his moist hands on his thighs.

'I'm sorry, Bénédicte. What did you say?'

'Guess when I bought this dress?'

Paul at first thought he'd misheard but the ex-nun was looking at him over her spectacles, beaming and nodding furiously. Paul didn't want her to look anywhere but at the precipitous road ahead and said the first thing that came into his head.

'Yesterday. You bought it yesterday because you wanted to look beautiful for me this evening!'

As soon as he'd said the words, he wanted to bite off his tongue, leap over the sheer drop and never be seen again, and he cursed his reddening cheeks. But at least Bénédicte's eyes were back on the road and her laughter tinkled around the vehicle.

'Prince Charming! At last, I've met my Prince Charming – and I just *knew* he'd be an Englishman. Now, be serious, young man. When do you think I bought this dress?'

Paul, still blushing hotly but happy as a sandboy, said, 'I give in, Bénédicte. When did you buy the dress?'

'In 1955.'

Paul thought he'd misheard and asked her to repeat.

'In 1955.'·

No, he hadn't misheard. He said nothing in reply because he didn't have a clue what to say.

'I've had this dress for forty-three years, monsieur. And tonight, I'm wearing it for the first time. What do you think of that?'

Paul didn't know what to think.

'Well, I'm flattered, Bénédicte,' he said, and dared to ask her why she'd never worn the dress before.

'I was saving it for a special occasion, of course.'

Bénédicte laughed so much that the hat slipped off her grey head and fell on to the back seat.

'And here we are,' she went on, 'La Grange.'

The car jerked to a halt. The only exterior evidence of La Grange being a restaurant was the elaborate and colourfully rustic sign that hung over the door; otherwise, it could still have been an old barn.

A middle-aged, buxom and laughing lady greeted her two customers at the door and her manner with the old lady proved her intimacy with and affection for Bénédicte. She bustlingly escorted them through the large and noisy restaurant to a table next to what in winter was a huge open fire. That evening the fireplace was empty of flames but the mantelpiece was covered with well-filled vases, farmyard paraphernalia, ornate silver candlesticks and what looked like old family photographs. Paul's mind flew back to another display of family photos and he once more thought about interrogating the lovely lady sitting opposite him. He really hoped he'd have the opportunity to do that. Madame Laval chatted to her customers about nothing in particular for a while and as she was leaving their table, she said, 'I'll send Jacqueline over with the menus.'

Paul could have sworn that Bénédicte winked at him. He must have been mistaken. Nuns (ex or otherwise, he imagined) didn't wink and certainly not at young men. He tried to avoid her twinkling, short-sighted gaze although it wasn't easy without appearing rude. He concentrated on the disappearing, waddling figure of Madame Laval and then his eyes feasted on a decidedly un-waddling figure walking towards them. The white-aproned waitress, a young woman of about twenty-two, had dark brown hair that hung in a lustrous plait down her back and was tied with a thin white ribbon. As she approached the table by the fireplace, her full lips broke into a smile and her large brown eyes crinkled at the corners.

'Bonsoir, Bénédicte.'

The young waitress bent and kissed her customer on both cheeks and the old lady wrapped her thin arms around the long, shapely neck and returned the show of affection.

'Jacqueline, I'm so happy to see you again. How are you and how are ...?'

When Jacqueline had convinced Bénédicte that her parents, her aunts and uncles and two brothers were in good health and that her sister and new baby were coming along fine, and that she, Jacqueline, couldn't have been better, Bénédicte finally introduced the waitress to Paul. He stood up rather awkwardly, held out his hand and damned his burning cheeks. Jacqueline smiled up at him and he fell in love with her velvet, crinkly-at-the-corner eyes and fresh, Alpine complexion. Her hand was cool in his and her grasp quite firm. Bénédicte explained that Paul was an English friend of the Beaulacs and was holidaying in their chalet and Jacqueline asked after the entire Beaulac family.

'Are you a musician, too?' she asked Paul, who had sat down again because if he hadn't, he suspected he might have fallen down.

'Yes, I'm ... I'm the ... erm ... the saxophonist. In the band. In ... erm ... in the ... in the Adam Beaulac Quartet.'

Jacqueline sucked in her breath and blinked at him and Paul noticed the length of her eyelashes – free of mascara – and the curve of her dark brows.

'That's wonderful,' she breathed. 'And do you know Adam's brother? Have you ever met Ben?'

'Oh, yeah. Of course. Many times. In fact.'

'Oh, I love his music. He's my favourite composer. I love his theme tunes for films ... sometimes Bénédicte and I go to the cinema together ... in Chamonix ... don't we, Bénédicte?'

In reply, Bénédicte thumped the table, the cutlery bounced and she grinned up at the waitress.

'Do you remember that film we saw last Christmas, Jacqueline? It was a real tear-jerker, wasn't it? And wasn't the music just ... just divine?'

And then the ex-nun blushed and giggled and said she shouldn't really use words like divine to describe earthly music, even if Ben Beaulac had composed it, it was very naughty of her. But it was true. Jacqueline giggled too and said that God would forgive her because Ben Beaulac's music was so beautiful and Bénédicte touched the gold cross at her throat and smiled and said she hoped that Jacqueline was right ...

Paul's stomach was beginning to make noises. Apart from the delicious brioche he'd had for breakfast he'd eaten very little that day. But if his stomach was temporarily starved his ears and eyes were being well and truly nourished. His eyes suddenly wandered to Jacqueline's left hand and he was foolishly relieved to see the absence of a ring. In fact, no jewellery at all adorned the waitress's body. Her dress was simple; blue cotton with short sleeves and almost obliterated by the pristine apron. Her tanned legs were free of stockings and on her feet were comfortable, no-nonsense white plimsolls. Paul's eyes feasted on the young woman who needed no ornament and his musician's ears rejoiced in her clear but soft and merry voice. And his stomach continued to rumble.

Eventually, Jacqueline tore herself away and wandered off to the kitchen, taking with her an order for two avocado salads and cheese fondue.

'Well, monsieur, what do you think?'

Bénédicte leaned across the table, her set of rather ill-fitting dentures beaming at her guest, her glasses slowly sliding to the end of her nose. Paul thought it was probably obvious what he thought and, anyway, the question was indiscreet and not very gracious. Maybe his own forthcoming interrogation would be acceptable after all.

'Don't you think she's beautiful? She is beautiful, isn't she? She's not married and it's unlikely she ever will be and it's such a shame ... Jacqueline was made for motherhood and ... and that kind of thing. The trouble with Jacqueline is ...'

At that moment the waitress re-appeared with the avocado and disappeared just as quickly. Bénédicte continued her eulogy and if Paul hadn't seen the woman with his own eyes, he'd have sworn that she was either inventing or exaggerating.

The meal was mouth-watering and the ambience at the table for two cheerful. Bénédicte never stopped delighting Paul with her forthrightness and sheer originality and he also welcomed every brief appearance that their waitress put in. After the delicious fondue and crème brulée dessert, Bénédicte ordered coffee and a digestif ('I can recommend the Poire William') and leaned back in her chair, replete. Across the now candle-lit table she watched the young Englishman surreptitiously gazing at the waitress, serving newcomers whom she evidently knew well.

'So, monsieur,' she said, none too quietly, 'when are you going to invite her out?'

'What?'

'Jacqueline. When are you going to invite her out? Don't you think it's completely ridiculous that a handsome young man like you spends his time alone in a chalet and a beautiful young woman like her lives alone in a small apartment over a butcher's shop? When are you going to invite her?'

'Invite her where, Bénédicte?'

Paul's embarrassment showed in the sudden flush of crimson in his cheeks and in his confusion, he knocked his cup of coffee off the table. Within seconds Jacqueline had arrived with a cloth and a sympathetic smile. She quickly disappeared and returned with a fresh cup of coffee and Paul mumbled his thanks, avoiding the waitress's eyes. Jacqueline, after another brief chat with Bénédicte, quickly scurried away. After a few moments silence a little voice piped up.

'And don't tell me you didn't do that on purpose.'

'What?'

'Full marks for trying but I'm not impressed.' Bénédicte leaned forward again and nearly knocked over her own cup and saucer. 'Would you like me to play Cupid, monsieur?'

'No! Thank you.'

Paul's voice was barely audible but firm. Bénédicte's spectacles were slowly descending to the tip of her nose yet again but she seemed totally oblivious. Paul, impotent as he was, didn't dare imagine how his unpredictable companion would play Cupid, and would refuse to let her even think about it. If he wasn't capable of performing his own dating rituals, nobody was going to do it for him. Not even a woman of God. The mischievous smile had slipped from Bénédicte's face and she was now gazing at him with an expression closely resembling those of the bovine occupants of the mountain meadows. Paul waited with bated breath.

'I'll be very careful, monsieur.'

Her voice was very low, accompanied by facial contortions.

'Pardon?'

'I'll be very careful. You know – diplomatic. She'll never suspect a thing.'

Bénédicte pulled down the skin under her right eye with a bony finger and winked.

'You can rely on me, monsieur.'

Paul's acute embarrassment, self-consciousness and sheer dread suddenly left him and he threw back his head and laughed, heartily. His unique companion was having the time of her life and, he had to admit, so was he. More so than he ever would with any beautiful, nubile young seductress. With Bénédicte he could relax – well, almost – and have fun. He didn't have to prove himself, he had nothing to fear. He could simply be himself.

And he suddenly realised what a sad reflection he'd just made.

Two things were unaccomplished that evening. Jacqueline, the lovely young waitress, didn't receive an invitation and Paul's planned interrogation on the Beaulac family didn't materialise. He slept fitfully that night. He woke up three times from strange, rather alarming dreams, the subject of which completely escaped him as soon as he was conscious. Although the following day was hot and sunny, he didn't venture very far. He got up late and, after a frugal breakfast, ambled down the mountain road to the village's only newsagent, taking a few photographs on the way. He was glad he'd splashed out on a decent camera before leaving Paris; the stunning scenery was certainly worth it. He'd already taken two rolls of films and was looking forward to seeing the results.

'Bonjour, jeune homme,' Claude Mercier greeted him as he entered the shop.

'Bonjour,' Paul grinned back and asked for his usual newspaper.

One or two local people were chatting in front of the counter and they drew Paul into their lively, bantering conversation which lasted a good half-hour. He spent the rest of the day reading, drinking too much strong coffee and trying to push all thoughts of a pretty young waitress and a revealing chest of drawers to the back of his mind.

When Bénédicte called that evening brandishing a bottle of Bordeaux and a bunch of flowers from her garden, he welcomed her with open arms. He was ready for entertaining company after a day of solitude. They sat on the balcony enjoying the red wine and they chatted about this and that and the subject eventually got round to their previous evening at La Grange and, of course, Jacqueline.

'She comes from Annecy but now lives in the village in a small flat over the butcher's shop. Have you met our butcher yet, by the way? No? Well, when you do, you be very careful what you say to him – unless you want all the Haute Savoie to know about it. Jacqueline's learned to be polite to him and no more ... "Bonjour, monsieur, how are you, monsieur? Please, thank you, monsieur. Au revoir, monsieur." That's all. And if he tries to ask her questions, she's learned to politely turn a deaf ear ... I remember once ... oh many years ago, I think he'd just opened his shop ... yes ... that's right ... I was at the front of a very long queue and somehow ... I can't imagine how ... he'd found out that I used to be a nun at the convent in Annecy. And, do you know, monsieur, as he was cutting my pork chop ... Or was it a lamb chop? I really don't remember. No, it was definitely a pork chop ... So, as he was serving me with my pork ... yes, my *pork* chop, he asked me why I'd left the convent. Can you imagine that, monsieur, in front of all those people? Of course, I didn't tell him because ... well, I didn't tell him. And since then, I've always been very, very careful ... and I advise everyone to do the same. I remember one day ...'

'Excuse me, Bénédicte,' Paul smiled at her, 'you were telling me about ... about Jacqueline.'

'Ah yes, so I was. Now, what on earth made me tell you about Monsieur Meylan? It must have been something you said ... So, where was I?'

'Jacqueline has a flat above the butcher's shop.'

'Yes, monsieur, she does. Now, how on earth did you know that? Anyway, the flat is very convenient for her but lonely. She sees her family in Annecy only once a month and there are very few young people in the village. It's so sad. And she's so beautiful, so very special.' The ex-nun paused. 'Don't you think she's beautiful, monsieur?'

Paul sipped his coffee and nodded; yes, he thought she was very beautiful.

'She nearly became a nun, you know. For a long time, she thought it was her calling – so she tells me. And then she had a change of heart, I don't know why. I often think she may as well be in a convent, the life she leads. Such a pity. Such a lovely girl.'

Paul said nothing and Bénédicte studied his face.

'And I sometimes have the feeling when I speak to you, monsieur, that you may as well spend your life in a monastery.'

Paul started and their eyes met across the short space between them. His cheeks burned and his moist, idle hands began to rub his thighs. Bénédicte's eyes twinkled at him and she pushed her recalcitrant, sliding spectacles back up her nose.

'You're a very handsome man, you know, and you're a pleasure to be with. You're pleasant, you're polite and you have a sense of humour. I imagine you have a lot to offer a young lady. Take my advice ... Don't live your life in a metaphorical monastery. It will be such a waste.'

They stared at each other and for a long time there was a silence that ended only when Bénédicte made a move to stand up and take her leave. Paul looked up at her and the previously unsaid words finally tumbled out.

'How well do you know the Beaulac family, Bénédicte?'

She slowly sat down again, her eyes glued to Paul's face.

'I think I know them very well; at least I've known them for a long time. Why do you ask, monsieur?'

Paul dislodged his eyes from her scrutiny.

'Did ... erm ... did you know the parents? I mean ... erm ... Adam and Ben's parents?'

'No, I didn't. Why do you ask?'

Paul took a deep breath.

'Well, there are some photos in my room ...'

The telephone chose that moment to ring, its loud bell resounding around the chalet. Lost in their own particular thoughts, they both jumped and Bénédicte laughed gaily.

'If that's my jealous inamorato, tell him I'm on my way home ... See you very soon, monsieur!'

With a wave of her thin, crêpey hand she disappeared down the steps and if Paul hadn't known better, he'd have sworn that the old girl had arranged for the phone to ring at that moment. She'd certainly been relieved to escape, that had been pretty obvious. He let out a few choice expletives as he marched to the phone.

'Allo?'

Paul took it for granted that the untimely call would be for a member of the Beaulac family but he was wrong.

'Bonsoir. Est-ce-que je suis bien chez la famille Beaulac?'

'Oui, monsieur. This is the Beaulac's chalet.'

Paul was about to add that the Beaulacs were absent when the caller asked if he was speaking to the young English gentleman. It was Claude Mercier, the newsagent, and he asked Paul if he'd missed anything since he got home. Paul frowned and foolishly looked around him.

'Missed anything? No, I don't think so.'

Apparently, he'd left his new, expensive camera on Mr Mercier's counter and although it had been spotted a while ago, he hadn't had time to call before now. He'd been run off his feet all day and suggested that one of his customers drop it off at the chalet the following morning. It would be no trouble to anyone who had transport ...

'Oh, that won't be necessary,' Paul said, not wanting to trust a complete stranger with his camera. 'I can walk down to the village tomorrow ...'

'Unless you were coming for anything special, that's not necessary. Don't worry,' he added, as though reading Paul's thoughts, 'your camera will be safe with any of my customers and I'll send you your newspaper, too. You can pay me the next time you need to come down here.'

Paul felt ashamed of himself. This was a small, friendly village not a large, anonymous capital city.

'Well, if you're sure it won't be any trouble ...'

'No trouble at all, monsieur. You'll have your camera back tomorrow morning. Have a good day.'

'You too, Monsieur Mercier. Thanks a lot.'

As he hung up, Paul's eyes fell on the assortment of family photographs arrayed on the piano. And he somehow knew that his anticipated, hopefully revealing heart-to-heart with the Beaulac's eccentric friend and neighbour was destined not to take place.

He slept a little better that night and woke up feeling refreshed the next morning. He got up at seven o'clock, had a brief and invigorating shower and opened his shutters to a bright, sunny day. He'd just finished his breakfast when he heard a vehicle pull up outside the chalet. That would probably be his camera coming home. How could he have left his camera on

216

a shop counter, for God's sake? Bloody twerp ... He ran upstairs, pulled on jeans and a clean tee-shirt and ran back down.

'Coming!' he called.

He pulled open the door and grinned into Jacqueline's pretty, smiling face.

She also wore jeans and a tee-shirt and her long dark hair hung loosely around her shoulders. She was free of makeup, her pink skin glowed healthily and Paul recognised the fragrance of vanilla.

'Ah. Jacqueline. Erm ... bonjour. Bonjour.'

'Bonjour, monsieur. You left your camera on the newsagent's counter yesterday and he asked me to drop it off for you ...'

Paul took the equipment out of her outstretched hands and smiled shyly back at her.

'Yes, he phoned me yesterday evening. I hadn't even noticed ... can you believe that? It's new, actually, I bought it just before I came here. I'm not an expert but I wanted to get some good pictures of the mountains and especially Mont Blanc ...'

He was babbling. He stopped. He looked at Jacqueline and she looked at him.

'Well, thanks. Thank you very much for bringing it back to me. That was ... very kind of you.'

'That's no problem,' Jacqueline continued to smile at him. 'I have a car and I'm not working until this evening so I had plenty of time. I have plenty of time. Today.'

Paul nodded in reply. Jacqueline still stood in front of him – *beautifully* – and they gazed at each other for several moments. Jacqueline finally turned away.

'Well, enjoy your day, monsieur, and ...'

She was heading down the path, out of the garden, out of his life.

'Jacqueline!'

She turned round. Paul's face was the same colour as the geraniums adorning the windowsills.

'Look ... erm ... I've just finished my breakfast. There's ... there's still some coffee in the pot. Would ... would you ... erm ... would you like some ... erm ... a cup of coffee?'

He was actually wringing his hands. Jacqueline hesitated. She frowned and then she smiled and walked back towards him.

'That will be nice,' she said, very quietly.

She followed him into the kitchen and he clumsily pulled out a chair for her to sit down. She smiled her thanks and placed her two hands on the table, looking around her. Her eyes fell on the quickly diminishing brioche.

'That looks like one of Bénédicte's delicious brioches,' she said, almost licking her lips. Paul turned from the half-empty coffee pot and grinned at her.

'It is,' he said. 'I'm hoping she'll give me the recipe before I go back to Paris.'

'Oh, I doubt that,' Jacqueline smiled. 'She can be very secretive about her cooking. She'll probably give you sixty- five brioches to take home with you, but not the recipe.'

'I must remember to buy another holdall in that case. Look, I'm sorry ... erm ... but there isn't as much coffee as I thought. I'll make another pot.'

'Oh, please don't bother,' Jacqueline smiled up at him and blushed. Paul was already blushing. Jacqueline stood up rather hastily and her chair fell over backwards and crashed to the floor. They both rushed to pick it up and almost collided.

'You see,' murmured Jacqueline, 'you're not the only clumsy one!'

'But your clumsiness is much more elegant than mine!'

'Oh, monsieur,' Jacqueline laughed.

'Paul.'

'What?'

'My name's Paul. Paul Atkinson. I'd ... like you to call me ... erm ... Paul.'

'All right. Paul.'

They were looking at each other and smiling, rather inanely.

'Look, I'll ... erm ... I'll make that coffee ...'

'No, Paul. Please don't bother. I've already had two cups this morning. I have ...' She stopped and blushed again and looked away from him. And then she moved away from him. Paul followed her.

'Yes? What do you have?'

'Oh no; it's nothing, really. I should go because ...'

'Please tell me, Jacqueline. What do you have?'

Apart from beautiful hair, perfect skin, gorgeous eyes and a charming smile.

'Well, I was going to say ... I have a better idea.'

Paul frowned. A better idea than what? He was still thinking about her hair, skin, eyes and smile.

'Tell me,' he urged, confused.

'Oh monsieur ... Paul. I was thinking that maybe we could perhaps have a picnic somewhere. I know some really lovely places and I have a car and I'm free all day.' She stopped prattling and blushed again. 'Oh, I'm sorry. I'm sure you're *not* free all day.'

Paul wanted to get hold of her, squeeze her tight and kiss those lovely, luscious pink lips. But, of course he didn't. He simply smiled.

'That's a *great* idea, Jacqueline. Of course I'm not busy; I'm on holiday and I'd love to have a picnic lunch with you. Shall we get some food from the village or make something here? And where are you going to take me?'

Jacqueline started to relax and she shrugged her shoulders.

'I thought we could go to a forest where there is a small lake and...'

'It sounds great. Shall I prepare something now?'

'*We'll* prepare something now. Do you have bread? Ham, cheese, salad, tomatoes, fruit? Apples will be good. Oh yes, and bottles of water.'

'Not wine?' Paul enquired, opening the fridge door.

'I'm driving,' Jacqueline grinned at him. 'But, of course, if you want to drink wine ...'

'No, but a couple of beers will go down very nicely in this heat. And water too, of course,' he added, with a sober look on his face. And Jacqueline laughed.

About an hour later, Jacqueline pointed out the distant, sparkling water as they drove through pine trees on a steep and stony track and the cacophony of birdsong.

'It's a lovely walk around this part of the lake,' Jacqueline said as they pulled their baskets and Tupperware boxes out of the boot. 'Perhaps we could do that now and come back later to have our picnic?'

'I'm following you!' Paul grinned at her, suddenly wallowing in the heat, the scenery surrounding him and the joy of his companion's company. He didn't actually follow her; they walked side by side and not quite touching, along the lakeshore and Jacqueline proved to be an excellent guide. Paul asked questions and passed comments and they quietly rejoiced in each other's company. After they'd been strolling on the uneven ground for about half an hour, Jacqueline stumbled over a large stone and Paul caught her arm and prevented a fall. She breathed in deeply, pushed her hair out of her eyes and avoided his gaze.

'Thank you,' she mumbled and Paul slowly released his grip.

'Okay?' he asked, frowning.

'Okay.' Jacqueline smiled.

And then they watched delightedly as a team of ducks suddenly flapped their wings, quacked in unison and left the water, soaring into the sky like as many small aircraft giving an aerobatic display. The lake glittered and rippled after their departure and a black swan appeared from nowhere and gazed at the onlookers disdainfully.

'I sometimes wonder if I'll ever want to go back to Paris,' Paul murmured, 'or any other big city.'

'Shall we go back to the car,' Jacqueline suggested after a few moments, 'and have lunch? I'm starving and we can walk around the other side of the lake after we've eaten. That's if you want to, of course.'

Oh, I want to, Paul said to himself, I certainly want to. And to Jacqueline he said, 'Race you back to the car. Last one there has to set the table.'

Paul was the first to arrive. When Jacqueline caught up, he was leaning against the car boot with his arms folded, grinning at her.

'If you'd left me your keys, I could have had everything ready by now,' he said.

'And here they are,' Jacqueline laughed, throwing the bunch of keys at him.

They sat on the water's edge while they ate their lunch and fed the ducks. They talked about Paul's life in Paris as a musician and Jacqueline's life in the Alps as a waitress. They asked each other questions, avoiding anything too personal, and they passed comments and made each other laugh. After their coffee, Paul stood up, gently pulled Jacqueline to her feet and they set off walking again, around the other side of the lake.

'How did you find this place?' Paul asked, taking his twentieth photograph. 'Have you been coming here a long time?'

'Since I was a baby,' Jacqueline smiled. 'My dad used to bring all the family here most weekends and sometimes we even camped. It was wonderful for us kids. We used to play all sorts of games in the forest – mum was scared to death sometimes – and dad used to go fishing on one of the boats. Mum was always quite happy sunbathing and reading, and in the evenings, she used to cook the most fantastic meals.'

Jacqueline suddenly stopped talking and Paul noticed the expression in her eyes.

'Do you miss your family, Jacqueline? I mean … I know they don't live on the other side of the world but if you don't see them often it could seem like that. Especially if you're really close.'

She turned and looked into Paul's face.

'I do miss them,' she said. 'I'm not unhappy living in the village and working at La Grange. Everyone's very kind and friendly.'

'But …' Paul prompted.

'But I'm not used to living alone and I don't think I ever will be. It probably sounds ridiculous to you. You left your country, your family, your friends, your language, everything. But my family is very important to me and … well, I'm not depressed, not at all, but I suppose I'm lonely. And when I say that I feel terribly guilty because I shouldn't feel lonely at all.'

'I have the impression there's a shortage of young people in the village.'

'Young people my age, yes. There are children and adolescents, of course, but most people my age have left and gone to Paris or Lyon to work … or another big city.'

Paul looked at her and kicked a stone as he walked. He stuffed his empty hands into his pockets and cleared his throat.

'And … erm … well, you don't fancy trying your chances in Paris?' he asked, looking away from her and into the distance. 'Or … another big city?'

'Oh no. I've never been to a big city. Well, of course I've been to a big city but I've never been to Paris. Well, not really … I could never imagine going to live there alone.'

'It's a hard city,' Paul agreed, 'especially when you're alone.'

Jacqueline stopped walking then and with her right hand pointed to the horizon.

'Look, Paul. Mont Blanc.'

Paul looked. In the distance, the Mont Blanc range stood in lilac glory under the sun's rays, the snow-capped peaks pink, and bright spots of yellow, red and orange hung bizarrely in the bright blue sky.

'Hang-gliders,' Jacqueline said. 'Have you been hang-gliding yet? No, I don't suppose you have. It's a really marvellous experience. I couldn't begin to describe it.'

She walked towards the water's edge and looked down at the variety of waterfowl that grumbled and chortled and paddled and fought and played on the lake.

'Another very good reason for not living in a big city,' she smiled up at Paul. He pulled a face, nodded slowly at her and inwardly sighed.

When they got back to the car Paul asked his companion if he could take a photo of her standing by the lake. She acquiesced and smiled into the camera and fooled around a bit and Paul took several different shots. Then Jacqueline offered to take a picture of him.

'I don't want you to break my camera!' he yelled.

The look that passed over Jacqueline's face was unfathomable and there was a short silence. Then she said, and very quietly, 'I won't break your camera, Paul. Actually … I'm quite adept at taking photos and I know …'

'Oh God, I … I didn't mean that,' Paul told her. 'I'm sorry, I didn't mean that at all. I … I meant to say I hope my ugly mug doesn't break my camera … not you … Actually, it's an English joke … probably a very bad English joke but …'

'Oh, I see.' Jacqueline smiled and her whole countenance changed. 'Well, in that case maybe I will break your camera. But I promise I'll try not to. Now, go over there and try not to fall into the water, please.'

'Don't worry, I can swim.'

'I'm sure you can but I don't want to ruin the photo. I don't want wet car seats, either. Off you go!'

On the way back to the chalet they laughed a lot and talked about the differences between British and French humour, British and French customs and, as they were driving up the mountain towards the chalet, British and French cooking. Suddenly, Paul knew he didn't want the day to end. He didn't want to suddenly find himself alone and no longer in Jacqueline's company. She stopped the car but didn't turn off the engine; if she didn't hurry home to get ready, she'd be late for work that evening. Paul knew he was going to have to drag himself away from her. He opened the passenger door and smiled at the driver.

'Thank you for a super day, Jacqueline. I've ... I've really enjoyed myself.'

'So have I, Paul,' Jacqueline almost whispered and blushed. 'It's been ... super. But I really must go now or I'll be very late.'

Paul racked his brains. He had to see her again; and the strange, unbelievable thing was that he thought she wanted to see him again. He thought she'd enjoyed being with him; that was the unbelievable impression she'd given him. He had to see her again, invite her, but where to? He didn't have a car. There was one restaurant in the village and she worked there, for God's sake. The nearest cinema was in Chamonix, a short drive away and he couldn't expect to use her car again. And offering to buy petrol sounded a bit crass. The only bar in the village belonged to the tobacconist, hardly a romantic rendezvous. Where could he invite her? A quick shin up Mont Blanc?

'Look, Jacqueline, I'd like to ... erm ... I'd really like to see you again. Soon. I was wondering whether you'd like to ... to have dinner with me? Here, at the chalet. I'll ... erm ... I'll cook for us. I'm no Cordon Bleu but if you bring a packet of indigestion pills you should be okay ...' He laughed and added that that was another sample of British humour. 'Would you like to have dinner with me, Jacqueline?'

'Yes,' Jacqueline replied and she, too, had to clear her throat. 'Yes, I would.'

Paul wanted to get out of the car and leap about and tell the world and then he remembered something.

'But you work in the evenings ...'

'Tomorrow is my evening off,' Jacqueline smiled at him.

'Oh? Ah. Excellent! Well then ... tomorrow. Seven o'clock. Is that ... okay with you?'

Jacqueline was nodding.

'That's perfect. Thank you. Can I bring anything?'

Only your beautiful self, Paul silently told her. Aloud he said, 'Only yourself. Oh, and maybe a packet of ...'

'Indigestion pills. I'll bring a good, reliable brand.'

Jacqueline laughed and suddenly leaned forward and kissed him on the cheek. They both blushed and Paul leaned forward and kissed her on the cheek and then, somehow, and neither of them knew quite how, they kissed each other – very, very lightly – on the lips.

'I really have to go now,' Jacqueline told Paul, still blushing.

'See you tomorrow. Seven o'clock. And don't be late,' Paul told Jacqueline, still blushing.

And then they both laughed and Paul bumped his head getting out of the car and Jacqueline looked sympathetic and Paul pulled a silly face and slammed the car door. He watched her drive down the mountain road and she waved as the car disappeared round the bend. And they both knew that they were very quickly but surely falling in love.

***

Paul spent the rest of the day tidying and untidying the chalet, rehearsing clever and witty chat up lines and planning a menu. It would have to be simple. Very simple. But adequate. She was French; she appreciated good food. So: entrée, main course, cheese, dessert. Oh Christ, what had he let himself in for? Maybe he could ask Bénédicte to do the cooking; he'd pay her to do the cooking, for God's sake. By the time he went to bed he'd managed to calm down a little and he'd decided on a plain but pleasant menu. Entrée – green salad. There was a lettuce in the fridge and just enough vinaigrette left in the bottle. Main course – spaghetti Bolognese, he was a dab hand at spag bol. There were tons of onions and plenty of garlic in the kitchen, all he needed to buy was the meat and tinned toms. Oh, and the pasta. So far so good. Okay. Cheese? Rebluchon, of course, and maybe a bit of brie. There was plenty of that in the fridge. And dessert. That could pose a serious problem. Maybe she'd settle for fruit or a yogurt? And maybe she wouldn't. Maybe she'd have to. And the wine? He mustn't forget the wine. A full-bodied red, maybe even Italian ... why not? And candles, they'd have dinner by candlelight. Of course. So, all he needed to buy was the meat, tomatoes, Italian wine ... and candles. Red candles. Paul finally drifted off to sleep in the early hours of the morning.

***

Paul's written shopping list was short – minced beef, tin of tomatoes, tomato purée and some kind of fruit tart from the 'boulangerie'. Oh, and the inevitable baguette, of course. He ate a late and lazy breakfast and, after checking for the umpteenth time the contents of the kitchen cupboards, he meandered down the mountain road, his thoughts on the evening ahead. He tried to think of other things; the scenery surrounding him, the weather, glorious now after the summer storm, his beguiling neighbour. But pleasant as these thoughts were, they couldn't annihilate his almost childlike anticipation of the evening ahead.

There were few shops in the village; apart from the newsagent and tobacconist, there were the ubiquitous boulangerie and chemist, the butcher and a small, general grocer. Paul bought most of his provisions – including a packet of long, red candles – at the grocers and then made his way to the butcher's shop, which he knew was the last building on the rue du Paradis, the road that led south out of the village. Jacqueline must have a great view from her bedroom window ... Paul felt the familiar aching in his abdomen at the thought of Jacqueline, together with sudden panic that he might just bump into her ... there was a short queue outside the butcher's and he tagged on to the end. The old man in front of him passed a remark about the weather, Paul replied and they lapsed into silence. Someone left the shop and the queue moved forward. The butcher started to serve his next customer, a young woman with a toddler, and he gazed at the child as his blood-stained hands chopped the pork.

'How old is he now, Madame Jarry?'

'He'll be two next month – and don't I know it!'

'A young man already! So, when can we expect to see his brother (or sister this time), perhaps?'

'What?'

'Jamais deux sans trois. Everything comes in threes, Madame Jarry. You've got two fine boys; you must be thinking about having a third. And don't wait too long, don't leave it too late. Now that his big brother's gone to school that little feller there needs a playmate – don't you, my lad?'

He swiftly wrapped the pork chops in greaseproof paper.

'By the way, you know Madame Bernard's expecting again, don't you?'

Madame Jarry juggled with the chops, her purse and her child. She didn't look at the butcher.

'No. I didn't.'

'A bit of a surprise, hein? Especially her husband being as he is. Word's getting around that ...'

Madame Jarry dropped the meat into a straw basket, left some cash on the counter, thanked the butcher and without looking at him, left the shop.

'He's worse than any old woman,' she murmured to the man standing in front of Paul.

'I always turn a deaf ear,' the old man replied. 'That way I don't get into bother.'

It was Paul's turn to be served.

'A kilo of your best minced beef, please.'

'Coming right up.'

The butcher shuffled to the window, selected the meat and threw it on to the scales, glancing at Paul out of his eye corner. He was a big man with ruddy cheeks and heavy jowls and his small eyes were almost hidden behind horn-rimmed glasses. There was no hair on his head but he sported a thick, grey moustache.

'You wouldn't be the young feller staying at the Beaulac's chalet?'

The man's previous conversation with his wary customer and his own recent conversation with Bénédicte were both fresh in Paul's mind. He merely nodded and started to whistle, his eyes flitting around the white-tiled shop.

'A bit lonely up there, isn't it? Not much for a young feller like you to do. I suppose Bénédicte keeps you entertained?'

'You could say that.'

The big, red, blood-stained hands were wrapping Paul and Jacqueline's meal in greaseproof paper.

'The old girl's as nutty as a fruitcake. Good for a laugh but you young stallions need a bit more than that, don't you? A bit of company at night to keep the bed warm, that's what a young stallion like you needs.'

He leaned forward and winked – Paul supposed it was a wink – and was thankful he was now the only customer, thankful there were no other ears than his.

'I bet you've got a companion at night in the capital, hein, a young stallion like you.'

Paul handed money over the counter and took the meat. He would have liked to ram it into the butcher's face.

'Yes, you're right there. I do have a companion in Paris. A wonderful companion. We make beautiful music together and normally we're inseparable. Unfortunately, though, I'm alone in the chalet and my companion is alone in Paris. But, not to worry, we'll be together again very soon. Thank you, monsieur, and goodbye.'

He bought a baguette and an apricot tart from the boulangerie and made his way back up the mountain.

The long walk after a more or less sleepless night had tired him and Paul slept for a couple of hours in the afternoon. He woke up at four o'clock and wondered how he could fill the hours until she arrived. He tried reading the newspaper but couldn't concentrate. He thought about paying Bénédicte a visit but decided against it. He mooched around the chalet and did nothing constructive at all. Later, he took an invigorating shower and dressed in a pair of clean denims and a pale blue tee-shirt. He hoped Jacqueline wouldn't be dressed up to the nines because they'd both feel embarrassed. But he'd only brought casual clothes with him. He prepared the Bolognese sauce, uncorked a bottle of Chianti and took the cheese out of the fridge. He set the table for two, placing the red candles in silver holders that he found tucked away at the back of a kitchen cupboard.

Paul was two very different people that evening. A virile, very excited young man waiting for the arrival of a beautiful, charming and very desirable young woman. Unfortunately, he was also a shivering, trembling, blubbering nincompoop. At seven-thirty, a third character invaded his already schizophrenic personality; a character who willed the dinner guest not to come, who prayed to Bénédicte's God to keep Jacqueline away, keep her at home in her flat above the butcher's shop. It would surely be better for him and definitely better for her. An evening spent with Paul Atkinson could only be a waste of her time and a disappointment. Yesterday's picnic must surely have been enough for any woman.

And the third character got his way in the end because Jacqueline didn't come. Paul paced every room in the chalet, looked out of every window. He turned the hotplate off and turned it back on again. He drank several glasses of wine and threw the empty glass against the wall. It shattered into a thousand pieces as had Paul's hopes. At midnight he went to bed. The following day he made sure that the drawers he'd ravaged were back in order. He stripped the bed, cleaned the chalet from top to bottom and packed his rucksack. He left the chalet in the afternoon, hitched a lift down the mountain and at the small, pretty Alpine station he changed his return ticket and left for Paris an hour later.

226

Chapter Seventeen

Helen answered only very vaguely Marie-Laure's indiscreet questions about her evening out with Paul Atkinson. Yes, she'd had quite a good time; they'd been to a crêperie in Montparnasse; she'd quite enjoyed his company and no, they hadn't arranged to see each other again. Fortunately, because of the good weather the salon was busy and the two women didn't have much time to chat. The forthcoming holiday in the Alps had been mentioned only briefly since the initial invitation; again, work prevented lengthy dialogues. But definite plans had been laid and Helen viewed them with a mixture of excitement and a kind of dread. Had Adam's suggestion to Paul been serious and, if so, would he take him up on it? And if he did, what would be the outcome for the four of them? There was another, even more anxiety-provoking thought that wouldn't leave Helen alone for very long. Ben's name hadn't been mentioned; not in relation to her. She was a fan of his music, full stop. Helen had no idea whether Adam had spoken to his twin about Marie-Laure's new English assistant, Helen Hartnell, and the fact that she was going to spend time at the family's chalet with them. How would Ben have reacted? And if Ben hadn't been told, if he was completely in the dark (as she hoped he was), would there be the unthinkable possibility that he and Kim-on-a-good-day would turn up in the Alps? She'd thought about tentatively broaching this alarming subject with Marie-Laure but never actually got round to it. The words just wouldn't come. And Helen asked herself if, in a masochistic way, she was in fact hoping that Ben – without his wife – would arrive at the chalet. And just supposing that Ben and Paul Atkinson were there at the same time? Why had her previous nondescript existence suddenly become so sickeningly chaotic?

One evening, after a particularly hectic and exhausting day, Helen got home at eighty-thirty to find a letter waiting for her in the letter box. The handwriting was now familiar and she mentally groaned. Why didn't Paul just accept how things were between them and that she wasn't interested in him? Why did he continue making a bloody fool of himself? She trudged upstairs with her post, wearily opened her door and poured herself a large glass of orange juice before even thinking about doing anything else.

Then she opened the envelope.

Dear Helen,

I enjoyed our evening together at the crêperie and I'm sorry it ended quite badly. It was my fault entirely and I'd like to apologise. I know how it must have seemed to you but I certainly didn't mean to upset you in any way. I'm afraid I'm not very good at relationships with ladies, it's the story of my life. I'm not feeling sorry for myself, by the way, just stating a fact! Maybe we could give it another try some time? I'd really like us to be friends – we did have a good evening together, didn't we? At least I did and I hope you did, too. This is my number if you ever feel like giving me a ring sometime – 01.40.20.64.90.

By the way, I won't be joining you at Adam's chalet. It would have been great – it's a beautiful part of the world and we'd have had some fun. But, to be honest, not all my memories of the Alps are happy ones and there's a very good reason for my not going back. But I won't go into that. Anyway, I'd already planned to go to Antibes with Serge for a month and I'd feel really bad if I let him down. And I don't trust his Mediterranean temper!

So, Helen, enjoy your holiday with Marie-Laure and Adam – on second thoughts, if I do fall victim to Serge's Mediterranean temperament, don't be too surprised if I do turn up! In the meantime, take care of yourself and don't forget, if you feel like giving me a ring it would be nice to hear from you.

Best wishes,
Paul

P.S. Do you have an email address? It would be an easier way for us to correspond!

Helen read the letter twice and once more found his correspondence ambiguous. Why had he bothered writing? Was there a cryptic meaning behind the seemingly innocent apology and the explanation of his holiday plans? Did he really intend showing up at the chalet if his holiday with Serge didn't work out? Did he honestly expect her to phone him? She screwed up the single sheet of paper and aimed it at the waste paper basket under the window. It missed and fell into a nearby plant pot. As Helen salvaged it and threw it where she'd intended to, she wondered, with some retarded curiosity, what possible reason he could have for not wanting to go back to the chalet. With her increasing tiredness she soon put the unwelcome letter to the back of her mind and, after a light supper, went to bed. She fell into a heavy sleep, strangely enough undisturbed by dreams. And to answer his postscript, no, she didn't have an email address. She didn't have a computer yet so why would she have an email address, for goodness' sake? Maybe in the not-too-distant future … It would be a quicker, cheaper way of corresponding with Jill, too. But for the moment, no, she didn't have an email address.

At the end of the following, equally hectic week, Helen got home to find yet another, thicker envelope waiting for her, standing upright in the letterbox. She groaned and mentally cursed as she took it out; and then she caught her breath and had to steady herself before climbing the one flight of stairs. Fifteen minutes later Helen would have given anything to be able to phone Jill but, unfortunately, her best friend had gone to Cornwall for a couple of weeks with her family; their annual summer holiday.

***

As Marie-Laure had predicted, the month of July was exceptionally busy and none too pleasant. Affluent women who were taking off for hotter climes and flesh-infested beaches flocked into the salon like migrating birds, needing to improve their appearance before they bared their bodies to all and sundry. Helen, tired, weary and often bored, wondered if she could ever face another pair of hairy legs and armpits or cellulite-beleaguered thighs. She felt like a human – and sometimes not-so-human – assembly line as one wanting-to-be-beautiful woman left and another walked in. The friendly ones talked about their holidays to come. The not so friendly ones simply lay there, allowing Helen's accomplished fingers and efficient tools to do their work. As the hot, stuffy days wore on and she became more exhausted and twice as irritable, she began to prefer the snobbish but silent clients. There was the occasional man, too, who wanted sessions under the sun-ray lamp in order to be already bronzed and 'beau' when he performed his first strut on the beach. Sometimes they even requested a facial or an epilation, imagining that a smooth-as-a-baby's-bottom body was preferable to a masculine display of chest hair. Helen laughed and told them that hairy men (within reason, of course) were far sexier than smooth-skinned and, of course, found herself in Marie-Laure's bad books. She was supposed to encourage the clients, not put them off.

'I agree with you,' Nathalie whispered in Helen's ear, 'Give me a gorilla lookalike any day. Oh, here comes trouble. Bonjour, Madame Fontenay, comment allez-vous?'

And Helen wafted back into Salon No. 2 to make Madame Fontenay's body suitable for the beach.

***

Towards the end of July Marie-Laure announced to Helen that, although the salon wouldn't close until the beginning of August, she and Adam would be leaving for the Alps at the end of the month.

'We have to prepare the chalet; it's been empty since the winter. So, you'll be joining us a week later, chérie.'

Helen felt a slight sense of panic. She had taken it for granted that the three of them would travel together and the idea of making her own way to the Beaulac's chalet was a bit daunting. However, she wasn't going to let Marie-Laure know that.

'Oh, I see. Right. But how will I get there?'

'By train, of course. The TGV to Lyon and then the regional train to our local village. And don't worry, you won't have to lug your suitcase up the mountain! We'll pick you up at the station.' She paused. 'You'll be capable of doing all that, I hope?'

There were times when Helen hated Marie-Laure to distraction and this was one of them.

***

Two evenings before Marie-Laure and Adam left Paris, they invited Helen for dinner to chat about the holiday and make some kind of itinerary. As the apartment was going to be empty for several weeks and most of the packing had been done, there was no standing on ceremony. Marie-Laure prepared a simple meal in the ample kitchen where they ate at the huge, scrubbed table. Although the three of them were mentally and physically exhausted, their conversation was loud, animated and peppered with laughter.

'I'll make some coffee,' Marie-Laure said, clearing away the dessert dishes. 'Decaffeinated, perhaps?'

'Good idea,' yawned Adam, 'let's have it on the balcony – may as well take advantage of the setting sun.'

Helen strolled on to the balcony and sat on the chair that Paul had occupied the last time. She started to think, rather more calmly now, about that less than successful lunch. This evening Paul's name hadn't been mentioned at all and she hoped it would continue that way. She'd felt relaxed, had enjoyed herself and was now very much looking forward to her holiday. The glass-topped coffee table stood in front of her; unlike the last time free of glasses and dishes of nibbly things. It wasn't entirely empty, though. In the middle stood a pile of correspondence that had been looked at and abandoned for whatever reason. Perhaps waiting to be answered. There was a large postcard on the top of the pile and, from where Helen was sitting, she thought she recognised the view; at least it looked familiar. She leaned forward to have a closer look and York Minster and the Roman wall greeted her curious gaze. Helen frowned at the unmistakeable view that she knew so well. A postcard from Yorkshire; had Jill been in touch with Marie-Laure and Marie-Laure hadn't mentioned it? In her last conversation with Jill, her friend had talked about Cornwall and had never disclosed sending, or her intention to send, a postcard of York, or anywhere else, to her ex-penfriend. As far as she knew, Adam and Marie-Laure knew no one else in Yorkshire; well, if they did, they certainly hadn't mentioned it. She was being paranoid. She was suddenly sorely tempted to pick the postcard up and glance at the signature but at that moment her hostess re-appeared with the coffee and a crystal dish filled with chocolate mints. As she placed the tray on the table, she shifted the pile of correspondence aside and Helen waited for her to refer to the postcard. She didn't. Her face gave nothing away. She poured the coffee and continued to talk about their forthcoming trip. And then Adam stepped onto the balcony. He slipped into the chair beside his wife and accepted the cup she offered him. He silently sipped his drink, listening to the two women and then his eyes moved to the post on the table. Helen silently gasped as she watched his expression change from contented and benign to anxious and agitated. He slowly stood up, unobtrusively picked up the pile of correspondence, tore up the postcard and threw the tiny pieces into the nearest bin. He took the remaining, opened envelopes inside the apartment, came back a little calmer and he and Marie-Laure exchanged a look that Helen would never have been able to interpret.

***

It was too late to make a phone call when Helen got home but as soon as she'd finished breakfast and a chapter of her book the next morning, she picked up the phone and dialled Jill's number.

'Hi, it's me.'

'Hello, you! You're an early bird for a Sunday morning.'

'It's ten o'clock here, remember. We're an hour ahead of you …'

'Ah yes, so this little bird won't get the worm, after all.'

'I'm not too early, am I? It's just that …'

'Don't be daft, of course you're not too early. It's Helen, Tom. He sends his love. What? Oh aye, we had a grand old time; at least, we all had a grand time except Caroline, who thought staying in a B and B in St Ives was on a par with a Neanderthal cave. She'd have preferred to stay here on her own but Tom and I weren't born yesterday. Anyway, we tried not to let her spoil our holiday ... too much. And, how are you?'

'Well, actually Jill, I'm ringing about a couple of things. Listen, have you recently sent a postcard to Marie-Laure? From York?'

'I haven't sent her a postcard from York and I didn't send one from St Ives either. Anyway, I don't have her address. Why do you ask?'

Helen briefly explained about the previous evening's discovery and Jill laughed.

'Sounds a bit dramatic, love. Why the heck are you getting so het up about a postcard from York?'

'It was weird, Jill. I didn't think you'd sent it when I saw Adam's reaction ... but I tell you what, I'd like to know who did.'

'You've got me wondering now. Well, let me know if you find out, won't you? Your life in the French capital seems to be getting curiouser and curiouser. What was the second thing?'

Helen took a deep breath and juggled the telephone and the paper in her hand.

'I've ... I've had a card from Ben.'

She listened for a few moments to Jill's silence.

'You've had a card from Ben?' Jill finally said. 'Benjamin Beaulac? Blimey! What kind of a card? Not from York, by any chance?'

'Very funny. Oh Jill, it's so lovely. And he's so obviously gone out of his way to find something really appropriate. Do you know the American artist, Norman Rockwell? Well, don't worry 'cos I didn't, either. I learned about him from Ben. Well, it's a reproduction of one of his paintings – Little Girl Observing Lovers on a Train.'

'Oh, Helen! Go on ...'

'Jill, I can't believe ... when I read it, I just couldn't believe what he'd written. What Benjamin Beaulac had written to *me*, Helen Hartnell, the bloody nondescript ...'

'Oh, Helen, for God's sake, stop it. Your mother ... well, tell me about it. Is it romantic?'

'Shall I read it to you?'

'Only if you really want to ... if it's too private ...'

'I want to share it with you, Jill. Oh, you haven't told Tom, have you? Or anybody else? No, of course you haven't. Sorry ... Shall I read it to you?'

'Hang on. I'm just making myself comfy so I can take it in better. Right …
I'm all ears, love.'

'Okay … "My dearest Helen, how are you, my love? Please forgive these
months of silence, it hasn't been my choice. My life has been far from
ecstatic over the past few weeks and correspondence of any kind with
anybody has been difficult, and with you impossible. I can say no more at
the moment. I can only hope that my life will change and improve but
there's a hell of a lot of tunnel in front of me yet. (Unfortunately, my love, it's
not the Channel Tunnel)."'

'Oh *Helen,* I can't believe this. It's incredible! Benjamin Beaulac … Go
on!'

'"Right now, I'm remembering our brief and (for me) ecstatic weekend in
Paris. I can't explain it to you but you touched something inside me where
no-else has ever come near. In spite of my romantic music, I've never
believed in love at first sight but I experienced it for the first time on that
train. And the feeling is still with me. I'm imagining you now, sitting alone in
your little studio, reading my card and remembering our weekend together.
At least, I very selfishly hope that you're alone until such time that we can be
together again. With my love, Ben."'

There was another, longer silence.

'It's incredible, Helen, and you know I don't mean that in a nasty way.
Who'd have thought that any of the old crowd from Firley would or could
have … but *you* have, haven't you?'

'I have what?' Helen asked, laughing.

'Well, you've … you've conquered Benjamin Beaulac … made him fall in
love with you … It's so romantic, Helen; romantic and pretty incredible, too.
You must be over the moon!'

'I don't think it's really hit me yet. I keep reading this card over and over.
I actually know it by heart now. But I'm worried, Jill, to be honest. He
doesn't sound happy, does he? He sounds as though he's got all the worries
of the world on his shoulders, and I told you how Adam behaved after he'd
been talking to him on the phone. He was obviously worried sick as well. I
wonder what's going on over there?'

'Where did he write from?'

'New York.'

'Well, write back to him and ask him …'

'Do you think he was daft enough to leave me an address? I can't write
back, Jill, and it's so bloody frustrating. I was just beginning to think it was
all over and I was getting over him a bit … just a bit … and then I received
this. And now I'm back to square one.'

'Why don't you ask Adam about him? Or even Marie-Laure?'

'You must be joking! You're the only person in the world who knows, Jill, and that's how it's going to stay.'

'Well, I reckon you'll be hearing from him again very soon; he's obviously not going to give up on you, is he?'

'But I won't be here for a month. I'll be staying in *his* chalet in the Alps ...'

Jill burst out laughing.

'It's ironic, isn't it? Absolutely incredible. Well, at least you can't complain that you're bored! And what about the other one? The sexy saxophonist? Sorry ... The cute saxophonist. Has he put his appearance in again?'

Helen told her friend about the letter.

'Well, he sounds like a thoroughly mixed up kid. But he does sound like a nice bloke, too. Don't hurt him too much, will you, Helen?'

'I just hope he doesn't turn up at the chalet while I'm there. Ben, too, for that matter.'

Jill giggled again.

'A duel at dawn and all that?'

Helen sighed.

'Do you remember when my mam said the only men I was capable of attracting were either idiots or bastards?'

'Oh, love, *please* forget everything that your mam ever said to you. And especially that nasty and totally untruthful remark. Anyway, it was donkey's years ago and ...'

'It could have been yesterday as far as I'm concerned, Jill. Look, I'd better go or I'll be going bankrupt. I'll send you a card from the Alps.'

'You'd better! Have a wonderful time, love, and be thankful you've got no bloody adolescent daughter to spoil everything for you. And if the two Mr Wonderfuls do turn up ...'

'I'll send them both to you by special delivery.'

'Please don't bother, love, I've got enough troubles of my own. Anyway, it's my turn to phone you next, after your holiday. Don't forget that postcard.'

'I won't. Love to everybody.'

***

On Friday, 30 July, 1999, Helen tidied and cleaned her tiny home and called her landlord, Henri Parisot, to let him know that she'd be away for a month. He had a key to the bedsit, of course, and would he mind popping in just to make sure everything was okay? Before she got ready for bed that evening, she opened the prettily decorated tin box that contained Ben's card, took it out and read it for the umpteenth time. What would he think if he knew she was going to spend her summer holiday at his family's mountain home? Or maybe he did know. Before she put the card back her lips brushed the Norman Rockwell picture that she knew Ben had specially chosen; and she remembered their own embraces, their own passionate kisses. He obviously hadn't forgotten them, either.

The train journey from Paris to Lyon took two hours and from Lyon to the village much longer but it was an unforgettable experience. The slow, chugging train stopped several times at isolated mountain villages and the people who got on and off were smiling, friendly, chatty. But Helen paid little attention to her fellow passengers; her eyes feasted on the incomparable scenery, the still snow-capped mountains, the majestic pine forests, the gushing waterfalls and clear, trickling streams. And she would have loved to be able to put pen to paper and produce a beautiful poem. She would have loved to be able to.

The train pulled into the small, picturesque station at four o'clock on Saturday afternoon and Adam was waiting for her on the platform. He wore beige shorts, a white tee-shirt, trainers and thick white socks. He already looked healthier than when Helen had last seen him. They kissed each other's cheeks and fondly hugged each other.

'It's good to see you here, Helen. I'm glad you came.' He pinched her cheek and grinned. These pretty little cheeks need a bit of colour to match those gorgeous blue eyes.'

Helen smiled at him happily.

'If I look as healthy as you when I leave here, I won't complain. It's not taken you long to get a tan.'

'Wait till you see my beautiful wife. I look positively pastel in comparison.'

Helen laughed and Adam took charge of her suitcase-on-wheels as they walked towards his parked car. Helen suddenly had a vision of his brother's hand pulling the same case onto the train that was to change her life. She pushed the thought to the back of her mind and concentrated on the very different world around her. Adam guided the car up winding, sometimes almost vertical roads and Helen was barely able to concentrate as he told her that Marie-Laure was preparing 'le gouter', the much-needed afternoon snack. The mountain air gave everyone hearty appetites. But Helen's eyes were hungrier than her stomach and she couldn't wait to explore this beautiful region of France.

Marie-Laure had prepared the 'gouter' on the balcony and after she greeted her guest suggested that they eat before Helen unpacked. Helen instantly fell in love with the view and was delighted to be told that she'd have the same view from her bedroom window – the first bedroom to the left at the top of the stairs. The main guestroom.

'We have lots of things planned for you,' Adam said. 'We know you need to rest but not all the time.'

'Tomorrow we'll stay at the chalet so you can acclimatise yourself,' Marie-Laure took over, 'and on Monday we thought we'd go to Annecy, see the lake, go shopping perhaps … and we'll show you the convent where Bénédicte used to be a nun.'

'Ah yes!' Helen grinned. 'The famous Bénédicte! When am I going to meet her?'

'Right now, by the look of it,' Adam muttered and raised his bronzed arm in greeting. Helen's eyes followed her host's gaze.

'Bonjour, Bénédicte. Comment-allez-vous?'

The old lady stood on the rubbly path that led from the road to the chalet. She wore black, orange and lime green Bermuda shorts, a black sleeveless tee-shirt with orange buttons and lime green ankle socks. An orange scarf was tied gypsy-fashion around her white hair. She clutched an aluminium-covered parcel in both hands. Marie-Laure and Adam exchanged a wry smile and Marie-Laure stood up.

'I didn't think we'd have long to wait,' she whispered, 'not when she knew our new guest was arriving. Now, chéri, do you think this is a brioche or a cooling-off tartiflette?'

'I'll put my money on the brioche,' Adam chuckled, 'the tartiflette usually comes later.'

Marie-Laure skipped downstairs to welcome their neighbour and made fresh coffee and the two appeared on the balcony a few minutes later. Adam stood up, held out his hand and Helen, her disbelieving eyes fixed on the newcomer's apparel, followed suit.

'I'm so happy to meet you!' Bénédicte cried, her new dentures performing a little tap dance in her mouth, her myopic eyes peering through stronger lenses. 'I'm always happy to meet my lovely Marie-Laure's friends.'

With her free hand she rigorously shook Helen's and the latter was surprised at the strength in the fragile-looking fingers. When everyone had sat down and had been served with coffee, Bénédicte handed her offering to Marie-Laure.

'For your breakfast tomorrow morning,' she beamed.

If Marie-Laure and Adam had taken bets, Adam would have won. A golden, succulent brioche was revealed when Marie-Laure peeled away the aluminium. She was euphoric in her thanks and explained to Helen what delicious titbits Bénédicte always generously provided, especially when there were guests at the chalet. Bénédicte settled back comfortably in her chair and scrutinised the English visitor for a long time.

'Ah, I remember so well the young Englishman who stayed here last year. Do you know, for the life of me I can't remember his name. He was always Monsieur to me. What was it? Ah yes, of course, Paul. Such a pleasant young man – would he be offended if I said he was cute? Paul was cute and so very charming but he seemed so … so lonely. Alone in the chalet and lonely. I really felt quite sorry for him. He loved my brioche, you know, and …'

'Everyone loves your brioche, Bénédicte.' Adam obviously wanted to change the course of the conversation.

'Don't flatter me, Adam! Ah, he was so lonely, Monsieur Paul. That's why I introduced him, very cleverly I thought, to Jacqueline because …'

'Would you like some more coffee, Bénédicte? Or how about …'

'I haven't finished this yet, thank you. Maybe later. Have you seen Jacqueline since you've been here? No? She's looking forward to seeing you both again. Such a pity that she and Paul … no, thank you, Marie-Laure, no more chocolate cake. I have to think of my figure, you know! And the way he disappeared so suddenly without a word. Such a shame. I couldn't make head or tail of it at the time. And Jacqueline was very reluctant to talk about … Oh look, there goes Monsieur Forestier from the village, I really must ask about his wife's operation. She's had a hysterectomy, you know … can you imagine, at her age? The poor thing. Cou-cou, Monsieur Forestier! Cou-cou, wait for me. I'm coming down … cou-cou, Monsieur Forestier!'

Bénédicte shot up so quickly and in such a flurry that her fragile chair toppled over backwards and she nearly followed it.

'Now look what I've done.'

She left her chair in its new position on the floor while she continued to 'cou-cou' and make agitated signals to the oblivious, probably hard-of-hearing Monsieur Forestier. However, once he'd acknowledged her conspicuous presence on the balcony, Bénédicte smiled, nodded her goodbyes to everyone and disappeared in a fleeting vision of black, orange and lime green, down the rubbly path.

The balcony fell into a rather stunned silence after the ex-nun had left and the three remaining figures watched as the couple on the road below chatted and Bénédicte's arms gesticulated wildly.

'She's a real character,' Helen smiled and put the fallen chair back on its feet.

'And a half,' Adam agreed.

'If there were more people in the world like her, the world would be a better place,' Marie-Laure murmured.

'But she's so un-nun-like,' Helen said. 'If it hadn't been for that gold cross hanging round her neck, I'd never have guessed ...'

'You ain't seen nothin' yet,' Adam laughed. 'Wait till she washes her hair.'

'What?'

'You'll see.'

The chatterers below finally parted company and Bénédicte looked up and gave a frantic wave before making her way back up the mountain. As they watched her retreating figure, Helen's thoughts flew back to her revelations about Paul the previous summer. She was dying to ask questions but the fact that Adam had so obviously wanted to change the subject, she held her itching tongue. She would save her questions for another day, maybe when she was alone with Marie-Laure.

'Right,' Marie-Laure suddenly stood up and smiled at her guest. 'I suppose you'll be wanting to see your room and put your things away. And I'll show you around the chalet. Come on.'

Helen followed her to her temporary bedroom.

'That's our bedroom at the other end of the landing,' Marie-Laure pointed out, 'and the one next to it is the other guest room. Normally we put ladies in there because it's much more femininely decorated, but we decided to give you a room with a view – don't worry, there's no extra charge! And this room here ...' her right hand tapped on the door of the room next to Helen's, 'is the haunted room. At least that's what Ben's kids used to say when they were tiny.' Her fingers stopped tapping, she leaned backwards against the door and a slow smile spread across her face as she looked at Helen. 'Actually, I think this room is haunted, too. We use it for storage now ... well, old junk, really ... Stuff that ... well, old relics from the dim and distant past. Oh yes, and I keep spare bed linen for the guest rooms in the chest of drawers in here. So, I'm the only one who sets foot in it now ... when I make up the guests' beds. Oh, and Kimberley, too, perhaps, but they haven't invited anyone here since ...'

She shrugged her shoulders and moved away from the door.

'Since what?' Helen breathed.

'Oh, I'm not going into that long story now. Here's your room ... step inside.'

Helen thought about the 'long story' when she walked into the bedroom that was hers for a month, but all ruminations were wiped away when her eyes fell on the picture postcard vista beyond the window.

'My God, Marie-Laure, this is unbelievable. It's out of this world. How do you ever manage to tear yourself away from this place?'

'I thought you'd like it.'

'Like it? This is ... this is paradise. Oh, Marie-Laure, thank you so much for inviting me here.'

Marie-Laure simply nodded, turned to leave the room and headed back downstairs.

'It's Adam you have to thank. He's the one who suggested inviting you. Okay, I'll leave you to unpack; there are plenty of coat-hangers in the wardrobe. Oh, and let me know if you need to do any ironing. Everything's downstairs. Have fun.'

As soon as she was alone Helen closed the door and looked around her room. The single bed stood against one wall, freshly made. The wardrobe was quite small but would be adequate for the few clothes she'd brought with her. Under the window stood a chest of drawers, on top of which stood a single vase of mixed flowers and nothing else. And no paintings, pictures or photos of any kind adorned either the walls or the furniture. But with such a magnificent view from the window, Helen supposed that no other decoration was necessary. As she began unpacking, her thoughts trailed back to the room next door and no one setting foot inside it except Marie-Laure and Kim-on-a-good-day who had had no guests there since ... since when? And what long story?

***

The first week of Helen's stay flew by far too quickly and every minute was filled. Apart from lazy hours relaxing on the balcony and gentle hikes in the glorious neighbourhood, they visited Chamonix and the foot of Mont Blanc, Annecy and its magnificent lake and even a day trip into Switzerland to visit Geneva. Helen was astonished to find she'd got sunburnt while knee-deep in snow; she developed a taste for fondue and reblochon cheese and she promised herself she'd see at least one marmot before returning to Paris. If Marie-Laure and Adam were tired and wanted to rest Helen was happy to go walking alone and she often bumped into Bénédicte on her solitary hikes. The eccentric and enchanting old lady always had the time to chat and never failed to delight Helen with her often outrageous appearance or outré conversation. Or both. She once had the pleasure of seeing the ex-nun after she'd washed her hair – invisible under the red and white checked tea-towel and prominent clothes pegs. Bénédicte had chatted ten to the dozen with her younger neighbour on that occasion, totally oblivious of the effect she was having. Helen didn't know how she managed to keep a straight face but as soon as she got back to the chalet her laughter exploded.

'I thought there were plenty of characters in Firley,' she giggled, for once forgetting the taboo she'd put on her village and former life there. 'But not one of them could compare with this lady.'

'She's a treasure.' Adam smiled, sitting tinkling at the old cottage piano. 'Everyone loves her and the village won't be the same after she's gone.'

Helen wondered if it was the right moment to ask what Bénédicte had meant when she'd vaguely spoken about Paul. Over the past few exciting days, she'd put the ex-nun's intriguing references out of her mind, but now they'd come back to her and she couldn't help but feel curious.

Before she had the time to speak, however, Marie-Laure announced, 'We're going to have dinner at the local restaurant this evening, Helen. La Grange; we've driven past it a few times, do you remember? We think you'll like it; it's typically Alpine and the food's excellent. Their speciality's fondue.'

'Great,' Helen grinned.

Marie-Laure was sitting at the kitchen table, idly turning the pages of a local newspaper. The soft, almost tuneless tinkling of the tinny piano drifted through the open door from the living room. Helen, thirsty after her walk, was helping herself to a large glass of mineral water. She was suddenly aware of Marie-Laure's eyes going over her, as she'd come to think of it.

'If you didn't bring anything suitable to wear for an evening out,' she smiled, and Helen felt the bile rise in her throat, 'I can lend you one of my dresses. We're more or less the same size.'

She yawned and turned her attention back to the printed page.

'I'll have to dig something out that they've never seen before at La Grange. Anyway, let me know.'

***

Madame Laval welcomed her three customers and showed them to their reserved table next to a window, with a superlative view of the valley below. Marie-Laure and Adam sat opposite each other and Helen had a seat facing the window. Before she sat down, she made a point of straightening the simple but elegant red cotton dress and adjusting the straps so that they didn't fall over her shoulder. She'd been hesitant about splashing out on such an unusual-for-her garment, feeling sure she'd never have the opportunity to wear it – it was far too dressy for the Bohemian atmosphere of the Cave Supérieure which constituted her social life. However, she'd finally been persuaded to purchase by the sales assistant's silver tongue and her own, unfamiliar, aching desire for possession. After she'd got home and tried on the exquisite dress in the privacy of her bedsit, she'd felt a little happier that she'd indulged herself but still unsure that she'd ever be able to wear it. This evening she'd been proved wrong and had breathed a sigh of relief when she'd taken it out of her small, temporary wardrobe. Marie-Laure's face had been a picture when Helen put her appearance in downstairs and the insipid lemon and cream frock that she'd 'dug out' lay untouched on the sofa. In spite of her small victory, Helen felt a touch of guilt. Maybe she shouldn't have worn the new red dress; maybe it would have been kinder and more in keeping to wear one of Marie-Laure's cast-offs. But Helen was becoming more and more weary of the 'in keeping' which automatically placed her in a subordinate position, one that was taken for granted by Marie-Laure. Marie-Laure, wearing a simple white shirt and cream linen trousers, examined her as she walked into the room. She pulled an unreadable face.

'Very pretty, chérie. But maybe it's a little overdressed for La Grange.' She shrugged and smiled. 'Anyway, we'll see.'

'I'll send Jacqueline with the menus,' Madame Laval eventually smiled and shuffled back to her kitchen. Two minutes later, in place of the elderly, plump proprietor, a much younger, slimmer and very pretty woman walked towards their table, carrying three large menus. She stood on Helen's right and a small bell began to ring in Helen's brain. Jacqueline. That was the name Bénédicte had used when she'd been mysteriously talking about Paul. She'd introduced Paul to Jacqueline and then ... Helen smiled up at the young waitress, whose looks were quite striking. But in spite of the professional smile there was a deep sadness in her brown eyes that seemed to reflect in her entire body. And her physical beauty was somehow marred by her lack of gaiety and warmth. She wore a plain blue cotton dress with a pristine white apron and cap that partially hid a head of dark brown hair cut short and layered around her face. She acknowledged her customers by name, but rather shyly and after she'd handed out the menus beat a hasty retreat. Helen had the impression she wanted no conversation, unlike her garrulous boss. She saw Marie-Laure and Adam exchange an unfathomable glance and then they both buried their heads in their menus. Helen's curiosity was growing. What was the mystery surrounding the waitress and Paul?

As the evening wore on the atmosphere became more relaxed and Helen enjoyed each new course more than the last. Marie-Laure and Adam knew most of the customers in the restaurant and several people stopped at their table either on arriving or leaving La Grange. Jacqueline was kept busy all evening but Helen noticed how she remained calm, smiling and relaxed with everyone – except the Beaulacs. Although she was pleasant and polite, she kept a certain reserve with them and Helen sensed some embarrassment on all their parts; but particularly the waitress's. So, as she was relishing her last mouthful of tarte Tatin, Helen was amazed to hear Marie-Laure say, 'Jacqueline, chérie, tell me, when is your evening off now?'

'Thursday. It's still Thursday.'

'Thursday. Right. Why don't you come and have dinner with us at the chalet next Thursday evening?'

Helen, herself surprised, watched the agitated expression on the waitress's face, her brain obviously working out how to decline with thanks.

'Yes, do come, Jacqueline,' Adam's initial puzzled frown had quickly transformed into a warm smile as he looked up at the waitress. 'It'll be a change for you ... and it'll be a change for my wife to serve you at table!'

'Oh, I think I might let our English guest perform that little duty,' said Marie-Laure, licking Chantilly cream off her spoon and looking at nothing in particular. Jacqueline stared at her and for a long moment her dry lips moved but no words came. She suddenly put her hand to her throat and audibly swallowed.

'Your English guest, Marie-Laure? Oh no ... no ... I ...'

'Yes, Jacqueline, our English guest.' Marie-Laure pointed rudely in the direction of Helen, who hadn't moved. 'Helen here, our English guest. You won't mind playing waitress for the evening, will you, Helen? I'll be cooking and Adam looking after the wine. Waitressing will be your contribution.'

Jacqueline's relief was almost tangible and a long silence suddenly hung over the table. Helen, furious and embarrassed for both herself and the waitress, didn't know where to look but finally her eyes focused on Jacqueline. She recognised and was surprised to see a fleeting look of sympathy there and gave her a small smile. It wasn't returned. Adam, whose eyes were fixed on his empty dessert dish, was the first to break the silence.

'Yes, do come to dinner on Thursday, my dear. We'd love to have you – and if anybody's going to do the serving, it'll be me. I'll be delighted to wait on three beautiful ladies.'

There was another silence and Helen watched and sympathised with Jacqueline's discomfort, but her mouth had dried up along with a little bit of dignity.

'Well, thank you. Thank you very much. What time would you like me to come?'

Jacqueline's voice was almost a whisper and her pretty eyes looked everywhere except at her customers.

'Seven o'clock. We'll look forward to seeing you.' Marie-Laure smiled. 'We haven't had the chance to chat for a long time, have we, chérie?'

'No,' Jacqueline agreed as she left the table and took their order for coffee to the kitchen.

***

No one spoke on the short journey home and they entered the chalet in silence, too. Adam yawned loudly and muttered that he was ready for bed, the mountain air always knocked him out, and Marie-Laure walked into the living room to close the shutters for the night. As she walked past the telephone that stood near the piano, its strident bell started to ring.

'Allo?'

Helen offered to close the shutters while Marie-Laure was speaking to the caller. But, in fact, she didn't speak, she merely listened – for what seemed like a very long time – and her sun-bronzed face visibly turned pale.

'Adam!' she eventually cried, 'please come ... it's Ben.'

Helen, motionless now in the middle of the small room, watched Adam running into the room and snatch the phone out of his wife's outstretched hand. She stood and watched him listening to his brother for a long time. She heard him say, 'We'll come. Yes, of course we'll come. Immediately.' She looked at Marie-Laure who'd sunk on to the sofa and then she watched Adam replace the receiver and walk quietly over to his wife.

'So. It's finally happened.'

Helen, panicky but superfluous and forgotten, quietly left the room and went upstairs. She got undressed, washed and got into bed. She lay for a long time with the light on, listening for signs of life but there were none and she eventually fell into a fitful sleep. When she went downstairs the next morning, the first thing she saw were two bulging suitcases at the foot of the stairs. Marie-Laure and Adam were sitting in the kitchen drinking coffee and not speaking. They both heard her footsteps and turned to look at her. Marie-Laure stood up and walked to the percolator, which was still warm and nearly full. In spite of expertly applied makeup, signs of a sleepless night were evident on her face.

'Helen, come and have some breakfast. Sit down ... there, that's right. Look ... Adam and I have to go to New York ... today, unfortunately. Our flight leaves Geneva at three o'clock. It's ... it's a family problem and we don't know how long we'll have to stay over there. But, look, you must stay here, we both want you to stay here and enjoy the rest of your holiday.'

Helen was inadvertently shaking her head.

'Oh no. No, I can't do that. I can't possibly stay here on my own … it wouldn't be the same and … and well, it wouldn't be right …'

'Of course it'll be right, Helen; it'll be perfectly all right and, anyway, you'll be doing us a favour. The chalet will be occupied. You can look after the plants for us and … well, keep the place clean. Please stay. We'll both feel terribly guilty if you cut your holiday short and there's really no need. Anyway, we may be back very soon … we simply just don't know at the moment.'

'Can I … could you tell me what's the matter? I mean … Is it anything very serious? Is … Ben ill … or something?'

Her voice trailed away and she watched Marie-Laure slowly shaking her head.

'I'm sorry, Helen, it's a very long story and we don't have either the time or the inclination to start telling you right now. We'll have to set off soon … it's a long drive to the airport. I'll try to phone you from New York … but I can't promise. Look, why don't you have some breakfast and think about the rest of your holiday … what you're going to do …'

'You'll enjoy yourself, Helen,' Adam broke in. 'You won't have any transport, that's true, but you enjoy walking, don't you? And there's always Bénédicte to keep you company. And she has a car, of course. She'll be able to chauffer you around, take you shopping. Don't you worry about anything at this end, and for God's sake, don't spoil your vacation by worrying about us. We'll call as soon as possible and we'll get back here if we can … if not, we'll see you back in Paris. Bénédicte'll lock up the chalet when you leave … Oh, and she'll definitely give you a lift to the station, so you don't have to worry about that, either. So, you make the most of your time here on your own. Okay? Good, that's settled then. At least we don't have you to worry and feel guilty about!' He smiled. 'Now, is there anything she needs to know, Marie-Laure, before we leave?'

'I don't think so. You're familiar with the chalet now, aren't you, Helen? Oh, I'll just show you how the washing machine works … and Adam, can you show her where to turn the electricity and water off?'

'Bénédicte can do that after she's left.' Adam was beginning to show signs of impatience. He looked at his watch, picked up both suitcases and headed for the door. 'I'll put these in the car.'

'And you know where to find clean sheets and towels. In the small room next to yours. In the chest of drawers. I usually put the blue or grey sheets on your bed but I don't remember which drawer they're in … you'll probably have to rummage around. But please do … rummage around in that room as much as you need, Helen … till you find what you're looking for.'

Helen opened her mouth to speak but the expression on Marie-Laure's

244

face prevented any reply. She suddenly felt someone walking very slowly over her grave.

'Right.' Adam was standing in front of her and had taken her two hands in both of his. 'Thanks for looking after our little home and just make sure you have a good time here. Okay?'

He kissed her cheek and strode out of the room, out of the chalet and down the uneven path to the waiting car.

'Goodbye, Helen,' Marie-Laure pecked her cheek. 'And do take care.'

She followed her husband's footsteps and Helen watched them climbing into the Renault and fastening their seat belts. They both raised their hands as the car skidded down the stony drive and onto the mountain road, turning left towards Switzerland.

'Goodbye,' Helen whispered and burst into tears.

Chapter Eighteen

Helen had started to sip her second bowl of coffee, not really tasting the freshly-percolated bitterness, when a familiar and welcome face appeared at the kitchen window. She leaped off her chair, unlocked the door and let Bénédicte into the kitchen. For once, she was rather soberly dressed in a plain cotton blouse and white trousers. Her head was free of remarkable adornment, her thin arms filled with what looked like homemade goodies, spilling out of a handle-less basket. She almost dropped the heavy item on the table and looked at Helen over the top of her spectacles.

'You're not going to starve just because your hosts have left you high and dry,' she said and the inimitable, badly-fitted-denture grin spread over her wrinkled face. 'There's brioche, bread, salami, reblochon cheese, some cherries – oh, and a bottle of Bordeaux to cheer yourself up if you're feeling lonely.'

Helen smiled her thanks.

'But I'm going to make sure you're not lonely! I'll take you everywhere you want to go ... I'll even take you where you don't want to go! You and I are going to have a whale of a time, Helen!'

Helen grinned back at the old lady, the only person in the world, she felt sure, who could have brought a smile to her face right then. She turned to the percolator to make fresh coffee and Bénédicte started to peel the aluminium away from the brioche.

'May as well eat it while it's warm,' she commented. 'And how about a glass of Bordeaux to wash it down?'

Helen gaped at the busy ex-nun.

'For breakfast, Bénédicte?'

Bénédicte once again looked over the rim of her glasses, grinned, winked and told Helen she mustn't blame her for trying.

'Well,' she added, sitting down and pushing a great slab of brioche towards Helen, 'if you're not game maybe you'd better save it for another occasion.' She winked. 'Who knows? Maybe you'll have a dinner guest one evening?'

And that reminded Helen of the invitation to the waitress, Jacqueline, for dinner the following Thursday evening. Her heart sank. Unless she rang the restaurant to cancel, she'd have to entertain the girl herself and she really didn't feel up to that. They didn't know each other at all and she'd had the impression that the girl was quite shy. Why was she fated to be thrown together with timid people? The two of them alone for an entire evening would probably be a nightmare for both of them. Apart from the Beaulacs – and Paul – and the fact that Helen had waitressed in a nightclub many moons ago (another of her brief, pointless and goal-less jobs), they probably had very little to talk about. She told Bénédicte about the invitation, expecting her to advise Helen to cancel and maybe offering to phone the restaurant herself. So, she was horrified to see the old lady's face light up.

'Excellent! I'm sure you and my Jacqueline will get along famously ... two lovely ladies together. I love Jacqueline dearly, you know, she's a very special person. But I feel so sorry for her ... She has no life out here in this small village, far from her family and friends. Well, her family is in Annecy, not very far away, but she only sees them once a month because of her work. I'm convinced she'd make someone a wonderful wife ... and mother, God willing.' Bénédicte crossed herself. 'But living out here she never has the opportunity to meet men. Or if she does meet a man, he's here one minute and gone the next ... tourists, climbers, that sort of thing. There was Monsieur Paul last year, for example. What a strange affair that was ... and I still haven't got to the bottom of it, worked out whose fault it was. I tell you what, though ...' Bénédicte leaned forward and adjusted her glasses, licked her lips, 'I was as mad as hell when I learned that Jacqueline had stood that nice Englishman up and he'd gone scuttling home like a beaten puppy. What was wrong with the pair of them? And Jacqueline became even more withdrawn, more insular after that little episode ...'

'What about her family, Bénédicte? You said "my Jacqueline". Is she a relative of yours?'

The ex-nun's glasses slowly slipped down her nose and she gazed at her breakfast companion with short-sighted but laughing eyes.

'Not in the true sense of the word, no. Jacqueline's family – in fact, her adoptive family – live in Annecy, as I explained. A big, boisterous, united family, but Jacqueline only sees them once a month. As I said, Madame Laval is very fond of her, very good to her, but even after working together for a couple of years, Madame Laval confesses that she doesn't know her waitress any more today than she did two years ago. It's not only shyness, it goes beyond that... Well, maybe you'll have more luck with her when she comes to dinner.'

By this time, the prospect of having dinner alone with the young waitress was quite alarming and, Helen had to be honest, she really was in no mood for difficult guests. It wasn't the right time. And then she had the idea (why hadn't she thought of it before?) of inviting Bénédicte to join them. But Bénédicte, unfortunately, had a meeting in Annecy that evening, at the Young Catholic Mothers' Association.

'Then I think it might be a good idea to cancel,' Helen said.

The glasses had slipped again and were thrust up the shiny nose by a furious finger.

'Absolutely not. What a nonsensical idea! Two lonely ladies needing company and you're thinking about cancelling ... never!' She picked up the bottle of Bordeaux and wiggled it in front of Helen's semi-amused face. 'After a few glasses of this both your tongues will be loose and there'll be no stopping either of you. And I wouldn't be surprised if Jacqueline ends up staying the night.' She leaned forward again and banged the bottle down on the table. 'I tell you what ... it always works with me. If you ever want to know my darkest secrets, Helen, open a bottle of good red wine!'

Helen laughed and tried to imagine what the old lady's darkest secrets could possibly be. And then she didn't know why she was so amused by the other woman's words; there were skeletons in everyone's cupboard. Why was Bénédicte so fond of the timid, friendless waitress? Why was she so eager for Jacqueline to improve her life, find a husband? But, intriguing as these thoughts and people were, the man Helen was in love with was suffering and in some kind of trouble on the other side of the Atlantic and she was desperate to know why. What misfortune had happened to him to make his brother and sister-in-law take off for New York, leaving their guest alone in their mountain home? She suddenly decided to plunge in at the deep end with her hosts' beloved neighbour.

'Bénédicte, how well do you know Adam and Marie-Laure?'

Bénédicte studied her companion for a while, a small frown on her face.

'What do you mean, Helen? Why do you ask?'

Helen, knowing she was treading on egg-shells, shrugged nonchalantly and smiled.

'Oh, no particular reason. I ... I just wondered if ... if you knew Ben ... Adam's brother in New York. He's ... he's obviously having problems at the moment, you know. Of course you know. Well, I was just wondering ...'

Helen's voice drifted away and Bénédicte sipped the final dregs of her coffee and made a show of wrapping what was left of the brioche into its aluminium. Then she stood up and, with no delicacy whatsoever, started to adjust the fastener on her trousers – the zip had started to work its way down. After a long time, she replied to Helen's question.

'I've never known the Beaulac family when they didn't have problems.'

Bénédicte picked up the dirty dishes, made her way to the sink and Helen thought she heard her muttering something about 'that villainous, destructive brother … ' She watched the thin, agile body piling the dishes into the sparkling, stainless steel sink, incongruous in the traditional, old-fashioned kitchen.

'Sorry, Bénédicte. I didn't hear you. What did you say?'

Helen's thoughts flew back to Ben's carefully chosen card, the delightfully suitable painting by Norman Rockwell … lovers in a train. His intimate, loving, carefully chosen words. And then his telephone call to the chalet and the quick departure of Marie-Laure and Adam. She suddenly felt nauseous and the blood pounded inside her head until she thought it was going to burst. She clutched the seat of her chair, for moral as well as physical support. She wished she hadn't asked Bénédicte to repeat; she didn't want to hear those words again plus any qualification she might add.

'Oh, nothing. Nothing at all. It's all history now.' The old lady sighed. 'I hope.'

She came back to the table, picked up the now empty basket and, after kissing Helen goodbye, moved towards the door. Helen suddenly felt a little afraid; she suddenly didn't want to be alone in the chalet on the mountain. She didn't want her neighbour – her new friend – to leave.

'Bénédicte – wait! Please. Look … when will … when will I see you again?'

Bénécicte's smile was back again and her last words and their hidden, sinister meaning were already a thing of the past.

'Every day, probably. At least once every day, more often if you like. You don't think I'd be able to resist a lovely, lonely neighbour like you, do you? Hey! I've just had a wonderful idea! Tomorrow we'll drive down to the village and take the Mont Blanc tram.'

'Take the what?'

Helen, all negative thoughts temporarily forgotten, gaped at this incredible woman.

'The Mont Blanc tram. You don't know what it is? Then you'll find out tomorrow. I'll pick you up at seven-thirty. Wear good walking shoes and warm clothes. Oh Helen, I can't wait! I'm so excited already!'

***

The Mont Blanc tram was a rack train that climbed to 2,372 metres, as far as the Nid d'Aigle on the slopes of Mont Blanc, chugging its way through the most breathtaking scenery Helen had ever seen. Dark green pine forests, snow-capped mountain ranges, gushing waterfalls and many coloured wildflowers all shared in an ambience of wonder and delight. The passengers all wore sturdy hiking boots, thick woollen socks, warm jackets. Bénédicte, sitting beside Helen on the wooden slatted seat, wore the necessary boots and socks and a Mickey Mouse sweatshirt with matching sun hat. She was totally oblivious to the amused glances she attracted in the busy carriage. Sitting next to her, Helen felt soberly and very inadequately dressed in a light cotton sweater, denim shorts and a pair of well-worn trainers. Bénédicte had looked aghast at her when she climbed into the car. Did she think they were going for a quiet stroll in pleasant meadows? Didn't she have more suitable clothes and decent boots? No, she didn't. She'd come to the chalet in the Alps for a relaxing holiday, gentle strolls in the mountains and with the clothes to fit; not for scrambling up Mont Blanc, or whatever. The last time Helen had worn heavy hiking gear had been on her treks across the Pennines … an age ago.

The two women hardly spoke during the steep ascent; they were both too captivated by the landscape. When the train finally pulled to a halt it was almost vertical. Everyone, mostly tourists in the region, jumped off and on to the slippery stony ground. Helen climbed off with less dexterity, more prudence and watched in wonder as the human mountain goats took off for even dizzier heights. Bénédicte soon made it very clear that Helen wasn't going to be one of them as she looked contemptuously at her ill-clad feet.

'For you it's not possible,' she said. Her bony finger pointed to a bar standing behind the stationary train. 'You go have some refreshment and I'll meet you back here in what … a couple of hours?'

Helen's vertigo had started to kick in as she looked around her and down into the valley below and was really quite relieved that she wasn't expected to follow. Relieved, but at the same time disappointed. She watched the small, determined, retreating figure in wonder and a lot of admiration. On the other hand, if she'd brought suitable clothes and boots with her … Marie-Laure, however, had never mentioned the Mont Blanc tram, it had probably never occurred to her. The city-elegant Marie-Laure probably didn't know the Mont Blanc tram existed. It took an incomparable woman like Bénédicte to think of it … and do it. Helen took her advice, refreshed herself with a cup of strong, hot coffee and a chocolate bar, took a few photographs and passed the time she had to kill chatting to other visitors, solitary people like herself who were either inappropriately dressed or lacked the stamina needed to tackle the terrain. As Helen sat on a rustic bench next to the platform, she was relieved to see Bénédicte's small, deceptively frail-looking body heading towards her. She was walking with and talking to another solitary hiker and raised her stick and grinned in greeting. She was pink and shining and brimming with health and vitality; and on her way back to civilisation she talked about her ascent, the people she'd met, the people she often met there and how, when she was a missionary in Peru...

'In Peru?'

'... I climbed to Matchu Pitchu.'

'And I suppose your next stop will be Kilimanjairo?'

'No. That was in 1949, just after I left the convent. Did I tell you I spent several years travelling around Africa? Charity and missionary work, mostly.'

'No, Bénédicte, you didn't.'

Well, I've never 'eard owt like it in me life; silly old bitch. Folk like that ought to be locked up, they're not safe. Why don't people just act normal instead o' tryin' to be different and makin' spectacles o' theirselves? If she wanted to be a nun, she should 'ave stayed a nun, locked up in a bloody convent. That's what I think. Helen breathed deeply before she asked her next question.

'Bénédicte, can I... can I ask you why... or under what circumstances... you... erm... you left the convent?'

The ex-nun's myopic, avian eyes squinted up at her and a slow smile eventually spread across her face. She took her companion's hand in her own.

'Like a lot of married people, Helen, I wanted to have my cake and eat it. I was married to God and loved Him deeply – and still do – but after eight years of devoting all my life to Him and only Him – in other words not living life to the full and not being able to participate and enjoy and revel in all that life and the world has to offer – I realised that I couldn't continue my chosen path. So, after a lot of thought, agonising and self-hatred I decided to abandon my chosen path and ... and lead a more, shall we say, a more normal life. So, I said a very sad and difficult goodbye to the convent and, while keeping my faith and my love of God, I became more ... shall we say ... normal.'

The laughter exploded out of Helen and she threw her arms around the far-from-normal ex-nun and kissed her; completely oblivious to the glances of the amused and very tired lookers-on.

***

Helen made no contact at all with Jacqueline before Thursday evening. Her conversation with Bénédicte had made her curious about the girl, even if the waitress's relationship with Paul disturbed her a little. In a kind of masochistic and selfish way, she was looking forward to talking to her that evening. Maybe she, too, knew the Beaulac family well, knew their history. Maybe she'd be able to provide answers to, up to now, unanswered questions.

On Wednesday morning Helen spent quite some time planning a menu and making a shopping list. Entrée: melon. Cheese: reblochon and one other. Dessert: ice cream, there was a carton of chocolate flavour in the freezer. And for the main course she hesitated between fish – a nice piece of salmon, perhaps – and pork. She had a lovely recipe for pork chops cooked in cider and apples – and finally decided on the meat. Most of her ingredients for the dinner were already in the kitchen so her shopping list was, in fact, very short. Bread and pork ... oh, and a bottle of cider. She knew there was a good butcher down in the village; both Marie-Laure and Bénédicte had sung his praises. She vaguely remembered Bénédicte linking him in some way with Jacqueline, but couldn't remember the details. No doubt he provided meat for La Grange and Jacqueline had to pick it up; something like that.

She wandered down to the village in the afternoon and easily located the butcher's shop on rue du Paradis – and the 'Closed' sign. She'd completely forgotten that, unlike Paris, provincial shops closed for a couple of hours after lunch. Helen looked at her watch. Two-thirty and the butcher opened again at three o'clock, so she had half an hour to kill. She continued walking down rue du Paradis and stood for a while gazing at the lush valley below and the snow-capped peaks in the distance. The rue du Paradis was well-named. This really was heaven. She found a grassy bank nearby, sat down, closed her eyes and when she opened them again it was just after three-thirty.

There were two elderly ladies standing at the counter when Helen walked into the butcher's shop. The first one, a stranger to Helen, was being served; the second lady was Madame Laval, the owner of La Grange. She turned round when Helen walked in and her face lit up in recognition.

'Ah bonjour, madame; ça va? Are you enjoying your holiday with Adam and Marie-Laure?'

Helen hesitated. Madame Laval was obviously unaware that the Beaulacs had gone away and she didn't feel it was up to her to discuss their business. She smiled at the large, pleasant woman in front of her.

'Yes, Madame Laval, I'm having a wonderful time. I just love the mountains. You're so lucky living here. I do envy you.'

'If I had a centime for every time a tourist said that to me, I'd be able to retire!' Madame Laval chortled. 'Parisians do appreciate our fresh air and the peace and quiet.'

'Well, I'm not exactly a Parisienne,' Helen grinned, 'but I do appreciate the peace and quiet! Not to mention the scenery.'

'You're English, aren't you? I think you must know Paul, Adam's young English friend who plays in his band.'

Helen nodded slowly, taken completely unawares. At that moment the first customer shuffled out of the shop saying, 'Au revoir, bonne journée!' to everyone.

'Au revoir, madame. I met Paul when he stayed at the chalet last year,' Madame Laval continued. 'Such a nice young man. Rather shy; but so well-mannered – and good-looking in a very English way. In fact, for me, he was a typical Englishman in every way – and that's a compliment, madame!'

Helen laughed.

'I'm not sure he's typically English,' she smiled, 'whatever that is. But he's … he's a special kind of man. That's true.'

'Will he be coming to the chalet again this summer?'

Helen slowly shook her head. She didn't like the direction the conversation was taking and didn't know Madame Laval well enough to let slip any confidences. She didn't want to let any cats out of the Beaulac's enigmatic and bulging bag.

'Oh, I'm not sure about that. He's been invited, of course … and … and it would be nice if he came … but …' She could think of nothing else to say without getting into deep water.

Madame Laval nodded sagely and cocked her head to one side, scrutinising the younger woman. Her demeanour had totally changed and Helen gasped.

'Well, if he does come, you'd better make sure he stays away from La Grange … away from the village … we don't want any more distress, we had enough last year.'

She then turned her attention to the big and ruddy-faced butcher who was patiently waiting to take her order.

As Helen carried her few purchases home her idle thoughts turned to other things than food. Adam and Marie-Laure had been gone a couple of days and there had been no telephone call. Maybe that was because of the time difference, but Helen somehow didn't think so. She also thought about her breakfast conversation with Bénédicte and the old lady's reluctance to talk about the 'villainous, destructive brother'. The words, coming back to her, brought on a slow nausea. Bénédicte was not a malicious woman; she was the epitome of kindness and generosity of spirit. Helen was convinced she wouldn't make censorious remarks about anyone without just cause. And again, her mother's seemingly prophetic words came crawling into her mind; the only men *you're* capable of attracting are either idiots or bastards. And why had the very pleasant Madame Laval suddenly and completely changed her attitude when she thought Paul might be going to the chalet? Oh, if only she were capable of writing poetry; if only she could put her pen to paper and write it all down in verse, get it all out of her system in the only way she knew – or had known – how. If only...

The phone was ringing when Helen got back to the chalet. She dropped the key in her haste to open the door, cursed and dropped it again because of the trembling in her fingers. Once inside, she threw down her shopping bag and snatched up the receiver, taking deep breaths at the same time.

'Allo?'

'Bonjour, Madame Beaulac. How are you?'

'I ... I'm afraid Madame Beaulac's not here at the moment. Can I take a message for her?'

In her disappointment Helen didn't recognise the young waitress's voice, or maybe she wouldn't have recognised it, anyway.

'Oh. I see. Well, Madame Beaulac invited me to dinner tomorrow evening and I was just calling to check that it's still okay.'

'Jacqueline, this is Helen ... Marie-Laure's friend. We met at La Grange the other evening...'

'Oh, yes. Yes, I remember. How are you?'

'I'm fine, thanks. Look, Jacqueline, there's a bit of a problem tomorrow evening. Well, not a problem exactly but ... well, Marie-Laure and Adam have gone ... have had to go to New York urgently and ... well, they don't know how long they'll be staying. So, there'll be just the two of us for dinner ... that's if you'd still like to come.'

Helen heard her own voice and thought she sounded ungracious if not rather rude.

'I'd really love you to come, Jacqueline. It'll certainly be better than having dinner alone and it'll ... erm ... it'll give us the chance to get to know each other a bit. Won't it?'

'Well, if you're sure it's no trouble,' Jacqueline all but whispered.

'Of course not! Anyway, I've just been out and bought food so you have to come,' Helen laughed.

'Well, thank you. Thank you very much. Can I bring anything?'

'Just yourself,' Helen replied, unoriginally, then added, 'and maybe a packet of Rennies,' as a witty afterthought, knowing the brand existed in France. The witty afterthought was greeted with total silence and then

Jacqueline said she really had to go because she was supposed to be laying tables for the evening's clientele.

'Right then,' Helen said, a little too brightly, 'see you tomorrow.'

The next time the phone rings, she told herself, it'll be a call from New York. But the phone didn't ring again that evening.

***

The fresh mountain air was starting to knock Helen out and on Wednesday evening she went to bed early and woke up at nine o'clock the next morning. She felt refreshed and as she stretched between the cool sheets, she felt the warm sticky dampness between her legs. Oh hell, no, she cursed aloud. Her periods were always regular, she could set her watch by them, but what with one thing and another this month she hadn't given them a thought. She leaped out of bed and cursed even more when she saw the dark red stain spreading on Marie-Laure's crisp white sheet. After a trip to the bathroom, she went back to her bedroom and tore the soiled sheet off the mattress. Now, where did Marie-Laure tell me the clean bed linen was? she asked herself.

She turned on the light in the room next door and wrinkled her nose at the fusty smell. The room was warm, heavy with lack of air, but she shivered. Her eyes travelled around the antique and unattractive furniture, cardboard boxes and unused household gadgets; knick-knacks and ancient toys. After several moments reflection she walked across the room to the hideous chest of drawers that stood facing her. The clean bed linen for the guest rooms was somewhere in there, in one of those drawers, she remembered Marie-Laure's instructions. But she hadn't said which one, had told her to rummage around. So ... she pulled open the top drawer. It was empty but for a sachet of potpourri. The second drawer was almost empty except for a neat little pile of pillow cases. She didn't need a pillow case, at least not yet. She pulled open a third drawer but with great difficulty, and then blinked. There were sheets, yes, piles of them, but sheets of paper. Paper that had at one time been white but was now yellowing with age; and writing that had also faded with the years. Helen's limbs began to tremble, her chest felt tight; maybe some answers to her questions lay in those ancient letters, documents, whatever they were. She jerked the drawer with clammy hands and it dropped with a heavy thud to the floor. And as it fell, the top layer of correspondence fell too, or rather slid out of the drawer and scattered at Helen's knees, as she was now kneeling. She cautiously picked up one of the envelopes and looked at writing that seemed vaguely familiar.

Firley
September, 1976

My beautiful Turtle Dove,

I've missed you so much since you left Firley and went back to France.
I can't stop thinking about you. You're on my mind all the time. Please
let me come to see you in Paris. I'll save up and stay in a cheap hotel –
you can come to me there. I'm thinking about our evening on the
moors together. You never forget your first time. Well, that's what they
say, and I know I'll never forget mine. I'm really glad that my first time
was with you.

Please write to me soon.
All my love,
Malcolm

And there were more; many more very similar letters. Short, not very well
written, not very well expressed, only full of frustration, love and longing.
Helen was numb, incapable of feeling more hurt, pain, deception and she
continued to read each letter thoroughly, dissecting each word, each
sentence, each beginning and each end and asked herself questions and
didn't listen to her own replies.

Dear Turtle Dove,

I was happy to have a letter from you at last – I thought you'd forgotten
me. Your letter – that I've read at least 1001 times, is at the moment
lying in my shirt pocket, next to my heart. When will I see you again?
I'm coming to France. I want to be with you. I want us to be together
again like we were that first – and last – time on the moors. I'm glad
you liked the photos – keep them safe from prying eyes. I'll do the
same. I thought about displaying one of them in Watts' window for all
the world to see – or at least all Keighley – but decided it wasn't a good
idea!

I love you, Turtle Dove, I love you, I love you. Je t'aime (is that
right?).

I love you,
Malcolm

Helen's senses had completely seized up as she read, re-read and finally put the letters back into their respective envelopes. There were cards, too, the kind of cards he'd never sent to her. Suddenly, her trembling hands were ferreting amongst the rest of the papers, searching for more words to torture herself with. She had to see, to read everything, to know everything. The envelope at the bottom and towards the back of the deep drawer was bigger and thicker than the others. She pulled it out and emptied its contents on to the floor. Seventeen- year-old Marie-Laure, alias Turtle Dove, looked up at her in various stages of undress and finally completely naked with the magnificent Pennines in the background. And the picture at the bottom of the pile seemed to stick to her clammy hand, not wanting to be discarded, wanting to mock. Once more, the wild, lonely Pennines were the background. And in the foreground the two of them; Turtle Dove and Malcolm, posing in front of his automatic camera, laughing, loving and completely naked.

Helen sat on the floor for a long time and didn't know that she was crying. Not that it mattered any more, it was history, it belonged to the past. But it had mattered then, at that time, in the hot summer of 1976 when all their lives had been turned upside down. And Marie-Laure had oh so blatantly lied to her, looked into her gullible, naïve, believing face and lied to her. 'Nothing happened between Malcolm and me,' she'd assured Helen and had denied ever having had a sexual relationship with him. And then, much later, she'd drawn Helen's attention to this room, this old and ugly chest of drawers. A forgotten room that nobody ever visited except herself. And she'd encouraged Helen to rummage around until she found what she was looking for. Or rather, as it turned out, what she wasn't looking for. Well, she'd found this ... this pictorial proof of Marie-Laure's lies and the once-upon-a-summertime couple's deceit. Now, as far as she was concerned, this proof belonged to her, and she carefully placed the evidence on her bedside table, upright against the heavy brass lamp and left it there, so that it would be the first thing she saw every morning and the last thing she saw before turning out the light.

After the initial torture and pain came the healthy anger and Helen wanted to retaliate, to lash out, to have her revenge. But that, of course, was impossible; impossible and futile. And then she wanted to take a leaf out of Paul's notorious book and flee, never to return. But she wasn't going to do that, either; at least not yet. She'd get through the day and the evening with Jacqueline and then she'd get her thoughts together. And she had a lot of thinking to do. If the phone rang, she wouldn't answer it; she wouldn't be capable of speaking to Marie-Laure at the moment; maybe never again. She needed to talk to someone, needed to talk about what she'd just lived through. But there was absolutely no one she could talk to; not about Marie-Laure's secret and sordid past. Not Bénédicte, not Jacqueline. There was always Jill, of course. Jill was the best person in the world to listen, sympathise and no doubt advise. She looked at her watch. Eleven o'clock. Even with the hour time difference Jill would be at work now. Anyway, she had enough problems of her own. Caroline had a new boyfriend and Jill didn't know who was leading whom astray but she was expecting something drastic to happen any minute; Darren (bloody stupid name, if you ask me, good, old-fashioned Tom had grumbled) was new to the district, so Jill supposed it was her wayward daughter who was doing the leading ... but it took two to tango ... and Jill was at the end of her tether. So, Helen couldn't burden her best friend with her heartache and anger when she had so many troubles of her own.

The phone rang twice that day and Helen heard it both times because she didn't go out at all. She got through the day by cleaning the chalet, watering the many plants and reading; or at least trying to read. She mentally willed her beloved neighbour to stay away and, miraculously, Bénédicte didn't put her appearance in that day. On the one hand Helen would have welcomed her with open arms because she desperately needed to talk; on the other hand, she couldn't talk to Bénédicte about what she needed to talk about. She prepared the table, the meal and herself in the early evening and the doorbell rang at exactly seven-thirty. Helen slapped a smile on her face and opened the door.

'Hello, Jacqueline. Come in.'

She stepped aside to let the young woman and her bunch of carnations into the kitchen. It seemed quite a while before Jacqueline put one foot in front of the other and moved forward. Helen had the impression she was nailed to the spot and two bright pink spots lit up her cheeks. Helen felt a twinge of discomfort as the girl's dark eyes scrutinised her with less than friendliness. Or maybe that was her imagination running haywire.

'Thank you,' Helen said, taking the diffidently-offered flowers, 'they're lovely.' And then, because she was at a loss for words, 'And did you bring the Rennies? I love cooking but, living alone, I don't get much practice and all my culinary delights usually turn out to be catastrophes.' She realised that she was babbling and added, 'Anyway, it should be okay this evening. It's a tried and tested recipe that's never been known to fail. Look, why don't you sit down while I put these in a vase and then I'll pour us an aperitif.'

Jacqueline pulled out a chair at the set table and sat down. She seemed to be concentrating very hard on the plate in front of her and Helen wondered if she'd committed an enormous faux pas when laying the French table. Jacqueline's silence continued, and as Helen quickly arranged the carnations in a ceramic jug her guest watched her almost furtively.

'That's a pretty dress.' Helen smiled, clutching at a straw. 'Yellow suits your dark colouring. Where do people round here buy their clothes, by the way?'

'Chamonix, Annecy, Sallanches. I don't have to bother too much about clothes because I always wear the same thing at the restaurant, it's a kind of uniform. It suits me ... it saves me time as well as money. And I never go anywhere exciting enough to get dressed up. It's just as well ... I don't earn enough to spend my money on fancy clothes.'

The sudden torrent of words took Helen by surprise and she stared at the younger woman. She placed the jug of flowers in the middle of the table and made her way to the drinks' cupboard.

'Me neither. Anyway, I prefer to spend my money on other things. Books, things for my bedsit ... Music. Much more interesting than trailing around clothes shops!'

She went into the living room and opened the drinks cabinet door.

'What would you like to drink? There's ... erm ... there's whisky ... gin ... Martini ...'

'If you have wine, I'll just have a glass of wine, please.'

'Will white be okay?'

Jacqueline nodded.

'That's what I'll have, too.'

Helen poured the drinks and sat down at the table opposite her unwanted, taciturn guest. They picked up their glasses, clinked and said, 'Santé'. Then they fell into silence. Helen glanced at the old clock on the kitchen wall, saw the hours ticking by and wondered how, verbally, to fill them.

'I ... erm ... I haven't seen Bénédicte today, which is unusual.'

There was no response from Jacqueline. Helen sipped her wine.

'She usually calls round at least once a day,' she continued, clinging on to what she thought could be a substantial straw. 'She's a wonderful character, isn't she? Unique. You know, she took me on the Mont Blanc tram and ...' and she recited her unforgettable trip with the ex-nun, hoping to entertain the girl but was rewarded with a rather watery smile and a slight shrug of the shoulders. Jacqueline obviously knew Bénédicte too well to be entertained by her eccentricities. Helen was beginning to wish that the old lady was there to help the evening along; she was going to need some prop unless things changed drastically. She watched Jacqueline take several more sips of her white wine and after a while the two red spots, which had gradually faded from her cheeks, came back with a vengeance. Suddenly, she hiccupped, giggled and put her hand to her mouth.

'Sorry!'

'Don't be. You can hiccup till the meadow ladies come home as far as I'm concerned.' The English expression translated into French sounded more than ridiculous and Jacqueline gaped at her.

'Till who comes home?'

'The meadow ladies. Cows. It's an English expression. Till the cows come home. Meaning a long time...'

Jacqueline looked to be deep in thought and a small smile was forming on her pretty lips.

'Meadow ladies. I like it.' She started to giggle again. 'I like this wine, too, but I daren't have any more because I'm driving.'

'You can spend the night here, if you like.'

Jacqueline stared at her again and Helen could have bitten out her tongue. Well, she'd very foolishly said it now and couldn't take the offer back.

'Thank you,' Jacqueline whispered and hiccupped again. 'But ... well, it's not really convenient.'

Relieved, Helen didn't argue; she stood up and went to check the pork that was sizzling nicely in the oven, the aroma tantalizingly filling the kitchen.

'That smells good,' Jacqueline said. 'I'm really hungry.'

'Excellent!' Helen grinned, suddenly beginning to feel a bit more relaxed. She took a dish of sliced melon out of the fridge and, as she walked back to the table, Jacqueline gazed at her with probing eyes.

'You don't live with him, then?'

Helen sat down at right angles to her guest and pulled the chair nearer the table.

'Sorry?' she said.

Jacqueline was blushing scarlet and her eyes flashed awkwardly around the kitchen.

'I've just realised ... a few minutes ago you said you didn't bother much about cooking because you live alone. So ... you don't live with ... with *him*.'

Helen thought it was just as well Jacqueline didn't want to drink too much alcohol; she was already talking in riddles.

'I don't live with who, Jacqueline?'

The two women looked at each other and Helen saw what she thought were tears at the back of Jacqueline's dark eyes. It was a long time before she replied, 'With … with Paul. Do you only … I mean, well, do you think you'll marry him?'

'Jacqueline, I don't have a clue what you're talking about. I'm not going to marry anybody; I don't even have … just a minute. Paul. Are you talking about Paul Atkinson? The saxophonist in Adam's band?'

Jacqueline's expression was a mixture of pleasure, pain and pure embarrassment. She nodded. 'Yes. Yes, Paul Atkinson.'

'I hardly know him, Jacqueline. Adam introduced me to him and he invited me out for a meal … once. He's … he's very pleasant and, well, I enjoyed his company. End of story. Why the devil did you think we were living together?'

'I wasn't sure if … if you actually lived together but I understood he was your man. If you know what I mean.'

The two red spots had spread across her face and neck and she couldn't meet Helen's mystified gaze. Helen's mind was racing … what sinister and cruel tricks had Marie-Laure been up to this time?

'What are you talking about, Jacqueline?' She picked up her fork and took a bite of melon but her eyes never left Jacqueline's face. 'Look, I think this needs sorting out, don't you?'

Jacqueline finally smiled shyly at her. 'You bought this evening's meal from the butcher in rue du Paradis, didn't you? My flat is – unfortunately – above his shop. In fact, he's my landlord and thanks to him I get to hear all the village gossip. It's his favourite pastime. Gossip.'

'But I hardly spoke to …'

'Apparently you were speaking to Madame Laval in the shop and my landlord was listening, as usual. Well, he must have got his facts wrong. He put two and two together and made fifty-six. I nearly didn't come this evening, you know.'

Helen stared at her.

'Why on earth not?'

The colour in Jacqueline's cheeks deepened and she giggled.

'I was jealous. One day last year Paul was in the butcher's and he told him that there was someone special in Paris. He'd already shown an interest in me. We spent a day together, in fact, just a day but it was enough for me to know I was …' Her voice lowered. 'I was falling in love with him and I thought, well, I foolishly thought he felt the same. And I couldn't believe that someone like him – quite a famous musician in Paris – could be interested in me. It was exciting and at the same time I felt that it was … well, right, somehow. I can't really explain. Anyway, I should have known better. Of course a man like that would have someone special in Paris and I didn't want to get involved, to get hurt. So, I decided it would be better not to see him again. There was no point. So – I know it was wrong and very impolite – but I just didn't turn up for the dinner he was cooking. And I never saw or heard from him again.'

'But, Jacqueline, Paul hasn't got anyone special in Paris. He hasn't got anyone, full stop. In fact, the poor bloke ... Look, I think this landlord of yours, this butcher, should mind his own damn business.'

'Do you like him, Helen? I mean, do you think he's a good person? Do you think he's *decent*?'

'Who, the butcher? No, I think he's a right bastard ...' Helen smiled. 'Sorry, only joking. Yes, I do think Paul's a good and decent person. He's painfully shy and difficult to get to know, but he has a lot of excellent qualities.'

Jacqueline sat in silence while Helen served the main course.

'I only met him twice,' she said, after Helen had sat down. 'but I don't know why, he really impressed me. He was a gentleman. An English gentleman.' Jacqueline suddenly laughed. 'That probably sounds silly to you but he was so polite, correct and he seemed genuinely interested in me. That was hard for me to believe and I was so ... so happy and when I found out he had someone special in Paris I took it very badly.'

'Well, I can assure you that there isn't anyone special in Paris. And why was it so hard to believe that Paul was interested in you, for God's sake?'

Jacqueline shrugged, looked at her and toyed with a piece of cooked apple on her plate.

'This is very good, Helen.'

'Thanks. Why was it so hard for you to believe that Paul was interested in you?'

Jacqueline made a despairing gesture that encompassed her whole body.

'I suppose I just don't have confidence in myself.' She paused and sighed deeply before continuing. 'I'm adopted, you know. Please don't misunderstand me, Helen, I love my parents very much. They've brought me up as their own daughter and given me absolutely everything. But when I found out I was adopted, I never felt quite the same. My parents have natural children, too; two boys and a girl and I could never accept that Mum and Dad loved me as much as them. It wasn't possible, wasn't normal, I always told myself when I was a kid. And my brothers and sister used to tease me and tell me I was different, not really wanted, that I didn't belong. And over the years I began to think – and I still think – that I'm odd, different and could never be special to anyone.'

'Oh, Jacqueline,' Helen whispered and there were tears in her eyes. 'Did your parents know that your brothers and sister said such terrible things to you?'

'No, of course not, I kept it to myself, bottled it up. And it was impossible for me to believe that a man like Paul could possibly fall in love with me ... and how could I possibly compare with the special someone in Paris? I even convinced myself that it had been Bénédicte's idea, knowing how she'd give anything to see me married with babies. I was convinced that she'd twisted the poor man's arm and he'd asked me out to please her.' Jacqueline's small voice trailed away. She smiled ruefully at her sympathetic listener and added, 'I couldn't bear that idea, that Paul had only invited me to please Bénédicte and that he was probably cursing her as well as me. Then I was told that Paul had someone special in Paris and I could imagine what that someone would be like. Beautiful, of course, intelligent, funny, probably very glamorous. So, I decided not to keep our second date.' She paused. 'When I was told you were Paul's Someone Special, I wasn't at all surprised. Everything seemed to fit.'

Helen stared at her companion, her mouth slightly open, her dinner almost forgotten. Beautiful, intelligent, funny, probably glamorous. Everything seemed to fit. You've no gumption, lass; you're hopeless; you can't do owt right; the only men *you're* capable of attracting are either idiots or bastards. But in the more recent past, 'If you knew how much you didn't bore me, Helen, I think you'd be very surprised.'

'Would you like to see Paul again?' Helen gently asked.

Jacqueline looked at her shyly and Helen watched the colour rising again in her cheeks. Very slowly she began to nod, which also managed to be a shake of the head and Helen felt slim young fingers clutch at her own.

'He nearly came here this summer,' Helen continued, not knowing if she was saying the right thing. 'Adam invited him but he'd already booked a holiday in Antibes with Serge, Adam's drummer. He really wanted to come, Jacqueline; the only reason he didn't was because he didn't want to let Serge down. That proves what a decent bloke he is, doesn't it?'

As she spoke, Helen knew that Paul's wanting to accept Adam's invitation had nothing to do with her being at the chalet but it had a lot to do with Jacqueline. She felt convinced of that now; and then his parting words came back to her before she'd escaped into her building and slammed the door. There was something he wanted to explain to her; something he needed to talk to her about. Or more like someone. She could have kicked herself ... Jacqueline's pretty, full lips suddenly widened into a sunny smile and her dark eyes crinkled around the corners. Something stirred inside Helen as she looked at the younger woman. She was a very pretty girl, stunning in her own way, and her shyness was endearing in its familiarity. But there was something else about her, something that Helen couldn't quite put her finger on.

'Do you know him well?' Jacqueline asked and Helen smiled to herself.

'No, not well. As I said, I've been in his company a couple of times and I've had dinner with him. And when I had dinner with him, I got to know him a little better. He seemed to loosen up a bit and we talked a lot about different things. He's a very nice man, Jacqueline.'

'And he's gone to Antibes for the summer.'

'Maybe not for the entire summer.'

There was a long silence then during which time Helen left Jacqueline to her thoughts and busied herself with the cheeseboard. When she sat down again her companion took the initiative for the first time and asked Helen where she came from, where she was born and thereby changing the subject. Helen was relieved.

'Yorkshire,' she smiled, 'in the north of England. It's a really beautiful region. It's not the Alps, of course, but ... What's the matter, Jacqueline?'

'Nothing's the matter,' she said, 'not really. But ... well ... I told you I was adopted. I was born in France, Paris to be exact, and my parents adopted me when I was six months old – and brought me to Annecy. My mum told me I'd been adopted when I was very young and it didn't really mean anything to me. But when my brother and sister started to ... you know ... I began to think about my real ... my birth ... family. My real father and mother. At first Mum wouldn't tell me anything, but in the end, I suppose she got fed up of listening to me. I found out that my real mother was French, a Parisienne and only eighteen when I was born, and my father was an Englishman – from Yorkshire. They met, apparently, when my mother was staying there with her English penfriend. It would have been in 1976.'

Helen waited a long time before she spoke and Jacqueline must have wondered what was going through her mind. When she could finally trust herself to speak, Helen asked, 'Do you ... erm ... do you know who your parents are? Their names, I mean.'

Jacqueline pulled a face, shrugged her shoulders and then smiled slowly, sweetly.

'No, I've no idea. At one time I would have liked to know but now it's not that important. Maybe one day I'll try to trace them but ... not at the moment; not for a while. I love my adoptive parents and there's no point in hurting them, is there?'

'No. Of course not.'

Helen avoided her eyes. They sat in silence for a while and then Helen, remembering her manners, offered the cheeseboard to her guest. They both selected reblochon and Roquefort, buttered chunks of crusty bread and concentrated on their food for a while. And then Jacqueline, obviously wanting to change the subject again, asked Helen what she'd been doing with herself since she'd been left alone.

'And have you taken many photographs?' she asked.

'Quite a lot,' Helen smiled. 'Especially when Bénédicte took me on the Mont Blanc tram. I hope they all turn out okay – I'm no professional.'

'Paul had a very good camera,' Jacqueline remembered. 'He left it on the newsagent's counter one day. That's how we ...' She shook her head. 'Oh, it doesn't matter. I'd have liked to see his photos, though.' She paused. 'When I was very young, I wanted to become a photographer. I always liked taking pictures, even when I was a little girl. I won a couple of competitions at school. Later, I wanted to enter the convent ... but that's another story and thank goodness I didn't. Anyway, Mum and Dad didn't encourage me in either aspiration. They didn't think photography was a suitable career for a girl, or so they said. Actually, I think they were afraid that I'd move to Paris and a life of debauchery – so I never became a photographer. I never became a nun, either. I became a waitress. And that's how I met Paul.'

Helen, after serving dessert, tried to pour the coffee without spilling too much. But the sudden summoning of the telephone caused her to spill quite a lot.

'Aren't you going to answer the phone?' Jacqueline asked when Helen didn't offer to move.

'No.'

Eventually the phone stopped ringing. Jacqueline continued to gaze at her hostess with something like a question mark between her eyes.

Chapter Nineteen

'Are you disappointed?'

'Yeah, of course I am, but to be honest I'm not really surprised. It's normal she wants to spend her holiday in France. I just hope she'll come at Christmas.'

'Don't bank on that, either,' said Tom. 'She'll probably be back in the Alps at Christmas – learning how to ski, heaven forbid. I tell you what, this chilli con carne's right champion, you can give my compliments to the chef.'

'And a nice tip for the waitress?' Jill grinned as she stood up and started to clear the table. She asked her tired husband if he wanted a slice of apple pie, at the same time pouring water into the electric kettle.

'Not for me, thanks. Just a nice cup o' tea, love.'

Tom yawned, stretched and asked Jill about her day, working part-time at the small library in Firley, and he told her about his own heavy day, the stressed and overworked computer programmer in the subsidiary of an American company in Leeds. They were always interested in each other's days and were never bored by their respective professional anecdotes.

'Let's have our tea in comfort in the living room,' Tom yawned. 'I need to put my feet up.'

'It's a sign of age,' commented Jill.

'No, love, it's a sign of infinite wisdom and acknowledgement of my just desserts.' He turned, the large blue, white and stained teapot in his two hands, and winked at his wife. 'And, anyway, I want to see what my kids are up to.'

His kids, Sharon who was twelve and Joey, nine, having already eaten their dinner much earlier, were sprawled on the floor in front of a far-too-loud television, rapidly changing channels, yelling at the top of their voices and bashing each other with the remote control. Tom walked across the room, Jill pulled a worse-for-wear coffee table in front of the sofa and Tom sat down.

'All right, you two, pack it in. If we lived near the cemetery, you'd be waking the dead.'

'Well, we don't live near the cemetery, do we Dad? So don't worry about it.'

Sharon didn't look at her father when she spoke to him but she did snatch the remote control out of her brother's weaker fingers and thwacked him on the head with it. Jill's sudden intake of breath was audible and she and Tom exchanged a glance. Tom would have let it go but Jill said, 'Let's have less of your cheek, Sharon, and a bit more respect for your father, please. You're getting more like your sister every day.'

Tom's mug stopped in mid-air on its way to his mouth.

'Speaking of which – or rather who – where is our Caroline?'

'Upstairs doin' her homework,' Sharon told him, still not looking at her father.

'Please don't lie to your dad, Sharon.' Jill's voice was soft but firm. 'Or anybody else for that matter.'

She put her Best Mum in the World mug on the coffee table, its contents untouched. She slowly stood up and walked towards the big bay window that looked on to the busy suburban street, with a view of the moors between the semi-detached houses opposite.

Jill hadn't changed very much in twenty-three years. She'd put on a little weight, there were tiny lines around her eyes and mouth and stray silver strands in her still-short brown hair. Otherwise, physically, she was still the same Jill. Tom, on the other hand, had changed almost beyond recognition. Over the years he'd become stout, thanks to Jill's excellent homely cooking, his customary pints at the Bay Horse, a sedentary job and a close relationship with his car. The little that was left of his hair was salt and pepper and his once mischievous and teasing eyes were now camouflaged behind horn-rimmed glasses. He looked a good ten years older than his forty-two. His bespectacled eyes quickly followed his wife across the room and he watched her doing nothing, standing by the window, playing for time.

'All right, where is she, Jill? What's she up to now? Has she had her tea?'

'No ... no, Tom. She hasn't been home.'

'Again.' After a slight pause, 'Has she phoned?'

'No.'

'I don't know why the bloody hell she wanted us to buy her a mobile phone when she never uses it.'

'She does use it. But not with us.'

The younger children were still lying on the thick brown carpet in front of the television, seemingly oblivious to the conversation behind them. But the screaming and whacking had stopped, at least for the time being they seemed to be interested in the same cartoon.

'What did she say when she left home this morning?'

'The usual "See you later".'

Tom groaned.

'For Christ's sake, I don't want a repeat of that last episode. If she's got herself another bloke, I'm not joking, I'll kill this one if he's anything like ... what was his name?'

Jill didn't supply the missing, forgotten and unimportant name. She stood in front of the windowsill, toying with a drooping begonia and battling with her own thoughts.

'This one's not like Stuart. He's better looking.'

Sharon didn't take her eyes off the screen as her shrill young voice piped up the information.

'What did you say, Sharon?'

Jill took a couple of steps forward.

'You heard. This one's better looking.'

Tom breathed in deeply, clenched and unclenched his now podgy fists and adjusted his glasses – a habit he'd acquired under stress.

'And who might "this one" be, young lady?' he asked. 'And please look at me when you speak to me.'

Sharon sighed deeply, rolled on to her side and looked up at her father.

'I don't know his name, Dad, but he's better looking than ...'

'I don't give a damn if he's better looking than Robert Redford ... Who the bloody hell is he?'

'Tom ...'

'Sharon. Who's this boy your sister's seeing? Your mum and I need to know.'

Sharon rolled her eyes dramatically and tapped the carpet with none-too-clean fingers, enjoying the small melodrama and her part in it.

'I don't know his name,' she repeated, 'but I've seen her with him, twice. Both times when I were comin' home from school – on them rocks on moor where Helen used to live. They were neckin'.'

She announced the last sentence with some elan. Tom stood up, stuffed his clenched fists into his trouser pockets, puffed out his ruddy cheeks and made a slow tour round the sofa. His heavy, clumsy feet knocked the coffee table leg and crockery clattered.

'Tom, love ... calm down.'

'I won't calm down, Jill. I've calmed down too often. That daughter of ours has got to learn.'

He stopped his strolling when he reached his wife and gazed levelly at her.

'I'm going to wait up for her tonight. You go to bed ...'

'No, Tom, I want to ...'

'You can speak to her tomorrow. I want to have *my* say tonight.'

Caroline Hopkins didn't come home until three minutes after midnight. She tried without much success to unlock and open the front door in total silence but she needn't have bothered because Tom's alert and prepared ears would have heard dust moving. The sixteen-year-old gently closed the door, locked it and tiptoed to the staircase. She was ready to make her soundless way to bed when her father's voice arrested her from the living room on her left.

'Caroline!'

Several moments passed before the door opened and Tom, red-eyed and grey-faced, standing in front of the fireplace, watched his eldest daughter skulk into the room. Caroline was as tall as her father but without his weight. She was very thin and the clothes she wore that evening – torn and faded jeans, tee-shirt and denim jacket – hung loosely on her skeletal frame. Her nut-brown hair, so like her mother's, hung long and lankily around her shoulders and her otherwise pretty face was spattered with adolescent blemishes. The collar of her denim jacket and her long hair failed to hide a large, ugly red mark on the side of her neck. She stood in the doorframe, sullen and defiant.

'Come here, Caroline.'

Caroline didn't move. Tom took two steps forward and repeated his command. Something on his grey face made Caroline obey and now she stood in front of her father, her large, brown and could-be-pretty eyes gazing unblinkingly into his.

'Where've you been?'

No reply.

'I insist that you answer me, Caroline. WHERE HAVE YOU BEEN UNTIL BLOODY MIDNIGHT?'

The eyes looked away now and looked everywhere but at her father.

'If I have to repeat myself one more time ...'

Tom was not a violent man; he'd never resorted to physical punishment, even when his children pushed him to the limit, but now he pulled his fists out of his pockets and subconsciously began to raise them. Caroline's gaze fixed itself on the unprecedented threatening hands.

'I've been out for a walk.'

'Oh, aye, of course you have. Till midnight.'

'We went ... we went to the pub.'

'Ah. WE. WE went to the pub. Now we're getting somewhere. And what pub did WE go to?'

'The Fallen Skittle – that new place on the other side o' Firley. Where all them new houses are.'

'And what have you been drinking, Caroline?'

'Coke.'

'Look, please don't lie to me ... I do have a sense of smell. What have you been drinking?'

'Rum and Coke.'

'All right. And how many rum and Cokes did you drink?'

'One. Well ... maybe three. So what?'

'So bloody what? Caroline, you're sixteen years old, you're under age ... and now, more to the point, who's WE?'

'I'm tired, Dad. I want to go to bed. I've to be up for school in mornin'.'

'You weren't tired when you were drinking rum and Coke in that pub, were you? And since when have *you* been worried about getting up for school?' Tom's face was livid now, his eyes bulbous behind the lenses and his fists making menacing movements at his side. 'Who's WE?'

'His name's Darren.'

'Ah. His name's Darren. And who is Darren? How do you know Darren?'

Tom's vicious eyes were now focusing on the increasingly reddening mark on his daughter's neck and Caroline's fingers involuntarily and unsuccessfully tried to hide it.

'I met him last week at the youth club dance; he's just come to live up here with his dad. He hasn't got a mother. She's dead.'

'How old is he?'

'Same age as me – about.'

'A kid, then. Right, young lady, you're going to listen to me and you're going to do exactly as I tell you. You're going to stop seeing this ... this Darren or whatever his bloody daft name is, as of now ... No arguments, please ... You're going to apologise to your mum for causing her a lot of worry and you're going to stay in every night till the end of your school term.'

'Dad! You're mean! You're mean and nasty and old! And you don't understand nowt. I won't stop seeing him. I like him a lot and ... he likes me. Anyway, he's different.'

Tom exploded.

'Different? Different from who, for God's sake? He takes you up on the bloody moors for a necking session, gives you a vulgar love bite and takes you into a pub to drink rum and Coke ... Oh aye, he's different, all right.'

'I won't stop seeing him, Dad. I won't. He's the only good thing in my life right now.'

Tom laughed, mirthlessly. 'The only good thing in your life. Look, lass, get yourself up those stairs to bed, get up in time for school tomorrow and come straight home tomorrow evening. Pass all your exams and then get yourself an interesting, worthwhile job that's well paid. Then you'll know what's good in life. And if I hear you've been seeing this Darren What's-his-Name again I'll ...'

'Darren Malcolm Jones. That's his name.'

Tom's tirade came to a grinding halt. He stood motionless, his eyes blinking at his daughter, his mouth open, his fists suddenly limp.

'Darren what did you say?'

'Darren – Malcolm – Jones.'

'And you said his father had just come to live up here?'

Caroline watched her father's changing demeanour with rightful curiosity.

'Yeah. So what?'

Tom briefly turned away from her baffled gaze and, thrusting his hands back into his pockets, studied his feet.

'Look – er – Caroline.'

The living room door suddenly creaked open and Jill, wearing a faded pink quilted dressing gown over a short pink and maroon nightdress, stood questioningly in the doorway. Her anxious eyes met Tom's across the room.

'How long how they been living up here?' Tom asked and Caroline continued to look mystified.

'I dunno. About six weeks, I reckon. Does it matter? Look, I'm really tired. I'm off to bed ...'

She turned round and tried to make her way past her mother.

'Wait a minute!' Tom's voice halted her steps again and his two womenfolk looked at him.

'I think I'd like to meet this ... this Darren. And his father.'

He suddenly started to grin and Caroline blinked uncomprehendingly at him, at the same time eager to escape while the going was good.

'Why don't you invite them next Sunday, love?'

'Tom!' Jill cried out but it was also a question.

'I think we're going to meet an old and long-lost friend, love,' Tom told her, and in spite of her mounting curiosity, Caroline didn't miss the opportunity to escape.

***

Darren Malcolm Jones was the spitting image of his father at the same age. The same size, the same fair hair that fell disobediently into his laughing blue eyes.

Malcolm Jones, however, did not resemble his son. The hair was still fair but cut very short and was far too sparse to be floppy. Deep lines ran across his forehead and between his nose and chin and there were pockets of loose flesh under his eyes. Unlike Tom, he hadn't put much weight on, he was gaunt and looked under-nourished.

'Well, hello there. Hi! It's ... well, it's good to see you again, Malc. It's really good to see you. Look, don't just stand there like a stuffed dummy, mate, come on in. Come in ... come in, Darren, lad.'

Malcolm and Darren Jones walked across the Hopkins' threshold for the first time, carrying a bottle of champagne and a box of chocolates. Tom held the door open and Jill stood slightly behind him, holding her hands behind her back and chewing her bottom lip.

'Hi. Hi there, Jill, love. Long time no see, eh? It's ... it's great to see you. Great. You look ... great. Both of you.'

For a few minutes the three of them stood gawping awkwardly at one another and then they were suddenly shouting, yelling, dancing and embracing while the two adolescents looked on, mesmerised. Sharon and Joey were, as usual, in front of the television set and Jill had to bludgeon them into politeness. Their children's misconduct was temporarily forgotten as the three adults enjoyed their lunch and caught up on the many lost years.

'And your wife?' Jill tentatively asked, after Malcolm had talked about his recent purchase of a town house in Firley's newly developed estate, and his plans to acquire the premises of what used to be Watts' photographic shop. The children had left the table, two of them to watch yet another totally unsuitable video, the two others to continue their up to now illicit relationship in the open air. But this time in the garden, within parental view. Malcolm had talked about everything and everyone important in the last twenty years of his life, except his marriage, his wife. Jill poured a second cup of coffee, settled herself back on her highly polished dining chair and watched the changing expressions on Malcolm's almost unrecognisable face. He stirred sugar into his, or rather Joey's, 'I love Leeds United' mug, for an interminable time.

'Annabel,' he finally murmured.

***

272

Annabel Marks had been a phenomenally beautiful and successful model when Malcolm was introduced to her. Celebrated freelance photographer as he was, he'd been hired by a leading car magazine to photograph the new model of a certain brand of British car, at an exhibition that took place in a shopping centre in a north London suburb. Annabel had been hired as the human model to display her semi-naked body in various positions inside and outside the vehicle. Malcolm Jones had enjoyed and excelled at photographing both models and had fallen instantaneously in love with one of them. The feeling was quite mutual.

Nineteen-year-old Annabel was blonde, blue-eyed with a body that created fantasies. Her family, the last in a long line of children's book publishers, had wanted a different professional future for their daughter, but as in all other aspects of her life, Annabel had got her way in the end. Although her parents would have preferred to see her doing more useful, intellectual work, they were pleased to see her successful and happy in what she did. Men had never been in short supply but Annabel, being in the position to pick and choose, had never lost her heart to any of them. However, when Malcolm focused his camera on her face with apparent professional indifference and later treated her to his most engaging smile plus an invitation to dinner, her disdain did a very quick disappearing act. Their love affair was vital, all encompassing, physically satisfying and turbulent. They were two magnets that electrified each other when they came together. After their hasty marriage, they both continued their respective careers and often came together professionally, which was also electrifying. Malcolm, a professional perfectionist, would tolerate no nonsense from his models, whether they were women, children, animals or cars. Annabel, after a lifetime of having her own way, was no easy person to work with and often a nightmare to live with. Their fights, verbal and occasionally mildly physical, gradually became more frequent, more intense, but their reconciliations were always worth the agony. Their small but charming house in Egham, Surrey, was as much a sanguinary battleground as a honeymoon haven.

After the birth of Darren things began to calm down. Annabel, completely devoted to her new son, gave up modelling and consecrated her time and energy on motherhood to the point of neglecting her husband. And herself. Her previously unfaultable face and nubile body became almost unrecognisable as the weight piled on and the war paint came off. Darren didn't care if she was beautiful or not, so she didn't have to bother. Malcolm spent more time working, often away from their less than happy home. And Annabel would frequently accuse him of infidelity. He had so many opportunities to be unfaithful while she was stuck at home nursing the baby ... and yet it was her own choice; she wanted to be 'stuck at home'.

'And were you unfaithful to her?' Jill breathed, her mind racing back further in time.

'No.' Malcolm smiled, ruefully. 'Believe it or not, I wasn't.' He paused and cleared his throat. 'But she was right – I certainly had plenty of opportunities.'

There followed a long silence and the three people avoided one another's eyes. Tom took off his glasses and slowly rubbed his eyes. Jill's fingers started to play with the edge of the white cotton tablecloth.

'What happened to Annabel?' she finally asked him, very softly.

Malcolm was a long time answering. His eyes travelled around the small, cosy dining room and rested on the still life picture of fresh fruit in a basket over the sideboard.

'She died – four years ago last month. Cancer. Breast cancer at first. She had a mastectomy and we thought ... we thought she was going to be okay. She was just about coming to terms with losing her left breast, it wasn't easy for her. I don't suppose it's easy for any woman but Annabel ... well, her face and her body had been her fortune, if you like.' He shrugged lamely and paused. 'Then they found the cancer had spread ... to her liver. She had treatment, chemotherapy, radiotherapy, and she suffered like I've never seen or want to see anybody suffer.' He played with and concentrated on his teaspoon. 'All for nothing. She died. In a hospice, in her sleep – peacefully – one night. All alone.'

There was a long silence.

'What did you do after she died?' Tom eventually asked. 'I mean ... did you stay in Egham ... what did you do?'

Tom simply couldn't imagine his life without Jill; she was his second backbone.

'Yeah, I kept the house in Egham but it was no joy, believe me. I worked my backside off just to keep busy; it was the only way I could forget. And I tried my level best to bring Darren up as his mother would have wanted. So that she would have been proud of him.' He suddenly grinned. 'I'm not so sure I did such a good job in light of recent events.'

'So, what made you come back to Yorkshire?'

It was a long time before Malcolm replied.

'It might sound daft but ... I needed to get back to my roots. A new start, I suppose. And I wanted Darren to know his roots, too ... I suppose.'

'You never came back when your mam and dad were still living here, did you?'

There was a note of regret and slight accusation in Tom's voice.

'Not as often as I'd have liked. Or should have done.'

'Are they still living in Kent? We heard that they'd moved down there a while ago.'

'My mother is but she's in a home now. She's got Alzheimer's … my dad died of a massive heart attack five years ago.'

'Oh, Malcolm, how awful. You've been through such a lot …'

Jill stood up, started to clear away the dishes and suggested sitting in the garden, making the most of the May sunshine. The two teenagers who were already in the garden decided to go for a walk.

'And where do you two think you're going?' Tom glared.

'Up on moors, of course. Where else is there to go for a walk round here? What else is there to do?'

It was Darren who answered him. Tom and Jill exchanged anxious glances.

'Well, make sure you're back by tea-time. No later than six o'clock. Okay?'

'Aw, D-a-d …'

'Okay?'

They opened the garden gate and crashed it shut without replying.

'Kids,' Malcolm grinned, seemingly unworried. He broke the silence that followed by mentioning the name that, up to then, had been carefully avoided by everyone.

'I … I don't suppose Helen still lives round these parts, does she?'

His voice sounded nonchalant but his eyes and shifting limbs told another story.

'Helen doesn't even live in England,' Jill announced and felt Malcolm's astonished expression before she saw it. 'She lives in Paris. Been there since last November.'

'Paris?' Malcolm's voice was barely audible, his eyes unblinking. 'What's she doing there, for God's sake?'

Jill took a deep breath and avoided the unsteadying gaze.

'Actually, she's working for a woman called Marie-Laure. You'll remember her better as Turtle Dove. My French penfriend.'

Jill felt Tom's surprised and angry eyes on her but didn't turn to meet them. Her own eyes were now fixed on her guest, sitting on the lawn in front of her deck chair. At his eventual and diffident enquiry, she told Malcolm how Helen came to be working for Turtle Dove in her beauty salon in Paris.

'Christ Almighty.' And after a while. 'And is she married? Helen, I mean. Is she … does she have anyone in Paris?'

Jill was loath to say no but she had to be honest. She'd have never heard the last of it if she'd blatantly lied in front of Tom.

'No, she's not married. And, as far as I know there's no one special ...' Jill suddenly stopped, conscious that what she was saying wasn't quite the truth, either. 'Well, there's no one special in Paris.' She hurried on, wanting to change the subject. 'It's a pity that she couldn't come over this summer. I invited her but she's going to spend her holiday with Turtle Dove and her husband, Adam ...' She hesitated over the name but decided not to elaborate. Beaulac was a name she wanted to avoid, 'at their chalet in the French Alps. Sounds good, doesn't it?'

'Does she ever come back?'

'Come back here? She's not been back yet but she might come to spend Christmas with us. At any rate, I hope so.'

Malcolm nodded his head again, staring at the lawn on which he was sitting and pulling at some stray weeds.

'And ... is she ... is she okay? I mean, she must be doing all right for herself if she's living in Paris.' He stopped and was obviously finding difficulty continuing. 'How ... well, how does she get on with ... with what's-her-name, Turtle Dove? Christ, I can't imagine ...'

'They must get on all right if they're spending their holiday together.'

There followed a stillness broken only by the twittering of the sparrows and the occasional creaking of Tom's deck chair, which seemed to have a problem taking his weight.

'I'd give anything to see her again, you know.'

'Who? Helen or Turtle Dove?'

Malcolm's wan cheeks suddenly flushed purple, his full lips slithered into a thin white line and he thumped the soft grass with a big fist. Jill visibly jumped and both she and Tom could easily imagine the furore in the relationship with his equally tempestuous wife.

'I curse the day I laid eyes on that penfriend of yours.'

Jill and Tom said nothing. They waited.

'She was a witch – a bitch and a witch and she cast a kind of spell on me; hypnotised me, if you like. After I met her, I forgot everything and everybody; I was like a zombie. I'll be perfectly honest with you, I wanted her body and soul and I think I'd have committed any crime to get them.' He paused and suddenly sniggered. 'Does that sound like your old pal Malcolm Jones talking? No, not to me it doesn't, either. She made the first move, you know. She called all the tunes and I followed – she was like the Pied Piper of bloody Hamelin – and I was ... no, listen, I'm not trying to make excuses for myself, I behaved like a perfect prick. I tell you, I was like somebody in a trance, under drugs. She was a witch. We … fucked (I can't say we made love) up there on the moors. It was my first time – go on, you can laugh – and I was shit scared. Scared and at the same time on cloud bloody nine. She refused to let me use anything, although I was well provided. I was scared … scared that there'd be repercussions … but I never heard of any. We wrote to each other, you know, after she went back to France. I wanted to go over there, pleaded with her to let me go see her, but she made it pretty obvious … she didn't want me to go. She could be quite … quite nasty … It all fizzled out in the end … I suppose she found some other poor sod to hypnotise.' He stopped and was breathing heavily. 'And you, Jill, do you still hear from the lovely lady?'

Jill shook her head, Malcolm's words tumbling around inside.

'She never contacted me again after she went home. And I certainly didn't write to her. Even if I'd wanted to, I wouldn't have betrayed Helen.'

There was another pause in the conversation then. After a few minutes, Malcolm asked if Turtle Dove had been in touch since Helen worked for her.

'No. Not a word. It's strange, I suppose, but neither of us has put pen to paper. It's as though our – friendship – never existed. And that's fine by me.'

Tom suddenly got up, stretched and disappeared indoors to organise some 'liquid refreshment'. Malcolm watched him go.

'You seem really happy … settled … you and my old mate,' he smiled. 'I'm glad. You've got some great kids, too.'

Jill grinned and pulled a face.

'Well, I'm not so sure about that. Caroline's been giving us a lot of sleepless nights, I can tell you. And your son's not helped either, recently.'

'I'll have a word with him,' Malcolm replied. 'Like father like son, I reckon.'

Jill felt compunction. 'Don't be too hard on yourself, Malcolm. You were young and foolish and, let's face it, Turtle Dove was absolutely gorgeous. And different, of course. None of us poor little Brits could possibly compare with her.'

'Don't you believe it. Helen was worth ten times … by the way, how's the old martinet? Is Dorothy still going strong?'

'Dorothy's dead,' Jill told him.

'Good God, I thought she'd outlive us all. So, what carried her off in the end?'

***

She loves to sit on the doorstep and read the evening papers
She loves to sit and gossip with more than willing neighbours
She loves to watch the serials and soaps on TV,
She loves all these activities
But she doesn't love me.
My interest in literature was very cleverly banned
Perhaps it was something that she didn't understand
And she complained that I always
'had a bloody pen in my hand'.
So – an academic life wasn't meant to be
For hopeless and nondescript little old me.

My boyfriends she loves to criticise
Never calls them the name with which they were baptised
And she makes a point of being rude and nasty
Because they're either idiots or bastards.

So – my childhood and later my adolescence
Were ravaged by the very presence
Of the woman who, though loathe I am,
I have to call – 'cos she is – my mam.

'Helen had written the poem – she couldn't even remember when or why, what had actually provoked her to write it – and had tucked it away with all her other little masterpieces in some drawer. One morning, Dorothy took it into her head to have a spring clean, a good clear out, something like that, and she found the lot of them. Whether she read all her daughter's poems nobody knows but she was found at the bottom of the bedroom stairs with that little masterpiece still clutched in her hand. Of course Helen, being Helen, blamed herself entirely for her mother's death. And since then, she's drawn a blank; she can't write poetry to save her life. She has a mental block. And she always says the poem was rubbish, anyway; should have been torn up or burned immediately; it was nothing to be proud of. But I'm not so sure; something must have happened to make her write it. Or maybe she just needed to purge herself of Dorothy's influence all those years. I don't suppose we'll ever know.'

Tom came striding across the lawn armed with cold drinks just as Jill stopped speaking. Malcolm helped himself to a can of beer off the tray and was grateful for the diversion.

'Cheers, Tom. Just what we need.'

He remarked that sitting on the lawn of a semi-detached house in Firley reminded him of his youth in Jill's parents' garden and there was in his voice a badly camouflaged wistfulness. He asked about Theresa and Jack, who were both still in good health and enjoying being grandparents. And he asked about Mandy and Tom proudly told him that his sister was embarking on an exciting new project but didn't want to say too much about it until it got off the ground; but she was happy to be working in Yorkshire again. Malcolm said he'd like to meet up with her again and Tom said he'd try to arrange something, although she was always run off her feet. But not as happy as you'd be to meet up with Helen again, Jill couldn't help but think. And she couldn't help but think either that Helen probably wouldn't be very interested in this new, older, mentally and physically life-scarred Malcolm. Especially when she had the famous, rich and dishy Ben Beaulac hot-footing it after her ...

By the time Malcolm had decided not to outstay his welcome, Caroline and Darren still hadn't come back from their walk. The May sun was slowly beginning to set over the hills and although it wasn't very late, Tom's curfew hadn't been respected. Caroline hadn't come home at tea-time.

'Aw, don't worry about her too much,' Malcolm advised. 'It's her age – she's normal. Experimenting with life. And don't worry about Darren, she'll be all right with him.' He attempted a laugh. 'He still thinks it's for peeing out of!'

'Oh aye, and who gave her that bloody red mark on her neck if it wasn't your Darren? You just said yourself like father like son.'

Tom and Malcolm were suddenly glaring at each other, the affection of re-found friendship making a quick exit. Jill suddenly felt weary.

'Oh, it's not only her carryings-on with boys, Malc. That's only part of it. It's her attitude to us, there's no respect, only a lot of aggression and cheek. She's started drinking and she smokes – although she thinks we don't know about that. She comes home at all hours and sometimes won't go to school. And now there's talk of drugs at the school. I'm at my wits' end, I really am. And I'm dreading the other two following in her footsteps.'

Malcolm noticed the tears welling up in Jill's tired eyes and saw the anxiety and despair in her movements.

'Look,' he said, 'if Mandy's in Yorkshire why don't you see if you can have a word with her? Professional-like, you know? She must know a thing or two about adolescent psychology.'

'I've thought of that myself,' Tom said and Jill turned to look at him.

'You've never said anything to me about Mandy having a word with her.'

Tom took off his glasses and wiped them for the umpteenth time on his tee-shirt.

'I wanted to bide my time; see which way the wind blew. I was hoping there'd be some improvement. Looks like I was wrong. I didn't really want to drag Mandy into our affairs but ... well, it might not be a bad idea to have a word in her professional ear. And keep it in the family, so to speak.'

By eight o'clock there was still no sign of either Caroline or Darren. Their parents walked up and down the street and in the nearby neighbourhood but the teenagers were nowhere to be seen. Malcolm said he had to leave and quietly told Jill and Tom to send his son home if he showed up with Caroline.

'And don't worry, I'll give him what for when he gets home.'

As Malcolm's paternal eyes wandered around, they drifted in the direction of the darkening moor. His fair eyebrows knitted together, enhancing the other deep lines on his face.

'Do you think Helen will come ... come home ... for Christmas?'

Jill's and Tom's thoughts were running on other, more urgent lines, and it took a few moments for Malcolm's incongruous question to sink in.

'Well, I've invited her, that's all I can say. Anyway, it's a long way off, isn't it? Anything could happen between now and then. I hope she'll come, though, I'm looking forward to seeing her ... on the other hand I wouldn't be surprised if she goes back to the chalet with Turtle Dove and ...'

'Where is this ... this chalet exactly?'

'I don't know *exactly*, Malc. Somewhere near Chamonix, if you know where that is. Mont Blanc. It sounds out of this world. Apparently. Turtle Dove ...'

'Damn Turtle Dove to hell.'

At that moment two familiar figures strolled around the corner, arms entwined, and giggling. Malcolm, with a curt 'Goodnight', moved forward in their direction without a backward glance. And Jill knew that Darren Malcolm Jones would be the brunt of his father's frustration and unwarranted wrath that night. She couldn't honestly say she was sorry.

***

I didn't do it. How many times has that short necessary sentence gone round and round in my head, along with the other one that means exactly the same. I'm not guilty.

Not this time.

Chapter Twenty

Even before Marie-Laure and Adam had left the chalet Helen had wanted to escape. From Ben. His presence was everywhere. On top of the old-fashioned cottage piano, together with Kimberley. On the bookshelves, on the coffee table. Ben – she knew it was Ben because he was with his wife and children – looked at her, watched her, smiled at, mocked her. She even imagined that his fingers created and played tunes for her on the old yellow and rather tinny keyboard. What did the composer say who found his lover in his chalet in the Alps? Snow good ... you'll have to go. Unable to share her silly Ben-joke with Ben, Helen was unable to laugh.

But now there were other, far more serious reasons for leaving, escaping. After her poignant but sickeningly enlightening dinner with Jacqueline and her own ghastly discoveries in the tell-tale drawers, how could she possibly stay under this roof? How could she consider returning to the beauty salon to work for Marie-Laure (Turtle Dove) Colombe-Beaulac? She couldn't. But before making any hasty and maybe regrettable decision, Helen was determined to be sensible, to work things out in a responsible, adult manner. She'd have to see and explain her sudden departure to Bénédicte, who deserved at least that little courtesy. And now there was Jacqueline; Jacqueline who looked on her as a friend, confided in her and who had suggested their seeing each other again before Helen left. In spite of what had horribly and so incredibly come to light, Helen liked the young waitress and, under other circumstances, would have welcomed her company. But if she made a friend of her now it would be a travesty, an attachment that couldn't possibly continue, and her conduct would be as discreditable as Paul's untimely disappearance. Paradoxically, Helen felt she couldn't have left without saying goodbye to her, either.

The telephone continued to ring the following day. After an almost sleepless night Helen felt drained and mentally exhausted and had neither the energy nor the inclination to venture outdoors. She spent the day lolling around, listening to classical music on the radio and unsuccessfully trying to read. Every time the telephone rang, she turned a deaf ear, refused to acknowledge its loud, raucous summons and eventually, of course, it stopped. However, by early evening, Helen's fraught nerves were on edge and when the phone rang about six-thirty, she tentatively picked up the receiver. From where she was standing, Ben's photo smiled at her and it seemed to her as though they had eye contact.

'Allo?'

Her heart was pounding and she could feel the sweat running down her forehead and the dryness in her mouth. She'd no idea how she was going to cope with this conversation as she waited to hear the news from New York.

'Et alors? I haven't seen you taking your walk today. Have you been out? Are you ill?'

'Ah, Bénédicte!' Helen smiled at the faceless but very welcome voice. She cleared her throat and wiped her forehead. 'No ... no, I haven't been out and I'm not ill. Just a bit tired, that's all. Look, Bénédicte, I've ... I've decided to go back to Paris.' And then straight back to England, home, she mentally added.

'Go back to Paris? No! But why? When?'

Because I've discovered that Marie-Laure Colombe did have an affair with my ex-husband-to-be and that your dear young Jacqueline is, with almost no doubt whatsoever, the fruit of their passion. Which means, of course, that Marie-Laure has lied to and deceived me and probably thoroughly enjoyed making a complete fool of me.

'Well, actually, you know, it's a bit lonely here without ... alone. And as I don't have a car I can't get around and ... oh, I'll be much better spending the rest of my holiday in my own home, Bénédicte.'

'Well, I think it's a great pity. Have you heard from Marie-Laure?'

Helen hesitated. She thought about the incessant ringing of the telephone.

'No. No, I haven't.'

She wasn't really lying, she told herself. In fact, she wasn't lying at all.

'How odd. I can't understand that. I think there must be something terribly wrong. Look, my dear, come and have dinner with me tomorrow evening. We'll have a nice long chat and if you're still determined to go back to Paris, I'll run you down to the station on ...'

'That's very kind of you but I wouldn't want to put you to that trouble.'

'It's no trouble at all. I only hope that, in the meantime, I can persuade you to stay here with us.'

'I really don't think so, Bénédicte,' Helen murmured. 'I know I'm doing the right thing.'

She suddenly felt tears welling in her eyes. Bénédicte was so genuinely kind, Ben was still smiling at her, together with his lovely wife, the evidence of Marie-Laure's deceit still lay in the room upstairs. How much more was she supposed to take, for God's sake?

'What time would you like me to come tomorrow evening?'

'Come early, my dear, about seven o'clock. I wonder if Jacqueline will be working tomorrow evening? I could invite her, too. We could have a party!'

'Jacqueline's evening off is Thursday.'

Maybe Jacqueline had more than one evening off. Helen didn't know and didn't want to know; at the moment her sudden panic prevailing over her sense of charity.

'Ah yes, you're right. A great pity; oh well, never mind. We'll enjoy ourselves, just the two of us. See you tomorrow then – and don't be late!'

***

Helen spent the early part of that evening in the kitchen, her unhappy thoughts her only companion. So, she'd made her decision to return to Paris and would be unable to go back on that decision even if she wanted to, as a second person was now involved. But her other and far more important decision was rather more difficult to make. Leaving her bedsit in Paris would not be as simple as leaving the chalet in the Alps. Leaving her job at the salon was going to be equally as difficult, but even more imperative. Their relationship – built on secrets, lies and false confidences – obviously couldn't continue. Helen could no longer trust the woman; she'd accepted her offer of friendship against her better judgement and her better judgement had been proved right. It was time to put a permanent end to a friendship that should never have seen the light of day. But she'd think about going back to England, back to Yorkshire, once she was back in Paris. One difficult decision at a time.

She left the kitchen as the light began to fail, went into the living room and turned on the soft, muted lamps that gave the room a golden glow. It wasn't quite dark yet and the sunset over the mountain peaks was achingly beautiful. Helen, however, felt cosier, safer almost, with the shutters closed and the lamps lit. She turned the television on at eight o'clock, for company, and in time to catch the evening news. There was nothing out of the ordinary happening in the world and Helen was debating whether to switch off the television and read, when Ben Beaulac's face suddenly filled the screen. Helen stared and sat like a sculpture, a figure in stone.

The impeccably dressed and soft-voiced newsreader, detached and phlegmatic, announced that the composer and pianist, Benjamin Beaulac, had for the first time in his professional life, appeared at a film premier on Broadway, (the composer of the theme tune) without his wife Kimberley at his side. After twenty-one years of marriage, Ben was suing his wife for divorce after having discovered that the father of the child she was expecting was her psychiatrist, who'd been treating her for depression for two years. Kimberley Beaulac was now living apart from her husband and co-habiting with her lover. There was a double tragedy in the celebrated Beaulac family, the newsreader went on to tell the country. Adam Beaulac, Ben's twin brother, had been involved in a road accident, a head-on crash with a young motorcyclist shortly after his arrival in New York, and was at the moment still in a coma in the ICU of a New York clinic. As soon as Ben left the cinema he was taken immediately to his brother's bedside.

Helen sat like a figure in stone for a long time after the news had ended. It was too much for her to take in, to digest, her brain seemed unable to function properly. And then, like a jigsaw puzzle, pieces started to move together, to begin to make some sense and then nonsense. The Norman Rockwell card and Ben's message; his phone call to Adam that had caused so much pain; the insistent ringing of the telephone that she'd ignored all day. Had the caller been Marie-Laure wanting to tell her and talk about Adam's accident? Or maybe it had been Ben wanting to ... but Ben probably didn't know she was at the chalet, probably didn't know that she was acquainted – she could no longer think of her as a friend – with Marie-Laure and Adam. She was being ridiculous; she didn't feature at all in this family affair, nobody would have given her a thought; it was just as well she was planning on leaving. She felt impotent tears gushing into her eyes and didn't know who she was crying for ... herself, Ben, Adam, Jacqueline ... The telephone rang. Helen's tears abruptly stopped, she hiccupped loudly and wiped her face on the back of her hand. For a while she didn't move and then she stood up on wobbly legs and with an unsteady hand took the receiver off the hook.

'Allo?'

Silence. She waited. It was obviously a bad connection from New York. And suddenly Helen was desperate to know who was at the other end of the line. And in her desperation, she shook the receiver and foolishly plucked at the wire.

'Allo? Allo?'

Nothing. She glared at the instrument in her hand, as though a face would miraculously appear there and when none did, continued to shake it in her trembling hand.

'Ah. Hello. Hello? Marie-Laure. Marie-Laure? Hello, is that you? Are you still there, Marie-Laure? For God's sake, woman, speak to me ...'

In spite of the interference on the line the voice sounded strangely familiar, and yet, Helen told herself, it wasn't possible, it didn't make sense. And then the line started purring at her and Helen stared at the receiver for a long time before replacing it on is cradle. It was after midnight when she finally turned off the lamps and made her way up the wooden staircase to her bedroom, for what she knew would be a sleepless night.

**

She didn't have a totally sleepless night but the little sleep she had was disturbed by strange and daunting dreams. She got up before seven o'clock the next morning and how she got through the day she couldn't have told anybody. She stayed in the chalet again, eating her frugal, unfinished meals on the balcony, haphazardly packing her suitcase and perversely praying for the telephone to ring. It didn't. She prayed for Bénédicte to appear, in spite of the fact they were having dinner together that evening. She didn't. Helen wondered if Bénédicte had heard the news and guessed that she hadn't, otherwise she would have put her appearance in. She hoped she wouldn't have to be the one to break the news of Adam's accident to her neighbour. She wasn't really in a position to do that as she didn't know any details ... and maybe Adam had died during the ... Oh God. In spite of her unanswered prayers, dishevelled brain and ceaselessly churning stomach, Helen got through the day. She spent most of the time cleaning and scrubbing, dusting and vacuuming; she wanted to leave the chalet sparklingly clean and tidy and she also needed to keep busy.

She stood on Bénédicte's doorstep at six-fifty, clutching a gift-wrapped parcel and a large bunch of yellow roses that she'd purloined from the Beaulac's balcony. Better to offer them as a cheap gift than leave them to die. The door was opened after several long moments and Helen's hostess stood in front of her, resplendent in black and white horizontally striped leggings, red plimsolls and a too-baggy turquoise sweatshirt that she'd tied at the waist with a long piece of string.

'But you look ravishing!' Bénédicte stepped aside to let her guest into her home and her myopic eyes explored Helen's slim figure. 'Far too sexy to spend the evening with an old ex-nun!' she added.

Helen smiled and bent to kiss the old ex-nun whose company was exactly what she needed that evening. She didn't think her simple white cotton dress was particularly sexy, only very comfortable and cool. And, In comparison with the ex-nun's apparel, extremely sober.

'You know, you're a very attractive woman, Helen, and I'm surprised that ... what on earth's the matter?'

'Haven't you heard the news, Bénédicte?' Helen decided to jump in at the deep end. But before she asked the question, she already knew the answer.

285

'What news, Helen? Look, come in and make yourself at home ... that's better. Now, what's this? What on earth have you been buying me? I'll put them in a vase immediately. Could you reach me a vase from the cupboard? No, that one over there. That's right. No, not that one, that's my winter vase ... and not that one, either. I only put flowers I *don't* like into that one. Take the one behind, the one with the crack down the side and the piece missing. Yes, go on, that's the one, that's right. Do you know, Helen, this vase belonged to my grandmother. It was a wedding gift from an old beau of hers. Her husband – my grandfather – never knew, of course. She told him it was a gift from a cousin three times removed who lived in Polynesia ... something like that. So, this vase is very special and I only use it for special flowers from special people. Here, could you put them in water, dear, you must be better at arranging flowers than I am – you live in Paris. Right. Now, what on earth have you been buying me, my dear Helen? Can I open it now? What beautiful wrapping paper, it's a shame to spoil ...'

Bénédicte's thin hand ripped the paper with something like glee, a total contradiction of her words.

'Oh, Helen, now this is far too beautiful for an old woman like me.'

The wrapping and ribbon fell to the floor and Helen, arranging the flowers in the ancient and decidedly ugly vase, watched the old lady's face as she examined the new crystal vase whose facets caught the light from the setting sun and glittered and sparkled in her gnarled fingers. Helen had purchased the vase in Paris, a 'thank you' gift for Marie-Laure before she left the chalet.

'Nothing could be too beautiful for you, Bénédicte,' Helen almost whispered and choked back the tears that had sprung into her eyes. Bénédicte quickly moved forward and planted a wet and trembly kiss on Helen's two cheeks. Helen then waited for instructions to transfer the roses to the new, far superior vase, but she waited in vain. Her old friend carefully placed her gift back in its box and then into the cupboard, to join the motley collection. The old and unlovely vase was obviously still the special one.

'Now,' Bénédicte said, heading for the antiquated and none-too-clean cooker where a spicy smelling sauce was bubbling away. She picked up a wooden spoon which could also have been her grandmother's wedding present, and started to stir, furiously, her eyes fixed on Helen behind the thick lenses. 'What news haven't I heard?'

Helen pondered over her words, not wanting to cause the old lady too much distress.

'You haven't had a phone call from New York, have you?' she finally muttered.

'A phone call from New York? Me? No, of course not. Why would Adam and Marie-Laure phone me?'

'You didn't ... see the news on television last night?'

A vision of Ben Beaulac's handsome but stricken face blurred in front of Helen's eyes. She explained, as briefly and calmly as possible, that Adam was in a coma in a New York clinic following a road accident. And, she very quickly added, knowing that she probably shouldn't be adding but she needed to talk about it, that Ben Beaulac was ... well, in the process of divorcing his wife because she was ... she was expecting a child to another man. Narrating the story, Helen wondered if the whole Alpine village wasn't bustling with the news and thought it a miracle that Bénédicte hadn't heard from another gossipy source. Bénédicte, however, had obviously been in the dark until then. She brandished the dripping spoon and moved away from the cooker to where Helen was still arranging the roses on the draining board. She took off her glasses, wiped them on her sweatshirt and gazed up at the younger woman. For a long time neither of them spoke and their breathing was audible in the still evening air.

'But this can't be true, Helen, it's not possible. You would have heard if such a terrible thing had happened to Adam – Marie-Laure would have let you know. You wouldn't have heard on the television news. She hasn't phoned you, has she?'

Helen pulled her eyes away from the sad, bewildered eyes of her hostess, who certainly couldn't be told the whole story. For so many reasons, for the sake of so many people, she couldn't be told the whole, complicated story. Helen turned her weary attention back to the flowers.

'Well, actually, the phone has rung a few times but ... well, every time I reached the phone, it stopped ringing.'

Helen hated lying to the woman she'd come to love. And then she remembered the one time she had answered the phone and a shiver of confusion and apprehension ran down her spine. Bénédicte suddenly started to look around her, to move and walk around the kitchen, wringing her hands and muttering to herself. Helen could smell burning coming from the cooker; an acrid, pungent smell instead of the original spicy aroma. Bénédicte, however, seemed oblivious. Helen picked up the discarded spoon and went to do some culinary rescue work. Her hostess watched her wordlessly for a while and then she suddenly whipped off her glasses and grabbed the hand that had taken charge of the stirring.

'But we must call New York, Helen! Of course! You do have a number there, I suppose? Marie-Laure must have left you a number to get in touch with them?'

Helen shook her head, a jerky, dizzying movement that to anyone else would have conveyed her distress. Bénédicte, fortunately, was inattentive.

'No, she didn't leave a number in New York. She – and Adam – had other things on their mind; they probably never gave it a thought.'

'What about Ben's number? Have you looked for it? It must be written down somewhere ...'

'I did think about that and I have looked for his number,' Helen lied, 'but I haven't found any phone numbers anywhere.'

'Oh Helen, we have to get in touch with them, somehow. We must find out about Adam. Is he going to be all right? Is he going to ... to survive? Poor Marie-Laure, she must be suffering so much ... And what did you say about Ben? He's divorcing Kimberley because ... she's having another man's child? But it's not possible. It's simply not possible, Helen. Kimberley needs Ben; she's always needed him. I simply cannot believe that she would ... would even look at another man. It's not possible. She loves Ben; she needs Ben. Why did they have to announce such ... such lies on television?'

She suddenly grabbed Helen's arm and stared up at her with frantic eyes.

'Ben has always been so supportive, you know. He's never let her down, all these years. And what about the poor children? I can't believe it. I won't believe it. Kimberley wouldn't even look at another man. You know, Helen, I'm convinced that the media invent these stories just to ... to spice up their act!'

Helen, in spite of everything, found herself smiling at the ex-nun.

'Remember Marie-Laure and Adam went to New York after ... after Ben's phone call. There was a tragedy ... or something ... in the family.'

'Ah yes. Of course. You're right.'

Bénédicte's grasp slackened then and the energy seemed to seep out of her; for once she looked like a frail, eighty-year-old woman. Helen marvelled at how personally she was taking the news. She must have felt very close to the Beaulac family. And then she remembered Bénédicte's mumbled and now contradictory lament about 'that villainous, destructive brother' and she wondered where her sympathies lay; with Ben or Kimberley. Maybe her sympathies in general lay with the two sisters-in-law rather than the twin brothers. In which case, Helen had no case at all. She also thought about the sad, adopted young waitress, whom Bénédicte was so fond of, and wondered if she knew more about the girl's history than she let on.

'Do you still want to leave tomorrow, Helen?' Bénédicte's voice was almost accusing. 'Do you still want to return to Paris at a time like this?'

Helen breathed in deeply, took Bénédicte's two hands in her own, squeezed them and looked deep into the misty, questioning eyes.

'I have to go back,' she said, praying to Bénédicte's God that she would understand and not judge. The gold cross on the splash of turquoise gleamed in the fading light. 'Look, I really don't have any choice. I have to leave the chalet ... I have to go home. It's ... well, it's very personal; that's all I can tell you, I'm sorry. But I really can't stay here any longer.'

In her confusion and to a certain extent, guilt, she was rambling and her companion now looked at her, her head on one side, a frown deepening the lines around her curious and sad eyes. She nodded slowly, not understanding at all but not probing either, merely accepting.

'Come on then,' she finally smiled. 'We'll talk while we're having dinner. Before it's completely ruined.'

***

They had dinner on the balcony, surrounded by pots of blood-red geraniums and many other plants and flowers that grew and hung and intertwined everywhere. Bénédicte had cooked beef in a spicy tomato sauce with mounds of fluffy rice followed by a well-filled cheeseboard and cherry tart to finish. They washed their meal down with a couple of glasses of rich red wine.

'Where did you learn to cook like this?' Helen smiled, swallowing another delicious mouthful and wanting to talk of other, less traumatic topics than the Beaulac family. 'Did you ... erm ... did you learn to cook in the convent?'

'Certainly not!'

Bénédicte beamed at her in sudden and obvious joy, either at the compliment or at the absurd suggestion that she'd learned to cook in a convent.

'My diet with the "bonnes soeurs" was less than frugal. No, my dear, my grandmother – the one with the naughty vase – taught me everything I know today,' she winked and bowed her head. 'And after I left the convent, I attended many different classes because I wanted to belong to and be a useful member of society. So, I learned cookery, handicrafts, first aid, painting. I painted the watercolour of Lake Annecy that hangs at the bottom of the stairs in the Beaulac's home.'

'Bénédicte, you really are a phenomenon, you never cease to amaze me. Is there *anything* you can't do?'

Bénédicte leaned across the table, gently fondled the yellow roses that

Helen had placed in the centre, winked and whispered, 'There are one or two things I've never tried to do, my dear. But I'm not dead yet.'

Helen had selected a slice of Roquefort off the cheeseboard and was carefully placing it on her bread when she heard the purring of a car engine on the road below. Bénédicte had heard it too, rather surprising in the otherwise quiet, empty late evening. They both looked over the balcony and a taxi was making its way along the winding, stony road, its yellow sign lambent in the Alpine twilight. It changed gear as it rounded the tricky bend beyond Bénédicte's home, and headed further up the mountain. When it had disappeared, the silence hung rather heavily around them.

'Where do you think he's going?' Helen asked, her curiosity aroused, knowing that dwellings towards the summit of their mountain were few and far between.

'Oh, he's probably dropped someone off in the village or at La Grange and now he'll be on his way back to Chamonix for more custom. It's a strange route to take, though, especially at night.'

La Grange and subsequent thoughts of its young waitress brought a sudden flush to Helen's cheeks. She didn't want to think about her, even less talk about her. She wanted the conversation to stay neutral, prosaic, and was glad when Bénédicte said, 'By the way, what time does your train leave tomorrow morning? I'll make sure you arrive at the station well in advance.'

'Well, if you're absolutely sure, Bénédicte, it's really kind of you and I do appreciate it. But I hate to put you to all that trouble ... I can always order a taxi. They obviously do come up here; we've just seen the proof.'

'Oh yes, of course taxis come up here from time to time. But I won't allow you to call a taxi, wait for it to come and worry if it'll be on time ... not to mention the expense ... I'd never forgive myself. What time does your train leave, Helen?'

'Half past seven. But I'll have to buy my ticket. I should have been going back to Paris with Marie-Laure and Adam in the car ... that was the plan.'

'Well, don't worry, you'll have plenty of time. By the way, does Jacqueline know that you're planning to leave?'

'No. No, she doesn't. Could you ... could you say goodbye from me, please? That would be ... I'd be very grateful.'

Their eyes met across the table and Helen would have given anything to know what was going on in her hostess's mind.

'She'll be disappointed,' her hostess replied. 'She likes you a lot. I bumped into her this morning, in the butcher's as a matter of fact, and she told me how much you'd impressed her. How fond of you she is. You and Paul both ... she seems to have a penchant for the English.'

Bénédicte stood up then and busied herself clearing the cheese dishes away and preparing the dessert.

'It's not surprising. Her biological father was English, you know.'

She tossed it out matter-of-factly, as though it were just a by-the-way in their conversation, which of course, for her, it was. Helen looked over the balcony at the descending darkness and could think of nothing lucid to reply.

'So that explains a lot, doesn't it?'

Bénédicte's hands were full so Helen quickly stood up and made a move to help her. The old lady, however, snatched her hands away, laughing, and a plate dropped on to the wooden floor and broke clean in two.

'Now look what you've done!' Bénédicte accused, grinning. 'Sit down and behave yourself!'

Helen did as she was told, sat down, behaved herself and had also composed herself by the time her hostess returned with the homemade cherry tart. Helen helped herself to a generous portion, as she was instructed to do. She complimented Bénédicte on her baking and then, as the thought struck her, asked her why she hadn't told Jacqueline that she, Helen, was leaving, when she saw her that morning.

'Because this morning I was still hoping I could persuade you to stay,' Bénédicte took a sip of unfinished wine. 'But I've given up hope of that.'

As she spoke her smile was such a mixture of sadness, reproach and incomprehension that Helen was sorely tempted to announce that she'd stay on at the chalet forever if the old lady wished it. She therefore decided that Jacqueline, as a topic of conversation, was the lesser of two evils.

'Do you know anything about Jacqueline's – biological – parents?' she heard herself asking and immediately regretted it.

Bénédicte had temporarily abandoned her dinner and was striking a match to a yellow candle in a glass bowl that stood next to Helen's flowers on the table, and it diffused an equally powerful fragrance. Night insects immediately began to flutter and drone around the sudden glow. Bénédicte sat down again and began to toy with the fruit tart in her dish. Helen's involuntary question hung in the air between them, along with the tiny moths.

'Not really. All I know is that Jacqueline's father was English, he came from a village in the north, I believe, her mother French, and she was born in Paris. Her mother was very young and, from what I understand, her studies were ruined because of the event. She had been a brilliant scholar, apparently, had a dazzling future ahead of her before her little folly. Jacqueline's adoptive mother told me those small details one evening while we were having a little heart-to-heart. I sincerely hope she never tries to find her real parents; it would bring a lot of heartache to the family and they deserve better than that. Her biological parents – whoever they are – could never have loved her more, or done more for her.'

Helen lowered her gaze and allowed Bénédicte's words to sink in before she attempted her next question.

'Do you think Marie-Laure and ... and Adam know about ... well, about Jacqueline's history?'

Bénédicte shrugged her thin shoulders and shoved her sliding spectacles back up her nose.

'I don't suppose they have the slightest interest in Jacqueline's history. Why should they? As far as they're concerned, she's the pretty young waitress at La Grange who's rather lonely, and they know I think a lot about her. They sometimes invite us together for aperitif at the chalet ... or something. But they never get involved. When they come here, they're usually on holiday. They come to enjoy themselves and that's what they do. And they usually keep themselves to themselves, they don't show much interest in other people's affairs. I suppose too much goes on in their own lives; so much misfortune, so many tragedies ...'

Her voice trailed away and Helen, her heart and brain hammering in unison, waited for her to continue, to qualify her tantalising statement. But the old lady's attention was suddenly caught by a foolhardy moth that had flown directly into the orange flame and whose fragile frame now lay frizzling on the table. Bénédicte struck it with a spoon to put it out of its misery. Helen flinched at the unexpected, violent action; 'so many tragedies' echoed through her mind as she watched her companion scoop up the corpse in her paper napkin.

It was almost eleven o'clock when Helen offered to help with the washing up before she left. Her hostess, of course, wouldn't hear of it.

'You go get a good night's sleep,' she said, escorting Helen to the door. 'You'll be up at the crack of dawn tomorrow. Look, when I arrive in the car, I'll toot my horn a few times to let you know I'm here and we can leave immediately. Unless ... well, are you sure you won't change your mind, Helen? It's not too late, you know, and the two of us could perhaps find a way of getting through to Marie-Laure in New York and ... well, two heads are better than one and ...'

'No, I'm really sorry but I've made my mind up and, anyway, I really don't have any choice. It's better if I go back to Paris, honestly. Please believe me.'

Bénédicte lifted her hands up in the air in acceptance and accompanied Helen to the bottom of her steeply sloping garden and the road that twisted down the mountain. They stopped at the roadside and breathed in the stillness.

'I think I'll walk down to the chalet with you.'

Helen shivered in the late evening breeze and it felt as though someone were walking over her grave.

'You'll do no such thing, Bénédicte. The road's reasonably well lit; I'll be fine. You go inside now, it's getting cold. And thanks again for a really lovely evening.'

They kissed each other on both cheeks, squeezed each other's hands and said, 'A demain.'

'See you tomorrow.'

***

As Helen approached the private track that led to the Beaulac's home, the first thing she noticed was the deep ridge of tyre tracks on the gravel, visible under the one bright lamp whose glow had helped her on her way. Her surprised and wary eyes looked for the familiar Renault that Adam always parked in the drive but no car was there. She remembered the solitary vehicle, the client-free taxi, purring up the mountain and Bénédicte's conclusion that the driver had probably dropped someone off. Something moved in the lower part of Helen's abdomen and she tried to ignore the sensation. The second thing she noticed, as she put one foot in front of the other, was the faint light visible through the slats in the shutters. Her heart seemed to stop beating at the same time as her feet stopped crunching and she felt bile come into her throat. The cool breeze blew into her face and she heard the fir trees swaying with its movement, the leaves rustling, the branches slightly groaning. For a long time she stood still, and then she walked forward until she reached the door that led into the kitchen. She thought about the insistent ringing of the telephone that she'd ignored and told herself it must have been Marie-Laure desperately trying to reach her, wanting to tell her that she was on her way back and to expect her at a certain time. And leaving behind her beloved husband unconscious in the intensive care unit of a New York clinic? And then she remembered the answered telephone call and the cracked, severed words in the strangely familiar voice that hadn't made sense. She'd thought about that a lot and it still didn't make sense. Helen slowly and with trembling fingers took the key out of her purse but it wasn't necessary. The door was unlocked. She slowly pushed it open and, as she entered the kitchen, her olfactory senses were assaulted; the smell of strong cheese, wine and something indefinable. The kitchen was empty but for still-dirty dishes on the table, a plate of half-finished cheese and a chunk of baguette, a half-empty bottle of Bordeaux and a dirty glass. Helen found difficulty breathing, the room was beginning to spin. She wanted to call a name but she didn't know what name to call. Marie-Laure? She had no desire to be alone in the chalet with Marie-Laure, even for a few night hours. And then she heard the music.

It didn't sound like the music of a celebrated composer and pianist, but the cottage piano was old and out of tune. Helen stood in the space between the kitchen and living room and looked at the man whose hands were tinkling on the keys. The broad back, covered now with a pale grey, sweat-stained shirt, the greying hair, much shorter than when she'd last seen and touched it, otherwise the same. She listened to the notes that the long, sensitive and expert fingers played and it was hard to imagine they were expert, that they had composed and played tunes that cleaved to people's minds for many years. But the piano was old, uncared for, the keys yellow, their sound tinny, proof of their antiquity and non-maintenance. The man was studying the sheet of music in front of him and more sheets of music lay scattered on the floor around the cheap, makeshift stool. Helen, subconsciously smiling now and every fibre of her body trembling, listened and watched and waited for the musician, the man, to sense her presence, to turn and find her standing there. She looked down at her simple white summer dress, the dress that Bénédicte had declared too sexy for an evening spent with an old ex-nun ... She felt perspiration on her body and wished she'd had the time to freshen up before ... Suddenly, the agile fingers shot across the keyboard in a kind of musical frenzy, the player slammed down the lid, cursed loudly, stood up and, pushing the stool aside with the back of his leg, whirled round. His eyes met Helen's across the short expanse of space. Helen waited for her heart to stop hammering, her limbs to stop shaking, waited for Ben to speak. He didn't speak, however, only his startled eyes corresponded with hers and then a slow smile began to play on his lips, awkwardly, as his fingers had manipulated the old keyboard. He ran a hand through his hair as his eyes dragged themselves away from hers and travelled the length of her body and back again, back to her waiting, unblinking eyes. He slowly cocked his head to one side and then opened his mouth as though to speak. But Helen, tired of waiting ... she'd been waiting for such a long time ... was the first to communicate.

'Ben!' she cried and it was almost a puppy's yelp of pain mingled with desire. She skipped across the room and, burrowing her face in his chest, she clung to him and continued to murmur his name, her voice barely audible, lost somewhere in the folds of his shirt, in his flesh and in her own tears.

'Oh Ben, it *was* you. I didn't believe it, it didn't make sense; it still doesn't make sense but it doesn't matter. I don't care. You're here; you've come and you've no idea how happy I am to ...'

And then she started to sob, deep hacking sobs, the effluvia of a variety of negative emotions finally erupting.

'Oh Ben. Hold me. Just hold me.'

'Hey there ...'

His words, too, were muffled, inaudible and disappeared into oblivion. As Helen continued to cling, his arms squeezed her to him and his right hand began to move slowly, soothingly, caressingly, through her damp and tangled hair. Helen's sobs began to slowly subside and she hiccupped loudly. She didn't offer to move out of his arms and he continued to stroke and squeeze her and then his hand moved out of her wet hair and to her wet, makeup-stained and, at that moment, unpretty cheek. Helen looked up at him, he looked down at her and words, Helen thought, were totally unnecessary. His slow, languorous smile said everything, as, no doubt, did hers. He kissed her then and Helen touched his face with unsure fingers and his kiss became more urgent, more demanding, more Ben. And then he swooped her up, simply slipped his right arm under her bottom and lifted her, supporting her body with his left hand.

'Let's go upstairs,' he said.

When they reached the landing, he wordlessly turned left and walked into Helen's bedroom. He gently lay her on the single bed and stood looking down at her, a strange, rather enigmatic smile moving about his lips. Helen held his gaze for what seemed a long time and then held her arms out to him and he slowly lowered himself beside her. His lips pecked at her skin like a starving bird while his fingers played on her body like an expert pianist's.

'Oh Ben.'

Helen closed her eyes and began to slowly kiss him back.

His lovemaking was more urgent, more demanding, more brutal than Helen remembered, but she knew how much he must have been through over the past few months and, as his specially selected card had suggested, he was very much in love with her; needed her. Oh yes, and he needed her now. Now that he'd lost his wife to another man and may, God forbid, be losing his twin brother. He needed her now. She returned passionate kiss for kiss, stroke for stroke, and incessantly called, spoke, whispered his name as her pleasures heightened.

'Ben, oh Ben, I've missed you. I've wanted you so much, Ben. I love you, Ben ...'

But Ben didn't whisper, speak or call out Helen's name in ecstasy; the only sounds she heard were the acknowledged, accepted guttural grunts of physical pleasure and the brush of his flesh on hers. Afterwards, curled up silently in each other's arms, Ben lay on his back gazing into blackness and Helen tied herself around him, her legs entwined with his, her arms thrown around him, still squeezing, still stroking. She waited for him to break the supernatural silence that had gone on far too long, to speak to, to verbally communicate with her now that the initial passion was replete, but the silence slowly gained momentum. Helen now desperately needed to talk to him but in view of Ben's post-coital taciturnity wasn't sure how to open tender and painful but necessary discussions. She finally resorted to humour; their personal, secret, Ben-and-Helen humour, as an opener, an ice-breaker, a lead to deeper, more sober conversation.

'Okay, Ben, what did the famous composer say who found an English woman in his alpine chalet?'

'Mmmm? What's that?'

Helen lifted her lips from his flesh, repeated, more loudly, more clearly. There was no response. Maybe she'd chosen a bad moment to tell a silly, tasteless joke. Maybe humour – even their personal, Ben-and-Helen humour – was the last thing he needed at the moment. She could have kicked herself; trust *her*. Every time you open yer mouth you put yer bloody foot in it. Why don't you think before you speak, lass, an' surprise everybody ...

'Snow good. You'll have to go.'

'What the goddam hell are you talking about?'

His voice rasped through the blackness and Helen, rigid, felt him untie his limbs and move away from her. She also felt a cold, creeping fear crawl from her toes to the roots of her hair. The bed groaned and he stood up.

'Ben?'

The light snapped on. Helen blinked several times before she saw the man she was in love with standing over the bed looking down at her in a way she hoped no man would ever look at her again. She slowly pulled herself into a sitting position, her eyes not leaving Ben's face, and subconsciously pulled the sheet over her nakedness. Ben didn't speak, only continued to look at her, his eyes bloodshot, the pupils dilated, and Helen thought she could see his breath as well as hear his breathing.

'Ben.'

The previous passion, the question in the whispered name had given way to a dull fear.

'Will you, for Christ's sake, stop snivelling that bloody name. Ben. B-e-n. B-E-N.'

The voice, the name echoed around the otherwise grave-quiet room and Helen fastened her eyes on the almost unrecognisable face, afraid she was going to vomit over the crisp, clean white sheet. And then, without warning, the hand that had stroked, caressed and loved her suddenly became a weapon and lashed out; once, twice ... again ... Helen lay gasping, unable to move or react. And then, she watched the long, sensitive fingers curl around the brass bedside lamp from where Turtle Dove and Malcolm gazed at her. She saw the photograph fall and felt the lamp's base slam into her face, her head. And as her mental and physical agony gave way to insensibility, a far away, familiar voice echoed down the narrow corridors of her ebbing consciousness.

'The only men *you're* capable of attracting are either idiots or bastards,' and then a faint noise like someone falling downstairs or running, perhaps running downstairs, and somewhere a door slamming.

Chapter Twenty-One

The school holidays, Jill had decided, were the worst. At least when Caroline was at school – and not playing truant – there was a certain amount of restriction. Jill and Tom at least knew where she was several hours a day, even if her behaviour there left a lot to be desired. During the school holidays, when Jill was tied to her books and Tom to his computer, Caroline could have been anywhere; she could be hitching her way to London for all Jill knew, and she wouldn't put that past her, either. She and Tom had hoped, when Caroline started seeing Darren regularly and he being Malcolm's son, that she'd at least try to mend her ways. Darren seemed to be quite a sensible lad for his age and they hoped he'd be a big influence on their daughter. In fact, it turned out to be the other way round; Darren was caught under Caroline's spell and she influenced him. In the three months they'd known each other, and since he and Malcolm had become a permanent fixture in the Hopkins' lives, Darren's personality had slowly changed, as Malcolm said, beyond all recognition.

'I hardly know him anymore,' he often complained to Jill and Tom, not directly accusing their daughter, but tactfully blaming the boy's age, lack of motherly love and influence, the upheaval of moving to the north and loss of his roots ... Perhaps it was normal that a lad his age would become unsettled, undergo a personality change. But behind his veiled excuses for his son's metamorphosis was Caroline, and both Jill and Tom realised it was in the name of friendship and fear of losing that friendship again that Malcolm kept his true feelings to himself.

The two teenagers spent most of their free time together, either at each other's homes or, on fine weekends and evenings, on the moor and in beer gardens around the village. Malcolm spent most of his weekends, at least Sundays, with his old friends. They went back to their old haunt, the Bay Horse, under new management now, of course, otherwise still the same, where they reminisced about old times and, inevitably, Helen's name often came up. They sometimes tried new pubs in Malcolm's neighbourhood, but always ended up back at the Bay Horse. Other pubs weren't the same, somehow. A lot of the old regulars remembered Malcolm and welcomed him into the pub's 'family', and he and Tom were invited to join the darts team and snooker club. Apart from social activities, Tom and Malcolm discovered a common interest that hadn't existed for them in their youth. They were both fanatical about their cars and spent many happy hours under each other's vehicles, investigating strange noises or whatever. Jill often cooked meals on Sunday, or sometimes they'd drive into Bradford and splash out on an Indian feast. Bradford had the best Indian restaurants in the UK, the three of them swore. The two younger children always came along, of course, always fighting in lumps, and sometimes Caroline and Darren, although they usually managed to find excuses to disappear. It was normal; teenagers never wanted to spend their weekends in their parents' company and neither Jill and Tom nor Malcolm objected to their wanting to do their own thing. They only worried about what that 'thing' might be and whether there would be any repercussions, scenes, as a result. They never prohibited, only made certain conditions and always asked questions, to which the insolent replies were never satisfactory. And then they always asked themselves questions and could never provide the answers. Their relationship with their children had become a kind of vicious circle, a mental game of hide and seek.

The summer arrived and instead of cooking hearty meals Jill started to prepare picnics for the two families and they often set off in their two cars for an unknown destination in the country – to walk, to eat their picnic, relax, enjoy the day. Sometimes they didn't take their cars, they just strolled across the moors with their rucksacks, fell down in a suitable spot and settled there for the afternoon. If Caroline and Darren had condescended to join them, they would disappear as soon as the food was finished, with warnings and unheeded instructions ringing in their pierced ears. Sharon and Joey always took some kind of technological game with them so they wouldn't get bored, Tom often slept, Malcolm ambled off alone to take endless photos and Jill took the opportunity to read. It had become a pleasant ritual over the summer weeks.

The only thing that marred Jill's pleasure and peace of mind in the renewal of her friendship with Malcolm was Helen. She would have to tell her eventually, of course. Helen would have to know that not only Malcolm but also his son was back in their lives with a vengeance and, apart from ongoing worries about Caroline and Darren, life was treating her well. But Jill didn't know how to bring the subject up. She didn't want to tell Helen on the phone when she couldn't see her face, see her reaction. She'd no idea how her friend would take the news; obviously she'd be very surprised – but would it be a happy surprise and a desire to meet Malcolm again? Or would the old (and understandable) resentment still be there and would that resentment overflow onto her and Tom and cause a breach in their friendship? That was the last thing she wanted. She had the impression that

Malcolm would have liked her to tell Helen, would have liked to speak to her himself, but Jill wasn't ready for that yet and didn't think Helen would be, either. Also, there was Ben Beaulac to consider; or rather Helen's rather obscure relationship with Ben Beaulac to consider. Helen was already confused and insecure and Jill didn't want to rub salt into her friend's sentimental wound. She managed to subtly change the subject whenever Malcolm brought Helen's name into the conversation and he eventually spoke of her less and less.

***

It was a Sunday towards the end of August. Jill had prepared a picnic for seven people, as usual. While she stuffed all the aluminium-wrapped edible goods into a large wicker basket, Tom was washing up the kitchen utensils and Sharon and Joey were, as usual, squabbling upstairs. Caroline, wearing extremely short shorts, a too-tight top, socks and clumsy trainers, lay on the settee watching a game show on television, waiting for her boyfriend and his dad to arrive.

'They're here!' Jill suddenly and very gaily called and Caroline leaped off the sofa, dashed to the door, wrenched it open and flung herself into Darren's thin arms.

'Hey, steady on,' Malcolm muttered, a not-quite-smile hovering on his lips. 'You nearly knocked him over. And me with him. Get yourself inside, Darren, you know we don't stand on ceremony here.'

'We're in the kitchen!' Jill called and then shouted for the younger children to come downstairs; they were nearly ready for off. She had to shout three times. And when she looked around for Caroline and Darren they were nowhere to be seen.

'They'll be in the back garden having a snog!' Malcolm grinned, but uncomfortably, and both Jill and Tom gave him a look that quickly wiped it off his face.

'Go look for them, will you,' Jill said, wiping her hands on a fresh, linen tea-towel.

Malcolm obediently slunk out of the kitchen and seconds later called that the kids were huddled together like two peas in a pod on the back doorstep, supposedly watching the little sparrows squabbling on the lawn. Jill heard her daughter's sarcastic voice in reply but couldn't distinguish what she actually said. She decided she was better off not knowing.

'Sharon! Joey! Get yourselves down these stairs or there'll be no picnic for you two! You'll be locked in!'

Malcolm, coming back into the kitchen, grinned at Jill.

'That's the way to speak to 'em!' he said.

Jill, however, didn't return his grin. She turned her face away from him and Malcolm couldn't help but notice the acute anxiety there.

'I'm not sure what's the best way to speak to them anymore, Malc. Or should I say to her, Caroline. I really am at the end of my tether.'

Before Malcolm could reply footsteps came clattering down the stairs and simultaneously two inert, bored-looking bodies emerged from the back garden. Darren's left arm dangled around Caroline's shoulder, his thin, boyish fingers almost touching her right breast. He beamed at his dad, defiantly or conspiratorially, Malcolm wasn't sure which. Caroline's clear blue eyes looked straight into his; there was no conspiracy there, only defiance. Malcolm impotently turned away. Tom gave some cartons of orange juice to Joey to carry and Jill handed some old bath towels to Sharon, something for them to sit on, on the coarse, dry moorland grass. Tom picked up the heavy basket and Jill marshalled everyone out of the front door, herself bringing up the rear and locking up.

The two younger children dashed on ahead as fast as they could with the weight of their charges, yelling and clouting each other and oblivious to Tom's remonstrances. Jill slowly walked behind them with Malcolm and he told her how pretty she looked in her blue Bermuda shorts and matching top.

'Is that the professional photographer talking,' Jill laughed, 'or are you trying to get round me?'

The three adults chatted and joked and Tom occasionally yelled at Joey and Sharon, and Jill more than occasionally glanced back at Caroline and Darren, who were lingering, lagging behind. Eventually they arrived at the end of what had been Dorothy and Helen Hartnell's street. The long row of grey terraced houses stretched away to their left and the endless green and purple wilderness to their right. Jill turned to follow the well-worn path across the moor and collided with Malcolm, who'd come to a standstill and stood gazing at the house on his left. Jill's soft eyes followed his gaze and her soft heart beat a little faster for him.

'It's changed,' Malcolm murmured, for the first time making reference to the house where he'd spent so many hours in his youth. 'It's unrecognisable ... almost.'

'Well, apparently a young couple bought it – Helen made a good sale there. First-time buyers, no property of their own to sell, no complications. They've done it all up since they moved in. A bit gaudy, isn't it?'

Malcolm continued to stare and finally turned away, shrugging his shoulders, playing at indifference.

'Just a bit,' he said.

They caught up with Tom, who'd strode onto the moor and was telling Joey off for throwing stones, or something, at his sister.

'Well, she started it!'

'No, I did not, you little liar, you kicked …'

'I don't care who started it,' Tom sighed. He put the basket down, took a tissue out of his jeans pocket and mopped his forehead. 'I'm telling you to stop. *Now.*'

Sharon clambered up and balanced herself on a convenient rock, twirled round a few times and then squinted behind her, into the distance.

'Where's our Caroline and Darren?'

'What?'

Tom whirled round and so did Malcolm. Sharon leaped off the rock, pushed her brother and they ran on ahead, bickering. Three pairs of anxious eyes searched the horizon in all directions but the two recalcitrant teenagers were nowhere in sight. Jill sighed deeply and passed a hot, weary hand over her face.

'Now what are they up to?'

'Don't worry, they're lagging behind, that's all,' Malcolm forced an unconcerned grin. 'Come on, they'll catch up with us when they're hungry. Let's keep going or the other pair'll be out of our sight as well.'

'They'd bloody better catch up or they'll know about it tonight,' Tom threw over his shoulder. 'Or at least my lass will.'

Caroline and Darren didn't catch up and only five people participated in the picnic that had been prepared for seven. Conversation was strained in spite of a great effort to be relaxed, jovial, to temporarily forget. The fact that they were sitting in more or less the exact spot where Malcolm had – in his own words – fucked Jill's French penfriend and afterwards taken photos of her, naked and totally uninhibited, didn't make the picnic comfortable for him. But at least the two younger children, who'd called a temporary truce, seemed to enjoy themselves. Very much.

***

There were three people waiting on the doorstep when they got home just after six o'clock. Caroline stood in her usual sulky stance, her long hair falling over her petulant face and Darren, a couple of feet away, on the other side of the man, less petulant, less sulky, more uneasy, more apprehensive. The man who stood between them and held each by the arm in what seemed like a vice-like grip, was Derek Ramsbottom, the local newsagent.

302

Jill felt the blood drain from her face when she saw the spectacle awaiting her and she came to a sudden halt in the middle of the street.

'What the bloody hell ...'

Tom didn't come to a halt, he raced forward with Malcolm at his heels.

'Good evenin', Tom,' Derek Ramsbottom greeted him, his round and normally smiling face as grim as death. 'I'm afraid I 'ave some very bad news for you an' Jill – concernin' these two 'ere. An' I'm right sorry it's me who 'as to tell you.'

Ramsbottom's Newsagents and Confectioners stayed open every Sunday until six o'clock, and as the shop had been slack most of the day – due to the good weather, no doubt, most of Firley had gone off for the day – it had been very easy for him to spot the two young miscreants helping themselves to sweets and chocolate. They thought they'd got away with it, the young buggers – till he caught up with 'em in the street. As soon as the two fathers approached, the big man loosened his grip on the two thin arms and finally let go, but neither Caroline nor Darren moved.

'As I say,' Derek Ramsbottom continued, heaving his heavy shoulders and thrusting his free hands into his brown trouser pockets. 'I'm sorry it's me who 'as to tell you.'

Jill was now standing in front of him, looking up at his bulk, a mixture of apology, disbelief and despair on her face.

'I don't know this young feller-me-lad but I do know Caroline an' I know she's been in bother before. Now, I'm not going' to press charges this time but may I advise you to do summat with 'er, Jill, before she ends up ... well, I don't 'ave to spell it out for you, do I?'

He looked at the three adults in turn, a long, steady gaze. Then his big frame moved towards the open gate but before he left the sorry party he stopped in his tracks, turned and addressed himself to Tom.

'I 'ope this business won't stop you buyin' yer papers or owt else from me shop, by the way. I still value yer custom – but you'd best keep that daughter o' yours away, that's all.'

Tom opened the door and watched everyone file into the house, his face blanched in spite of the early evening sun, his mouth a livid, tight line. He slammed the door after him and when everyone was in the living room, pushed Caroline down onto the sofa. His expletives echoed around the house.

'Just a minute, Tom, calm down a bit. This won't get anybody anywhere.'

Malcolm's voice was low, passive almost, yet despairing. He looked at the pretty young girl lolling on the sofa, his friends' daughter, his son's first girlfriend, and he saw that the accusation and Tom's tirade and threats had no effect whatsoever. Caroline's face was as impassive as if he'd been telling her the weather forecast. He looked across at Jill who'd just come back into the room after shepherding the younger children upstairs. He saw only despair on her face. And then he looked at his son, almost cowering behind the sofa, and he began to relax a little because there he saw contrition. When Tom finally stopped for breath, there was total silence. Something like a sob escaped from Jill's corner of the room and a sigh from Darren. And from Caroline – nothing. She made no effort to reply to her father's harangue, only gazed at him in defiance, and when he finally paused, she grinned at him and said, 'Can I go to my room now?' stood up and left.

Jill put a restraining hand on her husband's arm.

'No, Tom, let her go.'

Tom breathed in deeply, took off his glasses, wiped his bloodshot eyes and then focused them on Malcolm's son.

'Whose idea was it, Darren?' he gently asked. 'Be honest now, there's no point in lying and one of you must have instigated it. Who was it?'

Darren looked at his dad and then glanced at the other two adults; then he gulped loudly and looked at nothing and no one in particular.

'Come on, lad,' Tom urged. 'Was it Caroline?'

Darren continued to gaze at nothing.

'Was it Caroline, Darren?'

'Was it Caroline who wanted to go on a shoplifting spree or was it you, Darren?'

Malcolm's voice lifted his son's eyes to his. He slowly began to nod, his thin cheeks aflame.

'Yeah. Yeah, it was. It was … it was Caroline's idea.'

'Oh God, Tom, what are we going to do?' Jill sobbed.

Before Tom or anyone else could answer, the telephone rang. For a few moments it went unacknowledged.

'I'll go,' Tom finally said when it didn't stop ringing but Jill suddenly felt the need to escape from the room.

'No.' She took a tissue out of her bag that she'd thrown on an empty armchair, blew her nose and wiped her eyes. 'I'll get it.'

'Well, you'd better hurry up.'

The telephone stood on a table in the hall. Jill was gone for quite a while and the others could hear her muffled voice through the closed door. Nobody spoke and everyone avoided everyone else's eyes. When Jill came back into the room the two men noticed there was an unexpected calm about her, the ravaged look had almost disappeared. There was a small tremor in her voice, however, when she spoke.

'That was Mandy, Tom. Just ringing for a chat but ... I asked her to come and see us. About Caroline. We can have a good talk to her, professional like ... maybe she can give us some advice. Help.'

Tom was staring at her.

'And what did she say?'

'Well, she's too busy to come over this week but I said I'd meet her in Leeds next Tuesday evening. We're going to have dinner in a restaurant and I can ... well, you know, fill her in before she comes here. I think just the two of us, Tom, two women together. Anyway, I'll be a lot calmer if you're not there. You understand, don't you, love? You don't mind ...'

'I don't suppose I'll have to.' Tom sank down on the other armchair. 'Do you think it'll do any good?'

'I don't know, Tom, I just want to give it a try. A bit of professional help ... and keep it in the family at the same time. As you said yourself not so long ago, didn't you?'

'And you keep this to yourself, Darren, do you hear me?' Malcolm said and the subdued boy nodded his head. 'Right then, I reckon we'll be off now. I'll ... I'll give you a ring during the week, see how things are. And let's keep these two apart for a while, shall we? It won't do either of them any harm. Come on, Darren, let's have you home. Look, Jill, keep your pecker up, love, I'm sure this'll soon boil over.' He turned to Tom. 'And if your Mandy can help ...'

'Aye,' said Tom. 'If.'

Malcolm cuffed his old pal on the shoulder and was heading for the living room door when his eyes fell on a postcard propped up against a plant on the windowsill. A view of the Mont Blanc range against a brilliant blue sky and a multitude of flowers in the foreground. His hasty steps faltered and he nodded briefly in the direction of the picture.

'Good photograph,' he muttered to no one in particular. 'Mountains. I ... er ... I suppose it's from Helen?'

'Yes, it is,' Jill replied abstractedly. 'She's in the Alps with Turtle Dove and her husband. I think I told you they were spending their holiday together, didn't I? She's having a really lovely time ... absolutely bloody marvellous.'

Chapter Twenty-Two

If Malcolm's son had been contrite, Jill's daughter was not, and Jill entered the new, dimly-lit bistro in the centre of Leeds the following Tuesday with little optimism. She was rather late because of erratic public transport from her neck of the woods and Mandy was already sitting at their reserved table in the corner. She raised a welcoming hand and Jill hurried across the room with something that could have passed for a smile on her face.

Mandy in early middle age was still pertly pretty although less overtly sexy, thanks to more classical, if not exactly chaste, clothing. That Tuesday evening in late August, her blonde hair was tied back with a black ribbon and her contours were covered in a black cotton sleeveless blouse and cream linen skirt. Jill bent and kissed her sister-in-law, whom she hadn't seen for almost a year chiefly owing to Mandy's work, which now took up most, if not all, of her time. Although the two women had always got on, they had never become particularly close, never spent any time with their feminine heads together, had never shared confidences or even tittle-tattle. Their mutual love of Tom had really been their only attachment. Since their brief conversation on the telephone, Jill had had second thoughts about approaching Mandy the Psychologist on the delicate subject of her wayward daughter; maybe Mandy would be the last person to either sympathise or do any tangible good. Maybe it would have been better to consult an impartial outsider, if anybody at all. But it was too late now, the first tentative steps had been taken and Mandy had seemed interested and sympathetic on the phone. And she'd always been fond of Caroline, her brother's first-born, her first niece. Even so, it wasn't going to be easy divulging her daughter's seriously negative characteristics; apart from anything else they seemed like a reflection on herself, as a woman and particularly as a mother.

As soon as Jill, feeling decidedly frumpish next to her still-glamorous sister-in-law, sat down, a waiter appeared with menus and the first few minutes were taken up with ordering, changing their minds, re-ordering and handing the menus back to the pseudo-Italian waiter. As soon as this had been achieved, Jill smiled at her sister-in-law and said, 'So, the job's going well, Mandy. All your hard work's paid off. I'm really pleased for you and so is Tom. But we were both saying last night, apart from being difficult, isn't your work a bit, well, dangerous?'

Mandy wrinkled her nose and laughed. 'Well, I agree with you that my work's difficult; no doubt about that, I'm afraid. But dangerous? I hadn't honestly thought about that.'

Jill smiled again but at the same time gave a little shudder. 'Maybe I'm daft but, well, I can't imagine what it's like working with prisoners.'

'Ex-prisoners.'

'Okay, ex-prisoners. I mean, do they actually walk into your office, sit down and have a chat with you?'

Mandy laughed again.

'Yes, Jill, they actually walk into my office, sit down and talk to me. Sometimes it takes a while for them to feel at ease but, with a lot of patience and encouragement on my part, they do get there.'

'And ... well, what do they actually talk about? Their crimes or ...'

Mandy smiled.

'Of course they talk about their crimes, it's necessary. But they also talk a lot about their background, family and professional life, education, their social life before their imprisonment. They often find themselves completely alone after their release – their wives have left with the children or, if they've been in prison for a long time, there have been deaths in the family – and solitude's really traumatic for them, and can be dangerous. For them and for their future. So, they talk and I listen. And then I talk.'

'And you help them find work, too, don't you?'

'Help a bit, yes, but I collaborate with a national organisation that's specialised in finding jobs for ex-prisoners. I'm a psychologist and my function is to help these men – and sometimes women – to come to terms with themselves and the society they're a part of again. But I like to think I do my bit in helping them to find jobs – well, the right kind of work – too.'

Jill studied her sister-in-law for several moments while the waiter placed the avocado and crab starter in front of them. He disappeared with an enthusiastic if badly pronounced 'Buon appetito'. Jill and Mandy grinned at each other. Suddenly overcome with hunger they ate for a while in silence. Jill was again the first to speak. Although she hadn't yet broached the purpose of their meeting, she was genuinely fascinated by Mandy's work and it was also an excuse to postpone and work up to the distressing subject of Caroline.

'Do any of your prisoners get violent? I'm sorry, Mandy, but to me an ex-prisoner suggests violence in one way or another. It's probably unfair and sounds ridiculous to you, but ... well, when these men are alone in your office with an attractive woman, don't they get aggressive? Violent?'

Mandy smiled again.

'You'd be surprised how subdued most of them are. They've committed a crime, sometimes an atrocious crime, and they've lived behind bars for many years, in some cases. And the majority don't want to live behind bars again, believe me. And often it was a spontaneous offence in a moment of provoked anger, jealousy, even fear. A crime of passion, if you like. These men – the majority are men – aren't really criminals, they're human beings who've made a very big mistake. And, once they're released, they want to pay their debt to society in other ways by becoming decent citizens. Most of them. There was one occasion, though; one ex-prisoner I thought I knew well but … well, you never really know another person a hundred percent, do you?'

Mandy's previously enthusiastic voice trailed away to an almost incomprehensible murmur and her agitation showed on her face. Her eyes looked everywhere but at Jill.

'What happened?' Jill quietly prompted.

There was a brief pause before Mandy spoke again.

'He was very mixed up for a lot of reasons. I understood that but, although I listened, I wasn't able to talk him through his problems; they went too deep, too far back. At least I wasn't able to help him in the short time I knew him – it should have been a much, much longer time but our sessions were cut short the day he went berserk in my office.'

Jill's eyes widened and she put down her fork.

Mandy grimaced and rolled her eyes slightly.

'Don't panic; he attacked my desk and its contents, not me. Although I think I'd have been next on his list if he'd had the opportunity. Fortunately, I've got a secretary who's not only competent on a computer, she's also got a black belt in judo.'

'Good God.'

'But, as I said, Jill, that's the only real unpleasantness I've had to deal with – so far. Most of my clients are people who've made a big mistake, paid for it and are determined to make a new start in life – and they need a little help along the way. They need to talk, need someone to listen, they need psychological help. That's why they come to me. And – so far again – my career's flourishing. I made a wise move and I've no regrets.'

'I think you're wonderful, Mandy. I do admire you.' Jill smiled. 'And I think you're very brave. I know I couldn't …'

'Oh, don't shower too many accolades on me, Jill,' Mandy interrupted. 'Fortunately, Ma … that ex-prisoner was a particular case. He needs more help than I can probably give him.' She paused while she took a mouthful of delicious tagliatelle, dabbed her lip-sticked mouth with a green and red napkin, then said, 'Anyway, we met this evening to talk about you, not me. Or rather Caroline. So, what's the problem, Jill?'

Jill took a deep breath and then told her psychologist sister-in-law the problem, or rather problems, plural. It took a long time. The two women had finished their main course, dessert and coffee by the time she finished. Mandy didn't interrupt her once. When Jill finally stopped speaking and there were tears in her eyes, Mandy suggested paying a friendly, family visit to the Hopkins' home. Spend a Sunday with them, perhaps, and watch and listen to her niece. To begin with; and then she'd take it from there. She tried to reassure Jill that Caroline's wasn't an isolated case; she was sixteen with adolescent needs, worries, hormonal changes ... There were hundreds, if not thousands like her. Jill, however, wasn't convinced. Her daughter was unique ... at least as far as she and Tom were concerned. Mandy asked her if she thought it was serious with the Darren boy ... Malcolm's son. She vaguely remembered Malcolm Jones, her brother's mate when they were about Caroline's age. Jill said she didn't think her daughter was capable of getting serious with any boy. Anyway, so much the better, she was far too young.

'Yes, that's true,' Mandy agreed and recalled a long- ago conversation she'd had with her brother, begging him not to rush into an early marriage, to see a bit of the world, meet a lot of people. She made a gesture to the waiter, he nodded and hurried away to get the bill.

'Wasn't Malcolm going out for a while with that friend of yours ... sorry, I can't remember her name. A pretty little thing but ...'

'Helen. Helen Hartnell.'

'Yes, that's it. Helen. Poor kid, she never had much going for her, did she? I seem to remember she was under her domineering mother's thumb and a bit of a drifter ... couldn't keep a job, could she? In fact, it always surprised me that you two were such good pals, you were like chalk and cheese. I wonder whatever happened to the poor kid?'

'She lives and works in Paris now.'

'*What*?'

Jill smiled and gave a brief resumé of her best friend's life since Mandy had last seen her.

'I can't believe it, Jill. Well, you just never know, do you? And she's actually working for that dreadful French penfriend of yours? Little trollop if my memory serves me well. Thought she was a Brigitte Bardot duplicate. What was her name?'

Jill reminded her that her penfriend's name was Marie-Laure Colombe and that Malcolm had christened her Turtle Dove.

'Ah, yes, that rings a bell. Trust that daft devil!'

'But it stuck!' Jill laughed. And then she added, unaware of the explosion she was about to provoke, 'But she's not Colombe anymore. Her name's Beaulac; she's married to a jazz pianist, Adam Beaulac. I suppose you've heard of ... of Benjamin Beaulac, the composer? Well, Adam's his twin brother ...'

Jill stopped rambling when she noticed the sudden pallor in Mandy's cheek and the dismay, if not horror, on her face. The two women stared at each other across the table and Jill felt goosebumps crawling over her flesh. She waited for her sister-in-law to speak.

'Ben Beaulac isn't exactly Adam's twin brother,' Mandy finally murmured.

Jill subconsciously leaned forward. After a slight pause and clearing of her throat, Mandy continued.

'There were three boys born to Mr and Mrs Guillaume Beaulac in very primitive conditions in a hospital in Bombay. Triplets. Ben and Adam survived the difficult, premature birth in the, shall we say, less than a hundred per cent hygienic environment, and they grew into healthy babies and little boys. Maxwell – Max – the third, the last-born triplet wasn't so lucky. Because of the premature birth and lack of modern medical equipment he suffered some kind of brain damage – lack of oxygen, as far as I know. Nothing too serious but both his physical and mental growth were slow in comparison with his brothers and he was always way behind them in his studies. The family moved back to France as soon as the weak mother and the babies could travel and the boys were educated in Paris with frequent long visits to the US. Their mother was American, as you probably know. Ben and Adam developed a love of music at an early age and were encouraged to follow their chosen profession. They studied together at the Conservatoire National in Paris and Ben showed a particular talent for composition. The rest is history – excuse the cliché. Adam, who was a little less talented than his brother, concentrated on the piano and became equally well known in a more limited sphere. Unfortunately, the third brother, Max, showed very little talent for anything. He learned to play the piano but was only very average and later he developed an interest in art; took after his rather Bohemian mother who dabbled in watercolours. That was better, he had a certain gift, although Pablo Picasso had nothing to worry about! When Ben and Adam both left home to follow their careers, poor Max was left with indifferent parents and an insecure future. He'd shown a tendency to violence in his childhood, which was easily related to the brain damage – tantrums that went beyond the norm and occasional physical violence. As he grew older, his sexuality started to show, let's say, abnormal tendencies. In his adolescence, he was arrested several times for petty crimes – breaking and entering, burglary and general misconduct. In the beginning, apparently, his brothers were genuinely concerned and tried to help, but later in life they completely washed their hands of him. They preferred to keep him under wraps and made themselves known as the Beaulac twins; as far as the public was concerned, Maxwell Beaulac didn't exist. The parents had more or less washed *their* hands of him while he was still in the incubator; rather like a bitch rejects one of her litter.'

Jill was gazing at Mandy, her mouth open.

'But how do you know all this, for heaven's sake?'

'Can't you guess?' Mandy smiled. 'Max Beaulac is – or rather was – a client of mine. The first, in fact. He eventually left his indifferent family in Paris and bummed around Europe for a while, painting when he felt like it and doing whatever jobs came his way. He eventually settled in England, English being his second language, I suppose. London at first and then he moved north. He spent some time in Manchester and Liverpool and then decided to try his luck on the other side of the Pennines. He liked the countryside, the scenery, thought he'd be able to paint there. So, he rented a small flat in Bradford, did odd jobs here and there, nothing to speak of, and in his spare time he painted. Even set up a kind of studio in his flat. That was his downfall.'

'What do you mean?'

'Well, as I told you, Max had been arrested several times in France for minor offences, nothing too serious. Anyway, here in Yorkshire, I don't know where exactly, Max met – well, we'll call her Jane – a very attractive young lady, and for the first time Max decided to try his hand at painting a nude. Jane agreed to pose for him one fatal afternoon and it was all too much for Max; sexually, he was still an adolescent, you see. Jane claimed he raped her, Max insists it was mutual consent, that Jane provoked him, led him on. In his own words 'asked for it'. Anyway, the court put him down; four years. When he talked to me about that fatal afternoon, Jane could have led him on but I know only his story. But, in view of Max's history and mental state, there's a big question mark.'

'Did you see him often?'

'He was the first prisoner I interviewed – in prison – when I was still taking tentative steps towards my new project. The prison governor was very co-operative and helpful and allowed me to speak to several prisoners anonymously, to find my feet a little. Let me know what I was letting myself in for! Max Beaulac was the first prisoner I saw – after his release he contacted me and became my first client.'

'What happened to him? After his release, I mean.'

Mandy shrugged her shoulders and pulled a face.

'Before he went berserk in my office, he was talking about going back to France, to his roots, to find his way back into the Beaulac family circle. He'd always kept tabs on his brothers, followed their careers and family lives and they both kept in touch with him, sporadically. In fact, Ben actually visited him in prison a couple of times but it proved too distressing for both of them. But Max seemed to be a genuinely reformed character, really repentant and desperate to find his roots, become a Beaulac again. I encouraged him all the way, of course. But after the violent incident in my office, I never saw him again. He never came back.' She paused. 'I deeply regret that.'

'Where do you think he is now?' Jill asked.

'I can't be sure but I imagine he's somewhere in France. There was nothing and no one to keep him here, in Yorkshire. I only hope that, wherever he is, he's making a new and better life for himself. I'd like to think that I at least helped him to do that.'

For a few moments neither of them spoke and then Jill asked, 'Do all the brothers look alike?'

'Well, Max, apart from being slightly smaller, is the spitting image of Ben Beaulac, so I suppose he looks like Adam, too.'

Before they left the bistro, Mandy eagerly suggested a date and time to come and visit her niece and they both simultaneously held their fingers in the air and crossed them. For the first time in a long time Jill went home feeling something other than total pessimism.

***

Bénédicte finished watering her geraniums and turned her attention to her protegée, who was sitting on the balcony, staring ahead at the view she now knew so well. Helen's many facial injuries were still visible but the swelling under both eyes had gone down and the black bruises were softening to ochre. As were the other bruises disfiguring her body. Seven stitches were visible on her temple and her broken left wrist was still in plaster. She raised her glazed and bloodshot eyes to meet those of her old friend. Her hospitalisation in Chamonix had lasted one week, although she was still under medical surveillance and her departure to Paris, or anywhere else, had been postponed until the doctors were satisfied with her progress. She still suffered from blinding headaches and occasional double vision. Bénédicte had been more than happy to transform her chalet into a convalescent home.

The police, of course, had been notified, as had the Beaulac family in New York. A thorough investigation of the chalet had produced a small pile of documents that had been carelessly placed on top of the old cottage piano and had fallen behind; a European passport, a plane ticket purchased in Manchester and other official documents, all in the name of Maxwell Beaulac. Ben had answered the telephone when the Chamonix Commisariat de Police called his home; a call that on Ben's side of the world gave rise to long, involved and enlightening discussions with his sister-in-law. But Helen, thousands of miles away in the shelter and haven of Bénédicte's chalet, knew nothing of this. Her own interviews with the police were, as far as they were concerned, totally unproductive. Her recollection of that fateful evening was nebulous, to say the least; she remembered only being with Ben, loving Ben, and beyond Ben her brain would not function. But it wasn't Ben, they told her; it wasn't *Ben* Beaulac who had assaulted her and almost beat her to a pulp ... it was ... but Helen hadn't been able to take any of it in at the time; she only felt a mild thankfulness and relief that it hadn't been Ben. But if it wasn't Ben, then who ...?

In fact, Helen knew very little of anything anymore. Although not exactly suffering from amnesia, when she regained consciousness after twenty-four hours, it seemed as though she'd inflicted a kind of voluntary blank on her life over the past few months. She spoke only if spoken to, smiled if smiled at and when questioned nodded or shook her head and never used people's names. Her conversation, for want of a better word, was oblique, vague in all its aspects. During the hot, late-summer days she sat on the balcony and watched Bénédicte tending her plants or working in the garden. They ate sparse meals together and Helen tried to read, but this once-upon-a-time passion was too arduous a task for the moment. Bénédicte, inwardly panic-stricken yet trying to stay calm for her patient's sake, frequently made cloak-and-dagger calls to the hospital in Chamonix; and was assured that Helen's behaviour was normal. She'd taken a mental and physical battering and was making slow but sure progress.

Bénédicte smiled at her protegée and Helen looked up, blinked and smiled back. The old lady looked at the ridiculous shocking pink plastic watch on her wrist, announced that it was 'l'heure du gouter' and would Helen like anything to nibble with her tea? Helen smiled again and shook her head. Bénédicte was about to suggest 'a little something' – Helen's weight loss was a constant worry to her – when the telephone in the kitchen rang. She quickly disappeared. Fifteen minutes later she came back bearing a tray of tea, slices of lemon, brioche and the news that Marie-Laure would be arriving in Geneva at six o'clock the following evening. Adam was coming along nicely; he too had regained consciousness (what a pair they made!) with no permanent damage to speak of. His main problem now was a broken femur and two broken ribs. But he was capable of being left in the care of more than competent hospital staff while his wife investigated the troubles in France. Helen only stared at Bénédicte while the old lady busied herself with cups and saucers. She carefully placed a cup of hot lemon tea in front of Helen and waited for some kind of response, a reaction to her announcement. There was none. Helen acknowledged the news with her usual involuntary indifference. Bénédicte sat down opposite her patient, plopped two sugar lumps into her own tea and stared at Helen while she stirred.

'I'll be going to Geneva to pick them up at the airport,' she said. 'Marie-Laure isn't insured to drive the Renault – it'll have to stay at the airport for a while.'

There was a faint flicker of unprecedented interest on Helen's face.

'You're going to drive to Geneva? But that's impossible. It's ... it's in another country. It's too far.'

'Yes, that's right, Geneva is in Switzerland. Which is several kilometres up the road! It's not impossible and it's not too far, either.'

Bénédicte grinned and her eyes were twinkling. It was the first sign of animation she'd witnessed in Helen since her arrival from the hospital. The second was not long in coming.

'I often drive into Switzerland for one thing and another, you know. Petrol for one thing, it's cheaper there. Anyway, Geneva is only across the border – and I really enjoy driving; it's fun ... exhilarating. Look, why don't you come with me, Helen? Why don't you come to the airport with me to meet them?'

Helen was now gazing at the chatterer, a small frown between her bruised eyes.

'To meet "them"? Who are "them"? Will Adam be coming, too? Will he be able to travel?'

The old lady sipped her tea and took a hearty bite of brioche. So, Helen remembered Adam's accident, she remembered that he was in hospital. She slowly chewed her brioche, her excitement and thankfulness growing along with the returning interest and vitality in front of her.

'No, my dear, of course not. Adam is still in hospital and will be for a while. He can't walk ... broken leg and ribs. But he's much better, he's going to be fine. Don't you worry about our Adam, my dear.'

The curious eyes were still looking at her, waiting.

'So, who's "them"?' Helen repeated.

'Marie-Laure and Ben. I must admit I find it – shall we say – very gallant of Ben to leave his twin's hospital bedside and to travel all those miles to visit a young lady he's never even had the pleasure of meeting. But Ben has always been – gallant. Gallant and genuinely caring, so perhaps it's not surprising, really. And, after all, it was his brother who ...'

She slowly sipped her tea and watched a small blue butterfly dancing on her scarlet geraniums.

The following day there was a storm. Claps of thunder and a spectacular display of lightning gave way to sheets of torrential rain. Bénédicte pottered about the chalet and tut-tutted and oh-là-laà-ed and Helen, trying to concentrate on looking at magazines but with little success, watched the older woman with growing concern.

'Do you think you should drive to the airport in this weather?' she asked. 'I honestly don't think you should. I'll be really worried about you ...'

'They're expecting me, my dear, I'll have to go. But I think I'll make a start very soon and take my time.'

Helen smiled and nodded her agreement at this suggestion. Yes, please take your time, Bénédicte, take lots and lots of time. That's what I need now. So much time. How much time is there before I'll see him again? Will I be able to look at that face, that body again? The thought of looking at that face and body made her nauseous. And how much time before I'll see *her*? The woman who employed me, who pretended to be my friend, who lied to me. The mother of Malcolm's child (of that Helen had no doubts at all); the mother of Jacqueline, innocent Jacqueline who doesn't know her birth mother and yet does. Ben, am I going to see you again very soon? Will I be able to look at you, listen to your voice? What will you say to me, think of me? Have you already judged me and found me guilty?

'Helen? Helen, my dear, what's the matter? Helen, are you all right?'

The glazed, indifferent look was there again, the puppet-like limbs and the yellowish bruises glowed in the dim, silvery light.

'Helen? Why don't you come to the airport with me?'

But Helen was shaking her head before Bénédicte finished speaking. No, Bénédicte, I need time, time, time ... that's all I need ... She shook her head oh-so-slowly and looked up at the ex-nun.

'No,' was all she said.

Half an hour later Bénédicte dashed into the garden to the shelter of her faithful Deux Chevaux parked in front of her chalet. She wore a bright red patent leather raincoat, red Wellington boots and a yellow, flowery sou'wester pulled low on her forehead.

'See you later!' she called as she slipped into the vehicle.

In spite of her distress Helen couldn't help chuckling at the disappearing vision in the garden. Well, at least they wouldn't miss her at the airport. They, they ... Marie-Laure and Ben. Ben. Ben.

The car pulled away down the stony lane and on to the shining, river-like road where it came to a grinding halt. Helen saw the yellow flowers appear out of the window and waited for Bénédicte to bellow something at her. And then she saw a familiar figure approaching the old vehicle, brandishing an umbrella.

A few minutes later, Helen opened the door to Jacqueline, who wiped her rubber boots on the 'Bienvenue' mat and walked into the kitchen with a large and beautiful bouquet of pink and purple carnations. She kissed the invalid as she offered the flowers.

'Thanks very much,' Helen murmured and then remembered another bunch of flowers, yellow roses, given by her and arranged by her in a seen-better-days vase, and the evening that followed, and then the night.

'Would you put them in a vase for me, please? Bénédicte's vases are ...'

'I know where they are.' Jacqueline smiled.

She took the grandmother's wicked wedding present out of the cupboard and filled it with cold water. Then she began to arrange the blooms.

'This is one of my jobs at La Grange,' she told Helen. 'I always do the flower arranging for the tables.'

Helen simply nodded; she could think of nothing to reply. They both settled down at the kitchen table.

'And how are you now, Helen?' Jacqueline asked, a frown of concern between her lovely eyes. 'You're looking much better than when I last saw you.'

Helen stared at her.

'Better than when you last saw me? But that was ...'

She hadn't forgotten the last time they saw each other when Jacqueline's history had been disclosed and ...

'When you were in hospital.' Jacqueline was blushing. 'I came to see you but you were ... you were still unconscious.'

'Oh. Oh, I see. I didn't know. Well, that was ... really kind of you, Jacqueline.'

Helen tried to smile and swallow her unfair resentment and unreasonable jealousy of this lovely girl. This daughter of Malcolm and Turtle Dove, conceived no doubt on her and Malcolm's piece of earth. The unconscious instigator of lies, deceit and deep unhappiness. And yet, along with all the unjust negative accusations was pity and a genuine liking for the girl.

'I've just seen Bénédicte in the car; she told me she was going to pick

Marie-Laure up at the airport. It's so good of her to come and see you and leave Adam at a time like this. She must think a lot about you.'

Helen only bent her head and said nothing.

'Do you think you'll be going back to Paris soon?' Jacqueline's unexpected question was spoken softly, almost indistinctly, and she stumbled over the simple words. And then she repeated it more clearly.

'I hope so. As soon as the hospital gives the green light, I'll be going back to ... to Paris.'

'Have you any idea when that will be?'

Helen, in spite of her ongoing apathy and general unawareness, detected a note of urgency in Jacqueline's voice.

'No,' she replied slowly, studying her interrogator. 'Why are you asking, Jacqueline?'

The blushes suddenly came back with a vengeance and the brown velvet eyes darted around the room, looking anywhere but at Helen. They came to rest on the carnations between them.

'Do you ... do you think you'll be seeing Paul in ... in Paris?'

Helen passed a weary hand over her face and rubbed her sore, tired eyes.

'I doubt it very much. Why?'

Jacqueline, her cheeks scarlet, her eyes sparkling, explained to Helen that she'd like to send a message to him; she'd like Helen to give him a message from her, if possible, if she didn't mind. Jacqueline gazed at her like an eager young puppy, her face full of expectancy, clutching at the thread of hope that Helen could offer her. Helen felt drained and suddenly wanted to be alone. To sleep, to forget. To wake up in a bedroom in England, overlooking the moors, the Pennines; to forget everything, everyone that had been part of her life over the past few months.

'What's the message?' There was no interest in the question.

'Oh Helen, could you ask him to ... to get in touch with me? Write to me, phone me? I'll give you my address and number ... to give to him. I still think about him, Helen, I can't help it. I know it must sound so silly; we hardly knew each other. We didn't know each other at all, really, but ... well, that day we spent together was – for me – magic and I can't get it – or him – out of my mind. There was something about him and I ... I had the feeling he felt the same about me. I just knew ... I just knew ...'

The last words disappeared on a whisper but nonetheless echoed inside Helen's confused brain.

'But Jacqueline, you haven't seen him for such a long time. And, as you've just said, you hardly knew him. In fact, you don't know him at all really, do you?'

The words she spoke to Jacqueline reverberated in her own mind and brought with them a flood of more confusion. You haven't seen him for a long time ... but she'd be seeing him in a few short hours. He'd be walking through that door with Marie-Laure and Bénédicte in a few short hours. You don't know him at all, do you? She'd spent a train journey with him and a few idyllic days in his home. Only. She possessed a Renoir reproduction and a Norman Rockwell card, both given by Ben, both which she treasured. But she didn't know him. The proof was her battered and broken body because if she'd known him ... Paul and Jacqueline; Adam and Marie-Laure. Adam and Paul, fellow musicians and friends. Marie-Laure and Jacqueline, mother and daughter, oblivious and unsuspecting. Paul and Jacqueline; not possible, unthinkable. Helen could prevent the unthinkable from happening. Paul and Jacqueline; Marie-Laure and Adam; Marie-Laure and Jacqueline; Ben and Helen. Helen and Ben. He'd be walking through that door in a few short hours. Ben, whom she really didn't know at all.

I met and loved a stranger on a train
My heart and soul, my body, weren't equipped.
The stranger was the author of many a strain
And I only Little Miss Nondescript.

He would be found dead the next morning
Killed by boredom I gaily quipped,
He assured me that I wasn't boring
What a nocturne for this Nondescript.

The jokes we shared were corny, really
And because of them I flipped
Because we shared this 'something silly'
L'homme célèbre and his Nondescript.

I thought I knew the man I slept with
The man I laughed with, ate with and stripped,
With whom I lay naked and leaped into bed with
And never felt less like a Nondescript ... with.

But if I'd known him, I'd have recognised
The imposter who lashed and beat and whipped.
If I'd known him well, I would have analysed
And re-written this Nocturne for a Nondescript.

318

'I don't know *you* very well, either, Helen, but I like you a lot,' Jacqueline's cheeks were reddening. 'I like to think that we're friends.'

Tears welled into Helen's eyes and spilled down her maimed cheeks and Jacqueline leaped out of her chair, flew round the table and wrapped her arms around her.

'Oh, I'm so sorry, Helen, I didn't mean to upset you. I'm so silly and thoughtless and tactless. You're still not well and I'm not helping to make you better. I'm sorry.'

She pulled Helen towards her and squeezed the still-tender body.

'We are friends, aren't we, Helen?'

Helen, for reasons known neither to herself nor to the girl who was cuddling her, sobbed, and her aching body heaved and she told herself that, because she too wanted Jacqueline to be a friend, she could never initiate or encourage a relationship between her and Adam's saxophonist. When her tears had finally subsided and she'd composed herself and apologised, and after Jacqueline had made a large pot of strong coffee, they smiled shyly at each other, both wanting and needing to speak, to talk, yet not knowing what to say, how to begin. The only sound came from the percolator, which suddenly slurped to a finale and Jacqueline stood up.

'At least this will keep me awake when I'm working this evening.'

This evening, Helen thought. Ah, this evening.

'Is La Grange busy at the moment?' she asked.

Jacqueline nodded and pulled a wry face.

'It'll be busy until the autumn.' She paused. 'And then ... then I'm thinking of leaving.'

Helen's head shot up.

'Leaving? Leaving La Grange?'

'Leaving La Grange. And the Alps. I'm thinking of trying my luck in Paris.'

'Paris?' Helen heard herself insanely repeating. 'What are you thinking of doing in Paris?'

Jacqueline shrugged as she poured the coffee.

'The same. There's no shortage of restaurants in Paris, is there?' She paused again. 'But I've also been thinking of asking Marie-Laure about training to become a beautician. Why not? I think it'll be quite interesting and at least I'd meet a lot of people. Maybe I could even work for her ... and with you. That would be lovely.'

Helen winced and acknowledged the wry smile.

'And of course, there's Paul,' she said and Jacqueline gave an enthusiastic little nod.

'And there's you. And Marie-Laure. At least I'll have two friends. Three if I'm very lucky. If Paul still wants me. Will you help me now?'

'Oh Jacqueline, please don't ... look, please don't ask me to get involved. If it didn't work out, you'd blame me ... you and Paul both ... and you'd be right ...'

'No, I wouldn't blame you, Helen, I could never blame you ... how could I?'

'Then I'd blame myself and wouldn't be able to live with myself,' Helen exaggerated hugely. 'I'd blame myself for getting involved in the first place and interfering.'

'But you're being so pessimistic,' Jacqueline suddenly accused. 'You're assuming that it won't work out, that things will go wrong ... Look, let's be optimistic instead ... let's look on the bright side ...'

Helen smiled wearily. This conversation was going on too long, getting completely out of proportion, and she wasn't yet up to lengthy, emotional discussions. I'm not up to lengthy emotional discussions yet, Ben.

'Yes, let's look on the bright side. You go to Paris if that's what you want. Find yourself a job and somewhere to live and leave the rest to destiny. Not me. Okay?'

Her gentle smile softened the bluntness of her words and Jacqueline slowly smiled back at her.

'Okay,' she sighed. 'I give in. And I've decided that if I do move to the capital – my birthplace, in fact – that it will be the right time to do some investigating. I really do want to know who my biological parents are, you know.'

She was starting work at seven o'clock that evening and she left Bénédicte's home at five, to trek down the mountain in the still-pouring rain. Her car was temporarily in the garage being serviced. Helen hugged her as tightly as she could and thanked her for the visit, especially in such awful weather, and for the lovely flowers.

'I'll try to come again before you leave,' Jacqueline replied, 'and maybe the next time we meet it'll be in Paris.'

And maybe not, thought Helen, nodding and smiling enigmatically. They gave each other a final kiss on the cheek and Helen waved until the disappearing figure was well and truly out of sight.

***

The flight was nearing its end and he was glad that the woman sitting at his side had finally dropped off to sleep. She'd chatted during a great part of the

320

journey, if 'chatted' was the right word. Harried, perhaps, was more like it. She worried about this, that and the other. The feller they'd left behind and how he'd survive without her under the current difficult circumstances; what physical and mental state they'd find Helen in; how bad her injuries were; would she recognise them; how would she, above all, react to *him*? And that led back to the one she'd left behind. A vicious circle. When all he was concerned about was Helen. Helen, who had never really been far from his thoughts, in spite of separation and tragic events. And now he was a free man, single if not without ties, he was quite delighted and more than a little anxious about seeing her ... Helen ... again. And he wanted to concentrate his thoughts on the woman and their imminent meeting.

Helen had been made to suffer in her young life; any chance of professional or social success had doubtlessly been crushed by her mother's harmful influence plus the lack of a loving, encouraging father in her life. Recently, she'd suffered physically, although he didn't know all the details, nor the extent of her injuries. He'd know those details soon enough. His thoughts subsequently turned to himself because he'd been made to suffer, too. In spite of his fulfilled ambitions, professional success and public esteem, his personal life had been a fiasco. When he looked back on his youth and what he'd had going for him and the mistakes he'd made – or rather the one big mistake he'd made – he inwardly squirmed. And then he should never have got married; never have married the beautiful but unstable woman who'd been incapable of loving as he wanted, needed to be loved. Even her eventual illness hadn't brought them closer, as he'd hoped it would.

A deep masculine voice suddenly announced that the plane would shortly be arriving in Geneva and would passengers please fasten their seat belts. All at once he felt like a teenager again; gauche, inexperienced, excited about going on his first date. How many more hours before he'd be with Helen again? What physical state would he find her in? What would be her reaction when she first laid eyes on him? He did as he'd just been instructed to do, fastened his seat belt and gently nudged the sleeping figure at his side. They were about to land.

***

The rain had stopped when Helen woke up. The sleep had been so deep that her head ached and her eyes felt heavy. She made her way upstairs to the bathroom where she clumsily, with one hand, performed a kind of toilette. A not very efficient toilette but it was the best she could manage. And, anyway, what was the point of trying to make ravishing a ravaged face? Helen smiled into the small and simple mirror. The poetry was coming back, slowly but surely. And she had no intention of letting it get away again.

Thinking, as she now was, about writing, Helen began to wonder if Jill had ever received the brief and not very intelligible note that she'd dictated to Bénédicte just after her release from hospital. And if she'd be able to make head or tail of it. Helen hadn't wanted to worry her too much and had tried to minimise her injuries, but had let her know that she'd have to stay for quite a bit longer in the Alps and, without going into a song and dance act, the reason why. She'd thought of phoning her best friend, initially; if Jill had been trying to call her in Paris she'd be worrying about the lack of response. But she quite honestly hadn't felt either up to or capable of verbal communication of any kind and especially one that necessitated a description of what had happened since their last conversation. After a lot of thought, she'd decided on a letter, which turned out to be more a note and in Bénédicte's handwriting, which was one thing that did give away her age, plus the probable spelling mistakes in the foreign language she was writing. The letter had probably confused and upset Jill much more than any phone call would have done. It had been sent a few weeks ago and, so far, Helen had received nothing from Yorkshire. Maybe Jill had replied and the letter had gone astray, or was gathering Alpine dust in Bénédicte's letterbox at the foot of the garden. Collecting her post wasn't something that came naturally to the old lady; she received so little herself and therefore it was something she rarely thought about. Helen ought to remind her; maybe she really should phone Jill, too, although she didn't want to take liberties with Bénédicte's phone and the old lady would never accept payment, she was sure of that. Maybe Jill had never received the letter; maybe there had been postal strikes somewhere between the Alps and Yorkshire ... it happened. Her confused thoughts somersaulting around in her brain, Helen realised that Jill was the person she'd love to be waiting for now, the one person she would love to see walking through the door of Bénédicte's chalet. Jill, her best friend, who'd loved her for a life time, warts and all, and vice versa. Jill had always encouraged her to write; had loved her poems; had understood them, the simpler the better, she'd always said. She could relate to Helen's poetry and was convinced a lot of other women would have been able to, as well, given the opportunity. But she'd never been given the opportunity because her mam had called it 'scribbling' and had complained because she always 'ad a bloody pen in 'er 'and instead o' doin' summat useful'.

It was still there, the poetry, the need to get things off her chest and on paper. And now was the ideal opportunity, to occupy the long idle hours, to get her too-long-non-functioning brain working again. And God, did she have things to write about! Life in an Alpine chalet! The Mont Blanc range; life in a Parisian bedsit; a passionate weekend with a famous musician-composer ... that one, of course, had already been written. Thank God ... he hadn't broken her right wrist. Or her write wrist. Oh yes, the poetry was definitely coming back ... And then, of course, a night of passion and violence with the musician-composer's brother ... oh, she could really go to town on that one ... and afterwards waiting for the musician-composer to come to her, to walk through the door, take her in his arms and declare his undying love. Helen smiled, almost grinned to her ridiculous self. That wasn't poetry, that was bullshit, as the Americans, or even Franco-Americans born in India, might say. Now she was being facetious, far too facetious for the occasion, and the idea bewildered her. But, honestly, she really would prefer to be waiting for Jill right then. It was a difficult and absurd fact to digest but it was certainly a fact. She wasn't only apprehensive of Ben's imminent arrival; she was actually quite dreading it. She couldn't imagine how he would greet her, didn't even know his true intentions in flying to France with Marie-Laure, to see her. Concern for her health? Guilt because of the pattern of events? Genuine affection? True love? Bullshit again. Not possible after one, seemingly long- ago weekend in Paris after having just met. Love was time, knowledge, intimacy, tolerance, common interests, passion yes, warts and all ... Maybe she should start composing a poetic speech for Ben's impending arrival.

***

Bénédicte, who, thanks to an improvement in the weather and smooth traffic on the motorway, had arrived in good time in Geneva and stood amongst the crowds in front of the arrivals board. Two planes had landed at more or less the same time and their passengers bustled through the exit, pushing luggage trolleys, calming harassed children and waving at waiting relatives and friends. Bénédicte's eyes – better functioning now behind more powerful lenses – scanned the hurrying hordes for two familiar and beloved faces. At last, she recognised one of them and moved forward, her tiny body pushing people and excusing herself, her thin arms flailing wildly.

'Marie-Laure! Marie-Laure! Coucou! Marie-Laure!'

Unaware of the amused glances she was attracting, Bénédicte threw herself at the beautiful and elegant woman who bent to embrace her.

'I'm so glad you've come, my dear, so glad. It's so good of you to think of Helen at a time like this, when Adam needs you so much. How is he? When will he be able to leave the hospital? Will he ever be able to walk again? And what about the other driver – the motorcyclist – was he injured, too? Oh, Helen's so pleased you're coming home, so pleased.'

At last, the well of questions dried up and Bénédicte held Marie-Laure at arm's length and her small, avian eyes behind better lenses darted about her.

'Where is he?' she asked. 'Where's Ben?'

Marie-Laure slowly shrugged herself out of the old lady's grasp and started to walk away, pulling her large blue suitcase behind her.

'He's in New York. I'm alone. Where have you parked the car, Bénédicte?'

'Ben's in New York?' Bénédicte stood looking after Marie-Laure's disappearing back for a few moments and then moved forward. 'But why hasn't he come? Because of Adam? Did he decide to stay with his brother? I can understand that but ...'

'I'll tell you everything in the car. God, I'm so exhausted I might actually sleep in the car ... so don't be surprised if I nod off. I feel as though I haven't slept for six months.'

They didn't speak again until they were both strapped into the Deux Chevaux and the small red car was heading towards the Swiss–French border.

'Before you go to sleep, Marie-Laure, please tell me about Ben. He's not ill, is he? And what about Adam? Is he going to get better? Is he going to be the same man as he was before ... before the accident?'

Marie-Laure laughed but mirthlessly.

'Do you want to know about Ben or Adam? Adam is still in hospital and will be for a while. He's going to need rehabilitation before he'll be able to walk normally again. And he's not ...' Marie-Laure suddenly stopped speaking and turned her face away. Bénédicte glanced at her and waited a few moments before she reacted.

'He's not what, Marie-Laure?'

'He's not ... well, his behaviour is a little ...'

'A little ...?'

'Let's just say a little difficult. Since he came out of the coma, he's ... well, he's not quite the Adam I know and love. The doctors say it'll take time.'

'What do they mean?' Bénédicte frowned, trying to concentrate on heavy traffic as well as a disquieting conversation. 'What will take time?'

'To get back to his old self. The self that ... that I married, that you and I know and love. You see, he's had a bit of a personality change, if you like. Since he came out of the coma, he's ... well, the doctors say I'll have to be patient and ... and tolerant. That's what they say.'

Bénédicte's eyes darted between the road ahead and the passenger at her side, who obviously needed her full attention; she ought to pull over somewhere and park but there was no chance of that at the moment, not with this traffic. Someone hooted their horn at the Deux Chevaux, Bénédicte smiled apologetically through the rear-view mirror and raised her hands helplessly from the steering wheel in a kind of 'I'm sorry, please forgive me but ...'

'And what about Ben?' she asked. 'I suppose he wanted to stay with his brother and that's only natural. After all, there was really no reason for him to come to France, was there? Although I imagine he wants to find out about Max; get in touch with the police, that sort of thing. Actually, there is a very good reason for him to come to France ... to the Alps ... if he can help the police with their enquiries. Oh, Marie-Laure, it's been dreadful. Absolutely dreadful. Our little English guest has been through so much and you won't recognise her; although her injuries don't look quite as bad as they did. It's so good of you to leave Adam but it's also necessary that you're here, we both do need you, Marie-Laure. And I do wish Ben had come, it would be nice to have a man around the place. Even if he doesn't know our little invalid ...'

In spite of the jet-lag Marie-Laure suddenly seemed wide awake and very alert.

'Oh, but he does know her, Bénédicte. In fact, he knows her rather intimately. Our little invalid, as you call her, has been much cleverer and far more cunning than I'd ever have given her credit for.'

'Marie-Laure?'

'My dear brother-in-law picked Helen up on a train last year and they spent a sordid little weekend together in Paris. At Ben and Kim's home. Ben showed her the sights and gave her a very good time and I imagine it all turned Helen's head. She doesn't come from the same milieu, you know. Far from it. I don't think Ben had any intention of seeing the English trollop again after his dirty weekend but, as I say, our little invalid was very cunning. She found out ... I suppose that, when she was looking for a new job, her landlord, Henri Parisot, who's also our good friend, told her that the beautician Marie-Laure Beaulac was married to Ben's brother and she inveigled her way into working for me. She obviously thought it was the ideal solution to getting into contact with Ben. Can you believe it, Bénédicte? Can you believe that "our little invalid" could be so devious?'

Bénédicte's driving had slowed down and one or two horns hooted as the drivers tried to overtake. She frowned and her mouth was grim, magnifying the already deep lines on her cheeks. She felt totally confused, bewildered, but her mind was racing.

'I don't understand, my dear,' she said, after a long silence. 'Helen and

Ben, a married man? It's not possible. It's so out of character. Out of both their characters. And Helen isn't cunning, she's not devious at all ...'

Marie-Laure laughed.

'Oh dear, Bénédicte, the trouble with you is you only see what's on the surface, what people want you to see. You never scratch the surface to find out what's underneath.' Her perfectly manicured hand patted the old claw that clutched the steering wheel. 'It all came out after the French police contacted me, of course,' she continued. 'Ben reacted, shall we say, rather excessively to the name – Helen Hartnell. And the circumstances of the assault. He and I had many a long conversation, a few sleepless nights. I'm sure "our little invalid's" ears must have been burning. And, needless to say, Ben could no longer play the injured and cuckolded husband once this squalid story came to light. I suppose he could have denied all knowledge of Helen but, I must admit, he was totally honest and he did seem genuinely concerned about her. It was he who suggested coming to see her, to investigate the whole story. It was his brother who'd committed the crime, after all, and he had to follow that up. We even booked our tickets ... and then he started to have second thoughts and to ... to panic a bit. Adam needed him, too, especially as I wasn't going to be there, and Adam came first, of course. Every time. And Amy and Jeremy, they desperately needed him, too, in view of their mother's defection. The poor kids are still suffering from shock, for God's sake. And then we learned that the police had tracked him down ... Max, I mean ... in Lyon and he was in custody there. I saw the relief on Ben's face. Relief that Max had been arrested, of course, but also ... well, I think he felt he'd been exonerated from a task he didn't really want to do ... come to France and visit his brother's victim. A woman he wanted to wash his hands of. That's the impression I had, anyway. And then ... well, I made it clear to him how Helen had wheedled her clever way into working for me and it was so obvious why ... It was a means of being able to crawl her way back into his life; a means of pursuing him ... getting her claws on him again ... through me; through his family. That put the wind up him all right. I could almost see him running for his life and not in the direction of the French Alps. And then, right out of the blue, Ben's agent called and needed to speak to him about a concert that was being planned at Carnegie Hall. So that settled it. Our little invalid – as you call her – couldn't compete with that, could she? So, Ben stayed in New York. Work came first.'

Bénédicte said nothing at the end of her passenger's monologue. There was nothing to say. She could only wonder why, in relationships with the opposite sex, men – and women, too, no doubt – often behaved like idiots or 'des salauds'. Bastards. They behaved either like idiots or bastards. Or both.

326

She took her eyes off the road for a brief second, raised them to heaven and thanked God that she'd chosen a life of celibacy.

***

The express train from Geneva pulled slowly into the small and picturesque Alpine station as dusk was purpling the mountains.

'This is it,' Jill said. 'This is where we get off. Oh, I do hope Helen got my letter okay and there'll be some accommodation for us – somewhere.'

Malcolm pulled two small bags off the luggage rack and stood aside to let Jill pass into the aisle. She was wide awake again and raring to go after her nap during the flight.

'Well, if not, we can always squat in Marie-Laure's living room. It'll only be for a week. Only joking, love, only joking.'

'Your sense of humour hasn't improved with age, Malcolm Jones. I'm only too glad that Marie-bloody-Laure's tied up in New York with her husband – that's what I understood from Helen's rather confusing letter, anyway. She's the last person I want to bump into, thank you very much. I'm looking forward to meeting the eccentric Bénédicte, though.'

Malcolm threw their bags on to the small platform and jumped off the train.

'The only person I'm looking forward to seeing right now is Helen,' he said. 'God, I'm nervous, lass, I don't mind telling you. I hope we get at least a lukewarm reception.'

Jill stood next to him in front of the quaint station and looked around her, taking in the breathtaking twilight scenery and looking out for signs of a taxi. She grinned up at her companion and thumped the bump that was his belly.

'Well, I'll be getting a red-hot reception, there's nowt no surer as they say in Firley,' she told him. 'As for you, young man, well, you'll just have to wait and see, won't you?'

Chapter Twenty-Three

Marie-Laure was the first to notice the overflowing letterbox at the end of the drive. A few brightly coloured advertisements had already fallen on to the road.

'When was the last time you emptied your letterbox, Bénédicte?' she asked, wryly.

'What's the point?' her companion harrumphed. 'It's always either junk mail or bills. I pay all my bills by direct debit and have all my love letters sent to a PO box number in Chamonix.'

'Well, I think it's time it was opened,' Marie-Laure smiled, 'or you'll be accused of littering the mountain – which might lead to a hefty fine. And, generous as you are, you wouldn't like that, would you? Where's the key?'

The car came to a grinding halt in front of the guilty box, and at the same time Bénédicte opened the glove compartment and dropped a well-filled Mickey Mouse key ring onto her passenger's lap. Marie-Laure rolled her eyes heavenward, imagining that half the keys probably fitted locks from the dim and distant past. She picked out the smallest and handed back the rest, one of which was the front door key.

The door was locked, as Bénédicte had expected it to be. She knew that the latch would have been firmly dropped after her departure. Helen would certainly take no chances with security; of that she had no doubt whatsoever. She turned her key in the lock and gently pushed it open, calling out her protegée's name at the same time. Helen was sitting in the small, cluttered living room, in a corner of the old and well-worn sofa, crouching there like a tiny hunted animal, Bénédicte couldn't help thinking. She grinned as she approached but her cheerful greeting wasn't returned. Helen looked up at her with huge and wary, frightened animal eyes.

'Where are they?' she murmured, almost inaudibly.

'Well, Marie-Laure decided that my post needed to be rescued before I made a mess of the mountain, so she's out there doing me and my post a good turn ... and Ben ...'

Helen moved for the first time. She wriggled in her seat, more for something to do than the search for comfort. Her maimed eyes looked up at her hostess.

'Yes? Ben?'

'Ben hasn't been able to come, I'm afraid.' Bénédicte remembered Marie-Laure's revelation in the car; she felt the blood flooding her face, and the sudden dryness in her mouth prevented her from either telling the truth or kindly inventing. Footsteps behind Bénédicte caused Helen to raise her eyes and she saw Marie-Laure throw a pile of correspondence on to a convenient chair. Junk mail, a lot of it, but there were two envelopes that stood out amongst the garish colours of advertising; one long white one and one airmail. The silence that followed was audible; the three women froze in their respective positions and it was Bénédicte who made the first move.

'Well, I'd better throw this junk away and see what other gems are waiting to be opened. Marie-Laure, my dear, why don't you go into the kitchen and make us all a cup of coffee. I certainly need one and ...'

'Yes, I'll do that.' Marie-Laure obviously didn't need asking twice. She almost ran out of the room.

Bénédicte picked up the discarded post, sat in the chair and placed the papers in her lap. A distraction. Work for idle, arthritic fingers and scrutiny for a confused brain.

'Supermarket; DIY store; double glazing; pizza take-away ... Do people actually read this rubbish or am I the only person in the world to throw this junk straight into the recycling bin? Oh, what's this? There's a sale on at Le Soulier Sympa and trainers are half price. Just what I need ... I'll make a note of their number ... Marie-Laure, the brioche is wrapped up in the bread basket and you'll find butter and some blackcurrant jam in the fridge ...'

Helen hugged and cuddled herself and closed her eyes. Delicious as Bénédicte's brioche was, the thought of swallowing anything at that moment made her nauseous ... even the coffee. Why couldn't she be far away, alone on some small, warm island with only books and music for company and ... why hadn't Ben come? Was this relief, anguish, disappointment? Had she really been dreading seeing him or had she been fooling herself? She wasn't in love with him; she couldn't be, not after all this time, not after everything that had happened; she could never look at his face, his smile, his body again. She couldn't. It would be absolutely impossible. And yet she felt ... sort of let down and, yes, disappointed, anything but the relief she would have expected to feel. She hugged herself even more tightly in spite of the mild pain it gave her bruised arms.

When Marie-Laure came back into the room carrying a full tray, and seated herself in the chair next to the hostess, gently placing the tray on the floor and handing out cups, Bénédicte picked up the airmail envelope, and her fingers pulled at the seal. She concentrated on her task in order that she didn't have to look at the two other women; didn't have to participate in their unenviable conversation although her ears remained alert. Her whole senses, however, were very soon enveloped by what she held in her hand.

Apart from Helen's quiet 'Merci' when Marie-Laure gave her a cup, it was Bénédicte who finally broke the silence. While she'd been reading, her glasses had slowly slid down her nose and when she looked up, she pushed them back where they belonged and peered through the thick lenses. Her two guests looked and waited.

'This letter is from Ben,' she quietly announced.

Two lots of coffee slopped into two identical saucers.

'Apparently, Ben wrote this to me several weeks ago, when he discovered that Kim had been unfaithful.' She paused, her eyes flicking over the missive. 'Oh dear. He tells me that his marriage was unhappy for many years and that they stayed together for the children and for convenience. He was … quite distressed by Kim's infidelity and her pregnancy to another man; a man he'd met and … trusted totally. But he tells me that he has also met another woman who means a lot to him and he thinks and hopes that it's mutual. Because he loves me and values my opinion, because he values my opinion of him, he wanted to tell me himself and not to be surprised if he one day introduces a new young woman into the Beaulac's life. He thinks she and I would get on well and that I'd like her very much.'

At precisely that moment, the doorbell rang. Bénédicte's head shot up, her glasses slid down her nose and she frowned deeply before pushing them up again.

'Now, who on earth is this?' She looked and sounded almost angry, obviously discomfited by the unexpected intrusion. 'I'm not expecting anyone.'

She put the letter back into its envelope, placed it on top of the other simple white envelope which boasted a British stamp, stood up and made her way to the front door. She was gone for what seemed a long time.

The other two women sat and looked at each other across the room. They didn't want to be alone in each other's company; they both willed their hostess to come back very quickly.

'How's Adam?' Helen asked in English, after quietly clearing her throat.

Marie-Laure was breathing heavily, her breasts moving and her lips twitching oddly. Helen thought that she wasn't going to reply; she also thought – and she was right – that Marie-Laure wasn't going to ask her, Helen, how *she* was. Marie-Laure, who was so good to have left her husband in hospital in another country, to come and visit the invalid who'd been physically attacked, left for dead, while staying at the Beaulac's home.

'Adam is ... doing very well.' Marie-Laure replied, also in English, and continued in that language, as they often did. 'A few broken bones but he'll recover. I don't want to talk about Adam, Helen, I want to talk about Ben. About you and Ben, to be precise. Your ... er ... your relationship with my brother-in-law, knowing that he was a married man with children. Happily married or not, that's not the point, he was married when you met him and you willingly (or so I'm told) entered into a relationship with him. Encouraged an illicit relationship.'

The two women were gazing at each other now, their breathing heavy and audible, and they noticed neither Bénédicte nor the couple behind her, standing on the threshold between the room and the tiny hall.

'I didn't need to encourage him, not at all. It was mutual attraction right from the start. I met him at Waterloo and he changed his ticket so that he could sit with me on Eurostar. By the time we arrived in Paris, we ... well, we ... were in love. He rescued me from a filthy, unhygienic hotel where I was supposed to stay indefinitely and that's why he invited me to spend time at his home. The rest happened very naturally. Yes, he was honest, he told me he was married and had two wonderful children; he helped me to find a place of my own – through Henri Parisot. And he stayed in touch with me; not very often but his letters were warm, affectionate, made me hope that I might see him again. And I wanted that so very much. Of course I didn't tell you and Adam about it, Marie-Laure, how could I?'

'You were dishonest, Helen; dishonest and sly. You came to our home knowing that Adam was Ben's twin ... Ben's brother. You were deceitful ... cunning ... accepting our invitation for a holiday in the Alps, knowing that Ben owned the chalet, too. Perhaps in the hope he'd turn up there and ...?'

'No ... no, not at all. I didn't know Adam was Ben's brother the first time I came to your home. I'd absolutely no idea. I accepted your invitation to the chalet because it was kind of you to offer and I wanted to see ... to explore the Alps ...'

'And maybe you had ... designs on Adam, too?'

'Oh, don't be ridiculous, Marie-Laure, I was in love with Ben. I ... I'm still in love with him. I still love Ben. But ...'

'But what?'

'I don't know if I'd ever be able to look at him ... touch him again without thinking of ... It would take a long time. Such a long time. Oh God.' Then she looked Marie-Laure straight in the eye and said, 'And, let's face it Marie-Laure, you're the last person to talk about dishonesty, deceitfulness, aren't you? Oh yes, I did as you told me and I rummaged in your chest of drawers until I found what I was looking for – although I didn't know I was

331

looking for it at the time. The clean sheets were soon forgotten when I found those letters, those photos of you and Malcolm completely naked on the Pennines. Oh no, you didn't have a sexual relationship with my ... my future husband, did you? You didn't ... have Malcolm's baby and give her up because she would have ruined your brilliant future ... did you? Once she was adopted and out of the way, I'm sure you never gave her a second thought, did you?'

Bénédicte and the two new arrivals were silently standing in the doorway, a bemused Bénédicte understanding absolutely nothing, and then one of the party suddenly turned around and walked away. He quietly left the room and then left the chalet and disappeared into the fast approaching dusk outside. Two people hadn't even noticed his presence; they certainly didn't notice his absence. At the same time the other new arrival moved forward, her arms held out in front of her, tears in her eyes and a smile on her lips. Helen tore her gaze away from Marie-Laure and her new expression lit up the macabre, melancholy room.

'Oh my God. Oh my God! Jill!'

Helen moved then and held out her arms which were very quickly filled. At least one of her dreams had just, oh so beautifully, come true.

Epilogue

1

Henri Parisot looked up from behind the sparkling glass counter as the bell chimed in the entrance of a customer and a cool breeze blew into the shop. Henri's round, pink face lit up with genuine pleasure.

'Paul, my dear young man, this is a surprise. How are you? And how's the old saxophone?'

He shuffled in front of the counter and heartily shook hands with the young Englishman.

'Hello, Henri. The old sax is fine, thanks, and so am I. And you know that we'll be travelling together very soon. Ben's organised a Christmas and New Year concert in New York so we'll be away for a couple of weeks. I'm looking forward to it – and so is the old sax!'

Henri clasped his chubby hands together on his steadily increasing paunch, something between a smile and a grimace playing on his face.

'And Adam? Is he looking forward to going back to New York so soon? I should have thought it was the last place on earth where he'd want to spend Christmas.'

'As long as Adam's working, I don't think he notices where he is,' Paul laughed but the humour quickly disappeared from his face as his thoughts concentrated on the group's leader. Adam hadn't been the same person since his accident; his mood swings were extreme, leaping from kind, jovial, normal Adam to aggressive, even vicious, a totally unrecognisable Adam. It was no longer easy working with him but it must have been even more difficult living with him, if scenes he'd witnessed at the Beaulac's home were anything to go by. The once easy-going, as-near-as-dammit perfect husband had turned into a possessive tyrant, driven to fits of blinding, jealous rage for the slightest reason, and usually, no reason at all. Marie-Laure's harmless flirtations with her husband's fellow musicians had come to a brutal full stop. Paul hoped for all their sakes – and especially Marie-Laure's – that this cruel aftermath of Adam's accident would be very temporary. He didn't want to discuss Adam with Henri Parisot, however, and quickly changed the subject.

'Anyway, I'm looking for a flight case for the "old saxophone", Henri,' he said. 'if you have one.'

The sale and purchase were quickly transacted and Henri expected Paul to immediately take his leave. However, when the door opened and another customer arrived, Paul made no move to go. He mooched around the shop while the owner was occupied, examined various musical instruments and their accessories and nonchalantly hummed a rather tuneless tune. The customer, a long-haired youth with an untidy beard and studs in ear and nose, took his time examining electronic keyboards and asking a lot of questions. Henri threw several glances in Paul's direction, indicating for him to leave if he was in a hurry, but the saxophonist showed no inclination to say goodbye. A keyboard was finally put on one side for future collection, a deposit paid and the satisfied customer happily left the shop. Paul made his way back to the counter and Henri raised an enquiring eyebrow.

'Henri, you're still in the property business, aren't you?'

Henri smiled, confirmed that he was and added that business was booming.

'Well, I've been thinking about moving for a while now, you know – my place is like a postage stamp and I'd like to change districts ... somewhere a bit more salubrious. I was wondering if Helen Hartnell's old bedsit was still vacant ... and if it is, Henri ...'

The smile slowly left Henri's face and he held up a silencing hand.

'Ah but, Paul, my dear young man, I'm afraid you're too late. A young lady moved in only last week. She's just arrived in Paris from Adam's neck of the woods ... the Alps. A delightful young lady. Pretty, too.'

Paul sucked in his lower lip, pushed his hands into his jeans pockets and resignedly nodded his head. He'd thought he'd probably left it too late so wasn't really surprised, but that didn't alleviate his disappointment.

'Do you have anything else available?' he asked. 'On the Left Bank?'

Henri Parisot sighed deeply and raised his hands in the air.

'On the Left Bank no,' he apologised, 'but if my new tenant decides to leave the big city and return to the mountains – which unfortunately wouldn't surprise me – I'll certainly let you know.'

'Oh?' said Paul, his optimism rising again. 'Do you think there's a chance ...?'

'Well, she's a quiet, shy little thing and apart from Adam and Marie-Laure she knows no one in Paris.'

'She knows Adam?'

'Yes, she used to be a waitress in the village where the Beaulacs have a chalet. At the moment she's working in a seedy little bistro in the north of

Paris and hating every minute. But I believe it's temporary ... she's planning on doing a training course with Marie-Laure in the new year ... to replace Helen in the salon, you know. Unless she decides to go back to the mountains, of course ...'

Paul felt the sudden rush of blood to his cheeks, his heart beating a little faster. Henri was muttering about the year 2000 – a new century, a new millennium – bringing a lot of changes for a lot of people, and he hoped they'd all be good ones but he wasn't too sure.

'Is ... erm ... is her name Jacqueline, by any chance?' Paul managed to stammer. And if it is, why hasn't Adam told me about this? To save face, to prevent problems, to protect me, her, himself and Marie-Laure? There could be a hundred reasons; Adam was so unstable now ... He maybe hadn't even realised what Jacqueline's move would mean to him ... to Paul ... and hopefully to her ... Or maybe the new tenant's name wasn't Jacqueline.

Henri Parisot stared at him and nodded his head rather vigorously.

'Yes, as a matter of fact it is. Jacqueline. Pretty girl. Shy but ...'

'And you say she's moved into Helen's old bedsit ... she's already living there? Will she be at home this evening? No, you don't know that, of course. Sorry, Henri. Anyway, thanks. Thanks a lot. You're a pal. Thanks.' Paul was grinning now and his previously tired eyes were sparkling. 'Merry Christmas, Henri – and give your wife a big kiss from me!'

If Henri Parisot hadn't noticed the sudden sparkle in Paul's eyes, he certainly did notice him leaving the shop backwards, stammering profusely and tripping clumsily over the threshold. Ah les Anglais, les Anglais, he muttered to himself when the door finally closed and the bell stopped chiming.

II

Adam Beaulac pressed the entry-code to his building and was happy to step inside the warm entrance hall. The heavy door clicked shut behind him and he stood for a moment wiping his wet shoes on the mat and relishing the idea of being home again. Inside his building. About to take the lift to his floor, his apartment where his possessions and his beautiful wife were waiting for him. He hadn't realised how much his own property meant to him until he didn't have it anymore, until he was confined to a strange bed, a clinical room, unable to move, dependent, totally dependent. Thank God all that was behind him and he was a free man again – with a limp – but a free man who fully appreciated the good things in life; his home, his beautiful wife and very soon a working Christmas in New York. With family and friends and his wonderful wife; his wonderful wife who belonged to *him* – to Adam Beaulac – body and soul; who always had and always would – he'd make sure of that – belong only to him. Body and soul.

On his way to the lift, Adam stopped in front of the display of letterboxes, took a tangle of keys out of his pocket and opened the box marked 'Beaulac'. Ah, so Marie-Laure hadn't bothered to check the second post. There were four envelopes. He pulled them out without checking them because he had the impression they were all Christmas cards. Whistling an easily recognisable, keep-it-in-the-family tune, he pressed a button on the wall in front of him and stepped into the lift. As he stepped out of the lift, he almost collided with a neighbour and both men simultaneously said, 'Bonsoir'. Still whistling, Adam turned his key in the lock, opened the door and was greeted by the sound of bright feminine voices and laughter coming from the dining room. A pang of disappointment immediately made itself felt. Adam had been looking forward to an evening alone with his wife. They wouldn't have much opportunity to be alone before their trip because Marie-Laure was going to be busy both at the salon and at home in the weeks up to Christmas, and he and the boys were rehearsing almost twenty-four hours a day. This evening was the exception – he'd planned it. Once they arrived back on American soil they wouldn't have a minute to themselves, so this evening he'd planned – well, whatever his plans had been it looked like they were about to go up in smoke. He stood for a moment and took a deep breath, trying to control his rising temper. He remembered the small pile of envelopes in his right hand and his uninterested eyes scanned the gaily coloured ones before he placed them on a small, highly polished table that stood against the wall. The fourth envelope wasn't gaily coloured, it was brown and addressed to Monsieur Adam Beaulac, in frighteningly familiar handwriting. He turned the envelope over in his stiff, cold fingers and gasped at the thick, black writing in the French language, across the back.

Maxwell Beaulac
Prison Registration No. A12436
Cell Number 12

The feminine voices continued to prattle behind the dining room door. Adam slowly tore open the envelope and pulled out its solitary content. It was a long time before he began to function again.

***

The dining room door suddenly opened and Marie-Laure walked into the hall; tall, beautiful, glowing. The emerald kimono she wore flapped open as she hurried towards Adam. Adam took his hand out of his heavy grey overcoat pocket and slowly held it out to his wife. She took hold of the long, cold fingers and put them to her lips.

'You're frozen, my love, come in here and get warm. I have a wonderful surprise for you.'

She reached up and kissed her husband's cold lips and, still clutching the equally cold fingers, led him into the dining room where the beautifully decorated table was laid for three. Bénédicte was sitting at the table, facing him and wearing a scarlet lambswool sweater with huge black pom-poms that hung and swung in strategic positions – and a happy grin.

'Bénédicte!' Adam yelled. 'Well, I'll be darned! What on earth are you doing here? This is Paris, for God's sake!'

He limped across the room, leaned across the table and bent to kiss the old lady's cheek. Bénédicte explained that, as they were going to New York for the end of year festivities and not to the Alps as was their custom, she'd decided to surprise them with a short, pre-Christmas visit. Her first trip to the capital – what did he think of that? Adam thought that it was one of God's better miracles and how long would she be staying?

'Three days,' she replied, 'I know you're both very busy and it's a bad time but ... well, I just had to see you before you went away. I think we should put all recent misdeeds and misunderstandings behind us and concentrate on the future. A new century! A new millennium! And I know Marie-Laure agrees with me – don't you, dear? After all, you are the family I never had and families should always stick together, whatever life throws at them. So here I am. I hope you're as happy to see me as I am to see you two.'

Marie-Laure made a suitable reply. Adam took off his overcoat and draped it on the back of his chair before sitting down opposite Bénédicte, his wife sitting at the head of the table between them. They spoke for a while about indifferent things and then Marie-Laure announced that the dinner should be ready and she'd serve the entrée. It was at that moment that Adam remembered the abandoned cards on the hall table and Marie-Laure said she'd bring them in with the dinner. She was gone for several minutes and came back carrying a tray of paté and toast and three brightly coloured envelopes. She carefully placed the dish of paté on the pristine white tablecloth.

'Why don't you open the cards before we eat?' Adam suggested and his eyes never left his wife's face while she tore open the envelopes. After she'd looked at the cards and checked the signatures, she put them on the table between the dish of paté and Bénédicte's plate. Adam attentively watched her movements but neither responded to her remarks nor showed any interest in the seasonal correspondence. Marie-Laure asked Bénédicte to help herself to food but Adam's voice, slightly raised, halted the old lady's hand as it reached for the toast.

'Something else arrived in the mail this afternoon,' he said, slipping his hand behind him and into his overcoat pocket. And on top of the pile of Christmas cards, between the dish of paté and Bénédicte's plate, he tossed a photograph of an embracing, laughing and quite naked young couple, the girl instantly recognisable, the boy's features hidden by undisciplined hair; taken somewhere on the Yorkshire Pennines in the hot summer of 1976.

III

New York
2 November, 2001

Dear Helen,

I hope this letter find its way to you via your publisher.
You'll no doubt be surprised, maybe even distressed, hearing from me after such a lapse of time. However, after reading and thoroughly enjoying your poetry, I wanted to congratulate you on your success and felt that it would be a good opportunity to contact you again.
First of all, let me say how sorry I am that tragic circumstances beyond our control dictated that we were never to see each other again, at least for a very long time. I understand that your friendship with Marie-Laure has ended, which makes me happy and very relieved, to say the least.

Years ago, when Adam told me he was going to marry Marie-Laure Colombe, I was horrified and did my best to persuade him otherwise. He was totally captivated by her, as were a lot of men, and could see no further than the end of his nose. But I wasn't in love with her and I saw through all her wiles and machinations. However, Adam did marry her and he and I were almost estranged because of it. Thank God we had a strong and indestructible relationship so this didn't happen. When my wife left me and Marie-Laure and Adam came to New York

338

they stayed at my apartment, of course, and after my brother was hospitalised, Marie-Laure continued to stay with me. I suppose we comforted each other as best we could, under the circumstances. When she told me about you working for her and staying at the chalet, I was dismayed and alarmed because I knew how capable she was of making your life a misery and turning you against me. I never trusted her from the moment I met her and with good reason. Unfortunately, I was foolish enough to trust her with my packing before we were supposed to fly to France. I had an important meeting that day with my agent that I couldn't cancel. Marie-Laure and I were late leaving the flat and afterwards I realised that was another of Marie-Laure's ruses; she had an important phone call to make that lasted half an hour, and when we were in the taxi she found an excuse to go back to the apartment and stayed there for an inordinate amount of time. When we finally arrived at JFK, we had only an hour before the flight took off. And my passport wasn't in my case. Hadn't been packed.

Although Adam and I are still very close, I have promised myself never to have anything to do with Marie-Laure again. Under any circumstances.

I have been very busy with work over the past year, Helen, and a rather messy and distressing divorce. I don't know how you would feel about seeing me now after all this time and after all that happened to you at the vicious hands of a Beaulac. I didn't know how to find you, didn't know where you were, or how you would react to hearing from me, as a friend and even less as a lover. That remains to be seen. However, I'll remain hopeful and, in the meantime, I have a very different proposal.

For some time now I've been considering writing a stage musical for the West End in London. Friends in the business have approached me several times and after slowly warming to the idea I'm now 'raring to go', have already started working on some of the music and am feeling very excited about this new project. I'm now looking for a lyricist to write the words that will put the punch into my music and, after devouring your poetry, I've been wondering if you'd be willing to take on this work. I think your style, both the comic and the tragic, would be ideal for the musical's storyline. Please think about this offer, Helen, it will be a wonderful opportunity for you and will no doubt open many professional doors. It will mean that we would be working together for quite some time, of course, and to coin a phrase, I think we'll make a great professional team. You can write to me at my new address in New York, or even better, by email. Jaminlac@ Think it over carefully, Helen, and please contact me as soon as you possibly can. If your answer is negative – and I very much hope it won't be – then I'll have to start re-thinking.

I'll be looking forward to hearing from you, Helen, and in the meantime, take good care of yourself.

With my love and best wishes,
Ben (Beaulac)

P.S. I loved the one about the cockroaches!

***

Helen read the letter three times before slowly slipping it back into the blue airmail envelope. She gazed for a while at the view from her apartment in the fifth arrondissement, a small but sufficient and attractive place above her own small but successful beauty salon 'Les Ongles a l'Anglaise'. She picked up the mobile phone that stood on the desk next to her computer and punched in a number.

'Hello?'

'Hi, Caroline, it's me, love. Are you okay? Excellent ... And Sharon and Joey? Ah, so not much has changed there then! As long as they're happy in their squabbling and I'm sure they are! The time to worry is when they stop, I reckon! Is your mum there, love?'

'No, Helen, she's not home from work yet. Or rather, she's not home from the shops yet; she said something about looking for a new pair of shoes for work ... so I'm just getting the dinner ready. Well, dinner's a bit of an exaggeration but at least she won't have owt to do when she gets home. Do you want me to give her a message, Helen? Helen? Are you still there?'

Helen smiled at the changed and cheerful, at the moment, faceless voice.

'Yes, love, I'm still here. Look, will you tell your mam ...' she paused and breathed in deeply. 'Tell your mam that ... that I've just been made an offer that I shouldn't really refuse.'

THE END